A Poison Of Passengers

by
Jack Treby

Copyright © Jack Treby 2018

Published by Carter & Allan

The Author asserts the moral right to be identified as the author of this work

All rights reserved. No part of this publication may be reproduced, stored in a retrieval system, or transmitted, in any form or by any means, electronic, mechanical, photocopying, recording or otherwise, without the prior permission of the publishers

A Poison Of Passengers

Also by Jack Treby

THE HILARY MANNINGHAM-BUTLER
MYSTERIES

The Scandal at Bletchley
The Red Zeppelin
The Devil's Brew
Hilary and the Hurricane (a novelette)
A Poison of Passengers

The Pineapple Republic

www.jacktreby.com

Chapter One

'It's a bomb!' some fat idiot yelled, as I was heading for the exit. 'They've found a bomb!'

Until that moment, the evacuation had been proceeding calmly. We had risen from our tables, as directed, and made our way towards the rear of the building. There was no panic, no jostling, no anxious babble of conversation, just a well ordered movement of people obeying the instructions from on high. Admittedly, none of us had the foggiest idea what was going on, but in the absence of any concrete information we were content for the time being to do as we were told.

The banging of a spoon a minute or so earlier had been the first indication that anything was amiss. Leopardi's Restaurant, on the Upper West Side of Manhattan, was heaving with customers and it took a moment for the sound to penetrate the fog of animated conversation. A few dozen tables were spread out across the floor and a good hundred and fifty people were busily tucking in to various unsavoury dishes. The waiter holding the spoon was not far from my table, however, and when he lifted it and started bashing a silver tray in his other hand, I could not help but pay attention. He was a small fellow, smartly dressed, with an elongated moustache in the Italian style. That was hardly surprising, since this was an Italian restaurant. The man's voice was loud but firm.

'Ladies and gentlemen, if I can can have your attention.' A gaggle of waiters froze at the sound of his voice. This was clearly the head man. 'As a matter of some urgency, I must ask you all to vacate the premises immediately,' he said. That provoked an understandable reaction from the diners, though one of puzzlement rather than fear. 'There is no time to explain,' he insisted, as one or two hesitant questions were thrown at him across the floor. 'For your own safety, would you please make your way quickly to the exit at the rear of the building.' He gestured to a small corridor, normally curtained off. An arrow indicated that this was the way to the restrooms. Presumably, an exit of some kind was located just beyond that.

1

The waiter's tone was serious enough to brook no opposition and people immediately began to push back their chairs and gather up their possessions. 'Please move quickly,' he directed. 'This is a matter of some urgency.'

My companion, Terrance Greenfield, was already on his feet. He was an amiable fellow in late middle age, grey haired and distinguished, with a faintly receding hairline. His clothes were a little crumpled – that faded nobility common to many an Englishman abroad – and his brow was sporting a puzzled frown. He removed his napkin and placed it down on the table. Greenfield was not the sort of fellow to be perturbed by an unexpected development.

I was not quite so sanguine. The head waiter was doing his best to look calm, but some of the junior flunkeys were as white as the proverbial sheet. 'What on earth do you think's going on?' I asked Greenfield, as we circled the table and moved together into the flow of people now making their way towards the rear of the restaurant. Nobody was showing any signs of distress. This was an orderly retreat rather than a stampede. We might have been conducting a fire drill. Perhaps it *was* a fire, I thought suddenly, glancing around. But there was no sign of any smoke.

Greenfield scratched the side of his chin. 'Haven't the faintest idea,' he admitted, as we shuffled quietly along. His ignorance only made the matter more disturbing, so far as I was concerned. Terrence Greenfield was a big noise in the British secret service. It was rare for him to be in the dark about anything.

A few of the other diners were having whispered conversations. Leopardi's was a respectable establishment, but it wasn't exactly in the top tier. Bankers and office workers were rubbing shoulders with shopkeepers and the odd courting couple. The décor was similarly pleasant but uninspiring, with bright lights and flowered wallpaper. The tables now being abandoned were piled high with plates of spaghetti and other Italian monstrosities, and the sheer number of people crammed into the place made it a lively establishment at any time of day. Nine o'clock in the evening, however, was peak time, and I had to give credit to the good sense of my fellow diners as we made our way slowly towards the exit. Why we could not use the front of the building, I had no idea. The corridor leading to the restrooms was only wide enough to take two or three men abreast, but with a little consideration it would only be a matter of minutes before we had all passed through and out onto the street.

It was then that some fat idiot announced his theory about the bomb and all hell broke lose.

The cry was immediately echoed across the length of the restaurant. 'A bomb! A bomb!' Two words to strike fear into the heart of any New Yorker. We had all read the papers over the Christmas break and seen the horrific pictures. The bombing campaign had begun in earnest on Boxing Day 1931. But none of us had thought to be caught up in it like this. If indeed it was a bomb. 'We gotta get out of here!' some fool in a checked shirt yelled.

And then, all at once, we were in the middle of a stampede. The crowd, so calm a moment before, now became a desperate mob, determined to fight its way out of the building. I had barely had time to register the "B" word before I encountered a jagged elbow and felt a shoulder bashing heavily against me. I staggered sideways, almost losing my footing as I collided with a nearby table. 'For goodness sake!' I muttered, grabbing hold of the table top. Greenfield stepped across to help steady my arm. The ugly mass of now panicking diners were converging on that far corridor and fights were breaking out among the office workers, as people tried to force their way through. I saw one bounder pull at the dress of an elderly woman, attempting to shove her out of the way, but the solid looking woman fetched him a hefty wallop with her handbag and it was he who dropped to the floor. A little boy, out late with his parents, was screaming in fright, his mother having been swept away from him. A quick-witted waiter, who had managed not to lose his cool, swiftly gathered the boy up and pulled him to safety, through a second door marked "PRIVATE".

I caught a glimpse of gleaming metal behind the double

3

doors. That must be the kitchens, I thought. Another way out of the building.

A couple of other diners had spotted the opportunity and, abandoning the crowd, made their own, private escape. Greenfield met my eye and we quickly followed suit, through the hefty flapping doors. Behind us, there were cries of anger and distress. The kitchen itself was empty, however. The staff had already retreated through a rear door out onto the road. I could hardly blame them. We threaded our way through the kitchen and out into a dark side street.

It was a comparatively mild evening for early January, which is to say bitterly cold, but I didn't care. It was a relief to be outside. Could it really be a bomb, I wondered, looking back at the restaurant. What kind of scoundrel would leave a crate of dynamite in a public place? The slaughter would be indiscriminate.

A dozen or more people were now crowding up behind us, having followed us out through the kitchens. Many more were spooling onto the street to our left, via the bins bordering the restroom exit. There wasn't enough room on the pavement for so many people and the diners were already spilling out into the middle of the road, to the consternation of several passing taxi drivers. Horns were blaring angrily.

Greenfield and I threaded ourselves through the traffic and across the street, helping one young man who had tripped and narrowly avoided a motorcar. Finally reaching the far kerb, we turned around and looked back at the restaurant. My breath was a cloud of vapour in the air. There had not been time to gather our hats and coats but I was at least passably dressed in a smart jacket and waistcoat. Greenfield was similarly attired, but some of the womenfolk were in light cotton evening dresses. The waiter who had called the alarm now appeared to the right of the bins and began fielding a torrent of irate questions. In the distance, I could hear several police sirens as New York's finest raced towards the scene.

'Are you all right?' Greenfield asked me. 'You look like you've seen a ghost.'

'I'm fine.' I shuddered, gathering myself up on the far

4

pavement. 'Do you think it really could be a bomb?' Leopardi's was an Italian restaurant and Italians were behind the recent terror campaign. The ex-patriot community was at war, communists against fascists, and things had escalated just after Christmas when a series of letter bombs had been sent to prominent supporters of Mussolini. It was no wonder that the thought of a bomb had provoked such a panic.

Greenfield was perplexed. 'I don't know,' he confessed, in answer to my question. 'Leopardi's no supporter of fascism. Bombing his place makes no sense. He's a restaurateur. He has no interest in politics.' And hitherto, the bombs had all been aimed at individuals, not members of the public.

I gazed across the road, at the crowd still spreading out from the rear of the building. 'Well, somebody has a grudge against him.'

'So it appears. I don't like this at all.'

The police cars were now screeching to a halt, out of sight at the front of the building.

'I'm not exactly thrilled about it myself,' I muttered. 'Next time, Terrance, I think *I'll* choose the restaurant.'

Greenfield was too distracted to smile. 'Look, are you all right out here for a minute? I'm going to try to find out what's going on.'

I regarded the man in surprise. 'Well, yes, I'm fine, but...what are you going to do? You're not going back in there?'

Greenfield shook his head. 'I'll head round the front. See if I can find out what's happening. Won't be two ticks.'

I watched him move off. The fellow had a death wish. Of course, as a member of the security services, Greenfield was used to tricky situations, but there was no call this time to put himself in the line of fire. Whatever was going on at Leopardi's, it surely had nothing to do with us.

In hindsight, having dinner at an Italian restaurant on my last evening in New York was perhaps not the best idea. Terrance Greenfield was a colleague of mine, an amiable bean counter beavering away diligently on behalf of the British establishment. The Secret Intelligence Bureau had an office in New York and he was one of the senior men. I was quite fond of Greenfield, though I did not know him well. He was a good looking fellow in his later years, grey haired but with a warm twinkle in his eye. The two of us had met up at Leopardi's at eight o'clock and settled in a quiet corner, well away from the main entrance.

'Not enjoying the food?' Greenfield had asked, swirling a mound of spaghetti on the end of his fork as we moved onto the main course. He had recommended the fish, but I was beginning to have second thoughts. The damn thing was drenched in olive oil and goodness knows what else. I gave out a heavy sigh, looking down at the thing. The Mediterranean diet is supposed to do wonders for one's health, but I would happily have traded a few years of my life for a decent Sunday roast and a half bottle of whisky.

'Oh, it's well cooked,' I said, staring glumly at the oily monstrosity before me. 'I'm just having trouble picking out all the bones.'

'You should have gone with the spaghetti,' Greenfield said, bringing the fork to his mouth and expertly sucking it up; then he reached for his napkin and dabbed at his lips. His was the first friendly face I had seen when I arrived in the United States. I had flown over by Zeppelin the previous April. Greenfield had welcomed me to the New York office and helped me to establish my new identity. Mr Henry Buxton, no less, one of several aliases I had used in recent years. It didn't have quite the same ring as my real name – Hilary Manningham-Butler – but it was serviceable enough. I had returned to New York just before Christmas, after an horrendous few months in Central America, and Greenfield had been equally welcoming. The idea of a night out with him on my last evening in the Americas was an appealing one, even allowing for the unfortunate choice of restaurant.

'You'll like the dessert anyway.' Greenfield sat back in his chair. 'Leopardi makes the best ice cream in America.' I rolled my eyes and stabbed at the fish one last time. He could see I was not convinced. 'Well, you'll have no complaints about the Galitia, at any rate. The food onboard is first rate.' The RMS Galitia was a steamship departing for Southampton first thing tomorrow.

I had travelled on the ship a couple of times before, albeit some years ago. This time, I had booked myself a first class ticket. It was a bit of an extravagance but I could just about afford it. I'd had such a terrible time of late – in Guatemala and British Honduras – that I felt the need for a little luxury, even if it did stretch the budget somewhat. After two years away from home, I had finally decided to return to England. I was fed up gallivanting around the globe, getting caught up in other people's business. I had not exactly left the old country in a blaze of glory, but I was pining now for the home comforts and enough was enough. I had a new identity and a decent pot of money set aside. So long as I avoided my old haunts in London and the home counties, I would be safe enough.

'Well,' said Greenfield, 'I wish you Godspeed tomorrow.' He raised his glass.

The soda water the waiter had brought us had been augmented by a few drops of whisky from my canteen. We clinked the glasses together. It was an awful nuisance, having to bring one's own alcohol out to a restaurant like this. That was one thing I would definitely not miss about America: their ridiculous laws on alcohol. At least the waiters were happy to turn a blind eye. They had enough on their plate, with the rather loud clientele crammed into the place at this time of the evening. Leopardi's was a smart enough establishment but it was a far cry from the Ritz.

'There is one little favour you might do for us,' Greenfield added quietly, once we had taken a quick gulp from our glasses.

Here it comes, I thought. I did not for a minute believe I had been invited out this evening for purely social reasons. There is always a price tag when it comes to the British Secret Service.

Greenfield did not beat about the bush. 'There's a chap

travelling with you on the Galitia tomorrow. An American gentleman.'

'Oh?'

'Used to be one of ours. Did a bit of work for us during the war.' The Great War, of course. 'He's freelance now and got himself involved in all sorts of disreputable activity.'

'A gangster?'

'Well, after a fashion. Not one of the nastier ones, thank goodness, but we have standing orders to keep an eye on him. The people back home have given us a watching brief.'

'And you want me to keep an eye on him on the voyage to Southampton?'

'Just a fatherly eye,' Greenfield reassured me. 'Nothing too onerous.'

'You do realise, strictly speaking, I am no longer an employee of His Majesty's Government?' I had resigned my commission in Guatemala. Well, "resigned" is perhaps not the most accurate term. I had got myself into a bit of a pickle and had been forced to flee the country. My life of late had been one disaster after another.

'I appreciate that,' Greenfield said. 'But this isn't anything complicated or dangerous. Just a favour from on high. And it will stand you in good stead when you get back home.'

'I see.' Actually, that was important to me. My attempts to find work in British Honduras, the next country along, had been soundly rebuffed; and although I now had quite a sum of money put by, it would not last forever. At some point, I would have to throw myself on the mercy of my old bosses back in London. 'Very well. So who is this scoundrel?'

Greenfield reached into his jacket and pulled out a small photograph. He placed it on the table in front of me. I had just taken a mouthful of fish and I almost choked at the sight of it, a bone briefly lodging in the back of my gullet. I coughed and reached quickly for a swig of whisky.

'Are you all right?' Greenfield asked, with some concern.

'Yes, I...I just didn't...' I stared down at the photograph. That face. My God. It was as familiar to me as that of my own father.

'You recognise him?' Greenfield asked in surprise.

'Oh, yes.' I nodded and took another gulp of whisky. 'Lord, yes.' That rounded, boyish face and those sparkling eyes. It was unmistakable. 'That's Harry Latimer.' I coughed again, taking a moment to recover my wits. 'We're…erm…we're old friends.'

Greenfield pressed back in his chair. 'You know Latimer?' His brow crinkled slightly. 'That I didn't expect. It's a long time since he last worked for British Intelligence.'

'Oh, I've *known* him a long time. And he gets around, does Harry.' I bit my lip. The two of us had been friends since the war. I had first met him in New Orleans, a few days after the armistice; but I had never thought to see him again. The last time we had bumped into each other had been in England in the autumn of 1929. I had been caught up in a rather unfortunate series of events at a country house in Buckinghamshire. At the end of it, for reasons too onerous to go into here, I had been forced to fake my own death. As far as Harry Latimer was concerned, I was dead and buried. 'Look here, Terrance,' I admitted now, 'this could be dashed awkward.'

'How so?' Greenfield put down his glass and recovered the photograph, which he pocketed smoothly. He knew nothing of the Bletchley affair, of course, and I was not about to explain it to him. But I had to tell him something.

'Well, for a start, he knows my real name.' That was something almost nobody knew. 'You say he's travelling on the Galitia?'

Greenfield nodded. 'Booked a ticket just the other day. When we saw the name of the ship, we thought of you. That's why I suggested coming here. I gather this is a regular haunt of his. I was going to point him out to you.'

My eyes widened in alarm. 'He's here? Harry's here?'

'Yes. Just around the corner. Look, you can see his reflection in the mirror there.'

I glanced across the crowded room at the wide floor-length mirror. Sure enough, the familiar figure was reflected there, albeit from behind, the broad shoulders and the loosely cropped hair. My old friend, Harry Latimer, as I lived and breathed. He had ordered the fish as well. And he would get the shock of his life when he saw me. A phantom rising up from his past.

'No idea who he's dining with, though,' Greenfield added.

I blinked in surprise, as I recognised his companion. Her face at least was fully visible. 'That's Mrs O'Neill,' I said. She was a large, matronly woman in her early fifties. 'She's staying at the Alderley hotel, just down the hall from me.' I had booked myself into a pleasant room there for my last couple of nights in New York. 'She's travelling on the Galitia too.' The woman had made a point of introducing herself to me. 'Why she would be dining with Harry I have no idea.'

'Mr Latimer has an eye for the ladies, I understand.'

That was true enough. Harry did have something of a reputation in that respect. There were half a dozen irate fathers back in England who would happily see Harry Latimer keelhauled, and doubtless a similar number in the United States. 'Yes, but young and blonde,' I said. 'Not middle aged widows. Even rich ones.' Mrs O'Neill was not short of a bob or two, that much I did know. I brought a hand up to my face. 'Lord, do you think he might have seen me?'

'Who knows? If he knows you that well, you're going to have to say hello. It won't make any odds, from our point of view. You won't be able to avoid him, once you set sail.'

I dropped the hand. That was true. 'Lord, I was hoping for a quiet trip home.' I gazed across at the mirror once again. 'Perhaps I should bite the bullet and go over now.' If I had to say hello, I might as well get it over with. It might be quite fun, to see the look of horror on his face when I appeared before him. Harry did not like surprises and this would be the surprise of a lifetime.

Greenfield dismissed that idea with a wave of his fork. 'This is your last evening in New York. You can worry about Harry Latimer tomorrow. He probably hasn't even noticed we're here.' He put down the fork. 'Actually, I thought we could take in a show after dinner. Something a little risqué. I hear there's quite a good…what the devil?'

It was at this point that the head waiter banged his tray, some fool shouted 'bomb' and, moments later, we found ourselves part of the stampede.

Now I was out on the street and Terrence Greenfield was disappearing from view. If anyone could find out what was going on in the restaurant, it was our man in New York. I reached into my jacket pocket, to pull out my cigarette case. At that moment, a loud female voice called across to me. 'Mr Buxton! I thought it was you! Isn't it awful?'

I tried not to shudder as the familiar figure of Mrs Susan O'Neill bustled across the pavement towards me. She was an imposing woman, perhaps five feet four in height, stocky, and with lively darting eyes peering out from an otherwise bland face. She was dressed in an elegant silk evening gown, fashionably cut. It might have suited a woman half her age. It was certainly no protection from the cold. She had probably come out with a fur coat and a hat, but there had been no time to retrieve it from the cloakroom.

I pocketed my cigarette case and raised a reluctant hand in greeting. I had forgotten all about the woman, in the mad panic to leave the restaurant. 'Not an ideal evening,' I agreed. My eyes, however, were fixed on her escort, a handsome scoundrel who was smiling benignly.

'Do you think it really is a bomb?' Mrs O'Neill babbled. Her accent was a refined east coast American, but I flinched at the volume of it. 'Ought we to move further away?'

Her companion did not seem particularly concerned. 'Oh, I think we're safe enough here, Mrs O'Neill. Even if it is a bomb.' His eyes flicked back to the restaurant. 'If it was going to go off, I figure it would have done it by now.'

'Very likely,' I agreed, with a grim smile.

Harry Latimer returned my gaze with some amusement. He was a tall, broad shouldered fellow in his late thirties, a veritable bear of a man. He was handsome in a boyish way; perhaps not quite a matinee idol but a decent enough lead in a second feature. It was a little over two years since I had last seen him and he did not seem to have aged a day. Harry threw

11

me an easy smile. Oddly, he did not seem surprised to see me, which in itself was something of a surprise. Perhaps he had already clocked me back in the restaurant.

Mrs O'Neill's attention was focused firmly on the evacuation. 'We might have all been killed,' she burbled.

'Oh, we're safe enough out here,' Harry said, scratching an earhole. 'So, are you going to introduce me to your friend?' His accent, unlike Mrs O'Neill's, was a smooth transatlantic hybrid, not quite British or American. Years spent flitting across Europe had mellowed his speech patterns somewhat.

'Oh, yes, of course!' Mrs O'Neill exclaimed. 'Do forgive me. Mr Buxton, this is Harry Latimer. He's from New Jersey. Mr Latimer, this is a friend of mine from England, Mr Henry Buxton.' The word "friend" was stretching it a little. We had barely known each other for two days.

'Buxton?' Harry lifted an eyebrow as he thrust out his hand. He would not have heard that name before. It was one of many aliases I had used in recent years. Reginald Bland. Henry Buxton. I had even been Mrs Harold Bannerman, briefly, crossing from Guatemala to British Honduras. 'A pleasure to meet you,' he said.

'Er...likewise,' I agreed. Whatever the man was up to, he seemed content to present me as a stranger in front of Mrs O'Neill. Business always came first with Harry. If he was at all surprised at my unexpected return from the dead, he was not going to show it in front of his new best friend. The man had a superb poker face.

A gentle splatter of rain was beginning to fall on us. The woman started to shiver.

'Mrs O'Neill, you're freezing,' Harry observed, with a creditable stab at concern. He whipped off his jacket. 'Here, let me,' he said, placing the garment over her shoulders, to the delight of the middle aged widow. As he did so, his hands gently brushed the clasp of her pearl necklace.

'Mr Latimer is my guardian angel,' she purred. 'He saved my life.'

Harry waved away the compliment. 'You're exaggerating,' he protested lightly.

12

'I don't think we were in any real danger,' I declared. 'I suspect the front of the building is where the action would be, if there was going to be any.'

'Oh, not the restaurant,' Mrs O'Neill said. 'Would you believe it? Twice in one day!'

'The police too.' Harry Latimer grimaced, glancing across the street. A patrol man had just rounded a corner, moving in to take a few statements from some of the diners on the opposite side of the road. Harry tended to dance around on the wrong side of the law and was never happy when the boys in blue were in the vicinity. The senior officers would be at the front of the building by now, with the bomb squad if necessary. And Terrance Greenfield would be poking his nose in, finding out exactly what was going on.

'Twice?' I asked, not quite following.

'Oh, you won't have heard,' Mrs O'Neill said. 'Mr Buxton, it was dreadful. I was attacked, in broad daylight, just as I was leaving the hotel this morning.'

'Good lord.'

'The doorman was calling me a taxicab. I stepped out onto the side walk, when this horrible, horrible man, he grabbed hold of me.'

'To be strictly accurate,' Harry interjected, with the slightest of smirks, 'he grabbed hold of her purse.'

'Good grief. A robbery?'

'My handbag,' Mrs O'Neill confirmed, 'He snatched it from me, before I even knew what was happening. Then he ran off down the street. It was awful. If Mr Latimer hadn't been there...'

'I was just coming around the corner,' Harry explained. 'I heard Mrs O'Neill call out, I saw the bag and I realised straight away what was going on.'

I nodded grimly. I was beginning to understand only too well.

'I confronted the guy and managed to pull the bag away from him, but he gave me a good sock to the jaw and, I have to confess, that winded me. By the time I'd recovered myself, he'd run off.'

13

'Harry was so brave!' Mrs O'Neill gushed. 'My knight in shining armour. And do you know, he wouldn't accept a cent in reward?'

The hero of the hour shrugged modestly. 'Hey, I was just doing what any good citizen would do.' By this time, I was struggling not to laugh. It looked like Harry was up to his old tricks again. But Mrs O'Neill seemed oblivious to the deception. 'And I was happy to accept an invitation to dinner,' Harry added.

'And you'll never guess,' Mrs O'Neill continued breathlessly. 'Mr Latimer is booked on the Galitia as well. Isn't that a coincidence?'

'It certainly is,' I agreed, straight-faced.

By now, the rain was falling steadily. Mrs O'Neill pulled Harry's jacket tightly around herself.

'We ought to get you back to your hotel,' Harry suggested. 'Are you at the Alderley too?' This question was directed at me.

'Yes, on the third floor. Why, is that where you're staying?'

'No, I'm at the Waldorf Astoria, a little further on.'

'What, the new place?'

'Yeah, that's the one.' It had only been open a couple of months. 'Hey, would you mind, old man?' He glanced up at the sky. 'I think we should get Mrs O'Neill back to the Alderley, before the rain really hits.' The woman opened her mouth to protest, but Harry lifted a hand. 'We can send someone for the coats later on.' I had the impression my American friend was rather keen to move on, and not just for Mrs O'Neill's sake. The further we got from the police, the happier he would be.

I was less keen to desert my post. I couldn't just abandon Terrance Greenfield, even if it was pouring down. 'I was here with a friend,' I said. 'He seems to have wandered off somewhere.' The rain was falling quite heavily now. 'I dare say I can catch up with him later.' After all, I had been tasked with keeping an eye on Harry Latimer and – bomb or no bomb – I might as well make a start on it. 'Mrs O'Neill?' I extended an arm and the American woman took it gratefully.

14

'I'm so lucky,' she beamed, 'to have met two such *nice* young men.'

Mrs O'Neill was mistaken on almost every count. It was not luck that had led Harry Latimer into her life. It had been design. Harry and I were not exactly young, he was not exactly nice; and I was not exactly a man. Oh, I certainly looked the part – square jaw, broad shoulders, deep voice – but though I presented myself to the world as an English gentleman, the fact was that I had been born a woman. There was no malign intent in my deception. I had simply chosen to live my life as a man.

It was my father who had set the ball rolling. He had wanted a son and had insisted on raising me as a boy. When I reached adulthood, I had decided to continue the charade. It was a matter of convenience more than anything else. Men have always been afforded greater latitude than women and, in a society which routinely regards females as "the weaker sex", it was a source of some pride to me that I had managed to pass myself off so easily as a man. The physique helped, of course, not to mention the bandages restraining my rather modest chest, but it was the attitude more than anything else that helped to convince people, that effortless superiority so many men contrive to project, despite their obvious imperfections. The fact that I was able to replicate it and pull the wool over so many eyes gave the lie to their absurd prejudices. I had been a spy, a thief, a man about town, even – God help me – a detective, and though I seldom acquitted myself as well as I might have hoped, I had at least survived in the male domain on equal terms.

Harry Latimer's deception was altogether more tawdry. I had got the drop on that from the moment I had first caught sight of him at the restaurant; but it wasn't until we had settled Mrs O'Neill comfortably back into the hands of her companion, Miss Wellesley, at the Alderley hotel, that the matter had been formally broached. 'That poor woman,' I said, as we made our way along the corridor towards the elevator. 'She doesn't know what a viper she's invited into her nest. You haven't changed,

15

Harry.'

The American did not bat an eyelid as he pressed the call button. 'I can't imagine what you mean.'

'The purse snatching this morning. It was a set-up, wasn't it?' Harry shrugged, non-committally. 'Come off it, Harry. I know you too well. You wanted to effect an introduction. Get her confidence. Who was the purse snatcher? A friend of yours?'

Harry grinned. 'An acquaintance.' He rubbed his chin as the elevator arrived at our floor. 'He really did sock me one.'

'That must have been galling for you.' Harry was a past master at the art of fisticuffs. He could best anyone in a fight and he wouldn't enjoy losing out like that, even if it was just for show. 'Bit over the top, though, wasn't it? Couldn't you have bumped into Mrs O'Neill at the breakfast table or something like that?'

'Oh, sure, sure,' Harry said, as the lift operator pulled back the gate and invited us inside. 'If we'd been staying at the same hotel. But I figured I might as well make a show of it.'

'Presenting yourself as the hero of the piece.' We shuffled into the elevator and the doorman closed up the gate in front of us.

'That's about the size of it, old man.' The operator pressed a button and the lift began its descent. 'You know me too well.'

'Yes, unfortunately.' And I had a pretty good idea what he was aiming for too. I waited until we were out of the lift before articulating my suspicions. 'It's the necklace, I take it. The pearls.' I had noticed the chain hanging from Mrs O'Neill's neck the first time we had met. A good twenty or thirty pieces in all, on a simple string. If they were genuine – which I was sure they would be – they would be worth an absolute fortune.

Harry smiled slyly. 'Such a pretty thing, that necklace. It seems such a waste, hanging from the neck of a widow like Mrs O'Neill. I could put it to much better use.'

'I'll bet you could.' We moved across the foyer.

'Hey, you're not exactly lily-white, old man,' he observed, as we strolled casually towards the bar. 'Last time I saw you, you were heading for the morgue.'

'Ah yes.' I grimaced. 'That may take a little bit of explaining.' I was surprised Harry had left it this long before bringing it up. He was probably making a point of taking it all in his stride.

We moved into the saloon bar and settled down at a small table in a quiet corner. The bar was poorly named. There was not a drop of alcohol to be had anywhere. We ordered two glasses of soda water and, when they arrived, I pulled out my flask and topped it up with a spot of whisky. Harry did likewise, though he preferred brandy. 'Great minds think alike,' he said, pocketing his own canteen and lifting his glass. He sat back in his chair. 'So what's the story, Hilary?'

'Henry. Henry Buxton now.'

'Henry.' He grinned. 'How come you're not pushing up daisies?'

'It's a long story,' I admitted mournfully. Harry had been there at Bletchley, so he knew most of it. I explained the rest as best I could. The faked suicide, when things had gone against me. The help I had been given from on high.

'I figured at the time it was all a little too neat. And the Colonel...' Our former boss at MI5. 'He wouldn't have let you die. He always had a soft spot for you, old man. Can't imagine why.'

'It's thanks to him I got away at all. What about you?' Harry had had his own problems that weekend. 'You left England shortly afterwards, I take it?'

'I was asked to leave. The Colonel's not so fond of me. Told me to get out in no uncertain terms.' He shrugged cheerfully. 'The perils of a life lived to the full. It meant I had to miss your funeral. But I gather there was a good turn out.'

'Yes, so I heard.' I didn't like to think too much about that.

'Which reminds me.' Harry grinned again. 'You owe me ten shillings.'

I blinked. 'Ten shilling?'

'For the wreathe, old man. For the wreathe.'

I let out a snort. 'Is that all I was worth?'

'Hey, I wouldn't have bothered if it had been anyone else. So where did you go, when they carted you off? To Europe?'

'Yes. The south of France to begin with. Then I spent a few months in Gibraltar. Finally ended up in Guatemala, of all places, working as a Passport Control officer.'

'Jeez, you get about.'

'Not through choice. The job was a complete wash out. I left there in July and fished up in British Honduras. Just in time for the hurricane season.'

Harry mimed his surprise. 'You were there in *September*?'

'Yes.' I grimaced. 'Right in the middle of it.'

'Jesus. I read about that.' A hurricane had struck the capital city. 'The whole place was flattened, wasn't it?'

I was trying my best not to remember. 'It wasn't the hurricane that did the real damage. It was the tidal wave that came after it. My God, Harry, you should have seen it. Fifteen feet tall. I never saw anything like it. I was lucky to escape with my life.'

'How did you escape?'

'I didn't, in point of fact.' I coughed in embarrassment. 'I just shinned up the nearest coconut tree and hung on for dear life.'

Harry laughed out loud. 'You have got to be kidding me!'

'It's true, I swear. Any other tree and I'd have been swept away, but that one held fast. It was the aftermath, though. The absolute devastation.' I shuddered at the memory. 'It was awful, Harry. So many dead. I decided then and there, I was done with the Americas. My life has been an unmitigated disaster these last few years. I just want to go home, whatever the consequences. So at the earliest opportunity, I hopped on a plane and headed for New York.'

'I thought you hated aeroplanes.'

'I do. But needs must.'

'And now you're booked on the Galitia?'

'For my sins. Though what reception I'll receive when I

get back to England, I have no idea.'

Harry sucked in a breath with mock seriousness. 'It's not easy being a dead man. How do you manage for money?'

'I do all right.' Sadly, the bulk of my estate had been passed on to my next of kin, but I had not been left entirely destitute. 'I have a couple of small annuities the lawyers know nothing about. And I've kept myself busy, doing the odd bit of work for the old firm. I can't talk about that, of course.'

Harry nodded. 'Yeah, I know. Need to know.' He sat back in his chair. 'Jesus, Hilary. And I thought my life was complicated.'

'Henry, please. I am trying very hard to simplify things. Hopefully, once we're onboard the Galitia, I can start to relax.'

'No explosives allowed.'

'Well, exactly. And that's what I mean.' I waved my hands in the air. 'I can't even have a meal at a restaurant these days without all hell breaking loose.'

'I know the feeling. So what did Terrance Greenfield want with you?' Harry met my eye. For all his casual charm, there was always an edge to him where business matters were concerned. And Terrance Greenfield was definitely business.

'Ah.' I coughed again. 'You saw him there did you?'

'At the restaurant, sure.' So he *had* noticed us dining together, before the evacuation. 'I'm not going to miss a high up from the SIS. Don't tell me. He asked you to keep an eye on me, on the way home? Is that right?'

'Er…yes, something like that. Just the Colonel being nosey, I expect.' Harry had worked for MI5 during the war. The old firm had kept an eye on him ever since. It was in no-one's interests for Harry Latimer to end up behind bars. 'And I'm sure you're going to behave yourself onboard ship.'

'Oh, of course, old man. Of course.'

'When you're not conspiring to steal pearl necklaces.' I chuckled. 'So when are you planning to do the deed? You can't spend a week socializing with the woman onboard ship if you've stolen them on the first day.'

'No, I figure it's going to be a slow burn, this one. In any case, the necklace is just a side show. I was planning on leaving the country quite soon in any case. You're not the only one leading a complicated life. No, I think a nice sea voyage will do me the world of good.'

Harry had been looking rather shifty back at the restaurant, when the police had appeared on the scene. 'So what have you done? Robbed a bank or something?' I wasn't sure I wanted to know the details and I doubted Harry would tell me anyway.

'Oh, nothing like that, old man.' He smirked. 'You know me. I would never get involved in anything outside the law.'

I laughed loudly. He had said it with such a straight face. 'You're a rogue, Harry.' I raised my glass a second time. 'It's good to see you.'

Terrance Greenfield was on the other end of the line. A waiter had called me over to a public phone. Harry was sitting quietly, nursing a second brandy and soda.

'Sorry for disappearing like that,' I said, keeping my voice low. 'I bumped into Harry Latimer. I'm with him at the bar now. I thought we'd keep things on a social level.'

'Quite right,' Greenfield agreed. 'Was he surprised to see you?'

'I'll say. He saw you and I together though, so he knows what we're about. Knows I've been told to keep an eye on him.'

'That can't be helped. You stick close to him, regardless. Tell the Colonel everything when you get back to Southampton.'

'I'll do my best. What's happening at your end? Did you find out what happened at the restaurant?'

'Yes, in a manner of speaking. Everything's calmed down here now. I've spoken to the chief of police.' Being a member of the security services, even on foreign soil, had its advantages.

'And what did you find out? Was it a bomb? Did they call in the bomb squad?'

20

'They did. But it was all a hoax.'

'A hoax?'

'There was a package. Looked just like a parcel bomb, but there was nothing in it.'

'Lord.'

'I spoke to one of the waiters at the restaurant. Apparently, it was left on the doorstep at the side of the building. It wasn't sent through the regular mail. Someone off-shift saw it and brought it in. One of the waiters panicked when he realised it was the same sort of parcel he'd read about in the papers. It was the same size and had all the same markings. But the bomb squad were able to determine that there was nothing dangerous inside. Different weight, no obvious trigger. In fact, there was nothing in it at all, just packaging.'

'That is odd,' I said. 'So what have the police concluded?'

'They don't think it's anything to do with the communists. It's what they call a "copy cat". Someone reading about the letter bombs and doing it themselves.'

'Lord. You mean some sort of sick joke?'

'It looks like it,' Greenfield admitted. 'A little more than a schoolboy prank, though.'

'I'll say.' All those people struggling to get out of the restaurant. Someone could have been seriously hurt.

'There was one peculiarity though. That's why I thought I'd better call you. They found an address written on the package. Well, not an address, a name.'

'Oh?' I raised an eyebrow.

'It's all a bit awkward. The police are going to want to speak to her, I'm afraid. She's staying at the Alderley, didn't you say?'

'The Alderley? Who do you mean?'

'Your Mrs O'Neill,' Greenfield said. 'The parcel was addressed to her.'

Chapter Two

'Isn't she wonderful?' Mrs O'Neill gushed, as we stepped out of the taxicab. The docks on the west side of Manhattan were swarming with life. It was a mild January morning and the sun was beaming down on a veritable cavalcade of overcoats, fedoras and cloche hats. Mrs O'Neill was taking no chances, however, and was dressed in a heavy fur coat and muffler. Harry had been as good as his word, sending a boy back to the restaurant last night to collect her things. He was making his own way here this morning, from the Waldorf Astoria.

I turned back to the taxicab and offered a polite hand to a second woman as she stepped out onto the concourse. Cynthia Wellesley was Mrs O'Neill's paid companion, a fresh-faced English girl in her early twenties, dressed in a light overcoat and two piece rayon dress. She would be accompanying Mrs O'Neill on her European odyssey, having answered an advertisement in a newspaper just before Christmas. It was always nice to have someone to talk to, I supposed, though the American woman was not exactly shy when it came to conversing with strangers.

'Good morning!' she had bellowed at me, the day before last, when I had emerged bleary eyed from my hotel room a little after nine o'clock. I had barely got a word in before she had introduced herself and minutes later, much to my chagrin, I had found myself taking breakfast with the damned women. It never ceases to amaze me how forward some Americans can be. In England, even in a small hotel, we would have exchanged a polite nod and then settled at separate tables. There was nothing improper in her advances, however – she was a respectable widow – and politeness dictated that I show her some civility.

The taxi driver let out a cough and I reached for my wallet, as the women placed their hand luggage on the pavement and took a moment to peruse the energetic scene before us.

Even in 1932, the embarkation of a steamship was a

major social event and it was not just the passengers and crew who had turned out to witness the spectacle. We had arrived on the concourse just outside Pier 54, where the crowds were gathering for the morning's departure. The building was a long, brick built colonnade with several gated entrances. A steady stream of people were passing beneath the steel archway leading onto the pier, many of them friends and relatives of those about to depart, as well as the passengers themselves. It was the sight of the ship, however, with its four red and black funnels peeping above the roof of the building, that had caught Mrs O'Neill's attention. 'Isn't she marvellous?' she exclaimed again.

The RMS Galitia was a British built steamship, nine hundred feet from top to tail and almost a hundred feet wide. 'She is impressive,' I agreed, glancing back from the taxi.

'Oh, but you've travelled on her before,' Mrs O'Neill recalled.

'A long time ago.' Shortly before the war, in fact, on my first trip to the Americas. 'She was fresh out of the shipyard then.' I peered up at the funnels, a familiar and reassuring sight. 'She's worn well, by the look of her. You wouldn't think she's been afloat for almost two decades.' The Galitia had been ploughing a regular furrow between New York and Southampton for many, many years. During the war, she had even seen service as a medical ship.

Mrs O'Neill beamed. 'I'm so glad we were able to get tickets. The White Star Line is all very well, but the Galitia is something special, don't you think?'

'Indeed.' The RMS Galitia was a veritable grand hotel of the waves and I was looking forward to the voyage immensely.

Behind us, the taxicab chugged away in a cloud of smoke.

Mrs O'Neill's companion had not spoken a word since our arrival. I took a moment to observe the girl now as she stood listening to our conversation. Cynthia Wellesley was quite a serious minded young woman. Bookish, I would have said, albeit on the briefest of acquaintances. Brave too, coming all this way to America on her own. She had travelled here on an exchange, apparently, to study for a term at one of the American universities. Botany, no less, a subject which bored me rigid. She had confided in me, however, that she was a little apprehensive about the return voyage. That was probably why she had not come out to the restaurant last night; or perhaps she was allowing Mrs O'Neill the time to get to know Harry Latimer properly, without any unhelpful distractions. In the normal state of affairs, I knew which one of these women Harry would have his eye on. Miss Wellesley was quite a pretty young thing, blonde and wide eyed. Definitely Harry's type. 'I get so terribly seasick,' she told me. 'And this time of the year, the weather can be so rough.'

'It's not looking too disastrous at the moment,' I said, 'according to the forecast. How was the journey out?' Miss Wellesley had come to America the previous summer.

'It was quite mild,' she admitted. 'I was ill for the first couple of days, but after that it was all right. Just a question of finding my sea legs. Do you get seasick, Mr Buxton?'

'Not as much as I used to. It's aeroplanes that give me the real tremors.'

Her eyes lit up. 'Gosh, I've never been in an aeroplane.'

'Take my advice,' I said. 'Don't.' I had been sick on the journey over from British Honduras. If my man Maurice had not been there with a brown paper bag I might have splattered the entire cabin.

Mrs O'Neill had stopped speaking and was staring expectantly at the two of us. 'Do you think we ought to get in line?' she asked. 'Or should we wait for Mr Latimer?'

'You go on,' I said. 'I'll wait for Harry…er Mr Latimer. I want to have a last cigarette before I head in, in any case.' A big sign above the entrance made it clear that smoking was not permitted on the pier itself. The ship, thank goodness, had no such rules. As soon as we were out of port, we could smoke and drink as much as we liked. 'Are your friends here yet? I thought I saw a limousine leaving just as we pulled up.'

Mrs O'Neill nodded. 'I think so. We'll have to see.' An English couple, a lord and lady something, had booked a suite on B Deck. They had been staying with Mrs O'Neill for the last few months, apparently. I hadn't met them yet, though doubtless we would become acquainted over the course of the next few days. 'Come along Cynthia!' Mrs O'Neill called. 'We'll see you onboard, then, Mr Buxton.'

'I look forward to it,' I lied.

Miss Wellesley smiled at me as she moved to accompany her mistress. I watched the two of them go with some relief. Mrs O'Neill was a force of nature and better dealt with in small doses. I pulled out a cigarette and lit it quickly. I was glad that the woman had recovered her spirits, though, after the events of the previous day.

'Me?' she had exclaimed in disbelief, when I'd passed on the news about the letter bomb. I had popped up to the third floor last night to tell her what I had heard. 'It was addressed to *me?*'

'So I've been told.'

Mrs O'Neill was standing in the doorway of her hotel room, in a knee length silk dress, utterly flummoxed. 'But that's...it can't be.'

'The police will be on their way up shortly,' I warned her, repeating what Greenfield had told me on the telephone. 'Is there any reason you can think of why someone would leave a parcel there with your name on it? Is there anyone you've offended recently?'

'No-one, Mr Buxton. Unless...' She hesitated, looking up and down the corridor. 'My late husband. His business interests. I know they sometimes...'

At that moment, the lift pinged just across the way and the police arrived in the corridor. Two grisly looking detectives. Mrs O'Neill brought a hand to her mouth. It was the second time in less than a day that she had had to contend with the boys in blue, after the business with the handbag that morning. The first time she had spoken to a fresh-faced constable; but these fellows – as Harry would put it – were "the real deal".

The detectives flashed their badges and were invited into the hotel room.

I was left out in the corridor, but Miss Wellesley gave

me an account of the interview later on and Mrs O'Neill confirmed the details at breakfast.

The American woman was not suspected of any involvement with the parcel itself. The police thought it possible, however, that someone had added her name to the letter out of spite. Did she know anyone who might do such a thing? She told them there were a few people who might have held a grudge against her late husband. His business interests were quite broad and he had stepped on a fair number of toes in his later years. After his death, Mrs O'Neil had assumed responsibility for those businesses – albeit at arms length – so it was possible they might have decided to switch their attention to her. But why here and now she had no idea. Another possibility, she said, was her husband's connection to the Italian community. Ulysses O'Neill had been friendly with one or two prominent officials at the Italian embassy, though that was purely a matter of business. He had never been a supporter of Mussolini.

Happily, the police took Mrs O'Neill's statement at face value and voiced no objections to her leaving on the Galitia the following morning. If they found out anything more, or needed further information, they would contact her onboard ship, they said. The authorities had concluded – as Terrance Greenfield had already surmised – that the restaurant hoax was not directly related to the terror campaign. As such, it was no longer a priority. They were simply going through the motions with regard to Mrs O'Neill.

The whole business had drained the woman considerably, however, though she put a brave face on it at breakfast. Miss Wellesley was also fretting, about the forthcoming voyage, so it was left to me to normalise the situation. I was not best pleased having to play nursemaid over the toast and marmalade to a pair of virtual strangers, but I did my duty, waxing lyrical for some minutes about Europe and all the many sights they would see during the course of their trip. And now, thank the lord, Mrs O'Neill had regained her vigour, as she tootled off to board the steamship. Hopefully, from here on in, she would direct most of her attention at Harry Latimer.

I dropped the end of my cigarette and stubbed it out on the ground. My American friend was running a little late this morning. I looked up and caught sight of him hurrying along the concourse towards me. Harry smiled broadly as he came to a halt.

'Morning, old man. All on your own?' He glanced around. The crowd outside was starting to thin, as people moved through into the departure hall.

'Mrs O'Neill's gone on ahead. What kept you? I thought you'd be lapping at her heels this morning.'

'Any other morning I would be.' He had a suitcase with him under his arm, but was otherwise dressed in a smart suit, an overcoat and a rakishly angled fedora. Even in a hurry, Harry Latimer managed to show some style. 'I had a bit of an errand to run,' he added.

'Oh?'

'Picking up some specialised equipment.'

'What sort of equipment?'

He smirked and held up his free hand theatrically, forming his fingers and thumb into a small "O". 'Sort of round and about this size.'

I regarded him blankly for a moment, and then the penny dropped. 'Pearls,' I said, finally cottoning on. 'A set of fake pearls.'

He laughed, dropping his hand. 'Could be.'

So that was it. 'You've got hold of some fakes. And you're planning on switching them for the real thing?'

'That's the idea.' His eyes gleamed. 'Nothing like a bit of paste to fool the eye. A friend of mine's been working on them through the night. Luckily, all the pearls are the same size. He just needed to get the colouring right.'

'Wait a minute. How on earth could he know…?'

'Oh, he got a good look at them. Last night, at the restaurant.'

'At Leopardi's?' My jaw dropped. 'He was there?'

'Sure. The table just along from me and Mrs O'Neill. Had a perfect view of us in the mirror.'

'Good lord.' It seemed like an awful lot of people had

been dining at Leopardi's last night. 'You're thorough, I'll give you that.' I did recall seeing some bearded fellow sitting not too far from them. He had looked the artistic type. Was there anybody dining at that damned restaurant who didn't have a hidden agenda? But it was too late to worry about that now. I returned my attention to the necklace. 'How are you intending to make the switch? Does she ever take it off?' I had never seen Mrs O'Neill without the necklace. It was damned foolish of her to run around in broad daylight with such a valuable set of pearls hanging from her neck, but it was not my place to comment. The necklace had been a gift from her late husband and she liked to keep it close to hand.

'She's got to take it off some time,' Harry reckoned. 'At night or in the bath. The swimming pool perhaps.' He grinned. There was a full length pool onboard the Galitia, as well as a gymnasium. 'Don't worry, old man, I'll find an opportunity. And I'm not exactly in a hurry. We have six whole days onboard ship.' He stretched out his arms. 'And when I bid Mrs O'Neill a tearful farewell in Southampton, she won't have any idea she's even lost them.'

'You're sure these fakes will stand up to close scrutiny?'

'Oh, I'm sure. Pierre knows his business.'

'In that case, may I take a look?' I glanced down at his case.

'I don't have them with me, old man. Credit me with a little intelligence. I'm not going to waltz through customs carrying a string of fakes. No, they'll be slipped onboard by the back door.' He took a look at his wristwatch. 'Right about now. That's why I'm running a little late. Making a few arrangements.'

'You mean roping some poor sailor in to help you smuggle them onboard ship?'

'That's about the size of it.' He smirked. 'There's always some guy hanging around the docks who can do with an extra shot of rum.'

'Harry, you're incorrigible.'

'I like to think so.' He grinned again.

'Mind you, I think you missed a trick, turning up late like this. You should have been here to see Mrs O'Neill onboard. If you want access to her boudoir, you're going to need to keep in her good books.'

Harry pulled a face. 'I'm hoping it won't come to that. Although, now you mention it, she is sharing a room with the delectable Miss Wellesley...'

I laughed. 'You keep your mind on the job, you dirty devil! Miss Wellesley is a respectable young girl.'

'No harm in looking, old man.'

'I doubt Mrs O'Neill will take kindly to you making eyes at her paid companion.'

'Oh, I'll be as good as gold,' Harry assured me. 'You know me. Business comes first. Hey, how did Mrs O'Neill manage with the police last night?' Harry had not hung around for long at the bar after the detectives had arrived.

'She was a little shaken, but she's fine now.' She had gone straight to bed after the interview, but Miss Wellesley had knocked on my door and given me an account of what had happened. 'The bomb was a hoax, so they're not too concerned about investigating it. Apparently, her late husband was a friend of some bigwig at the Italian embassy, which might explain the name on the envelope. Well, I say friend, a business acquaintance. Mr O'Neill was big in shoes, apparently. Exporting to Europe.'

'Yeah, so I've heard.'

'It takes some talent, selling shoes to the Italians, but apparently he managed it. Anyway, the police think the whole thing was down to some fool with a grudge against Mrs O'Neill's late husband.'

'That figures,' Harry agreed. 'How long is it since he died?'

'I'm not sure. A year or two, I think.'

'Well, it couldn't have been the real bombers, in any case.'

'I suppose not. They'll have gone to ground by now, I should imagine. Plotting their next atrocity.' It was appalling that people like that could get away with terrorising people on

29

such a scale. This was meant to be a civilised country.

'You mean you haven't you heard?' Harry regarded me with some surprise.

'Heard what?'

'It was in all the papers this morning.'

'I didn't have time to look.' I had been too busy soothing Mrs O'Neill's furrowed brow.

'They caught the bombers yesterday evening. It was in the stop press. They've got them under lock and key.'

'Good lord. Yesterday?'

'Yeah. So the cops were right. The business at the restaurant couldn't have had anything to do with them. Not if the parcel was hand delivered.'

'That's true.' I scratched my chin. 'So who were they? The bombers?'

Harry shrugged. 'Communists, like everyone said. Italians, targetting a few prominent friends of Mussolini.'

'Trying to target them.' I grimaced. It was not the fascists who had been blown to kingdom come, but two postal workers. 'Those poor men at that post office.'

'Yeah, that was too bad.' The other bombs had been defused, thankfully. 'Still, justice will be done, old man. It won't be long before those guys fry.'

I screwed up my face. 'You have a knack for a distasteful phrase. Anyway, we can put all that behind us now, thank goodness. It'll be plain sailing from today. And you can concentrate all your energies on Mrs O'Neill and her necklace.'

'Yeah, I guess so.' He nodded, pulling out his ticket and examining it briefly. 'Hey, look, though, I may need a little help with that.'

'Oh, no.' I raised my hands. 'If you want to steal her necklace, that's your affair. I'm happy to turn a blind eye, but I'm definitely not getting involved.'

'Oh, not *involved*, old man.' He looked up. 'I wouldn't ask you to do anything illegal. But I may need someone to distract her attention, when I make the switch.'

'And why on earth would I help you?'

'Out of the goodness of your heart?'

I threw him a look.

'Well, you do owe me a favour, old man.'

'Actually, I think we're even at the moment.'

He rolled his eyes. 'All right, all right. I'll owe *you* a favour.' That was what I wanted to hear. For all his criminal tendencies, Harry would always pay up on a debt. Eventually. 'I just need someone to make up the foursome. You, me, Mrs O'Neill and Miss Wellesley.'

'Mrs O'Neill does have other friends onboard.'

'Yeah, I know. I've met them. But I need someone I can trust. Don't worry, old man. I'll make it worth your while.'

'All right, Harry.' Actually it might be quite fun. It had been a long time since I had been involved in a bit of innocent skulduggery. It would make a nice change from the more serious mayhem of the last few months. 'Just so long as it's understood, I want nothing to do with the actual theft. I want to slip back into England quietly, not under police escort.'

'Understood.' He pocketed his ticket and looked at the queue outside the gate. 'So, shall we head on in?'

'No time like the present,' I agreed, picking up my luggage.

'You know, I think Mrs O'Neill is really taken with you,' he said, as we moved towards the gate. 'Wouldn't stop talking about you yesterday. I think a little romance might be in the air.'

'Harry, that's not funny.'

'Hey, you could do a lot worse. She's drowning in dough. Her husband left her a fortune and I think she may be on the lookout for husband number two.'

That was the conclusion I had already come to. 'Well, she can damn well look elsewhere.'

The bulk of the luggage had been sent on ahead from the hotel. My man Maurice had packed everything up last night and given it over to the staff at the Alderley for conveyance to the docks. He had come on ahead, as there had not been room in the taxicab for all of us.

An automated conveyor belt on the right-hand side of the pier was ferrying some of the baggage up into the side of the Galitia. A number of crewmen were lifting the bags from a large trolley and dumping them with reasonable care onto the rotating belt. The noise of the machinery, however, was as nothing compared to the general hubbub within the enclosure.

'It's just as I remember it,' I said to Harry, as we threaded our way towards the customs post. There were three sets of people queueing, with first class naturally given priority; but hundreds of well wishers were also assembled on the near side of the barrier, making their farewells and clogging up the whole area. Several children were skipping about carelessly in front of us. One woman was saying goodbye to her husband – I presumed it was her husband, since they were canoodling shamelessly in front of everyone – and from the ship itself we heard the cries of the seamen, shouting instructions across the way. 'Well, perhaps not as many people this time.' In the old days, when steerage made up the bulk of the passenger list, thousands of people would have been crammed in here, ready to be packed onboard ship. The pier was still busy, but the boarding time had been cut as the passenger numbers had dropped. Even the Cunard people, it seemed, had been affected by the economic downturn.

Harry handed his passport to a sober looking official. I caught a glimpse of the name as he passed the booklet across. "G Harrington Latimer". Not quite his real name but close enough. If he was skipping the country – and I had the sneaking suspicion that he might be – then he was only doing it under partial cover of darkness. Whoever had provided the forgery had done a good job. The customs man returned it without a second glance.

My own passport was genuine, though the name on the cover – Henry Augustus Buxton – was a fake. I gave a quick prayer of thanks to Terrance Greenfield as I handed the document across. Technically speaking, I was not breaking any laws today.

Ahead of us, the first class passengers were beginning to make their way onto the ship. A covered gangway ran a short distance between the pier and the outer wall of the steamer. A smartly dressed officer at the bottom of the ramp was checking the tickets. Mrs O'Neill and Miss Wellesley were just heading up the gang plank. By the look of it, the passengers with rooms on the port side were being processed first. I pulled up for a moment, as I spotted another figure waiting patiently in line. It was my valet, Maurice, a grim looking Frenchman in his mid fifties. He looked as white as a sheet. I felt a small pang of sympathy. His fear of boats was even greater than my fear of aeroplanes. But the man was steeling himself nonetheless.

Harry caught my gaze and peered across at the greying figure. 'Who's that?' he asked, as we pocketed our passports and shuffled through the gate.

'My valet, Maurice. Just boarding the ship.'

Harry grinned. 'You've got a new guy, huh?'

'A Frenchman, yes. He's been with me a while now.' Over two years, in fact. Maurice had been with me since Gibraltar. 'Not too keen on ships, though.' I fumbled for my ticket as we moved to join the back of the queue. In truth, I had not been sure whether he would be coming with me at all. The valet had been prevaricating over the matter for some weeks. It had been simple enough on the way out – we had crossed the Atlantic by Zeppelin – but an ocean liner was an entirely different kettle of fish. Maurice, it transpired, had been on a similar ship during the war, which had been sunk by a German U-boat. Since then he had had a morbid fear of all things nautical. Not that he had bothered to mention this to me until fairly recently. At Christmas, however, he had received a telegram from France informing him that his mother was seriously ill. The doctors had given her just a few months to live. If he wanted to return home to see her before the end, he had no choice but to hop on a steamer; and so he had reluctantly agreed to accompany me back to Europe.

I had been in two minds whether to buy him a first class ticket. I was not made of money and there was something to be said for banishing the fellow to third class and forgetting about him for the duration of the journey. The last thing I needed was a morose Frenchman cluttering up the place, even if he had good reason to be upset. A cabin steward would be on hand to change the bedsheets and polish the boots, and I would not need any home cooking on a ship like the Galitia. All the same, there were some things that a steward could not take care of. I would still need to dress for dinner and Maurice was one of a very small number of people who knew the truth about my sex. That was something even Harry didn't know. For all his many faults, Maurice had an attention to detail which far exceeded my own fumbling hands. And so I had booked him a berth on the same deck as my own. A separate cabin, though. There were limits to my consideration.

It was only after I had shown Maurice the tickets that he confided to me the full truth about his wartime experiences. He had been onboard the Lusitania when it had been torpedoed in 1915. He had been coming back from America with his then employer, a French diplomat. That man had drowned and Maurice had only just escaped with his life. The incident had scarred him terribly. The RMS Galitia, of course, was the Lusitania's sister ship, the last of the great pre-war Cunard liners. If I had known this a week earlier, I would have booked with another company. That was the trouble with Maurice. He never told me anything unless he absolutely had to. However, having paid through the nose for these tickets, there was no question of returning them; and so here we were, boarding a steamship, the both of us, for the first time in over a decade.

Harry could not make out anything odd in the man's manner, as we edged closer to the gangway. 'He looks okay to me.'

'He doesn't like to show his feelings,' I said, as we prepared our tickets for inspection. The valet's battered face was granite-like in its immobility, but the firmness with which he grabbed the handrail gave a fair indication of his true feelings. 'Trust me, he's terrified.' The Frenchman moved slowly up the gangplank. 'It's going to be a long old trip,' I suggested, looking down at my ticket once again. Unlike my man Maurice, however, I was rather looking forward to it.

The steam whistle let out a long, low blast, followed by three short toots. The engines were already throbbing and, a few moments later, the ship began its slow reverse out of the docks and away from the pier. I tightened my grip on the window frame as the movement vibrated through my arms and legs and the wooden floorboards began to sway gently beneath my feet. A gaggle of energetic well-wishers were grinning across at us through a selection of square holes in the pier opposite, cheering and waving, and for a brief moment I had the peculiar impression that they were moving and I was standing still; then my stomach turned itself over and my mind quickly reorientated itself. It was always the same when a ship started moving. It would take everyone a few minutes to find their bearings. Around me, the other first class passengers were crowded at the open windows along the entire length of the starboard promenade, watching with varying degrees of enthusiasm as the great steamship slowly pulled back into the Hudson river.

The promenade was a long covered way, stretching a good third of the length of the ship. Steps led up into various cabins and other rooms. I caught sight of Harry Latimer, a good fifty feet downwind, conversing with Mrs O'Neill, who he had quickly located. He caught my eye, across that distance, and smiled mischievously. Evidently, he was making up for lost time. Mrs O'Neill was oblivious, waving enthusiastically at the crowds through the open window, though to my knowledge there was no-one here to see her off.

The American passengers were easily distinguished from their more restrained European cousins, their louder voices and rather manic hands marking them out as reliably as their garish clothing. It was pleasing to reflect, however, looking across the solid, elegantly wrought deck, that this was a British built ship and I was now one step closer to home. I have never been one to succumb to the disease of nostalgia – I am all too aware of the many faults of my fellow countrymen – but, after two years away, just stepping onboard the Galitia – even hearing the loud guttural cries of the crewmen as they went about their business – I felt a warm glow of familiarity. It might take a minute or two to find my sea legs, but it seemed to me that I was now on home turf.

'Look at the tiny boats!' a little girl gurgled happily, peering over the lip of the window and observing the tugs guiding us out onto the river. She saw me watching her and waved a podgy hand. I am not overly fond of children but, caught up in the moment, I allowed myself to wave back. I took one last look through the windows at the Manhattan skyline – a farewell glimpse of the Empire State Building and the other now familiar landmarks – and then turned and headed back to the foyer.

I had moved further down the promenade than I had intended and I had to thread my way through the babbling crowds and along a pleasant garden lounge before arriving on the gently carpeted floor of the foyer. The landing here was all marble columns and wrought iron elevators, but an elaborate staircase wound down to the lower decks. I exchanged polite nods with a few other passengers as I contemplated briefly whether to use the lift, but B Deck was only one floor below. The walk so far had already served to inoculate me against the sway of the ship, so I decided to bite the bullet and risk the stairs.

A steward was hovering near the bottom step 'May I help you sir?' he asked, stepping forward. He was a fresh-faced youth in his early twenties, with small eyes and big teeth, dressed in the traditional Cunard grey.

I looked down at the piece of paper. 'Er…B61, I think.'
'Just along here, sir, on the starboard side.'

The key was already in the door. It was a pleasant, roomy space, a far cry from the cramped Zeppelin cabin I had shoe-horned myself into on the way out to America. This was proper first class accommodation, light and airy. I stepped inside and gave a sigh of satisfaction. The word "cabin" did not do it justice. In the literature it was referred to as a "stateroom" and I could see why. There was a bed set against one wall, with actual legs and a wooden bedstead, rather than the regulation bunk. A window off to the left had a rectangular frame and pretty floral curtains, in place of the traditional port hole. Best of all, on the right hand side, there was a private bathroom. I had paid a little extra for that. I had learnt my lesson on previous trips. Given my peculiar lifestyle, it was better where possible to keep away from public lavatories.

My luggage was resting smartly at the side of the bed. 'There are towels in the bathroom and a spare blanket in the closet if you need it,' the steward informed me. 'If you need anything else, just give me a bell at any time. My name's Adam.'

'Thank you, Adam.' I reached into my pocket for a coin, but stopped myself just in time. For all the splendour of the accommodation, this was not a hotel and Adam was not a bellhop. Gratuities could wait until the end of the trip. 'Oh, there was one thing you could do,' it occurred to me suddenly.

'Sir?'

'My valet has a cabin not far from here. I don't know the number, I'm afraid. Somewhere amidships. His name's Maurice Sauveterre. French fellow. Looks like a tombstone. I was wondering if you could provide him with an extra key?'

'Maurice Sauveterre.' Adam fixed the name in his mind. 'Of course, sir.'

'He might need to pop in here from time to time.'

'I'll arrange it for you.' The steward moved out into the corridor. 'Oh, excuse me, miss.'

A young woman had come to a halt just outside the door. 'Is this B61?' she asked, hesitantly.

'That's right, miss.'

I caught sight of her face. 'Miss Wellesley!' I called out, in surprise. 'Are you lost? I thought you were on the port side.'

'Yes, I am. I'm awfully sorry.' Cynthia Wellesley raised a hand in greeting. 'I am starting to feel a little light headed.' She wobbled slightly and reached out to steady herself on the frame of the door. She was looking a little green around the gills.

The steward was hovering to her left. 'That's all right, Adam,' I said. 'Please come in, Miss Wellesley. Sit yourself down.' Adam made a tactful retreat and Miss Wellesley stepped tentatively through the doorway. 'You are looking a little peaky.' The motion of the ship was beginning to take its toll. At my direction, she sat herself down on the edge of the bed, to the left of the suitcase.

'I'm sure I'll be fine in a minute.'

'Can I get you a glass of water?'

'That would be most kind.'

I reached for the jug on the bedside table and poured out a glass, which I handed across. Miss Wellesley knocked it back in one. She was a slender thing, tallish and nicely dressed in a two piece rayon number. She must have nipped to her room, before calling on me, as she was no longer wearing her coat. 'Thank you,' she said, recovering her composure. She handed the glass back to me. 'You're very kind.' Her eyes met mine with a sincere smile. For all her quiet nature, Miss Wellesley did not strike me as being particularly shy. It had taken a fair amount of pluck to travel the world like this all on her own and she had had no qualms about stepping into my hotel room last night, to report back on the interview with Mrs O'Neill. Neither was she reluctant to enter my cabin now without a chaperone. Miss Wellesley was a thoroughly modern girl; and all the better for that. Just so long as she didn't start throwing up over the carpet. 'I hope you don't mind me coming to see you like this,' she said. 'I wanted to ask your advice. I couldn't think who else to talk to.'

'Advice?' I coughed, not quite understanding.

'You've been so kind to us these last couple of days. Myself and Mrs O'Neill. Helping to put our minds to rest. Soothing our ruffled feathers.'

'Well, I do my best, of course.' Not that I had had much choice in the matter. That's the trouble with showing kindness to people. You do it once and they expect you to do it again and again. I pulled up a chair. 'What's on your mind, Miss Wellesley?'

'I...' She hesitated. 'I think I may have done something terrible.'

'Oh?'

'Mrs O'Neill has had such a terrible time, these last few days. The purse snatching and then the restaurant. Being interviewed by the police.'

'Yes, it's been very trying for her.'

'And you saw how she was at breakfast. She's trying to put it all behind her, but if anything else were to happen…' Miss Wellesley took a gulp of air. She was clutching a small piece of paper in her hand. 'I haven't known Mrs O'Neill that long. Barely more than a week or so. But in that short time, I've become rather fond of her. I would never do anything to hurt her.'

'I'm sure you wouldn't.' My eyes narrowed, wishing the girl would get to the point. 'But you say you've done something you regret?'

She nodded unhappily. 'As you know, we've been sharing a suite at the Alderley for the last few nights.'

'Yes.' An impressive set of rooms, judging by the glimpse of it I had had through the doorway.

'I rose early this morning,' Miss Wellesley continued. 'Earlier than Mrs O'Neill, and I noticed a small piece of paper had been pushed underneath the door of the suite.'

I glanced down at her lap. 'You mean, that piece of paper?'

'Yes.' She nodded and handed it across. 'I should have told Mrs O'Neill about it. It was addressed to her. But it's such a vile…such a horrible thing.'

I unfolded the note and scanned it briefly. 'Good God,' I spluttered, unable to stop myself.

'If Mrs O'Neill had seen that, she would have been horrified,' Miss Wellesley asserted, not without good reason. 'And she was so anxious to get away this morning, to put everything behind her and start her European adventure. If I'd shown her that, she might have felt obliged to call the police. Again.'

'The third time in 24 hours.'

'Yes. And if they'd come to talk to her, she might have missed the boat.'

'Yes, I do see that.' I looked up. 'So you kept it from

her?'

'I did,' Miss Wellesley admitted. 'I suppose it was wrong of me not to show it to her straight away, but I…I just thought…'

'You thought she'd been through enough. I understand.'

'And now I don't…I don't know whether to show it to her at all. To admit that I kept it from her. And…and to worry her even more, now that we're all here onboard ship.'

I sat back in my chair. 'Yes, I see your dilemma. Although I must confess, I'm not sure what to suggest.' Try as I might, I could not disguise the irritation in my voice. Why did the damn girl have to get me involved in this? I had no more idea what to do about it than she did. 'Well, look. Whoever slipped this under the door of your room, I imagine we've left them far behind by now.'

'You don't think I should tell Mrs O'Neill?'

I shrugged, glancing out of the window. The ship was now pulling out of the river and into the sea. 'They can't do her any harm out here. And as you say, there's no point upsetting her unnecessarily.' I looked down at the note again and shivered slightly. Apart from the name, the paper contained only one simple statement, in typed capital letters: "NEXT TIME," it said, "IT WILL NOT BE A HOAX".

Chapter Three

Sir Richard Villiers sat back in a comfortable padded armchair and surveyed the smoking room with something less than satisfaction. 'Oh, I grant you, the décor hasn't changed,' he conceded, dropping his pipe briefly from his mouth. 'The Galitia is still the finest ship afloat. Nothing to match it anywhere else in the world. No, it's the passengers they're letting on these days.' He wrinkled his nose, shifting his glasses up a good half an inch. 'Too many riff raff getting into first class, that's the problem.' He sighed. Sir Richard was an odd looking man in his mid fifties. He had grey, close cropped hair and a thin face dominated by a pair of heavy spectacles. His suit was finely cut, however, and there was no mistaking the aristocratic attitude.

'You'll like this guy,' Harry had teased, when we arrived together at the Carolean Smoking Room a little after eleven. 'He's even more of a snob than you are.'

Sir Richard was one of a small party of guests who had been staying with Mrs O'Neill at her town house in Boston for the past few months. Sir Richard had been a business partner of her late husband, apparently; and a good friend to boot. Harry had met the fellow a couple of days ago at the Waldorf Astoria, where they both had rooms. The American handled the introductions, when we arrived at the smoking room together.

The Carolean was a pleasant, well lit chamber, a good fifty feet across, with oak panelled walls, several cosy recesses and an elaborate fireplace. Wooden floorboards were covered over with hand-made Persian carpets, and a portrait of James II was hanging above the mantelpiece at one end. Light streamed in from a set of high windows above each alcove.

Sir Richard was surveying the scene with distaste. 'They'll let anybody in these days,' he concluded.

I sat back in my armchair and took a slow drag of my cigarette. 'I suppose they have to take anyone who can pay for a ticket.'

Sir Richard puffed unhappily on his pipe. 'But where

will it end, that's what I want to know. Where will it end?'

'It seems quiet enough at the moment,' I observed. Perhaps a dozen people were spread out across the saloon, in a space that could easily have accommodated many times that number. I tapped out the end of my cigarette. The Carolean had the feel of a gentlemen's club and, despite Sir Richard's assertion, none of the other guests looked particularly out of place. 'The whole ship seems a little quiet.'

'Barely a hundred and fifty of us in first class,' Sir Richard grumbled. 'According to the passenger list. In my day it would have been nearer five hundred. But it's not the quantity,' he asserted. 'It's the *quality*.' He pushed his glasses up against his nose once again. Harry was right: the man was a snob. Not that he didn't have a point, of course.

'It was the third class boarding that surprised me,' I said. 'When I last travelled on the Galitia, just after the war, everyone was packed in like sardines; but judging by the queues at the dock today, there don't seem to be many more people in second or third class than there are up here.'

'Maybe things are becoming a little more democratic,' Harry Latimer put in, cheekily.

'Heaven forbid!' Sir Richard shuddered. 'But you're right, Mr Buxton. Passenger numbers have fallen drastically in the last couple of years, especially below decks. It's not just the depression. The third class market was collapsing anyway.' He removed his pipe, seeing that the end had gone out, and relit it quickly. 'There's no such thing as steerage these days. That's why they're introducing this "tourist class".' An upmarket version of third class. Sir Richard harrumphed. 'Damn fool notion. But it was steerage that paid the bills and without it, it's difficult to see how ships like this can survive. It's all the Americans' fault.' He waggled his pipe. 'No disrespect to you, Mr Latimer. Once they decided to pick and choose which of the "poor and huddled masses" they let in, everything ground to a halt. What with that and the depression, we may well be seeing the end of the ocean liner as we know it.'

I stubbed out the end of my cigarette. 'I do hope not,' I said, with some feeling. 'It's got to be better than aeroplanes.'

There was vague talk in some circles of establishing a transatlantic airline some time in the future. Harry smirked, knowing how much I hated the damned things.

'But it's the people that make the difference,' Sir Richard continued, unable to let the idea drop. 'All these American tourists. Present company excepted, of course. You seem a decent, sober chap, Mr Latimer. But it has to be said, too many of your countrymen treat the place like nothing more than a floating bordello. Loud and boorish, that's the only way to describe them, even at this time of day. I'm sorry to say it, Mr Latimer, but most of them don't seem to be able to handle their drink.'

Harry nodded and drained a glass of brandy, which a flunkey had brought across. 'Well, we don't get a lot of practise these days.'

'That's your own damn fault.' Sir Richard snorted. 'Bloody silly law. There's nothing wrong with alcohol, so long as it's consumed in moderation.'

Harry nodded seriously. 'I think a lot of Americans are coming around to that way of thinking.' He put his glass down on a side table and sat back in his armchair. 'Although some people have made a lot of money out of prohibition.'

Sir Richard frowned. 'Criminals, you mean? Well, that's as good a reason as any to get rid of it. But what you Americans don't seem to understand is that there's a time and place. Boorishness in a public house is perhaps unavoidable, but there's no call for it here, in a civilised environment.' He gestured across the saloon. 'I'm talking generally, of course.' The Carolean just now was not exactly a hive of activity. 'You'll have to forgive me, Mr Latimer. I'm not getting at you. You have behaved impeccably. Stepping in like that yesterday morning, when that blackguard tried to rob Susan out in the street.'

'I was just doing my duty, sir.'

'And doing it very well.' Sir Richard regarded Harry for a moment, his expression thoughtful. 'You know, I think she may be developing a bit of a soft spot for you.'

'I don't think so, sir,' Harry said. 'I think she may be

43

more interested in Mr Buxton here.'

Sir Richard peered across at me, his brow furrowed. 'Yes, there may be some truth in that.' He leaned back in his chair. 'She does seem rather taken with you, Mr Buxton. You want to be careful, the pair of you. Susan has had a difficult time of late and I think she may be on the look out for a new husband.'

I shuddered at that idea, but Harry chuckled. 'We shall consider ourselves duly warned.'

'That's another thing,' Sir Richard complained. 'All the women onboard.' He gestured vaguely with his pipe. Apart from myself, there was not a single woman currently seated in the smoking room. 'Brazen young hussies, travelling alone, looking for excitement. Wouldn't have been allowed in my day.'

'And ageing widows looking for husbands,' Harry put in mischievously.

'Oh, that's a little different. Susan is the picture of respectability. Even if she does talk too much. And she does have a companion with her.'

Harry's eyes lit up. 'The delightful Miss Wellesley.'

'Yes, pretty young thing.' Sir Richard sucked on his pipe. 'Doesn't say much, though.'

'I think Harry has his eye on her already,' I said.

Sir Richard coughed. 'That doesn't surprise me.'

'You're not married yourself?' I asked.

'I was. My wife died a few years ago. Couldn't be bothered to go through it all again. Not really a woman's man, you know.' That I could well believe. 'Listen, we're having a few drinks in the old stateroom before supper this evening. I'm sure Susan – Mrs O'Neill – would like to see you both there. If you'd care to pop along? Nothing formal. Just a few cocktails.'

'That's very kind of you,' I said. 'We'd be delighted.' And bizarrely, I meant it. I had been starved of polite society for so long, it was pleasant to be back in the fold. Sir Richard was a trifle opinionated, but it was clear that he came from good stock; and it was agreeable – at long last – to be conversing with an equal. Harry was right. I was a snob and I

44

didn't care who knew it.

A young fellow appeared at the far end of the saloon. At the sight of him, Sir Richard grimaced. 'No peace anywhere,' he muttered. 'This is my secretary, Mr Ernest Hopkins.'

'Mr Hopkins.' I nodded my head as the man approached us. Harry just smiled.

'Sorry to disturb you, Sir Richard.' Hopkins was a thin, freckled fellow of about twenty-five. 'I've completed the figures you asked for. You wanted to see them as soon as they were complete.'

'So I did,' Sir Richard said. He tapped out the end of his pipe and rose reluctantly to his feet. 'Gentlemen, you'll have to excuse me. Business is calling.'

Harry and I made the appropriate noises.

Sir Richard grabbed the notebook from Mr Hopkins and then turned back to us briefly. 'The Reynolds Suite on B Deck,' he said. 'Six o'clock. On the port side. You can't miss it.'

Maurice was brushing down a pair of trousers as I returned to my room. A suitcase was open on the bed and the valet was busily tidying away my things. 'Afternoon, Morris,' I declared cheerfully, closing the door behind me. I always called him "Morris" rather than "Maurice". It was a long standing joke. I had just got the lift up from D Deck, after a rather pleasant lunch at the Louis XVI, and was in an unusually cheerful mood. Mrs O'Neill had been babbling away at me for an hour and a half, in the company of Harry and Miss Wellesley, but she had now gone off to the gymnasium for an hour of physical jerks. I had declined the invitation to join her. 'I want to let my lunch settle first,' I had lied. I have never been much of a one for physical exertion. Harry was looking to go for a swim in the pool with Miss Wellesley and I was content to leave them to it. I was hardly in a position to parade around in my bathing suit in any case. I would be much happier, this afternoon, taking a quiet turn around the deck. But first I had stopped off at a small kiosk and bought myself a bottle of whisky. That was the source of my good humour. I moved across to the bedside table,

45

put the bottle down and grabbed a tumbler. 'You got hold of a key, then?' I asked Maurice.

'Yes, Monsieur.' The valet was a battered looking fellow, smartly dressed, but with a manner bordering on the funereal.

I poured myself a glass and settled down happily in an armchair by the window. I sipped a mouthful of the nectar and closed my eyes, savouring the taste of it. This was proper scotch, not the Canadian fabrication I had been forced to consume over the last few months. 'Just been down to lunch,' I told the valet. 'The food was excellent. I think you'd approve.'

Maurice moved across to the closet and pulled out a hanger. 'If you say so, Monsieur.' When it came to nosh, my man was even more of a stickler than I was. That's the Frogs for you.

A couple of jackets were already hanging up inside the wardrobe but, in truth, there was not much luggage to unpack. I had lost most of my possessions in the hurricane, those that had been sent on to me from Guatemala. When I arrived in New York, I was carrying barely more than the clothes I stood up in. My entire wardrobe had had to be replaced. Maurice had taken care of that; he had a better eye for clothing than I did. The only personal possession I had managed to retain was my silver fob watch and that, sadly, was on its last legs. When I got back to England, I would be starting afresh, in almost every sense.

'Have *you* eaten anything?' I asked. The servants had a separate sitting from the rest of the passengers.

'No, Monsieur. I was not hungry.'

I regarded the man sourly. 'You have to eat, Morris. I don't want you fainting all over the place.'

'No, Monsieur.' He moved back to the suitcase.

I took another sip of the whisky and felt the warm glow spread down to my stomach. It really was a fine malt. 'How's the room?' I asked. It seemed only polite to enquire. I had booked Maurice a small cabin amidships. It was a somewhat basic affair, without a porthole or a private lavatory, but decent first class accommodation nonetheless; and not exactly cheap.

'It will suffice, Monsieur,' the valet replied, pulling out

46

one of my shirts. Maurice was not one to enthuse about anything. There was an edge to the comment, however. Despite his professional manner, it was clear that the valet was struggling somewhat with life onboard ship.

'It's only for a few days,' I muttered. 'The sea looks calm enough. We'll be home before you know it.'

'Yes, Monsieur.' Maurice hung up the shirt, then opened a drawer at the base of the closet and moved back to the suitcase to pull out my under things.

'Plenty of time for you to get home and see your mother.' This elicited no response at all. 'Did you send them a telegram, your family, to tell them you were coming?'

'Yes, Monsieur.' Again, he did not elaborate. Maurice was a man of few words and those had to be prised out of him with a pair of pliers.

'Have you decided if you're going to fly?' The Galitia was travelling directly to Southampton, so he would have to make his own way across the channel.

'No, Monsieur.'

I flicked my eyes upwards. The man had already had a week to think about it. 'Well, either way, you'll have to pay for it yourself.' I had shelled out enough money on his behalf already. Again, there was no response. Normally, Maurice's lack of conversation was a positive boon – there is nothing worse than a chatty servant – but this afternoon it was starting to grate. Despite the whisky, my mood was beginning to sour. 'Look, Morris, I appreciate this is difficult for you. But you need to put it out of your mind. Focus on the job.'

'Yes, Monsieur.'

'You're not the only one with problems, you know.'

'No, Monsieur.'

I reached into my jacket pocket and pulled out the piece of paper Miss Wellesley had shown me this morning. This would take his mind off things, I thought. 'Cast your eye over this.'

The valet closed up the drawer and moved across. He pulled out a pair of reading glasses, unfolded the note and scanned it briefly. 'Most peculiar.'

'Miss Wellesley showed it to me this morning. You've met Miss Wellesley? Blonde thing. Five foot five.'

'Yes, Monsieur.'

'She came here first thing, in a bit of a state.'

The valet looked up. 'She came to the cabin?'

'Yes, shortly after we set sail.' I outlined the salient points of the conversation; how Miss Wellesley had discovered the note under the door at the Alderley hotel.

'Most curious, Monsieur.'

'Yes it is. She enquired at the desk, at breakfast time, but they knew nothing about it. The night staff had all gone home by then of course. But this, coming immediately after the hoax bomb. It has to be connected somehow. Somebody has it in for Mrs O'Neill.'

'It would appear so, Monsieur.'

I stared down at the bottom of my glass. 'At least we know they're not on the ship with us. Whoever the scoundrel was, we'll have left him well behind by now.'

Maurice gazed thoughtfully at the note. 'Not necessarily, Monsieur.'

'What do you mean, "not necessarily"?'

The valet took a moment to consider his words. 'It may be nothing, Monsieur, but when I was collecting the key to your room, I happened to overhear a rather curious exchange.'

'An exchange?'

'Yes, Monsieur. At lunchtime, between two of the stewards. They were discussing a female passenger.'

My eyes narrowed. 'Gossiping, you mean?'

'Yes, Monsieur.' It was par for the course below stairs, sadly. There was little that anyone could do to prevent it. 'As I understand it, this particular passenger had received an anonymous letter, of a rather unsavoury nature.'

'Another one?' I boggled.

'Yes, Monsieur. Apparently, it was slipped under her door this morning, while the woman was away from her room.'

'Good lord.' I scratched my head. 'Did she make a complaint?'

'No, Monsieur. But one of the ladies maids was

48

overheard discussing the matter, in the canteen.'

'I see. And the note was definitely delivered onboard the Galitia?'

'Yes, Monsieur.'

I reflected on this for a moment. 'Do you know who the lady was?'

'No, Monsieur. Nor do I know the precise contents of the letter. However, as I understand it, the note was typed rather than hand-written. And it was in capital letters, like this one.'

'Good lord.'

'That at least is what the steward said.'

I bit my lip. 'That can't be a coincidence, Morris.'

'No, Monsieur. It cannot.'

'But this note.' I grabbed the paper back from him. 'This was delivered to the Alderley Hotel, before we left. I assumed whoever sent it intended it as a parting shot, for Mrs O'Neil. But if somebody else has been receiving similar letters, aboard ship....' I gazed across at my man.

'Yes, Monsieur.'

'Then that means whoever wrote this note, whoever sent that hoax bomb, then...they're onboard here with us.'

The valet regarded me grimly. 'Yes, Monsieur,' he agreed.

A heavy object collided with my left ankle. The secretary, Mr Hopkins, had opened the door to the sitting room and a small cat had raced in from the hallway and smacked straight into me. 'Good grief!' I exclaimed, nearly spilling my drink. The animal sprang back, equally alarmed, and then hissed loudly at me, baring its fangs.

'Matilda, no!' Lady Jocelyn Wingfield snapped sharply. The cat was a small, rat like thing with short grey hair and thinly lidded eyes. 'Bad girl!' She glared down at the animal. 'You know you shouldn't be in here!' Matilda was unrepentant, however. She slipped around the edge of the sofa and came to a halt beside Harry Latimer.

The two of us had arrived at the Reynolds Suite

49

promptly at six o'clock. The apartment was a luxury three bedroom affair on the port side. The sitting room alone was significantly larger than my own cabin. There was no sign of a party in progress, however. Only Sir Richard Villiers and his sister were there to greet us. Lady Jocelyn Wingfield was a tall and rather severe looking woman in her early fifties. Her grey hair was curled around a thin, unfriendly face. Piercing blue eyes bored into anyone she looked at, though her greeting was hospitable enough.

'Are we the first?' I asked, as Harry and I shuffled through the open doorway. The sitting room was an elegantly furnished space, large enough to accommodate a good seven or eight people. There were dark mahogany walls, a hefty fireplace and luxurious carpet underfoot. A plethora of paintings adorned the walls; all reproductions of works by Sir Joshua Reynolds. There was a drinks table, a couple of padded armchairs and a comfortable sofa. Several hefty wooden doors led off to the other rooms, which were connected together by a short hallway. This was, without doubt, the best accommodation the Galitia had to offer, an elegant and very expensive set of rooms. I did not know exactly what sort of business Sir Richard was involved in, but whatever it was he was clearly doing very well at it.

'Yes, do come in.' Sir Richard pushed up his glasses, gesturing us forward. 'Just us at the moment.' I could hear a quiet murmur of voices coming from an open doorway leading out onto the verandah, but it did not sound loud enough to be Mrs O'Neill or her companion. The American woman had a separate "stateroom" just along the way. 'This is my sister, Lady Jocelyn Wingfield,' Sir Richard said.

The lady extended a bony hand. 'A pleasure to meet you.' She was dressed in a smart, ankle length evening dress, well cut but understated in pale blue.

Sir Richard was in a dinner jacket, with waistcoat and dicky bow; but with the thick glasses and close cropped hair he looked more like a bank manager than an aristocrat. 'The others are out on the verandah,' he said. 'We can go through in a moment. But I'll get you both a drink first. Jenny, would you mind?'

A servant girl was hovering by the drinks table, dressed in the traditional black and white. Lady Jocelyn's maid, presumably. The girl poured us both a glass of an insipid looking cocktail.

'You'll like this,' Sir Richard declared, as Harry and I were presented with the triangular glasses. 'Discovered it in Boston. It's called "Goodnight Vienna". After the musical.'

I took a sip and tried not to wince. The drink was far too sweet for my taste.

Harry was more polite. 'Very nice,' he lied. 'Smooth, if a little sugary.'

'That's the apricot,' Sir Richard said.

'My brother has always had a rather sweet tooth,' Lady Jocelyn observed. 'So, Mr Buxton, what brought you to the Americas? I gather you've been here for some months?'

'Yes, indeed,' I said. 'Just business. Nothing terribly exciting, I'm afraid. And yourself?'

'I came over in October. My husband died last year and Richard thought I could do with a change of scene.' The brother nodded. 'He was coming over on business and thought I might like to accompany him. To spend Christmas here.'

'With Mrs O'Neill?'

'Yes.' Lady Jocelyn did not sound enthused. 'It was a kind thought. But I am looking forward to returning home.'

The conversation was cut short by the arrival of Ernest Hopkins from the hallway. He was the freckled fellow who had dragged Sir Richard away from the smoking room this morning. 'Ernest, come and join us,' Sir Richard called. 'You've met my secretary?'

'Briefly,' I said.

It was at this point that the cat had rushed forward, through the open doorway. The damn thing must have been lurking in one of the bedrooms. Having assaulted my left leg, she came to a halt beside Harry Latimer and began rubbing up against him.

'Bad girl!' Lady Jocelyn admonished again. 'I do apologise, Mr Buxton. She's not supposed to leave the bedroom.' The woman shot an angry but silent glare at Mr Hopkins, who must have left the door open.

'That's quite all right,' I said. 'No harm done.'

'She seems quite taken with you, old boy.' Sir Richard looked down at the animal, who was brushing herself against Harry's leg and purring loudly. 'Doesn't usually like strangers.'

Harry chuckled. 'Oh, I have a natural affinity with animals.'

'They have such a lot in common,' I teased. I could not help but regard the cat with a less sympathetic eye, however. 'I didn't think animals were allowed onboard ship. Apart from the mousers.' Matilda, for all her rat like appearance, was clearly not a ship's cat.

Sir Richard poured himself another cocktail. 'You're right, of course. Strictly speaking, she should be down in the hold, but Jocelyn won't be without her.'

'She's a sensitive soul,' Lady Jocelyn asserted. 'And she doesn't cause any trouble, do you Matilda?'

'The stewards are happy to turn a blind eye,' Sir Richard said, 'as a personal favour.' A man of Sir Richard's standing could always expect a certain latitude in these matters, especially if there was the prospect of a hefty tip at the end of the voyage. 'So long as she stays put, in the suite.'

'You brought her with you from England?'

'Indeed. She has been a great comfort to me these last few months,' Lady Jocelyn said.

The cat moved away from Harry and jumped up onto the sofa. 'Didn't she have to go into quarantine?' Harry asked.

'Not on the way out,' Sir Richard said. 'Might have to on the way home, though. They changed the rules a few years back. Used to be just dogs but now it's cats as well. Damn silly law. In my day...'

Lady Jocelyn cut across him. 'Jenny, will you get Matilda a saucer of milk and return her to the bedroom? Ernest, you must be more careful about leaving doors open.'

The secretary apologised sheepishly.

The maid reached across to take the cat from the sofa. Matilda hissed at her and a claw lashed out, scratching the back of the girl's hand. Jenny dropped the animal back onto the cushion. 'The little bleeder,' she muttered, without thinking.

'Jennifer! Mind your language!'

'Sorry, miss.' The girl tried to grab the cat again and the animal promptly bit her. 'Ow! Bloody thing!'

Lady Jocelyn was incensed. 'Jennifer, I will not tell you again. You will mind your language in front of our guests. Now be off with you.'

By now, the maid had a firm grip on the animal. 'Yes, miss,' she mumbled as she scurried out of the room.

'I do apologise,' Lady Jocelyn said. 'There is no excuse for bad language. Not in polite company.'

'Hey, it's not a problem.' Harry was never one to take offence. 'Believe me, I've heard a lot worse in my time.'

'I used to have a maid called Jenny,' I said, watching the girl disappear. 'Back in England. A housemaid.' I polished off the cocktail. 'She was a bit of a handful too.'

A man and a woman were seated on a couple of wicker chairs either side of a square table. 'Have you met my cousin?' Lady Jocelyn enquired, as we moved through onto the verandah. I recognised the man. He had a dog collar and a voluminous grey-black beard. He had been playing shuffleboard on the promenade earlier this afternoon. I had come across the contest when I had gone out for a stroll. I had wanted a bit of time to myself to think. The business of that note was playing on my mind. I had stopped to watch the game and seen the vicar brandishing his cue stick with some relish. Shuffleboard was a popular pastime on a ship like this, a strange hybrid of croquet and bowls. The woman seated to his left I did not know. The wife, presumably. She was short and mousy, in her mid fifties, like most of the company. The two rose to their feet at our arrival.

'The Reverend Hamilton-Baynes and Mrs Hamilton-Baynes,' Lady Jocelyn introduced us. 'This is Mr Henry Buxton. You've already met Mr Latimer, of course.'

The vicar extended a warm hand. He was a sprightly

fellow, slightly older than his wife but with a shock of curly black hair and a full beard. 'Delighted to meet you.'

I returned the compliment and greeted his wife in similar fashion. The verandah was a comfortable rectangular space, with large windows facing out to sea. The sun had set some hours earlier – it being midwinter – so the area was now illuminated by electric lights. 'I saw the match this afternoon,' I told him. The reverend had been up against a young American. 'I was going to put half a dollar on you.' The officer next to me had been insistent that the American was bound to win, but I had thought otherwise. Shuffleboard was a game of skill rather than strength. Unfortunately, the crew were prohibited from gambling, so I was unable to place the bet. That was just as well, as it turned out. The foreigner had pipped the vicar with a last shove of his disk.

The Reverend Hamilton-Baynes chuckled. 'I thought I had him at the end, but it was not to be. Super fun, though. Do come and join us.' He gestured to the seats. We pushed ourselves awkwardly into the space surrounding the coffee table. 'Mr Latimer, I have something to show you.' The vicar reached down to the side of his chair and pulled out an elegant wooden box.

I shot Harry a questioning look.

'I was talking to the padre at lunch yesterday,' Harry explained. 'He's bringing back a rather special souvenir from America. He promised to show it to me.'

'It's not for me, you understand,' the vicar said. 'One of my parishioners.' He placed the box on the table and unclipped it, pulling the lid open with child-like enthusiasm. Inside, nestled on a bed of silk, was an antique pistol, in polished wood and metal.

'Good lord!' I exclaimed. 'Is that a musket?'

'It's a flintlock,' Harry said, leaning in. 'May I?'

'Be my guest.' The vicar beamed, his teeth shining out from beneath the bed of hair. He had a rather full beard and, unlike the hair on his head, it was flecked with grey.

Harry lifted the gun and cradled it gently. 'It's genuine,' he said, examining it closely. 'I'd say late eighteenth century.

No maker's mark, but definitely US manufacture.'

'So I've been told.' The vicar nodded eagerly. 'Isn't it marvellous?' He must have noticed my rather perplexed expression as he added hurriedly, 'You must think it very strange, a man of the cloth showing such an interest in antique weaponry.'

'Not at all. Everyone has to have a hobby.'

'It's not for me, you understand. I wouldn't know the first thing about it. But one of my parishioners is an amateur historian. He has one of the finest collections of antique weaponry in England. Absolutely splendid, it is. When he heard I was travelling to America, he asked me to keep an eye out for anything from the eighteenth century. The war of independence and all that. I saw this in an antique shop. It was frightfully expensive, so I telegraphed him and asked what he thought. He told me to buy it. He'll be jolly pleased when he sees it.'

'It's a fine piece,' Harry agreed, handing the weapon back.

'Harry – Mr Latimer – is quite an expert on guns as well,' I said. Although his reasons for knowing about such things were not quite as lily-white as the vicar's friend.

A rap at the far door heralded the arrival of Mrs O'Neill and her companion. Lady Jocelyn absented herself from the company to greet the new arrivals. There was room on the verandah for five or six people, but eight or nine would be pushing it a little.

The Reverend Hamilton-Baynes returned the musket to its box. I was surprised he had been allowed to bring it onboard. 'You didn't have any trouble getting that through customs?' I asked.

'No, no,' the vicar declared. 'It has a certificate. In any case, I doubt it would actually fire after all these years. I wouldn't have the first idea how to use it, even if it did.'

Harry smirked. 'I'll have to show you some time.' He rose to his feet as Mrs O'Neill and Miss Wellesley appeared in the doorway. They were both dressed for the occasion – quite garishly, in the case of Mrs O'Neill – and Sir Richard had furnished them each with a glass of his vile apricot cocktail.

55

'Well, here we all are!' he declared. And that was the party complete.

Harry vacated his seat and, with a few of the group, moved back into the sitting room. Mrs O'Neill made a beeline for the chair next to me. Lady Jocelyn and Sir Richard joined us on the wicker chairs.

'So how long have you all known each other?' I asked, once we had settled ourselves down.

'Oh, for a long, long time,' Mrs O'Neill gushed. 'My late husband, Ulysses, was in business with Sir Richard.'

'Yes, I remember you saying.'

'He was a good friend,' Sir Richard said. 'It was a great shame when he passed away. But he was ill for a long time.'

'I think of him every day,' Mrs O'Neill declared, stroking the pearls hanging from her neck. 'He gave these to me, for our twentieth wedding anniversary. I keep them with me always.'

'They're worth an absolute fortune,' Sir Richard said. 'I keep telling her, she should keep them under lock and key, but she won't listen.'

'Oh, but I'm perfectly safe here,' Mrs O'Neill insisted. 'With all these fine men to protect me.' She gestured to the assembled gathering.

Lady Jocelyn Wingfield sat back in her chair. She did not look convinced by the sentiment.

The clock ticked closer to eight and the party began to mutter about making their way down to D Deck for supper. Harry was deep in conversation with Miss Wellesley in the drawing room, and I doubt either of them noticed as I slid by into the hallway to answer a call of nature. It seemed we had split off now and I had been lumbered with Mrs O'Neill for the evening.

Cynthia Wellesley had recovered her composure somewhat over the course of the day. The seasickness seemed to be a thing of the past and, after our little talk this morning, the girl seemed to have put the business of the anonymous note out of her mind. I wished I could be quite so sanguine; but then, she had not heard about the second note. I was in two minds whether I ought to tell somebody about that. If there was some sort of lunatic onboard ship, it might be prudent to inform the authorities. But I didn't want to get Miss Wellesley in hot water with her employer; and I had no reason to believe anyone might be in any actual danger. Words are cheap, after all. Perhaps I would have a quiet word with Harry in the morning, and see what he thought about it. If I could prise him away from Miss Wellesley.

'Hey, why not call me Harry?' the fellow schmoozed as I passed the two of them by. 'We've known each for such a long time. It must be at least twenty-four hours.'

The girl smiled shyly. 'All right. Harry.'

'And may I call you Cynthia?'

'If you'd like to.'

The poor girl. It was text book stuff. In half an hour, he would be calling her "honey" and by the end of the evening they'd be canoodling outside his stateroom door. I had seen it so many times before. I still couldn't quite fathom the influence Harry had over so many women. Oh, he was handsome, to be sure, with those twinkling eyes and boyish good looks, and he certainly dressed well, but any fool could see the calculation in his eyes. The honey words were just a means to an end. I shook my head and moved across to the bathroom.

As I was completing my ablutions, some minutes later, another whispered conversation was taking place, out in the corridor. The Reynolds Suite had two bathrooms and three bedrooms, connected to the drawing room by a private hallway. The vicar and his wife presumably had one room, which meant Lady Jocelyn must be sharing with her maidservant, and Sir Richard with his secretary. Not an ideal arrangement, by any standards but, as I had discovered, it was useful to have one's staff on hand. It had not done much for the mood of Lady Jocelyn, however.

'That wretched girl,' she muttered, her voice wafting under the bathroom door. She must have returned to her room briefly to pick up her handbag. Everyone was now preparing to leave for supper. 'Embarrassing us in front of our guests. It won't do, Richard. It won't do at all. As if we don't have enough to worry about.'

Sir Richard was sympathetic. 'I'll speak to her in the morning.'

'Tell her if she doesn't buck her ideas up, she'll be out on her ear in Southampton. I'm not putting up with any more of it. This trip has been a disaster.'

'Hardly my fault, old girl,' Sir Richard protested. 'I wasn't to know what would happen.'

'I thought we could put all this behind us, once we were aboard ship. But now this. They've followed us here, Richard. It might even be someone we know. I can't bear it.'

'Stiff upper lip, old girl.' Sir Richard was speaking quietly, so as not to be overheard by anyone in the sitting room. 'If they had any teeth, they wouldn't resort to letter writing. In my day…'

'And you have to invite two complete strangers over for cocktails. What on earth were you thinking?'

'They're friends of Susan's. And you'd met the American chap already.'

'In passing. That's hardly the point, Richard.'

'Susan asked if they could come. I couldn't bally well say no, now could I?' That was news to me. It looked like Harry was right. Mrs O'Neill was determined to maintain close relations with the two of us.

'But we barely know them from Adam,' Lady Jocelyn said. 'And Susan only met them a couple of days ago.'

'They seem decent enough, as far as it goes. That's the trouble with first class these days. You never know what you're going to get.'

'Mr Buxton seems presentable,' Lady Jocelyn conceded, 'for a man of his class.' I blinked in surprise at that comment. What the devil did she mean by that? 'But as for the American, I don't like the look of him at all. Far too smooth. And he's being far too attentive to Miss Wellesley.'

'Yes, I can see the danger signs there,' Sir Richard grumbled. 'In my day, girls knew what to watch for. Kept well away from charmers like that. Still, she's not our responsibility.

Come on, my dear, we can't keep our guests waiting. The dinner gong will be sounding any moment. Best foot forward, put on a brave face and all that. In a few days, we'll be back in old Blighty, and all this will be forgotten.'

And with that, they moved across the hallway and returned to the drawing room, where the other guests were now assembled. I left it a couple of minutes, finishing up my affairs in the bathroom, and then slipped quietly in behind them. My absence had not been noticed. The conversation I had overheard had confirmed one important point, however. The rumours Maurice had stumbled across were true. Mrs O'Neill was not the only one receiving poison pen letters. 'Wouldn't resort to letter writing,' Sir Richard had said. And that was proof positive that, whoever was sending these letters – and whoever had arranged that hoax bomb – they were definitely here, aboard this ship.

Chapter Four

The Reverend Hamilton-Baynes was bashing away at a portable typewriter. I could scarcely miss the tall, heavily bearded cleric as I made my way through the writing room towards the Palladian Lounge on A Deck. It had been something of a late night for all of us and I had opted to skip a formal breakfast in favour of a much needed lie in. In fact, aware of the possibility of a sore head, I had booked a tray of food in advance, to be delivered to my room at nine am sharp. I had barely eaten any of it. The combination of alcohol and dancing the night before had taken a greater toll than I had anticipated. Now, staggering out into the wider world, here was the damn vicar, as bright as a button, tapping away between me and the sanctuary of the lounge. There was no chance of slipping by without acknowledging the fellow, so I called out as hearty a 'Good morning!' as my fogged cranium could manage.

The Reverend Hamilton-Baynes looked up from his typewriter and smiled a toothy smile. His white teeth shone out particularly brightly against that thick grey-black beard. 'Good morning, Mr Buxton. How is your head?'

'Dreadful,' I muttered. In point of fact, I had not drank all that much and I had been in bed well before two o'clock. No, it was the dancing that had been the killer. It was some years since I had last attended a formal dance and I had forgotten how exhausting they could be, especially after a heavy meal. 'I just need a bit of peace and quiet for an hour or so,' I said. 'To get my head together.' Hamilton-Baynes nodded sympathetically. He did not seem at all affected by the previous night's excesses, though he had been up at least as late as I had. 'Preparing a sermon?' I asked, peering across at the typewriter. A wall of text was printed across the sheet in front of him.

'My second one this morning. I like to keep ahead. Sir Richard was good enough to let me borrow his typewriter.' He pulled up the sheet. 'This one's about the value of music in uplifting the spirits.'

'Bringing us closer to God?'

The reverend beamed. 'That's the ticket.'

'You were certainly making the most of it last night,' I said. Hamilton-Baynes had been like a maniac on the dance floor. 'You put the youngsters to shame.'

'If only that were true! I confess, I enjoy it all far too much. But it's one of life's little pleasures, isn't it?'

'I suppose so,' I agreed dubiously. 'I think I'd rather play shuffleboard.'

'Yes, that's a lot of fun too.' Hamilton-Baynes nodded vigorously. 'A marvellous diversion on a ship like this.' It was certainly a popular pastime, one of many such games laid on for the amusement of the passengers in first class. A dazzling array of recreational activities were available to us: sports, competitions, even a series of formal lectures for the more sedentary passengers. There was little chance of anybody getting bored.

'Will you be be playing again today?' I asked the reverend. 'I'm sure you could beat that American fellow if you had another crack at him.'

'I may well do at some point. He's a splendid chap. Boxed for his county, you know. I told him I used to do a bit of that myself, in my school days. Actually, he's invited me to the gym this afternoon, for a bit of sparring.'

'Good lord.'

'Nothing formal. The chap's half my age! But it'll be super fun getting back into the gloves again.'

'Right, yes.' An image of the bearded vicar popped into my head, in shorts and a vest, with boxing gloves on his hands, like an animated *Punch* cartoon. 'Well, good luck. I may come along and cheer you on.'

'Please do.' He turned back to the typewriter as I moved away. 'Oh and I hope your head clears soon.'

So do I, I thought, so do I.

I continued on into the lounge, trying to free my head of that bizarre image. A boxing vicar. There were less holy activities, I supposed. Actually, I have always quite enjoyed boxing. There is nothing like watching a couple of hefty oafs giving each other a good pummelling. But the gambling opportunities were somewhat limited and sport without gambling, I have always felt, is like a champagne flute without the bubbly. Perhaps I could muscle in on a game of poker instead. A few likely card games were always in progress somewhere onboard ship. I would ask Harry to join me, if he promised to behave himself. He did have a habit of shuffling the decks somewhat in his own favour. But that could wait until later. First of all, I would settle down in the Palladian and have a quick glance at the morning paper. Maurice had picked me up a copy of the Cunard Bulletin, a specially printed news sheet.

I found myself a suitable chair and unfolded the newspaper.

The saloon was a different place in daylight. The Palladian Lounge was an elegantly fitted great hall, some seventy feet across. A huge wagon-shaped ceiling rose up a good eighteen feet above the central section, between two rows of ionic columns. The ceiling was decorated with elaborate reproductions of seventeenth century artwork. Chairs and tables were spread out across the hall. The floor was covered with finely woven carpet. There were few people about at this hour and those that were were dozing happily or quietly reading.

A waiter came by and I gestured for him to bring me a whisky and soda. Hair of the dog and all that. I was still half asleep and my head was throbbing unconscionably.

When Adam, the cabin steward, had knocked on my bedroom door at nine am, it had been a rude awakening. It seemed to me that I had barely closed my eyes from the night before.

'Good morning, Mr Buxton!' the damned fellow had bellowed with unnecessary jollity as he pushed open the door. 'I have your breakfast for you.' I had wrenched a crusted eyelid open and peered across at the blurred figure as he gestured to a trolley resting out in the corridor. 'Freshly cooked, just this minute.' The smell of bacon and eggs wafted into the room, and my stomach churned. 'Where do you want it, sir? On the bed?'

'No, on the table,' I croaked, reaching groggily for a glass of water.

'Very good, sir.' He placed the tray down neatly next to

the jug. 'It's a lovely morning. A little chilly on deck but bright sunshine.' As if to emphasize the point, he pulled back the curtains and the light streamed into the cabin, smacking hard against my face. 'Is there anything else I can do for you?'

There is nothing quite as irritating as a perky servant first thing in the morning. 'No, that'll be all thank you,' I informed him darkly. On any other day, I might have forgiven him his youthful exuberance, but just now I was really not in the mood. I was almost pleased, twenty minutes later, when Maurice arrived to help me dress. He at least could never be described as perky and would keep his opinions on the state of the weather to himself.

The whisky did its job and I settled down quietly with the newspaper. The Palladian was all but dead now, a far cry from last night.

The electric lights had been dazzling then, after supper; the floor bursting with activity. The chairs and tables had been cleared from the centre to create an enormous dance floor. There had been a live band, a seven piece orchestra made up of officers and other crew members, moonlighting for the evening. At supper they had played chamber music down in the restaurant on D Deck, before reassembling upstairs as a modern dance band. They were at one end of the hall, on a raised semi-circular stage. A good seventy or eighty people had taken to the floor as the band struck up. The dancers had done their best to fill up the space, but in truth the hall could comfortably have accommodated four times their number.

All that dancing. I shuddered at the memory. I had been forced up onto the floor myself on more than one occasion. It was bad enough throwing oneself about on solid ground, but on a swaying ship, on the first day out, it was more than a little tricky. I had not adjusted to shipboard life as well as I had hoped. I had done my duty, however, accompanying Mrs O'Neill for the first dance and Miss Wellesley for the second. The younger woman had really found her feet over the course of the day. After the first couple of jigs, however, I had made my excuses and headed for the side lines.

The vicar's wife, Margaret Hamilton-Baynes, expressed

some sympathy. 'You're looking quite exhausted,' she observed, as I collapsed into a chair, downed a quick glass and gestured at a nearby flunkey for a refill.

'Feeling my age, I'm afraid,' I admitted glumly. 'I can't get the hang of these modern dances. I can just about manage a waltz, on a good day, but I'm woefully out of practise.' I took a moment to catch my breath. 'You'll have to forgive me for not asking you onto the floor.'

'That's quite all right.' Mrs Hamilton-Baynes smiled warmly. 'I'm taking a short break myself.' She was a short, mousy woman in her early fifties with pinned-back hair and a puffy but not unattractive face. There were a few lines around her mouth and eyes, but on the whole she had worn better than I had, despite being ten years my senior.

The truth was, I was woefully out of condition. I had lost a few pounds in British Honduras but I had put them straight back on in New York. And the plentiful, well cooked British food on offer at the Louis XVI restaurant was not doing me any favours at all.

The Reverend Hamilton-Baynes swirled past us in a blur of energy, his white teeth flashing us a toothy grin. 'Your husband looks as if he's enjoying himself,' I observed, with some surprise. I had never seen a man of the cloth so nimble on his feet. He was outpacing his partner, Miss Wellesley, by some considerable margin. Harry Latimer had already danced with the young woman, and was now over at the bar, talking to some stranger or other. Mrs O'Neill was still on her feet, too, sporting a garish floor length evening dress in yellow and green. I didn't recognise the fellow she was dancing with. A young American, judging by the hair. I don't think she had much idea who he was either. She had drunk quite a bit this evening and the alcohol was unshackling the last of her inhibitions. Not that she had had many to start with.

'Joshua loves to dance,' Mrs Hamilton-Baynes informed me, with obvious affection. 'Any excuse he gets. If we need to raise money to repair the church roof, it will always be a charity ball, not a raffle or a jumble sale.'

'How long have the two of you been married?'

64

'Nearly thirty years now. We have three children, a girl and two boys. All adults. Doing very well for themselves.' Mrs Hamilton-Baynes spoke with a quiet pride. 'It's been a happy marriage.'

'And Lady Jocelyn is your cousin?'

'A distant cousin, yes. The poor relations.' She smiled again. 'Sir Richard was kind enough to invite us over. Jocelyn's husband passed away last August and he thought the trip would help to take her mind off things. Mind you, she only agreed to come if she could bring Matilda with her.' That blasted cat. Mrs Hamilton-Baynes chuckled quietly. 'We've always been close,' she said. 'I think that was why we were invited along. Jocelyn and I grew up together at Burlingford.'

'Burlingford?' I did not recognise the name.

'Burlingford Hall, in Worcestershire. The country seat. We were like sisters. Jocelyn can seem a little distance at times, especially with strangers, but she has a heart of gold.'

I'll take your word for that, I thought. Lady Jocelyn had certainly kept her distance from Harry and I over supper – the Reynolds suite had its own set of tables in the restaurant – and seemed in no hurry to reacquaint herself with us in the ballroom, now that her duties as hostess had been discharged. I glanced across at the great lady, who was sitting at a small table on the opposite side of the hall. Sir Richard was to her left and he at least raised his glass as he caught my eye. From this distance, he really did look more like a bank manager than a country squire, especially with those chunky glasses of his. Neither he nor his sister had yet got up to dance.

'And what about you, Mr Buxton, do you have a wife?'

'No. No, I was married once, but…she died, I'm afraid.' It was easier to lie than to explain the truth. There had been a marriage, back in England some years ago, but it had been a sham, of course, a mere matter of convenience. I tried not to think of it these days.

'I'm so sorry.' Mrs Hamilton-Baynes sympathised. 'I'm sure you will find someone else.'

'Lord, I hope not. I don't think I'll marry again.' Not if my life depended on it. 'I'm quite content as I am.' And that, at least, was the God's honest truth.

'Mrs O'Neill seems to have taken a shine to you. You could do a lot worse.' She laughed gently, catching sight of my horrified expression. The vicar's wife was not above a little teasing, it appeared.

'I'm sure there must be other, more eligible men onboard ship.'

'Like your friend Mr Latimer, perhaps? I was surprised to hear the two of you had only just met. You seem to know each other so well.'

'I...know the type well enough,' I extemporised. 'I don't think Harry's the marrying sort either.'

'Should I be concerned for Miss Wellesley?' Again, there was a flash of humour in her eyes.

'She seems a sensible enough girl. I'm sure she can take care of herself.' She was an adult, I wanted to say, and how she behaves is up to her. But Harry had an uncanny knack of bending people to his will. So much for business coming first.

The orchestra came to the end of *Puttin' On The Ritz* and the dance floor briefly cleared.

Miss Wellesley swept straight across to the bar and Harry greeted her warmly.

Mrs Hamilton-Baynes was not the only one to notice the couple's growing closeness. Mrs O'Neill had commented on it to me, during the opening number. She did not seem at all perturbed, however; not when she had me to focus her attentions upon. I would have to have a word with Harry about that. I appreciated he was in no hurry to complete his grubby business with the pearls, but I had not agreed to entertain Mrs O'Neill all on my own.

Harry leaned in and whispered something in Miss Wellesley's ear. Would he make a move on her tonight, I wondered, or would he leave it a day or two? I suspected he would wait. He was a scoundrel, but he was not completely lacking in manners. A steward moved across the floor towards him. Harry looked around and the man handed him a sheet of paper. He opened it up and scanned it briefly, then nodded and turned back to Miss Wellesley.

At this point, my view was blocked by the looming figure of Mrs O'Neill. 'Oh, Mr Buxton, isn't it wonderful?' she gushed. 'I do love a good dance.' Despite the alcohol in her system, the older woman remained perfectly steady on her feet. 'You mustn't sit there on the sidelines all evening.'

'I'm afraid I'm not the greatest of dancers.'

'Nonsense! I think you manage much better than you give yourself credit for.'

Mrs Hamilton-Baynes tried not to laugh as, once again, I was dragged up onto the floor, shooting daggers at Harry as I was swept across the ballroom by the damned American woman. I must have danced three dances in a row, before she would allow me a seat; and then she talked at me for a further forty minutes. Her voice was beginning to slur however, the combination of rich food, dancing and her unfamiliarity with alcohol finally taking its toll. At half past twelve, I summoned Harry across.

'Time to get her home,' I said. I had no desire to escort Mrs O'Neill back to her stateroom on my own. The woman was having difficulty even standing up, but with Harry's help I was able to get her back to her cabin and off to bed.

'You're looking a little the worse for wear yourself,' Harry observed, as we moved back out into the corridor.

'Are you surprised? You're a devil, Harry, leaving me in the lurch like that.'

'Hey, I appreciate you taking over from me. I think Mrs O'Neill has decided you're the better bet, old man. You can play along for a day or two, can't you?'

'No, I damn well can't. If you want to have your way with Miss Wellesley, that's your affair. But you can do it without my help.'

'I intend to.' He smirked.

'Look, why not switch the pearls now? She's out for the count. She'd never notice.'

'It can wait a while. I'm in no hurry. Besides, I have other fish to fry this evening.'

'Yes. I've noticed. One for the road?'

He grinned. 'Hey, I thought you'd never ask.'

67

We knocked back a final glass at the bar and, shortly after that, I headed off to bed. Harry had no intention of missing the last waltz, however, so he remained behind, chatting to Miss Wellesley. What time the two of them retired to bed, I have no idea.

My eyes were drooping now. The newspaper had failed to grab my attention. There was one small paragraph about the New York bombers, who had been formally charged, but there was nothing else of any interest. I pulled myself back up in my seat. Perhaps I should take a walk out on deck, I thought, to clear my head. But first, I would return to my cabin and have another look at that note.

A laundry trolley was blocking the corridor. A stewardess in a grey uniform and white cap was gathering together a set of fresh sheets outside an open doorway. She smiled at me as I came by and bobbed her head. My room was up ahead. I was not sure if it had been cleaned yet. Only male stewards were allowed into the men's cabins and there was no sign of Adam. I reached the door and was just grabbing the handle when a flicker of movement caught my attention off to the right. Some fool was crouching down in the corner there, his hands extended, shuffling about. I regarded the fellow with some amusement. 'Mr Hopkins?' I called out. It was Sir Richard's secretary. 'What on earth are you doing?'

Ernest Hopkins started at the sound of my voice. 'Mr Buxton,' he said, pulling himself up in embarrassment. He was a thin fellow in his mid twenties, with auburn hair and a freckled face. His suit was a little crumpled, having been on his hands and knees for some time. 'You haven't seen a cat prowling around here anywhere have you?' he asked.

'A cat?' It took me a moment to catch his drift. 'Oh, you mean Matilda? That rat like thing?'

Mr Hopkins nodded wearily. 'She slipped out of our suite about twenty minutes ago. Lady Jocelyn's in a fury. Sent me out to look for her before the stewards find her. I've been searching everywhere.' The young man did not sound happy.

'I'm meant to be working this morning,' he grumbled, 'but I get sent out for the cat.'

I could understand his aggravation. 'Couldn't they get the maid to do it?'

Hopkins shook his head. 'Jenny refused to come. Her hand's still bleeding from last night. She doesn't want to get bitten again.'

'That's understandable, I suppose.'

'Her ladyship is furious. Jenny must have left the door open this morning. I'm sure she didn't mean to. But the slightest crack is enough for Matilda.'

I glanced up and down the corridor. The stewardess had disappeared inside one of the rooms and, apart from her trolley, there was no sign of life. 'Probably caught the scent of a mouse,' I suggested. 'Not a terribly clever idea, bringing a cat onboard.'

'No. But if you do see her...'

'You'll be the first to know,' I assured him. Mind you, I was damned if I was going to help him recapture the animal. I did not share Harry's affinity with animals.

'I just hope to goodness she hasn't got into one of the other staterooms. There'll be hell to pay if she has. I'd better just try along here.' Hopkins moved past me. 'Good morning, Mr Buxton.'

'Good morning,' I said, watching him go. The poor fellow. The stewardess had come out of the room she was cleaning and bobbed at the man as he passed her by, but Hopkins was too distracted to notice. His eyes were on the carpet.

I smiled, as I glanced down a side corridor and caught the briefest flicker of a feline tail heading towards the port side. There the little devil was. I was about to call after Mr Hopkins – to tell him the news – when a door sprang open midway along the corridor and the cat bolted in alarm.

A stout middle aged woman came barrelling out of the bedroom. It was Mrs O'Neill. I regarded her in surprise. That was not her cabin. 'Oh, Mr Buxton! You must come at once!' she exclaimed.

'Mrs O'Neill? What is it?'

The woman was distraught. 'You must come quickly. It's Mr Latimer.'

'Harry? What is it? What's wrong?'

'Oh, Mr Buxton. It's awful!' Her voice cracked in despair. 'He's…he's dead!'

Chapter Five

There are some people you expect to live for ever. When my father passed away in the spring of 1913 I confess I did not shed a tear. We had never been close and a world without him in it was, in truth, something of a relief. But when my old nanny died, some years later, it was a different matter. It felt like a rock had been removed from under me. Nanny Perkins had guided me through my formative years, a strict but sympathetic figure. She had retired before the war and, aside from the odd letter, I had not heard from her in years; but somehow the knowledge that she was still alive was a source of great comfort to me; and when she was gone, it felt like something was missing from my world. It was the same with my valet – my first valet – Thomas Hargreaves. He had looked after me through my adolescence and into young adulthood. I had presumed he would be with me for life. And then, one day, he had died, and once again it felt as if a part of me had been cut away. Some people affect you like that. Harry Latimer was one such person.

We had first met in New Orleans in the winter of 1918. He had been trouncing all comers at a poker match in a bar somewhere on the outskirts of the city – this was in the days before prohibition – and one of the other players had quickly become suspicious. This particular fellow was six feet six and built like a tank. He accused Harry of cheating and a fight had broken out. It was an entertaining spectacle. My money was on the giant, but Harry had brought the man down with half a dozen blows, then grabbed all the cash and ran. I had chuckled quietly to myself about that for some days afterwards. Of course, I had no notion that I would ever see him again. But then, a week or two later, I bumped into Harry in another bar on the other side of town. At the time I thought it was a coincidence. In fact, he had settled on me as a potential "mark". I was to be the victim of an elaborate con, and he would have fleeced me of several hundred dollars if my wife had not stepped in at the last moment. Elizabeth had a far better eye for a scoundrel than I did. Harry had accepted defeat but managed to redeem himself, when Elizabeth was not looking, by offering up a racing tip which he assured me could not lose. That tip paid off, to the tune of fifty dollars – on a one dollar stake – and, after that, we became firm friends. I have never been able to resist a rogue, although I should perhaps make it clear that I was never attracted to Harry in a physical way. Back in Europe, we would bump into each other on a regular basis and each time we met up, it would be as if we had never been apart. Harry was always getting tangled up in some dubious scheme or other – he would sell anything to anyone, no questions asked – and I would often be called upon to help out, if he got into trouble. Then, when my finances took a sudden dive – as they frequently did – he would be on hand to return the favour. In truth, Harry Latimer was the closest thing to a friend I had in the whole world. Meeting up with him now, after more than two years apart, it had felt natural to slip back into the old routine. Harry was always there. He was a scoundrel, a conman, a thief, and a womanizer; but above all he was a good friend. And now he was dead.

I stared down at the pale figure in the bed, the head nestled firmly in the centre of the pillow. It was impossible, it was absurd, it could not be true. But it was. His plump, rounded face looked serene, as if he were asleep; but Harry's skin was pale and cold to touch. When Mrs O'Neill had broken the news to me out in the corridor, I had been certain she was mistaken. She must have got it wrong, I thought. Harry had probably just passed out and Mrs O'Neill was making a drama out of nothing. But then I moved into the room and saw the body – the pale figure in the striped pyjamas – and my blood ran cold. His eyes were closed and the bedsheets neatly held in place, but there was no sign of life. I went through the motions quickly, checking for a pulse or any signs of respiration but there was nothing to find. Harry Latimer was dead. He had probably been dead for some hours. And at that point, the shock hit me and I let out a quiet moan of despair.

How on earth could it have happened? My brain struggled to get a grip on the idea. How could he be dead? Had he had a heart attack? A stroke? Harry was not an old man; he was younger than I was. Thirty-nine, forty this year, on the cusp of middle age. He should have had years ahead of him. And then, a horrible thought flickered across my mind. Could it be that he had not died naturally? I shivered at the idea. Please God no, I thought. Not Harry. But I had stumbled across so many dead bodies of late, people who had met their ends in violent and unnatural circumstances. And I could not look at him lying there without thinking, what if...? But Harry, of all people? Oh, he had his enemies. Men he had conned, women he had jilted, criminals he had double crossed. But surely they would not strike him down here, in his cabin, in the middle of the Atlantic, miles from anywhere? I clenched my hands together. The possibility could not be dismissed. A sudden anger welled up inside me. I was meant to be looking after him. If he had been killed, if someone had done this to him, then they would pay for it, whoever they were. My God, I would make them pay.

It took me a few moments to calm myself; then I looked around the cabin, searching for any sign of a disturbance. This was one of the cheaper rooms on B Deck, nicely furnished but rather small, with a simple chair, a washbasin and a functional bedside table. A single bed with a smart wooden headboard took up most of one side. There was a jug of water on a small bedside table, with an upturned tumbler, but no sign of anything out of place.

Mrs O'Neill was sobbing loudly in the doorway behind me. I regarded the woman with sudden suspicion. 'What were you doing in his room?' I asked her.

She wiped her eyes. 'Cynthia asked me to look in. Harry wasn't at breakfast. We were going to invite him up to the garden lounge. I knocked but there was no reply.'

'I wasn't at breakfast either,' I said.

Mrs O'Neill attempted a shaky smile. 'I was going to look in on you next.'

'How did you get in here, though? The door wasn't locked?'

'No, it wasn't.' The catch on the inside had not been

thrown. Mrs O'Neill sniffled again. 'How…how did he die, do you think?'

'I don't know.' I gazed down at the body. There was no blood or any signs of a struggle. 'We need to fetch a steward. We ought to….' I stopped, glancing back at the door and catching sight of a dark figure hovering in the corridor outside. 'Morris, what are you doing here?'

The valet stepped forward. 'I heard voices, Monsieur. I am in the cabin next door. Is something the matter?'

'It's Harry. Harry Latimer. He's dead.'

'Dead?' The valet blinked.

'Yes. He must have…he must have died in his sleep. Look, make yourself useful.' I was doing my best to pull myself together. 'Fetch a steward. No, better yet, get a doctor.'

'At once, Monsieur.'

I poured out two glasses of whisky. 'Water?' Mrs O'Neill nodded and I added a quick splash from the jug before handing it across. She received the glass gratefully. Maurice had gone off in search of the doctor and we had retreated to my cabin. Mrs O'Neill had been starting to feel a little faint. It might have been better to wait at the scene until the doctor arrived, but my room was only a short distance away and it was better not to clutter up the place unnecessarily. Luckily, the cabin boy Adam had come by as Mrs O'Neill and I moved out into the corridor. I told him what had happened and asked him to keep an eye on the room.

'Make sure no-one goes in there until the doctor arrives.'

'Of course, sir.' He would let me know the moment he turned up.

I downed my glass and poured myself a second. A shell-shocked Mrs O'Neill was seated in the chair opposite me. She sipped her whisky gently, her hands shaking as she held the glass. 'I can't believe he's dead. Really dead.'

I sat down on the bed and knocked back the second glass. 'Dear God,' I muttered, dropping the tumbler to my lap.

It was still not sinking in. I had seen so much death of late, but most of the people who had died had been strangers to me, or at least casual acquaintances. The devastation I had witnessed in British Honduras had unnerved me like nothing else – all those bodies piled up in the streets – but even then they were a formless mass, unknown and unidentified. I pitied them, but I could not grieve for them as individuals. The same was not true of Harry Latimer.

'He seemed so full of life,' Mrs O'Neill gushed. 'So charming and so handsome. Life can be so cruel sometimes.'

'I thought he'd see me out,' I admitted, revolving the tumbler in my hand. 'He played fast and loose, but he…he always came out on top.'

Mrs O'Neill placed her glass on the floor and wiped her eyes. 'He was a good friend to you, wasn't he?'

'Yes, I…' A wave of despair bubbled up inside me but I fought it back as best I could. 'Yes, he was.'

'You must have known him for a long time.'

'I…yes.' I righted the tumbler and looked up. 'You guessed?'

'You were on first name terms, almost from the moment I introduced him to you,' she said. 'I thought…I thought perhaps you must have met before.'

I closed my eyes. There was no point in concealing the truth any longer. 'Actually, I've known him for years. I'm sorry. It wasn't our intention to deceive you. We met purely by chance. Harry…' I tried to think how to phrase the matter delicately. 'Look. You're probably going to find this out at some point anyway, but Harry…he was not all that he seemed. He…er…he didn't always act from the purest of motives.'

Mrs O'Neill nodded again. 'I suspected as much. I've never been particularly bright, Mr Buxton, but when a handsome man some years younger than me pays me that kind of attention, I know it isn't because he enjoys my company. I've never been a beautiful woman…'

I made the appropriate noises of disagreement but Mrs O'Neill waved them away. The woman was not quite as deluded as I had first supposed.

'I'm a rich woman and men often show an interest in me. I know their motives are not pure. But it can be lonely on your own. And it is still flattering when a man pays you attention.'

'He did like you, I'm sure, in his own way.'

'He was far more interested in Miss Wellesley.' Her face erupted in a sudden panic. 'Oh, Mr Buxton, what are we going to tell Cynthia? She'll be so upset. She was forming quite an attachment to him. Whatever am I going to tell her?'

'The truth,' I said, with a gentle shrug. 'That's all we can do. He liked her and now he's dead.' I suppressed a shudder at the finality of that thought.

'I was watching them together, last night. They seemed made for each other. I thought...I thought, well Mr Latimer could court Cynthia and you and I could...could...' Her face fell. 'Well, now is not the time for that.' She started to cry again, this time uncontrollably. I reached down to my jacket pocket and pulled out a handkerchief. The last thing I needed was waterworks in my cabin. Mrs O'Neill took the cloth gratefully. I have never been at ease, comforting distressed women and, truth to tell, this time I was not sure who was the more distressed. 'Life is so unfair. Anyone I ever care for...' She gave the handkerchief a good blow and I placed a tentative hand on her shoulder. All at once, she flung her arms around me and buried her head in my chest. I did my best not to flinch – I have never liked hugging – but the hard, racking sobs of Mrs Susan O'Neill were an echo of my own feelings.

'Is the doctor inside?' I asked.

'Yes, Monsieur.' Maurice was hovering in the corridor, his expression grim. It was probably unfair of me, sending him off like that across the decks to fetch a doctor, but he had done his duty, in surprisingly brisk order. There is nothing like a tragedy to bring out the best in people. 'He arrived some minutes ago. How is the Madame?'

'Upset, as you'd expect. A stewardess is looking after her.' Adam had popped his head around the door to tell me that the doctor had arrived. I had left Mrs O'Neill – with my handkerchief and a second glass of whisky – in the capable hands of the laundry woman. 'It's hit her hard,' I said. 'And me too.' I heaved myself up against the wall next to the valet, staring at the closed door of the cabin. The doctor was inside, with the head steward, examining the scene. 'My God. Harry of all people.'

'I am very sorry, Monsieur.'

'So am I, Morris. So am I. I was supposed to be keeping an eye on him. Making sure he didn't get into any trouble. And now this…' Lord. What was I going to tell London?

'You knew Monsieur Latimer for a long time?'

'Pretty much forever.' I sighed. 'Since the war anyway.'

'And you believe he died in his sleep?'

'I don't know. It looks that way. But he was younger than me. In better shape, too.'

'Outward appearances can be deceptive, Monsieur.'

'Yes, I'm aware of that, Morris. But this…' I waved a hand. 'It doesn't feel right, somehow.'

'You suspect foul play?'

'Lord, I hope not.' Just for once, I thought, it would be nice if someone could die of completely natural causes. 'There was certainly no sign of a forced entry. No struggle. No blood. He looked so peaceful, lying there. I suppose it could have been natural causes. There's a first time for everything.' My eyes began to film over. 'But if anything untoward did happen, Morris. If some blackguard…' I was beginning to shake once again, the rage boiling up inside me. 'If someone killed him, then I swear to you, Morris, I'll have them. I'll have them on the end of a rope, no matter what it takes.' My body was shuddering now, some sort of delayed shock kicking in. I had the unaccountable urge to thump somebody very hard. I have never been a violent woman. I have always been content to leave it to the other fellow to deliver the killing blow. But some things are simply beyond the pale. And a world without Harry Latimer was unconscionable. I banged my fist against the wall at my back. A lavatory flushed and there was an embarrassed harrumph from some oaf on the other side. That's the terrible thing about death; the way that life carries on regardless, not even pausing. Harry was lying dead and someone not fifteen feet away was attending to his toilette, completely oblivious. It was like a painting I had once seen, The Fall Of Icarus. There the poor fellow was, his wings melting from the heat of the sun, plunging to his death, and there everyone else was, getting on with their lives, not even noticing.

My melancholy was cut short by the door handle in front of me, which twisted around as the door opened. A man popped his head out. 'Mr Buxton?' This was the doctor, a tall, youngish man in a smart officers' uniform. 'Bartholomew Armstrong.' He thrust out a hand. I had seen the fellow about on deck, but I had not realised he was a doctor. That uniform was deceptive. 'You were a friend of the deceased?' he asked.

'Yes, yes I was.'

'I'm sorry for your loss. It's always very upsetting when somebody dies suddenly like this.' The doctor's face exuded calm regret, a professional but sincere manner. He was not a handsome man – his eyes were too small and far too close together, and his ears stuck out rather – but he had a dignified bearing. Behind him, through the door, I could see the head steward, standing soberly at the end of the bed. A sheet had been pulled over Harry's head.

'Yes, indeed. Oh, this is my man Morris.'

'We've met. I understand it was you who discovered the gentleman?'

'Me? No, it was Mrs O'Neill. A friend of his,' I babbled. 'Harry wasn't at breakfast, and she came to see if he was all right. He had a bit of a late night last night.'

Doctor Armstrong nodded. 'Yes, so I understand.'

I cut straight to the point. 'What...when did he die?'

'Judging by the state of the body, I would say about three hours ago. Perhaps between seven and eight o'clock in the morning.'

'And is there any indication...?' My voice trailed off. Was there any indication of how he had died?

'I'm afraid it's too early to say. I've conducted a brief examination, but I'll have to perform a post mortem to determine the specific cause of death. Tell me, did he have a heart condition at all?'

I frowned. 'Not that I'm aware of. He certainly never talked of it. Although, to be honest, I hadn't seen him for a year or two before this trip. He certainly wasn't complaining about anything. Why, do you think that's what may have...done for him?'

'There are some indicators of heart trauma.'

'A heart attack?'

'It's a significant possibility. Most likely, it would have happened in his sleep. He wouldn't have suffered unduly.' There was the bedside manner on display, the gentle reassurance. 'I'm afraid there will have to be an enquiry. A death onboard ship, particularly a man in his middle years, there are procedures to a follow. It's all quite routine.'

'You...don't think there was anything suspicious about his death?' I had to pose the question at least.

'No, not at all, but we have to be thorough. It's purely a matter of routine. We have a security officer onboard, a Mr Griffith, who'll examine the scene. He'll probably want to speak to you at some point. He's a good man. A red cap during the war.' A member of the military police force. 'He'll need to speak to you and Mrs...O'Neill was it?'

'That's right.'

'And anyone else who might have known Mr Latimer or associated with him. Any next of kin we should know about?'

'I don't think so. There's a girl...Miss Wellesley. Cynthia Wellesley. She was quite taken with him. She'll have to be informed.'

'Of course.'

'She may well have been the last person to see him alive.'

'I have the room next door, Monsieur,' Maurice volunteered. 'I believe the two of them returned here in the early hours. Perhaps two am.' The valet was a light sleeper, so it was not surprising that he had overheard them out in the corridor.

'I see. And was there...?' The doctor hesitated. 'Forgive the indelicate question...were you aware of any intimacy between them? It could have a bearing.'

'There was no intimacy, Monsieur.'

'But an awful lot of dancing before they went to bed,' I chipped in.

'I see. And did you happen to hear anything else, during the night?'

'No, Monsieur. Nothing at all.'

'Well, thank you for your help, both of you. The head steward and I will take things from here.'

'What will happen to...to the body?'

'He'll be taken down to the surgery so I can begin the post mortem. And the room will be locked up, until Mr Griffith has a chance to look at it.'

'Will you...let me know what you find? The results of the post mortem, I mean.'

'Yes, of course.' Armstrong smiled politely. 'It may not be for a day or so, I'm afraid, but I will let you know.'

'Thank you, doctor.'

The steward was coming out of the room. Armstrong waited patiently as the man locked up the door, then gave us a quick nod and the two of them went on their way. The officials were taking charge of the situation and there was nothing more I could do.

Nothing more, except to break the news to Miss Wellesley. Never volunteer for anything, that is what the army people say, and I have always found it a good rule to live by. Unfortunately, more often than not, one finds oneself volunteered by default. 'Oh, Mr Buxton, what can I say to her?' Mrs O'Neill had lamented, between sobs, in my cabin. 'She's so young. She's seen so little of life. You and I, Mr Buxton, we've known death, but that poor girl...'

'Would you like me to come with you?' I offered, somewhat reluctantly.

'Oh, would you?' In the circumstances, I did not really

have a choice. 'That would make it so much easier. You're such a kind man, Mr Buxton.'

'Call me Henry,' I said. Having already spent some minutes in the woman's crushing embrace, we could probably dispense with the formalities.

'Henry.' She smiled bleakly.

We met up with Miss Wellesley in the garden lounge on A Deck. She was sitting in one of the boxy wicker armchairs there, amid the colourful potted flowers, with a pot of tea on a table, engrossed in a book. The garden lounge was moderately busy, the sea visible through the large windows lining the starboard side of the ship. A group of men at the far end were engaged in a game of cards. I envied them. Breaking bad news is never a happy duty, especially when you haven't fully come to terms with the matter yourself. Miss Wellesley smiled at the sight of us and closed up her book. 'You were a long time, Mrs O'Neill,' she said, rising up politely as we arrived at the table. 'I'm afraid the tea will be cold now.' Cynthia Wellesley was a slender, pretty girl in her mid twenties. She was dressed demurely but her eyes flashed a lively greeting. 'Good morning, Mr Buxton. Is everything all right?' In that one look, she had observed our sombre expressions.

'I'm afraid not,' I said, as we took our seats around the small, square table.

'What's happened?' Miss Wellesley returned to her chair, her voice flecked with concern.

'It's Mr Latimer.'

'Harry? What's wrong?'

'Something terrible has happened,' Mrs O'Neill said, unable to hold herself back.

And so we broke the news. I have to say, the girl took it remarkably well. There were no tears, no histrionics. That is the difference, of course, between the American and the British constitution. We grieve, but we do so in private. There was no doubt, however, at the shock Miss Wellesley felt at this unwelcome news. 'I was only speaking to him last night,' she breathed. 'We said goodnight. He seemed in such good spirits.'

'The doctor seems to think it might have been a heart

attack,' I said. 'He didn't mention any pain to you? Any discomfort?'

Miss Wellesley shook her head vehemently. 'No, none at all. I can scarcely believe it. I've never met such a healthy man. So kind and courteous.' She stared down at the tea pot on the table. 'A little forward, perhaps, but that was just his way.'

'He was always fond of the ladies, was Harry,' I said.

'Mr Buxton has known Mr Latimer a little longer than either of them admitted to us,' Mrs O'Neill explained.

'Yes, I thought that might be the case. He spoke very fondly of you, Mr Buxton.'

'But he didn't seem out of sorts at all, last night?' I asked.

'Well….' The young woman considered for a moment. 'He did seem a little distracted, now I come to think of it. He disappeared for a short while, about an hour or two after supper. He said he needed to freshen up.'

'He went to the bathroom?'

'I imagine so. I was still on the dance floor, with the Reverend Hamilton-Baynes, but thinking back, he was gone rather a long time.' Her brow furrowed again. 'It might have been twenty minutes, almost. But then he came back and we danced again.'

'This was before we put Mrs O'Neill to bed?'

The American woman blushed at the reminder of her inebriated state.

'Yes, about eleven thirty, I would think,' Miss Wellesley said.

A steward had delivered a note to Harry at around that time, I recalled. 'You don't remember him receiving a piece of paper do you? A note, over by the bar?'

'I don't think so. A note?'

'Yes, I saw somebody hand it to him. One of the stewards. That must have been about eleven thirty.'

'I don't recall.'

'And it must have been shortly after that that he went off.'

Mrs O'Neill was alarmed. 'Oh, Mr Buxton…Henry.

You don't think there might have been…have been something untoward about his death?'

'No, no, no,' I assured the woman hastily. 'I'm sure there wasn't.' There was no point distressing her any further. 'The doctor was pretty firm about that. Almost certainly a heart attack, he said. The poor devil. But I have been hearing some odd things recently, about letters being received. Typewritten notes of a distasteful nature.' I exchanged a meaningful glance with Miss Wellesley. She had the decency to blush. 'And I wondered whether the note he received might have been something of that sort.'

'Oh, Mr Buxton. You've heard then? About the pen letters? The poison pen letters.'

'A little. I don't know the details.'

'Pen letters?' Miss Wellesley stared at her employer in surprise. 'You've been receiving poison pen letters?' The girl may have discovered the note back at the hotel but that was as far as her knowledge of the matter went, it seemed.

'Yes, I have. Oh, Cynthia, it's been so awful. I didn't want to burden you with it. But surely none of that can have anything to do with Mr Latimer. We only met a couple of days ago.'

'It might not be connected,' I said. After all, the note Harry had received had been hand delivered, not shoved anonymously under a door. 'But I think it might help if you explained a little.'

'Of course. I…yes.' Mrs O'Neill took a moment to collect her thoughts. 'It started some time ago. Letters received through the post. Vile letters. Mostly aimed at my husband.'

'Typewritten letters?'

'Yes. They upset him terribly. Whoever wrote them, they seemed to know everything about him. We thought at the time they must be from an employee. Well, a former employee; someone with a grudge against him. My late husband was a hard task master, where business matters were concerned. Then, after he died, the letters stopped for a while. But when Sir Richard and his family came here, over Christmas, they started up again. Letters to him and to his sister.'

Miss Wellesley was stunned. 'I had no idea,' she said. It was curious that the American woman had chosen not to confide in her. But then, they had only known each other a short while.

'And what did they say, these letters?' I leaned forward.

'It was all kinds of intimate, personal things. It's too distressing to talk about. It spoilt our Christmas.'

'Did you report them to the police?'

Mrs O'Neill shook her head. 'No. The letters…the information they contained was too personal. Almost as if it was from a member of my own household. That was why I… why I decided to go to Europe. To get away from it all. And then the restaurant…the bomb….after that, it became even more urgent. I had to get away, don't you see?'

I nodded. That, presumably, was why she had not told the police the whole story. 'But whoever sent those letters – and that bomb – Mrs O'Neill, it looks like they may be onboard this ship.'

'Oh, Henry. They can't be true! Whatever do you mean?'

'Well, Lady Jocelyn has received at least one threatening letter, since we boarded the Galitia. I heard her talking about it to her brother, last night.'

'But that's not possible!' Mrs O'Neill rocked back in her chair, horrified. 'She can't have. She would have told me.'

'I'm afraid it's true. A typewritten note, just like you said. But it's worse than that.' I glanced across at Miss Wellesley. 'I'm sorry to do this to you, Miss Wellesley, but I think in the circumstances…' The girl looked down at her lap and nodded softly. 'You also received a note. It was delivered to your hotel room yesterday morning, just before you got up.'

Mrs O'Neill frowned. 'I don't understand.'

I reached into my jacket, retrieved the piece of paper the young woman had given me and handed it across.

Miss Wellesley watched closely as the older woman opened it up. 'It was pushed underneath the door,' the girl explained. 'I didn't want to frighten you, so I hid it away.'

Mrs O'Neill shuddered. '"NEXT TIME IT WILL NOT

BE A HOAX",' she read out loud. 'And this was before we set sail?'

'It was,' I admitted grimly. 'And now at least one, or possibly two other people have received similar letters. Which means that whoever organised that bomb at Leopardi's, they may well be onboard this ship.' And, I added silently to myself, there was a distinct possibility that they had done for Harry Latimer.

Chapter Six

I lit up the cigarette and took a long, heavy drag. It had been a hell of a morning. I had barely had a moment to myself – in all the confusion – to stop and think. I closed my eyes and let the smoke fill my lungs. I am not usually a heavy smoker, but today the soothing effects of tobacco were sorely appreciated. I had retreated to the Carolean, to gather my wits and to give myself a bit of a breathing space. The smoking room was all but empty right now, as most of the passengers were down at lunch. I exhaled a cloud of smoke and opened my eyes. What the devil was I going to do? I would have to contact Terrance Greenfield in New York and let him know what had happened. If he hadn't already heard. Doubtless telegrams would be firing across the Atlantic, a well worn routine when a passenger died at sea. What would London think, when they heard that the man I was supposed to be keeping an eye on had expired on my watch? It would not reflect well on me. God, what a mess. I took another puff of the cigarette and coughed.

Just twenty four hours previously I had been sitting in this same alcove, conversing with Harry Latimer, after Sir Richard had toddled off with his secretary. It seemed, with the benefit of hindsight, that we had not had a care in the world, as we stubbed out our cigarettes, pulled ourselves out of the padded armchairs and made our way along the Long Gallery towards the elevators.

I had taken my time, admiring the paintings on the walls – there were some particularly fine royal portraits along the way – but Harry was dismissive.

'These are all reproductions,' he said. 'Just a load of fakes.'

'Rather fine fakes,' I thought.

'But not the real deal.' Harry's interest in art extended only as far as their financial value. 'They wouldn't risk the originals on a steamship. The insurance companies would never allow it. It'd cost them a fortune if the ship went down.'

'That's a happy thought,' I said. 'Typical insurance

people, valuing paintings more than people.'

'People are a dime a dozen, old man. Each of these paintings is unique. The originals, I mean. They're irreplaceable. You wouldn't want to lose them.'

'I'll remind you of that when we're running for the lifeboats.'

That was Harry all over. Always business. He was one of life's schemers and, like any good criminal, he always kept his cards close to his chest. The more I reflected on his death and all the other peculiar incidents which had taken place over the last forty eight hours, the less credible it seemed to me that he could simply have died of a heart attack.

But what was the alternative? I tapped out a bit of ash into a nearby ashtray. Could he really have been murdered? Quite a few people across various continents might have been happy to see him six feet under. Yet there was nothing at the crime scene to suggest foul play; no smoking revolver or bloody knife. Harry had been lying in his bed, as peaceful as a lamb. That did not preclude the idea of murder, however. Homicide did not necessarily have to involve actual violence. He might easily have been poisoned. I pondered that unhappy possibility for a moment. There had been no signs of distress; his face looked utterly serene. Any toxin would therefore have to have been slow acting; and, if such a poison had been employed, a post mortem would surely uncover it. Chemicals in the blood and all that. At least, I hoped it would. If Harry had been poisoned, though, how would it have been administered? Had somebody spiked his brandy at the bar last night, or contaminated the water jug by his bed? That would be the obvious thing to do. I grimaced, an unwelcome memory bubbling up in my mind. I had some experience of interfering with a person's drink and it had not ended well.

I tapped out the end of my cigarette and considered the practicalities of such an idea. Who would have had the opportunity to do it? There were only a handful of people onboard ship who could have gained access to his cabin without arousing suspicion; always assuming that the poison had been administered there. The stewards, mainly, and perhaps the odd acquaintance. What motive would any of them have had? Aside from myself, there was barely anybody onboard who even knew Harry. The occupants of the Reynolds Suite had been virtual strangers until last night. He had known Miss Wellesley and Mrs O'Neill a little longer than that, but neither of them struck me as credible suspects. The older woman was, admittedly, not quite as clueless as I had first supposed – she had managed to deduce that Harry and I were old friends – but her distress at discovering his body had struck me as entirely genuine. As, for that matter, had Miss Wellesley's reaction, when we told her the news.

The younger woman had been the last person to see Harry alive, of course, which meant she would have had the better opportunity; and for all the girl's apparently sweet nature, she did have a brain in her head. A student of botany, no less. That fact sparked a related thought: if she knew all about plants, she might also know a little about poisons. Most toxins were plant based, were they not? In theory, therefore, she might know the right combination of herbs with which to spike his drink. I chuckled to myself, dismissing the idea at once. Miss Wellesley was hardly likely to carry a set of herbs around with her, on the off chance that she might want to kill somebody. Besides, what possible motive could she have? She and Harry had only just met. Or perhaps – it occurred to me now – she might have lied about that. Harry had been less than honest about our friendship, after all. Perhaps he and Miss Wellesley had known each other for some time but had kept quiet about it for some reason.

If it had to be one of the women, though, Mrs O'Neill struck me as the more likely suspect. Maybe she had got wind of Harry's scheme to steal her necklace. What exactly had she been doing skulking about in his bedroom like that? Had the door really been unlocked? It seemed unlikely to me. The woman had had the opportunity but what would have been the point of killing him? If you discover somebody is a thief, you call the police, you don't poison them. And, of course, more to the point, with all the alcohol she had knocked back last night, Mrs O'Neill would have been out for the count until breakfast in any case.

Perhaps I was barking up the wrong tree. If Harry had been murdered, the culprit was more likely to be somebody I didn't know; some scoundrel lurking in the background. There could be any number of people aboard the Galitia Harry might have had dealings with. One of the stewards, perhaps, or a member of the crew who might have known him on the sly. If he had been killed, it was probably as the result of some scheme or other he had been involved in, some criminal he had upset, cheated or wronged. Gangsters, perhaps, back in America. Could that be it? Could it have been a "hit" of some kind? My mind drifted back to the hoax bomb at Leopardi's. Harry had certainly been spooked by that, though he had done his best to hide it. He had been rather anxious to get away afterwards, too. At the time, I had thought that was because of the police; but it could just as easily have been some local gang. One of them slipping aboard, maybe somebody in second or third class, and then creeping upstairs and doing the deed in the dead of night. Yes, that might be a plausible sequence of events.

I rubbed my eyes. What about the poison pen letters, though? Was all that just a coincidence? According to Mrs O'Neill, she and her late husband had been receiving these letters for several years, on and off. She had asked me not to mention the fact when I spoke to the detective fellow, and I had some sympathy with her request. Telling the boys in blue – or their local equivalent – would only muddy the waters and serve to embarrass Lady Jocelyn. Besides, if the first of those letters had been sent in 1928 or 29, as Mrs O'Neill claimed, then Harry could not possibly have been responsible. He would have been in Europe at the time. Admittedly, the man had received a suspicious looking note of his own last night, in the ballroom, but I had no reason to suppose that this was one of the regular pen letters. A malicious writer would not send a note via a steward, when it could so easily be read by anybody and the perpetrator traced. More likely it was a summons of some kind. Miss Wellesley had said that Harry had disappeared for a short while afterwards. Some other business, then, that I knew nothing about? And maybe that was what had got him killed.

Any further analysis was cut short by the arrival of Sir Richard Villiers. Having eaten his fill at the restaurant on D Deck, he had come up to the Carolean for a quiet drink and a smoke. He glanced across the hall. The smoking room seemed to have filled up rather in the last few minutes. The lunch time servings were coming to an end. A good half an hour must have passed by while I had been contemplating Harry's death. I tapped out my cigarette in the ashtray and was surprised to find it was my third of the day. A couple of ageing Americans were mumbling to each other on a settee in the centre of the hall and a retired colonel was dozing in a far corner, his cigarette gently fizzling away on its ashtray. Sir Richard's gaze swept across them and then fixed on me, tucked away in a small alcove off to the left. I struggled not to grimace. That was the last moment of quiet I would be allowed this afternoon. Sir Richard raised a hand in greeting and strode across to join me. 'Mr Buxton,' he said, his chunky glasses sparkling in the light from the high windows above us. By now, he would have heard about Harry's death, and his expression was suitably grave. 'How are you feeling?' he asked, coming to a halt in front of me. 'You weren't at lunch.'

'I wasn't hungry,' I said. In truth, I could not bear to face the company at table; all those sympathetic faces.

'I don't blame you, old boy. A terrible thing to happen.' He sat himself down next to me and pulled out his pipe.

'Dreadful,' I agreed. I gestured to the empty whisky glass in front of me and he nodded. A waiter jumped to attention as I indicated the glass and ordered two more.

Sir Richard filled the end of his pipe and lit it expertly; then he sat back in his armchair and took a long suck. 'Life and death. It's a rum do, isn't it?'

That was an understatement. 'I've seen so much of it lately,' I said. 'Some people you think will be there forever. Nanny Perkins. My old valet, Hargreaves. And Harry. Even if you don't see them for years on end, you know they're there. And when they die...' I trailed off as the waiter arrived with two whiskies.

Sir Richard reached forward for his glass. 'Best not to think about it too much.' He slurped at the drink. 'Stiff upper lip and all that.'

'You're right, of course.' I downed the whisky. 'Sorry, I didn't mean to be maudlin.'

'You have every right, old boy. I barely knew the fellow, of course, but it's hit Susan hard. Shock, I suppose. You know what women are like. They can't help themselves, the poor dears.' He placed his tumbler down on the side table. 'She couldn't eat anything at lunch. She's gone to have a lie down.'

'Probably the best thing for her,' I said. 'She has been through rather a lot lately. The bomb. The attempted robbery. And those letters too.' I shot Sir Richard a knowing look. If I had to talk to the fellow just now, I might as well find out what he knew.

His expression darkened. Sir Richard had a thin, grey face which matched his short, close cropped hair. 'Oh, you've heard about that?' He adjusted his spectacles. 'Dastardly business. It's put a pall on the whole trip.'

'It's not just Mrs O'Neill who's been receiving poison pen letters?'

'No, we all have, ever since we arrived in the Americas. It's a damn foolish way to conduct yourself. In my day, if you took against someone, you'd jolly well tell them to their face. Anonymous letters, not the done thing at all. A woman's way of fighting.'

I suppressed a scowl. I was not in the mood for such blatant male chauvinism. 'You think a woman sent the letters?'

'As to that, I couldn't tell you. But they've caused no end of upset.'

'What sort of things do they say? If you don't mind me asking?'

Sir Richard growled. He reached into his jacket pocket and pulled out an envelope. 'This is the first one I received, back in October. Don't know why I hang on to it. I've destroyed the rest. But this one. I don't mind telling you, Mr Buxton, it makes my blood boil.' He handed me the envelope. It was a regulation post office affair. The address was type written on the front.

I pulled out the letter inside. Again, it was standard issue note paper, the kind you could pick up in any "dime store" in America. The capital letters, however, were instantly familiar.

"SIR RICHARD, YOU ARE NOTHING BUT A LEECH. YOU COME HERE AND RUIN OUR LIVES. YOU TEAR OUR BUSINESSES APART, YOU LEAVE OUR WORKERS DESTITUTE. YOU STRIP AWAY THE WEALTH AND TURN YOUR CHEEK WHEN PEOPLE ARE DYING IN THE GUTTER AND YOU KNOW IT IS YOUR FAULT. BUT YOUR SINS WILL FIND YOU OUT AND YOU WILL PAY FOR IT. ALL THE MONEY IN THE WORLD CANNOT PROTECT YOU IN THE FACE OF THE ALMIGHTY."

I looked up. 'Religious sort?'

Sir Richard shrugged. 'Apparently.'

My mind flashed back to the Reverend Hamilton-Baynes, sitting at a typewriter in the writing room. Could he have something to do with this? 'It's pretty grim reading,' I admitted, staring down at the paper. The typeface was somewhat familiar too. I had half a mind to pull out Mrs O'Neill's note and compare the two, but I thought better of it with Sir Richard looking on. I read through the text again. 'It sounds like a disgruntled employee. What does it mean, tearing businesses apart?'

'That's an odious phrase.' Sir Richard puffed at his pipe. 'What I do is perfectly legitimate. I'm a businessman. I buy up failing companies, strip away the dead wood and sell them on. You can't blame me for the companies failing in the first place. That's their own damned fault, if they don't run the things properly. In my day, people took responsibility for their failings.'

'But people have ended up in the street?'

'It's unavoidable, with the economic downturn. But I discharge all the responsibilities. A week's notice. References where appropriate. Then sell off the assets and make use of them in any way I see fit. It's business, old boy, purely business.'

'But somebody's obviously aggrieved.' I returned the letter to its envelope and handed it back to Sir Richard. He pocketed it sourly. 'And this was the first note?'

'Yes, a few days after we arrived.'

'And Lady Jocelyn...she's received a couple of these as well?'

'More than a couple. They've been very unpleasant.' He scowled. 'Not the sort of thing I could possibly discuss with anyone. But Jocelyn's a brick. She can handle anything. She's the exception that proves the rule where women are concerned. But they were pretty near the knuckle, I can tell you.'

'And neither of you received any letters before you arrived in America?'

'No.'

'Did you inform the police?'

'Heavens, no. We don't want to involve anyone else. Far too upsetting. All sorts of unfounded allegations being thrown about. But we did make a few discreet enquiries. Had a proper look at the envelopes. Each letter was posted in a different post box, all within a three mile radius of the house.'

'Mrs O'Neill's house? In Boston?' That was interesting. 'Which suggests it could have been a member of the household.'

Sir Richard inclined his head. 'One of her people, we thought. Her late husband and I were in business together.'

'He was in shoes, wasn't he?'

'After a fashion. That was one of the more profitable off-shoots of a company we acquired a few years back. We sold that one on for quite a hefty profit eventually. Actually.' Sir Richard leaned in closely and lowered his voice. 'My secretary wondered if it might not be Susan herself who was sending the letters.'

'Mrs O'Neill?' I did not try to hide my surprise at that suggestion.

'There were some rather intimate details in there. Difficult to see how anyone else could have known.'

'And the letters to her husband, when he was alive?'

93

'The thought did cross my mind. But it was absolute poppycock, of course. They were devoted to each other. Susan wouldn't demean herself in that way. And, of course, she's received quite a few letters herself.'

'So I understand. And she could hardly be responsible for sending that parcel bomb to herself. Not with her own name on the envelope.'

'Well, quite. Over here!' Sir Richard called out abruptly. The secretary, Mr Hopkins, was hovering at the far door. The man spotted us and lifted a hand. The sleeping colonel roused briefly, harrumphed at the sudden noise, and then closed his eyes again.

Hopkins moved across to the alcove.

'Good lord,' I exclaimed, catching sight his face. 'What happened to you?' There were scratch marks across his left cheek.

'Matilda,' he confessed glumly.

'That blasted cat.' Sir Richard chuckled. 'He found her down on C Deck. Put up a bit of a fight, didn't she?' Hopkins nodded.

For the first time that day, I found myself chuckling too. 'Bad luck!'

'Jocelyn dotes on that damned cat. Can't stand the thing myself. Much more of a dog person. You know where you are with a dog. Yes, what is it, Ernest?'

To my surprise, it was me that the young man addressed. 'I was sent to find you, Mr Buxton. One of the officers, a Mr Griffith, wishes to speak to you.'

It took me a moment to place the name. 'Oh, the security fellow, you mean?'

'Yes, that's right.'

Sir Richard glowered. 'He was talking to Mrs O'Neill just before lunch. Impertinent fellow. In my day, people like that knew their place.'

'I'll be along shortly,' I said. 'Once I've finished up my cigarette.'

'Of course.' Hopkins hovered for a moment, clearly wanting to join us but not sure whether it was appropriate.

Sir Richard rolled his eyes. 'Go on then,' he said. 'You're probably due a break. You don't mind if Ernest joins us?'

'No.' I would not begrudge anyone a shot of tobacco.

Hopkins sat himself down and pulled out a packet of cigarettes. He was in quite an awkward position on this trip. He was an employee but he wasn't a servant. He existed in that netherworld – like a governess or a poor relation – someone who isn't below stairs but who nevertheless lacks status. It was not a position I would like to find myself in. But the fellow seemed amiable enough.

'We were just discussing those damn pen letters,' Sir Richard explained.

Hopkins hesitated as he lit his cigarette.

'Mr Buxton knows all about them,' Sir Richard declared. 'No harm in filling in the details. You received a couple yourself, didn't you?'

Hopkins nodded carefully. 'They weren't very pleasant, I'm afraid.'

'What did they say? If you don't mind me asking?'

The young man grimaced. I had the impression he would have preferred not to answer, but with Sir Richard there he could hardly refused. 'They rather impugned my integrity, I'm afraid.'

'Said he was cooking the books!' Sir Richard roared. I had not heard him laugh before. He received a couple of disapproving looks from the Americans. Now who's being too loud, I thought mischievously.

'It was very hurtful, Mr Buxton. I have always been scrupulously honest.'

'Of course you have. Absolute poppycock.'

'We thought it must be a member of Mrs O'Neill's household,' Hopkins went on. 'But now I'm not so sure.'

'You've received another letter since we left New York?'

'I haven't, no, but I gather Lady Jocelyn has.' Hopkins must have been the one that maid was talking to, when the steward overheard their conversation. What had he been doing in the servants' canteen, I wondered.

'Yesterday morning,' Sir Richard confirmed. 'It was slipped under the door, shortly after we arrived.'

'And Mrs O'Neill has received one too,' I said. 'So whoever is behind all this, they must be onboard this ship.'

'I did wonder if your man Latimer might have had something to do with it,' Sir Richard said. 'Forgive me for speaking ill of the dead. But he did appear out of nowhere somewhat.'

'It's not Harry's style. He was like you, Sir Richard. If he had a problem with anyone, he'd confront them eye to eye. With raised fists if necessary.' He had known how to handle himself, had Harry. 'He wouldn't send letters like that. No more than I would.'

'Well, anyway, it looks like he died in his sleep,' Sir Richard concluded, 'so I'd appreciate it if you didn't say anything to this detective chap about it all.'

'The pen letters?' I nodded. 'No, Mrs O'Neill has already asked me not to mention them.'

'Don't want to muddy the waters. Mr Latimer didn't receive anything of that sort, did he?' Sir Richard asked.

'No. At least...'

'There you are then. And there's no call to upset Susan any further.'

'Or Lady Jocelyn,' the secretary put in firmly. He reached a hand up to the cut on his cheek.

Mr Griffith was a short, thickset man in his late forties, with greying hair and heavy sideburns. 'It's kind of you to see me, sir,' he said, sitting back in the wicker chair and flipping open his notepad. 'This won't take long.' He was in uniform – the standard dark jacket and peak cap, although the cap was resting now on the table between us – but the uniform did not sit well on him. Griffith had more of the air of a police sergeant than an officer. As the ship's security man, that probably boded well. If there was anything untoward about Harry's death, it was this fellow's job to sniff it out. He pulled a pencil from his breast pocket and looked across at me. 'I gather you knew Mr Latimer well. What kind of a man was he?'

I sat back in my own chair, gazing out for a moment across the promenade. He had chosen a quiet spot on the port side for the interview, well away from prying ears. It was a little chilly out here, even with the windows closed. I scratched my ear briefly, wondering how I ought to reply to the question. If Griffith hadn't already made contact with the authorities in New York, he would be doing so shortly, so there was no point in concealing the truth. 'He was a…colourful character,' I confessed tentatively. 'Larger than life. Good humoured.'

'Honest?' Griffith met my eye; a sharp, penetrating gaze.

I hesitated. 'Not entirely.' I had the impression Griffith already knew the answer to that question. 'He…wasn't one to play by the rules.'

'So I gather. We found this in his suitcase.' The man reached down to a bag at his side and pulled out a small wooden box, plain and unvarnished. He placed it on the table. I had not seen it before. Griffith opened it up and allowed me to view the contents. I had to work hard not to smile. Several dozen white pearls on a bed of cotton.

'Pearls?' I said, trying my best to sound surprised. Each pearl was loose but there were small holes on either side, through which a necklace could easily be threaded. I looked up. 'Are they real?'

'They're paste,' the officer said. 'If they were real they would be worth an absolute fortune. Now why would a gentleman like Mr Latimer be carrying around a set of fake pearls?' He met my eye again. It was another test. Griffith was no fool, it seemed. I hesitated a second time, not wanting to incriminate myself. 'I notice Mrs O'Neill wears a rather fine set of pearls,' he prompted. So he had guessed the truth already.

I took a heavy breath. 'Harry was not an honest man,' I said. There was no point dissembling. This fellow was too clever by half. 'I don't want to speak ill of the dead, but he didn't always operate on the right side of the law.'

'He was a crook?'

'Er...well, yes. A *petty* crook. Not that I knew anything about it.'

'Of course not, sir.'

'But it's possible that his acquaintance with Mrs O'Neill was not entirely innocent.'

'He was after the jewels?'

'It's possible.' I frowned, gazing down at the fakes. Griffith had said he had found them in his suitcase, but Harry had not brought them onboard himself. He had enlisted somebody – presumably a member of the crew or some grunt below decks – to slip them past the customs men. At some point, that person had obviously delivered his cargo and Harry had stashed the pearls away. But perhaps – it occurred to me now – they had not been delivered immediately. Maybe that was what the note had been about last night. Perhaps whoever it was had finally got into first class and was arranging to deliver the goods. That would explain why Harry had slipped away for twenty minutes. If the smuggler was not allowed on the upper decks – an ordinary seaman, perhaps – then meeting up late at night would be a good idea, when most of the guests and other staff were either in the ballroom or in their beds. That might also explain why Harry had been so reluctant to switch the pearls, a short while later, when we had put Mrs O'Neill to bed. If he had only just received the box, he might not have had time to properly prepare them. Yes, it all made sense. And that meant the whole business of the note might well be entirely benign, and certainly unrelated to anything going on in the Reynolds Suite.

Mr Griffith coughed politely, startling me out of my reverie. I cleared my throat, to cover myself. 'I should perhaps make it clear, Mr Griffith, that I hadn't seen Harry in years. It was pure coincidence that we bumped into each other on this trip.'

'I'm sure it was, sir.' He closed up the box. 'And how long had you known the gentleman?'

I sat back in my chair. I felt like lighting another cigarette, but that would only serve to demonstrate how ill at ease I was. I did not want to provoke the man's suspicions any further. 'About ten or fifteen years, I think.' I tried to make the reply sound casual. 'We met just after the war. I was living in America then. I came back to Britain in the early twenties, and when he came to Europe we would meet up from time to time.' In fact, the last time we had met, he had been selling guns to some rather dubious people in the South of France; but I was not about to tell Griffith that. 'We never talked about his business,' I lied. 'I knew better than to ask.'

'I see.' Griffith scribbled in his notebook, not looking at me now. 'And when was the last time you saw him?'

'Last night. Mrs O'Neill had had rather a lot to drink and we put her to bed. Then we went back to the dance floor. That would have been about half past twelve, one o'clock.'

'And what did you do then?'

'Well, I'd had quite a bit myself, so I had one for the road and then headed off to bed. I gather Harry went to bed at about two, or perhaps a little later.'

Griffith looked up, his eyes narrowing. His ruddy complexion only served to accentuate those pale blue eyes. 'And how would you know that?'

'My valet, Maurice. He has the cabin next door. He heard them come in.'

Griffith flipped back through his notebook. 'Ah yes, a Monsieur Sauveterre.'

'That's the fellow. He heard Harry and Miss Wellesley saying goodnight. She must have been the last person to see him alive.'

'Not quite the last, sir,' Griffith said.

'Oh?' Who else had he been talking to?

'One of the stewards saw Mr Latimer at about six o'clock, in his pyjamas. Coming back from the bathroom. At least, that's how it appeared. Answering a call of nature.'

'I see. One of the stewards?'

'Yes, sir. A Mr Cooper. He was just coming on duty. Adam Cooper.'

'Adam?' That was my steward. 'He kept that quiet.'

'He didn't recognise him at the time. Mr Cooper only has responsibility for the starboard rooms, not the midsection.

It was only when he saw the body that he remembered the incident.'

'And this was at six am?'

'That's right. You sound surprised, sir.'

I hesitated. 'It's just that the doctor said the time of death was between seven and eight.'

'That's correct.' An hour or two afterwards.

'But if he was up and about just before that, answering a call of nature, then…' I shuddered. 'He might have been awake when he…when he had the heart attack.' He might not have died in his sleep.

'I'm afraid that's possible, sir.'

Lying in bed, dozing happily, and then a sudden, intense pain and his heart giving out, though whether through poison or bad luck remained to be seen. 'God, poor Harry.' It was not the way I would choose to go.

'He might well have dropped back to sleep, sir. He might not have known anything about it.'

'Lord, I hope not.' There was a brief silence. Griffith was staring calmly at me. Like any good policeman, he knew when to speak and when to be silent. Doubtless he could see the cogs whirring away in my head. Finally, I asked the obvious question. 'Do you think…do you think there was anything untoward about his death?'

Griffith took a moment before replying. 'It's too early to say, sir. Do you have any reason to be suspicious?'

'No. I mean, he consorted with all sorts of dubious people, but none of them would be here, onboard ship, would they? And there was no sign of any struggle?'

'None at all. Apart from this box, there was nothing out of the ordinary in the room that I could determine. I will keep an open mind, but as things stand, there's nothing to indicate any foul play. Sometimes, in my experience, the simplest explanations are often the right ones, sir.'

That was not my experience at all, but I kept that thought to myself.

'Mr Latimer was a crook,' Griffith asserted bluntly, 'but criminals are not immune to medical conditions. It is possible he simply had a heart attack. We will have to wait to hear the results of the post mortem. In the meantime, I have several other people to talk to.' He flipped shut his notebook, returned his pencil to his breast pocket and rose to his feet. 'Thank you for your time, Mr Buxton.' He held out his hand, and I rose up to shake it.

'Not at all. If there's anything else you want to know…'

His eyes met mine firmly once again. 'I know where to find you,' he finished. And with that, he pottered off along the promenade in search of his next victim.

I lingered for a moment, returning to my seat. The man had such an unnerving look. It seemed to pierce straight through you. What was it the doctor had said about him? A red cap in the Great War. I pitied any soldier who had tried to desert under his watch. But at least the investigation was in good hands. Whatever the truth of the situation, this man Griffith would get to the bottom of it.

Chapter Seven

'A lecture? On steam propulsion?' I boggled.

'Yes, Monsieur.' Maurice was dusting down my evening jacket. It was a little after seven. 'I had not fully appreciated the complexities involved.'

'In steam propulsion?'

'Yes, Monsieur. It was a most informative lecture.' He brushed off the shoulders of my jacket with his usual expert eye. 'The chief engineer had assembled a small array of models to demonstrate the principles involved.'

'Did he now?' I regarded the valet with some irritation. Maurice had always had an interest in obscure subjects, but this was taking the notion of an enquiring mind a little too far. 'Well, I'm glad you've had a productive afternoon,' I grumbled. 'For heaven's sake, Morris. I know I told you to get out and stretch your legs...' (I had been rather firm on that point, in fact. 'Don't stay in your cabin all day, wallowing in self pity,' I had told him.) 'But there's a time and a place. A friend of mine's just died.' I glared at the man as he laid down his brush.

'I am sorry, Monsieur. I did not think you would object.'

I flopped back onto the bed. 'It doesn't matter.' If attending a lecture or two helped take his mind off things, then I suppose I could not really object. 'It's just...I don't know. It's infuriating, everyone carrying on like this, as if nothing's happened.' Life on the Galitia was continuing serenely, without a care in the world. Nothing had been cancelled, not even the lectures. 'Do people even know somebody's died?'

'I do not believe so, Monsieur.'

Granted, there had been no formal announcement, but with Mr Griffith out and about interviewing people, I had thought the news might have spread by now. I pulled myself back up. I was supposed to be dressing for supper. Having skipped lunch, I was now starting to feel a little peckish. 'Nobody was talking about it? At the lecture? Over tea and biscuits?'

'No, Monsieur.'

'What about below stairs? Has there been any gossip there?'

'No, Monsieur.'

'What, none at all?'

'None that I am aware of, Monsieur.' That surprised me. I thought at least the staff would have commented on a dead body in their midst. 'A death onboard ship is not an unusual occurrence,' the valet pointed out. 'It would not normally be a subject for discussion.'

'They were gossiping readily enough about the poison pen letters yesterday.'

'Yes, Monsieur.' When somebody had overheard the maid talking about it in the canteen. 'But that was a rather more unusual affair.'

'More unusual than a passenger dying? Yes, I suppose you're right.' I wondered idly if Lady Jocelyn was aware that her maid had been gossiping about her, even if it was just with Sir Richard's secretary. 'Oh, did I tell you? Sir Richard showed me another one of those letters. He's been receiving them too, apparently. It was a nasty piece of work.' I leaned forward and pulled Mrs O'Neill's note out of my jacket, which was now hanging on the chair. 'Not dissimilar to this one. Typewritten, capital letters. Longer, though. More specific. And sent through the mail.'

Maurice looked up. 'And the typeface was the same?'

'Well, it was typed, if that's what you mean. But they all look pretty much the same, don't they? Typewriters.'

'No, Monsieur. There are significant differences.'

'What, between models, you mean?'

'Yes, Monsieur. But also between the individual machines. Each typewriter has its own unique characteristics.'

'Does it?'

'Yes, Monsieur. The alignment of the keys can vary significantly from one machine to another. No two typewriters will ever be exactly the same.'

'I'll take your word for that.' There was no end, it seemed, to the obscure subjects my valet knew all about.

Typewriters, for goodness sake.

Maurice reached into his pocket to pull out his reading glasses. 'If I may?' He gestured to the note. I shrugged and handed it over. The valet took a moment to examine it. 'You see, Monsieur. The letter "W" here, in the word "WILL".' He held the note so I could see it and indicated the letter in question. 'The top of the "W" is slightly higher than the top of the "I" or the top of the "T" in the previous word.'

I regarded the note dubiously. 'Is it?'

'Yes, Monsieur. You see? I noticed it when I examined the letter before.' That was typical of Maurice. He had always had a good eye for detail. But I was struggling to see the relevance of it.

'How on earth does having a misplaced "W" help us at all?'

'It would not, Monsieur, if we had only the one letter to examine.' Which was presumably why he had not mentioned it before. 'But if you were to compare this to the letter Sir Richard showed you, you would be able to see if they were typed on the same typewriter.'

'Well, of course they were typed on the same typewriter. There's only one person sending these damned letters. This isn't helping, Morris.'

'No, Monsieur. But knowing the idiosyncrasies involved could help us to identify the typewriter concerned, and thus the person responsible for sending these letters.'

I sat back for a moment. 'Yes, I see what you mean. But there must be dozens of typewriters aboard ship. Every time I pass through the writing room, there are half a dozen people clacking away. We can't check them all.'

'No, Monsieur. We would need to find some way to narrow the possibilities. But if Sir Richard's letter was sent through the post, before he left America, and it was typed on the same typewriter as this one, then that might prove a useful starting point.'

'I suppose so. The Reverend Hamilton-Baynes has a typewriter,' I recalled. 'No, wait a minute. He said he borrowed it from Sir Richard. And presumably they would have had that with them when they were staying at Mrs O'Neill's place.' I scratched an ear hole. 'So anyone might have had access to it.'

'Yes, Monsieur. If that was the machine that was used.'

I took the note back from Maurice and pocketed it; then reached for my fob watch and checked the hour. 'I ought to start getting dressed,' I said.

'Yes, Monsieur.' The valet removed his reading glasses and stowed them away.

I pulled off my shirt and handed it to him, scratching irritably at the bandages underneath. They always started to chafe a little against my chest as the day progressed. 'I can't see how it helps us, though. I can't very well go nosing about the Reynolds Suite on the off chance. And to be honest, Morris, I'm not altogether sure these pen letters are worth the trouble. I'm pretty sure they have nothing to do with Harry's death.'

'You believe he may have died naturally after all?'

'Mr Griffith seems to think so. And he's no fool.'

'He is an intelligent man,' Maurice agreed.

'Too clever by half, if you ask me. We'll have to wait for the autopsy, but I'm trying to keep an open mind. I didn't say anything to him about the letters.'

'Monsieur?'

'Mrs O'Neill asked me to keep quiet. And anyway, if Harry was killed, I'm pretty sure it must have been the result of some criminal activity or other. Some mad scheme Harry got himself into. He must have bitten off more than he could chew.'

'There is another possibility, Monsieur.'

'Oh?' I peered across at the valet. What had he thought of that I had not considered?

'Monsieur Latimer worked for the intelligence services during the war, did he not?'

'Yes. What of it?' I had sketched out Harry's dubious past and Maurice knew all about my own secret service connections. 'That was years ago.'

'And those same intelligence services asked you to keep an eye on him on this trip.'

'Yes, but purely as a matter of routine. Harry did some important work for them during the war. Don't ask me what it was. He's never talked about it.'

'Perhaps it was something that the British government would not wish to enter the public domain.'

I stared at the fellow suspiciously. 'What exactly are you suggesting, Morris?'

'It could be that someone in authority wished to make sure that he did not speak about his experiences, whatever they might be.'

I regarded the man in horror. 'An assassination, you mean? Morris, that's ridiculous.' I snorted. 'I don't know how you Frogs behave, but the British secret service does not kill people.'

'Perhaps not. But there are always rogue elements, Monsieur...'

'Yes, but...look, that was all years ago. During the war, before I even met him. However, I do know quite a few of the people he worked with. Decent, honourable men, who've been keeping a fatherly eye on him for years. Protecting him. Why would that change now?'

'I do not know, Monsieur.'

'No, it's absolute rubbish, Morris. You do talk drivel, sometimes.'

'Yes, Monsieur.'

'You mark my words, if it was murder, then it's a criminal gang of some sort. Maybe somebody else after the pearls.'

'Pearls, Monsieur?'

'Er...never mind.' That was one bit of the story I had not discussed with Maurice. My valet had an irritatingly firm moral compass and I knew he would not approve. 'I don't wish to discuss it any further.'

'No, Monsieur.' He helped me into a fresh shirt and we dressed quietly for the next few minutes. The silence lingered, however, and in the end it was I who broke it. 'So if they're not talking about Harry below stairs, what are they talking about?'

Maurice buttoned up the front of my waistcoat. 'I believe the main topic of conversation today has been Lady Jocelyn's cat.'

106

'What, Matilda?' I laughed.

'Yes, Monsieur.' He removed a fleck of dust from the front of the waistcoat. 'I understand there is some irritation that the animal should be allowed to wander freely across the decks. I believe representations have been made to the head steward.'

I sniggered again, my mood improving by the second. 'Oh, lord. He's going to speak to Lady Jocelyn?'

'Yes, Monsieur.'

'That won't go down well.'

'No, Monsieur. But if the animal is not kept within the confines of the Reynolds Suite, it will have to be confined to the hold.'

'What, in a cat box?' I chuckled. This was getting better and better. 'I'd pay good money to see Lady Jocelyn's face when they tell her that.' I stood up and pulled back my arms as Maurice helped me into my dinner jacket. There is nothing quite as enjoyable as watching a member of the British aristocracy losing her rag. 'Well,' I said, 'if that's all people have got to worry about, then perhaps it was natural causes after all.'

It could sometimes be a little chilly on the promenade, so I was grateful the following morning to settle myself a little way back from it, in the Long Gallery, as I awaited the arrival of Doctor Armstrong. I had ordered a pot of tea and settled myself into a comfortable armchair opposite the sash windows looking out onto the port side promenade. I had supposed the gallery, connecting the Palladian Lounge with the Carolean Smoking Room, would be one of the quieter places to talk, but even here a steady stream of people were making their way up and down, admiring the many works of art lining the mahogany panelled walls. The message I had received, via Adam, was that the doctor would meet me here at eleven o'clock. I had questioned the young steward about Harry and he had confirmed what Mr Griffith had told me about seeing him when he came on shift, though Adam was unable to provide any further information. And now, the results of the autopsy were about to be revealed. I sat nervously and poured myself out a small cup of tea. Just for once, I resisted the temptation to add a tot of whisky.

I had arrived some minutes early for the appointment, with a copy of the Cunard Bulletin to hand. Whenever anyone wandered past, I could bury myself in the news sheet, to discourage them from starting a conversation. The damnable informality of an ocean liner was proving a particularly onerous burden just now. There was little news to read, however. The Bulletin was mostly advertisements and notices about activities onboard ship. Today's lecture, apparently, was on the subject of "Cordon Bleu" cooking, whatever that was, delivered by the head chef. I hoped Maurice would not get any ideas. He had far too much of an enquiring mind for my taste. Three lectures in three days. The first, apparently, had been on the subject of "Human Anatomy". And the man who had delivered that lecture was, I now saw, hurrying towards me along the gallery.

'Mr Buxton.' Doctor Armstrong raised a hand in greeting. 'I'm sorry to keep you. A couple of last minute patients.'

I rose up to greet him. 'That's quite all right. Nothing serious, I hope.'

'No, no, just the usual scrapes and bruises.'

'The work of a doctor is never done.' I gestured for him to take the armchair on the opposite side of the table. 'I appreciate you taking the time to see me.'

Armstrong removed his cap and sat himself down. 'That's quite all right. All part of the service.' He was a smartly dressed fellow with broad shoulders and a mop of wavy blond hair. His face was a little bland, with pin holes for eyes and a stub of a nose, and the less said about his ears the better, but he held himself with a quiet confidence that was immensely reassuring. I have never much liked doctors – for obvious reasons – but Armstrong struck me as one of the better sort.

'Would you care for a cup of tea?' I asked. 'The pot's still warm.' I folded up my paper and reached for the china.

'No, thank you. I won't.' He settled into his chair, as I poured myself out another cup. 'How have you been?' he asked. 'This must have been a trying time for you.'

'Yes. I've been in a bit of a fog, to be honest.' I reached for the sugar. 'You've...er...you've completed the autopsy, I understand.'

Armstrong nodded gravely. 'Yes, last night. I've been typing up the results, in between patients. It can take a while.'

'Do you have lots of patients on a voyage like this?'

'A few. Usually nothing too serious. The occasional bruised limb, when people don't mind their step.'

I sat back in my chair and took a slurp of tea. 'But not too many deaths? Generally speaking?'

'It's more common than you might think, on a voyage of this kind. But it's usually older passengers. The change in routine can sometimes...well, bring things to a head.'

I nodded. 'And Harry?' I was anxious to get to the point.

Armstrong looked down. 'The same, I'm afraid.'

'So it *was* natural causes?'

'I'm afraid so. Mr Latimer's heart was in a bad way. He must have been aware of it. He would have been in some pain, the last few days.'

'He never gave any indication of that.'

'No. Some people have a way of concealing these things. It's odd, but sometimes they even manage to hide it from themselves. There is one crumb of comfort, though: it looks like he did die in his sleep. So at least he wouldn't have suffered unduly.'

'That's a mercy,' I agreed. 'You'll forgive me for asking, but...you're absolutely certain there was no possibility of foul play?' I couldn't help but pose the question. My mind had been so alive with theories of late that I couldn't quite let the idea go. That's the problem with having been involved in so many murder investigations: you always assume the worst.

'I examined the contents of his stomach,' Armstrong reassured me. 'There was nothing untoward there. A fair amount of alcohol in his bloodstream, but no more than you'd expect after a heavy evening.'

'A lot less than some,' I ventured.

'And no signs of any other toxins. No drugs or

poisonous substances. Although to be honest, Mr Buxton, if you'd seen the state of his heart, you might not have bothered to look.'

'The poor bastard,' I muttered, unable to moderate my language.

'Well, quite.'

There was an awkward pause. I put my tea cup down on the table. So it was true. Harry Latimer really had died of a heart attack. I slumped back into my chair. Poor Harry. 'So what happens now?'

'Well, Mr Griffith is completing his enquiries. He's been in contact with the authorities in New York. Mr Latimer was apparently known to the police there. He even had some connections with the local mafia. A colourful figure, by all accounts.'

'That's the polite way of phrasing it.'

'According to Mr Griffith, he has been wanted in connection with various historic felonies in other states, but nothing recent that they were aware of. There was no outstanding warrant for his arrest in New York. Mr Griffith has examined the stateroom and spoken to everyone onboard who knew him. With that and the results of the post mortem, he agrees that there is no reason to suppose there was anything suspicious about his death.'

I nodded. It wasn't quite what I had expected to hear, but it was a relief nonetheless. 'What will happen to…to his body?'

Armstrong gazed across at the windows. 'Well, there are two options. We can keep him on ice and arrange a funeral in Southampton. Or we can arrange a burial at sea. Unfortunately, we haven't been able to trace any living relatives to ask how they would like us to proceed.'

'Harry wouldn't care either way,' I thought. 'He wasn't sentimental like that. Best just to get it over with, I would think.'

'That will probably be my recommendation. The captain's not too keen on sea burials – he thinks it unsettles the other passengers – but I can probably bring him round to it. Just

110

a quiet affair in a day or two, once we've completed all the paperwork.'

I nodded again. 'You've been very helpful, Doctor Armstrong.'

'Just doing my job, sir.' Armstrong smiled sadly. 'Just doing my job.'

Chapter Eight

Mrs Hamilton-Baynes was not wearing a bathing suit and neither was I. Even if it had been practical for me to do so – which, given my peculiar lifestyle, it certainly was not – I had no desire to put my body on public display. There were plenty of other people assembled at the swimming pool on E Deck who felt differently, however. I had not expected to find myself among such a crowd this afternoon. I had planned for an altogether quieter time, in the aftermath of my conversation with Doctor Armstrong. A poker game somewhere, perhaps, to take my mind off things. There was a regular game over in the garden lounge each afternoon.

Unfortunately, Mrs O'Neill had other ideas. 'Oh, Henry!' she exclaimed to me, in the restaurant at lunchtime. 'We mustn't allow ourselves to be maudlin.' This was as we were mopping up the dessert. I had passed on the results of the autopsy and Mrs O'Neill had had several courses over which to ponder her response. 'We must put on a brave face,' she decided, her arms folded implacably across her bosom. And for her, that meant – of all things – a swimming competition.

The crew of the Galitia were running a series of events to celebrate the forthcoming Olympics in Los Angeles. A respectable crowd had gathered around the pool. Thankfully I would only be expected to observe and not to participate in the competition. Mrs O'Neill had dragged me down here to offer moral support to the Reverend Hamilton-Baynes. The vicar had cancelled his boxing match the previous afternoon, as a gesture of respect, but today there would be no stopping him. The sight of the man in his striped knee length bathing suit enthusiastically warming up at the side of the pool was enough to provoke a smile from even the most jaded of spectators.

'He's very athletic, your husband,' I observed, to Mrs Hamilton-Baynes. With his voluminous black and grey beard and the pale white skull cap, the poor fellow looked more like a cleaning implement than an Olympic swimmer. He was already at the far end of the pool, preparing for the first event: the over forties short swim. From the look of the competition, it would be a walkover. Despite the unfortunate attire, the vicar was easily in the best shape. 'I'd put money on him,' I said, with a slight shake of my head. The more I saw of the man, the more he surprised me. A boxer, a preacher and now a swimmer. Was there no end to his talents? He had even promised to give Miss Wellesley a lesson in shuffleboard, after the young woman had confessed she had never played the game. Despite his advancing years, the vicar was a walking dynamo.

'You're very kind,' Mrs Hamilton-Baynes said, returning my smile. She was a short, slender woman in her early fifties, with a pleasant open face and dark, neatly pinned hair. I had joined her at the far end of the pool, well away from Mrs O'Neill, who was standing midway along, to better observe the swimmers. 'I shouldn't put any money on him, though,' the vicar's wife advised, with a touch of humour. 'He wouldn't want you to lose out.'

'It wouldn't be the first time,' I said. My thoughts drifted back to the match I had stumbled across on the first afternoon, when some American had bested the vicar at shuffleboard. I had tried to get one of the officers to place a bet, but he had refused. Actually, it had been that doctor fellow, now I came to think of it. I hadn't known him at the time. It was his loss, though, not taking the bet. 'I'm not the world's greatest gambler,' I admitted.

The over forties were now lining up, all five of them in their stripy knee length drawers, taking their place at the far end of the baths. The pool itself was long and narrow in the Roman style, not deep by any means but graduated, as these things are. A low roof hung over the entire area. The crowd was gathered along the nearside of the pool, in front of the changing cubicles. Most of them were fully dressed but a few were in bathing suits; those taking part in later competitions. A set of wooden columns broke up the crowd along the length of a white marble floor. The first contest was to be a two length sprint, with lanes marked out for each of the competitors. It would likely be a brief affair, but energetic. The gym instructor, with his handlebar moustache, was standing by with a whistle and stopwatch at the far end.

'Now Harry,' I continued, still thinking about the gambling. 'He'd never place a bet that he wasn't sure he could win. Rather defeats the purpose of gambling, if you ask me.'

Mrs Hamilton-Baynes regarded me sadly for a moment. 'You were very close to him?'

'In some ways. Oh, here we go!' The instructor had blown his whistle and the swimmers had plunged forward into the warm water without a second's hesitation. The Reverend Hamilton-Baynes was on the near side and got off to a good start. The crowd roared, Mrs O'Neill waving her arms enthusiastically, while Mrs Hamilton-Baynes looked on with quiet amusement.

'Do you swim?' she asked, taking her eyes from the contest for a moment.

'Not if I can help it,' I said. 'Come on, reverend!' Even without a bet on, I found myself unexpectedly engaged. 'Look, he's edging ahead.' The swimmers were approaching us now, hands grabbing onto the nearside of the pool as they flipped over to begin the second leg. It was neck and neck between the reverend and one other fellow, a heavily whiskered gentleman who was puffing laboriously. The battle of the beards, no less. Damnation, why wasn't somebody organising a book here? Or a sweepstake at the very least. As the two men streamed towards the finish line, the second fellow began to nudge ahead. The gym instructor blew his whistle and, having paid close attention to the edge of the pool, declared the whiskered man the winner. The crowd applauded enthusiastically. I turned back to Mrs Hamilton-Baynes. 'Bad luck. He nearly had him there.'

The vicar's wife was unperturbed. 'He'll be happy with second place. He was worried he might come last.' She smiled. 'Swimming is not his strongest suit.'

I scoffed at that. Hamilton-Baynes had put in a pretty convincing performance. 'He'd put a fair few Olympians to shame.' Mrs O'Neill had been right to drag me down here this afternoon. Despite my best efforts, I was beginning to enjoy myself.

'You're glad you came?' Mrs Hamilton-Baynes asked.

'Absolutely.' It was not quite racing at Newmarket, but it was an admirable diversion nonetheless. I glanced at the smiling faces of the crowd. At the far end of the pool, the vicar was being helped out of the water. 'I'm surprised Sir Richard and Lady Jocelyn aren't here,' I said. I would have thought they would have turned out to offer a little encouragement.

'I don't think they would enjoy it just now,' Mrs Hamilton-Baynes said. 'They're not in the best of moods at the moment.'

'Oh?'

At the far end of the hall, the vicar was being handed his towel. Various supporters were slapping him on the back and congratulating him on his performance.

'I'm afraid there was a bit of a contretemps after lunch,' she explained.

'An argument? Between the two of them?'

'No, not between them. Between Jocelyn and her maid.'

'Ah. You mean, the one she's sharing a room with?'

'Jenny Simpkins, yes.'

'Never easy, bunking down with a servant.'

'No, I suppose not. But they're also sharing with Matilda, the cat.' Mrs Hamilton-Baynes' eyes flashed with gentle amusement. 'Jocelyn absolutely dotes on her. Unfortunately, she got out on deck yesterday morning. The head steward wasn't at all happy.'

'Yes, I heard about that. Gave poor Mr Hopkins quite a scratch.'

'The steward came to see her. Jocelyn, I mean. He told her if Matilda got out again, she would be put down in the hold. I think if it had been anyone else, he would have done it then and there. But Jocelyn was incensed. She's devoted to that cat. Matilda has been her only source of comfort, these last few months.'

'Since her husband died?'

'Yes.' The woman nodded seriously. 'She gave strict instructions to Jenny and to Ernest to watch themselves every time they went in and out of the door. But somehow, Matilda managed to get out again this morning.'

'Oh, lord.'

'Ernest found her, thankfully, before anyone saw, but Jocelyn was furious. She accused Jenny of letting the cat out deliberately. She's given her her notice. It's all very awkward.'

'Her notice?'

'It's been brewing for some time.' Mrs Hamilton-Baynes sighed. 'Jocelyn has never really liked the girl. She says she's far too insolent. And talks far too much. Also, she thinks she's rather too fond of Ernest. Of Mr Hopkins.'

I lifted an eyebrow. That was the first I had heard of that, though it did not surprise me.

'They're sweet on each other, I believe. But Jocelyn won't allow it. She doesn't think it's right for a servant to carry on like that. Making eyes at a secretary.'

'No, it is rather bad form,' I agreed. Servants were not supposed to have private lives. It got in the way of their work. I was lucky with Maurice. He had never shown any interest in such things. 'So Miss Simpkins has been dismissed?'

'I'm afraid so.'

'That's going to be a bit awkward, isn't it, if they're sharing a room?'

'It's not ideal. But she'll be working out her notice period.'

'Perhaps they could swap,' I thought. 'Put Miss Wellesley in with Lady Jocelyn and the maid in with Susan. If she doesn't object.'

'That might be a good idea,' Mrs Hamilton-Baynes agreed. 'But it's Jenny I'm worried about. Jocelyn can be a little stubborn sometimes, and she's adamant she won't provide a character. She'll pay the girl her dues to the end of the week, but nothing more. And without a reference, the poor girl won't get another job. She'll be destitute.'

'Doesn't she have a family?'

'Her parents disowned her. She has no-one. I wish there was something I could do.'

I could not think of anything to suggest. The life of a servant is never an easy one.

The Reverend Hamilton-Baynes was now moving along the side of the pool, drying himself off with his towel and accepting the commiserations of various strangers. A huge smile radiated out of that heavy beard as he locked eyes with his wife. At the far end of the pool, the gym instructor was already preparing for the next race. These were the younger men, and my eye strayed briefly at the sight of them. A bathing costume, for a man or a woman, is never flattering, but some people can carry it off better than others, particularly the young. Mrs Hamilton-Baynes, however, had eyes only for her husband. 'You'll have to excuse me,' she said, pulling away. 'I should congratulate the returning hero.'

'Be my guest.' I smiled.

The body was wrapped in a light cotton shroud, laid on top of a short ramp, which led over the side of the ship. We had gathered on the aft deck, in the open air, to pay our last respects to my old friend. It was a reasonable turn out, on a chilly morning, mostly staff and crewmen, with a few friends and acquaintances, but very few people who really knew Harry. A garland of flowers had been placed on top of the shroud. I had insisted on that. Harry had sent a wreathe to my funeral. It was the least I could do to return the favour; and the garden lounge on A Deck could do without a few of its blooms. It would have amused Harry no end to know that I had stolen some of them.

'I am the resurrection and the life, saith the lord,' the Reverend Hamilton-Baynes intoned, dressed now in respectable black robes and with an appropriately sombre expression. Mrs O'Neill, similarly attired in black silk, was clutching hands with Miss Wellesley off to his right as the comforting drone continued. Mrs O'Neill was sobbing quietly. It was surprising that the older woman, who had already buried one husband, should react so forcefully, whereas a young slip of a thing like Miss Wellesley was holding herself together. But such are the vagaries of constitution. Both women had helped me with the flowers, weaving them together into a fine bouquet. I had not told them where they had come from.

117

Mrs Hamilton-Baynes was observing her husband with quiet pride as he worked his way through the service. Lady Jocelyn and her brother were close by, suitably stone-faced, though in the case of her ladyship that was pretty much her default expression. She had one of those faces that could not help but look severe.

'He that believeth in me, though he were dead, yet shall he live.' Hamilton-Baynes had a prayer book resting in his left hand, but he knew the words by heart. How many people had he buried? I wondered. 'And whosoever liveth and believeth in me shall never die.' It was kind of the reverend to conduct the service. There was a resident dog collar man onboard ship, but Hamilton-Baynes had thought the personal touch might be more appropriate. He might not have known Harry well, but at least he could speak from personal experience. A peculiar fellow, Hamilton-Baynes, certainly unlike any Church of England vicar I had ever met, but I was gradually coming to admire him and his charming, modest wife. In his naive enthusiasm for life, the reverend was probably closer to the ideal of the mother church than many another more overtly pious individual. There was no one better to see Harry Latimer on his way to the afterlife.

The mourners stood around respectfully as the wind whistled through our hair. The sea was a little rough this morning, though the sun was peeking through the clouds above us, and everyone had dressed up against the cold. Maurice had insisted I wear my thickest overcoat and that was proving its worth. The valet had offered to pay his respects, along with the other mourners, but I had absolved him of the responsibility. It was a decent thought, but I didn't want him having a fit or fainting and embarrassing me, up here on deck in the open air. Better for him to stay buried down below, well away from the sight of the sea.

Actually, the turnout was rather better than I had expected. Alongside the people who knew him, there were a number of stewards and seamen, some of whom had carried the litter out onto the deck. I wondered idly if one of these fellows had helped Harry to smuggle his pearls onboard. Doctor

Armstrong was here too, alongside the head steward, and the captain of the Galitia, Steven Curtis, a grim, austere figure in a crisp naval uniform.

The only people who seemed out of place were standing over by the hatch. Two hefty looking brutes had appeared from nowhere early on in the service, while the rest of us had been singing a rather tuneless hymn. They were tall and broad shouldered, dressed respectfully enough for the occasion, though their suits looked a little rough and their faces were hard masks of flesh. I leaned in to Mrs Hamilton-Baynes, after the hymn had concluded. 'Who are those two?' I asked. But the vicar's wife had no idea. Someone from second or third class, perhaps. I did not like the look of them one little bit.

'For as much as it hath pleased Almighty God to take unto himself the soul of our dear brother here departed,' Hamilton-Baynes continued, as the service moved inexorably towards its conclusion, 'we commit his body to the deep; in sure and certain hope of the Resurrection unto eternal life, through our Lord Jesus Christ.' He muttered a few final words and then the inevitable 'Amen.' I repeated the word, along with the rest of the congregation, and felt my stomach lurch. I have never been much of a one for religious ceremonies – I am not a regular church goer – but at moments like this, I could understand their value; the comfort and reassurance they give, a much needed sense of continuity in the face of oblivion.

A couple of crewmen stepped forward to grab hold of the ramp on which Harry's body lay. I looked away for a moment. The two strangers were staring grimly ahead, their hands held in front of their waists, as the shroud with its garland of flowers slipped softly from the ramp. I turned back just in time to see the cocoon slip off the far end and plummet out of view. Such was the noise of the wind that none of us heard the sound as the body hit the water. But that was it. Harry was gone. I turned back to look at the two men, but they had also departed.

The note was as blunt and as cowardly as all the others, and just

119

as personal. "YOU ARE NOTHING BUT A LEECH," it said. "YOU ATTACH YOURSELF TO VULNERABLE WOMEN, HOPING TO BLEED THEM DRY. YOU HAVE NO SHAME AT ALL BUT YOUR SINS WILL FIND YOU OUT." Maurice had discovered the envelope on the mat while I was attending the funeral. He had been returning a couple of darned socks. The note must have been slipped underneath the door. When I popped back briefly after the service – to pick up a spare handkerchief to replace the one Mrs O'Neill had just borrowed – my valet was waiting for me. He had not presumed to open the envelope but he had taken note of the cover. The words "MR HENRY BUXTON" were typed on the front. 'The same capital letters,' he observed, as he handed it across.

'The same displacement too,' I said, scanning the message inside.

'It is from the same typewriter, Monsieur. There can be no doubt.'

'"YOUR SINS WILL FIND YOU OUT". That was what it said in Sir Richard's letter.'

'Perhaps the writer is a religious man,' Maurice suggested. 'Did you not say that the Reverend Hamilton-Baynes uses a typewriter to compose his sermons?'

'Yes, he does.' I looked up from the note. 'But I can't see him bottling up anything like this.' I was reluctant to pin the blame on the vicar. I was starting to quite like the fellow. 'He doesn't strike me as the type.'

'A religious man must place the concerns of his flock above those of himself. Who knows what turmoil resides beneath the surface?'

'Of Hamilton-Baynes?' I scoffed. 'You do talk rot sometimes, Morris. He's not the sort of man to have an inner life. Far too busy for that. But I suppose it could be someone close to him; someone else in the Reynolds Suite.'

'Mrs Hamilton-Baynes?' Maurice suggested.

'No. I don't think so. I don't think that woman has an unkind bone in her body.' She had shown great sympathy for the plight of her cousin's servant; more sympathy than I would have allowed. I returned the letter to its envelope. 'I suppose I ought to be flattered, that the bounder's attention has extended to me. I don't think much for his timing, though. Today of all days. Do you have that handkerchief?'

'Yes, Monsieur.' The valet reached down to a drawer and produced a fresh piece of cloth, which he folded up and placed in my breast pocket.

'How do I look?'

Maurice reached forward and flattened down a stray wisp of hair. The wind had been a little strong up on deck. 'You will do, Monsieur.'

I had no further time to think about the note. Sir Richard and Lady Jocelyn had organised a small reception over in the Reynolds Suite, in the aftermath of the funeral. It would be rude of me not to put in an appearance. I left Maurice behind to lock up the bedroom and hurried across the deck to the port side.

The gathering was already in full swing. The Reynolds Suite was the ideal location. There was plenty of room and a fair few people were scattered across the lounge, chatting happily away. Lady Jocelyn greeted me at the door. A couple of stewards had been drafted in to serve the drinks and the nibbles. There was no sign of the maid, who was presumably now *persona non grata*, but Lady Jocelyn led me through the crowd and made sure I was properly attended to. 'It's very kind of you, arranging all this,' I said.

'It was the least we could do. I hope the service was to your satisfaction.'

'First class,' I said, waving away the offer of an apricot cocktail. 'Harry would have been proud.' In fact, my old friend would not have cared one way or the other. A game of cards and a bottle of brandy, that would have been a far more appropriate send off for a man like Harry. But it was a kind thought, nonetheless. 'I must have a word with the reverend and thank him for the service.'

'He is always happy to help,' Lady Jocelyn said. 'He is an unusual man, Joshua, but he does rise to the occasion when required.'

Damning with faint praise, I thought. I wondered if

Lady Jocelyn had disapproved of the marriage between him and her cousin. It was difficult to tell with a woman like that. Her gaunt face and cold blue eyes gave nothing away. 'It was a good turn out too,' I added. 'Thoughtful of the captain to put in an appearance.'

'Yes, I thanked Steven personally,' she said. I resisted the temptation to comment on that. First name terms with the captain. No wonder the head steward had granted her one last chance with the cat.

Sir Richard Villiers had spotted me from the far side of the sofa. 'Help yourself to food, old boy,' he said, coming across. 'Plenty on offer. What did you think of the service?'

'Very good,' I said. 'A good turnout.' The conversations at these functions had a tendency to be a trifle repetitive. 'Didn't recognise everyone there though.'

'No, a few odd looking coves about,' Sir Richard agreed, with evident distaste.

'Those men who appeared at the back, by the hatchway. Did you see them?'

'Yes, I saw them. Rough looking sort.'

'You don't know who they were? I'd not seen them before.'

'No idea, I'm afraid,' Sir Richard huffed. 'Actually, I asked the steward about them. He said they were from third class. Didn't know anything more.' The knight took a sip of wine from his glass and glowered at the memory. '"Gatecrashing" that's what the Americans call it.' His eyes bulged behind those ridiculously large spectacles of his. 'Wouldn't be allowed in my day. People should stick to their own part of the ship.'

'I suppose they were just paying their respects.' But it worried me, that there were people onboard who knew Harry well enough to turn up to his funeral but who were strangers to me. Perhaps, though, they were just sightseers; the kind of people who popped up at other people's weddings, just to have a look, or to sit in the public galleries during court cases. 'It bumped the numbers up at least.'

'I'd have had them banned,' Sir Richard said. 'A funeral

should not be a public occasion. I tell you, Mr Buxton, when I pop my clogs, many years from now, there'll be no riff-raff at my funeral. Just family and close friends. Perhaps the odd business associate.'

'And a few servants?'

'The housekeeper maybe. And my butler, Dawkins, if he's still with us. But nobody else. They can stand in for the household staff.'

There was a knock at the far door and the captain of the Galitia made his entrance, taking off his peaked cap as he stepped through into the sitting room. Sir Richard and Lady Jocelyn excused themselves and went over to greet him. I slipped around the sofa and headed for the back of the room, filling up my plate from a table of food and peering out onto the verandah.

Mrs O'Neill was sitting at one of the boxy tables there, with Miss Wellesley to her side. 'Oh, Henry!' she exclaimed, her eyes lighting up at the sight of me before I had the chance to retreat from view. I was beginning to regret moving onto first name terms with the woman. 'What a dreadful day.' Mrs O'Neill was still clasping my handkerchief in her left hand. Her glossy black dress rippled in the sunlight from the port windows.

'Dreadful,' I agreed, bowing to the inevitable and coming forward to take my seat. 'Thank you for your help with the flowers, both of you. They were very nice.'

Mrs O'Neill beamed with pleasure. 'It was the least we could do.'

'And how have you been managing, Miss Wellesley?' I asked, as I settled myself down.

The girl had a sandwich in her hand and another on a plate in front of her. 'It still hasn't sunken in,' she admitted. 'I feel such a fraud.'

'A fraud?' I didn't follow.

Miss Wellesley dropped the half eaten sandwich onto the plate. 'Everyone's been so kind. But the fact is, I didn't really know Harry that well. I liked him, of course. Very much. But we were only just getting to know each other. I should be grieving but I...I just feel numb.'

I could sympathise with that. 'We all cope in our different ways. And life goes on. Not just for us,' I added grimly, reaching a hand into my jacket pocket. 'You'd think on a day like this our resident poison pen writer would give us a break.'

Mrs O'Neill's eyes widened. 'Henry, you don't mean... another letter?'

I pulled out the envelope. 'Slipped underneath the door, while I was burying an old friend. Can you credit it? Some people have no respect.' I had been in two minds whether to broach the matter with the two women, but Mrs O'Neill at least had a right to know, since so much of this affair had been centred around her.

'I'm so sorry,' she said. 'I had no idea things would spread like this.'

'It's hardly your fault,' I assured her, handing the envelope across.

'But why would they target you?' Miss Wellesley asked. 'I assumed it was a family matter.'

'Evidently, whoever it is has taken a dislike to me as well.'

Mrs O'Neill removed the letter from the envelope and scanned the text in horror. 'Oh, Henry! How awful for you. And on such a day as this.'

'You realise what they're implying? That I'm a money grabbing interloper, and that I'm only talking to you because I'm after your money.'

Miss Wellesley was appalled. 'That's preposterous,' she said.

'Somebody obviously thinks it.'

'Well, I certainly do not,' Mrs O'Neill reassured me, reaching across to place a hand on my knee. 'Goodness, Henry, you're one of the kindest, most thoughtful men I've ever met. That anyone could suggest such a thing. It's awful.'

I appreciated the sentiment, if not the hand. 'I suppose I should be flattered they think I'm worthy of attention. No one likes to be excluded.'

Miss Wellesley smiled at that. 'Will you inform Mr Griffith?' The security officer.

'I don't think so,' I said, taking the note back from Mrs O'Neill. 'It's pretty thin stuff. If anything, it confirms what Sir Richard said. Whoever writes these letters, they're just a coward. They're no threat to anyone. We should ignore them.'

'You're quite right, Henry,' Mrs O'Neill agreed. 'I wish I had your strength of character.'

I returned the letter to my pocket with apparent indifference; but on the inside, I confess, I was seething. Somebody was playing a nasty game. And the thought that it might be somebody here, in this very apartment, spitting venom at all and sundry from behind a cloak of anonymity, was particularly galling. I was not altogether convinced that anyone in the Reynolds Suite was responsible, but I could not be sure. They were a mixed bunch, after all.

There was, however, one simple way to determine the truth.

Chapter Nine

A trip to the lavatory, I always find, is the perfect pretext for a bit of snooping. I am not a naturally devious woman, but some years spent working for the security services has taught me a few useful tricks. When it comes to ferreting out other people's secrets, there is nothing quite as helpful as a formal social gathering. With so many people milling about in the main rooms, talking and drinking, it is simplicity itself to slip away and have a poke around. Strictly speaking, it was not my responsibility to investigate these damned letters, but the whole thing had put me in something of a sour mood. It was high time somebody got to the bottom of it. If I could locate Sir Richard's typewriter and rule that out as the source of the correspondence, then at least I could be assured that nobody here was behind it. I would have to be quick, though. In a big house, if someone is caught snooping, there is always the excuse of having got lost; but in the relatively cramped confines of the Reynolds Suite there would be no such cover.

The hallway was about fifteen feet long, with a water closet at either end and three bedroom doors along one side. The two end bedrooms projected out beyond the confines of the hall, with one at the living room end, the other towards the prow of the ship; and both these doors were shut as I moved into the hallway. Matilda would be locked up somewhere in one of these rooms, so I would have to be careful. The last thing I wanted was the cat getting loose. The middle door, thankfully, was slightly ajar, so I would try that one first. I glanced up and down the corridor, to make sure no-one else was about, and then pushed it open.

It was a twin room, with two beds on the right-hand side, a chair and a dressing table with a large ovoid mirror. There were several small paintings decorating the walls – reproductions of works by Sir Joshua Reynolds, naturally – and a window opposite with a view out onto the promenade. And there, on a small desk next to the closet, was Sir Richard's typewriter. I smiled with relief. For all my delusions of professionalism, I had not been sure I would be able to find it. These things are often packed away out of sight, when they are not being used. I poked my head out the door, before moving across, to make sure the corridor was still clear. I don't like to take these things for granted. I have never been much at ease with this kind of activity, though the worst that could happen on this occasion would be a strict telling off; and that I could bear well enough.

The typewriter was a mass market Olivetti, of the type found in countless studies and drawing rooms across the civilised world. My old valet, Hargreaves, had had one similar to this. There was no paper in the drum and nothing lying to the left or right of it on the table. That was unlucky. I could probably find a bit of plain paper, but I couldn't risk spooling and tapping out anything on the machine itself. There is no such thing as a quiet typewriter. I would just have to dig around the room and see if I could find some old correspondence. It was Sir Richard's Olivetti, so this had to be his bedroom; which, as I recalled, he shared with his secretary. In all likelihood, therefore, this was where they conducted a lot of their business.

Could either one of them have been behind the letters? I wondered. At first thought, it seemed unlikely. Both men had been victims of the scoundrel, whoever he was, as had everyone else hereabouts, with the possible exception of the maid. But perhaps the perpetrator might have sent a letter or two to themselves, as a cover. It would look suspicious if they were the only person in the group not to receive one. Could Sir Richard Villiers himself be behind them? The man was full of bluster, with an angry heart that might well suit this kind of attack, for all his public displays of contempt for the perpetrator. And the most recent crop of letters had only started when he and his companions had arrived in the Americas.

What about Mr Hopkins? If anyone in the household had reason to be resentful, it might be that young man. A disaffected employee, accused of fiddling the books. He had a bit of thing for the maid too, according to Mrs Hamilton-Baynes. Could that be the main reason for his resentment? The

127

original letters, though – those received by Mrs O'Neill's husband – had been sent several years ago, and I doubted Hopkins had been in Sir Richard's employ for that long. He was in his mid twenties, after all. Neither did he strike me as someone bottling up his emotions; tactful, yes, but not resentful, except perhaps where Matilda was concerned. Besides, in my experience, venom spitting was an occupation of the elderly, not of virile young men.

In any case, there were plenty of other residents of the Reynolds Suite who might have had access to this particular typewriter. Lady Jocelyn, for example. Who knew what horrors she was bottling up? The Reverend and Mrs Hamilton-Baynes I had already considered; and much as I might like to dismiss the possibility, I knew for a fact that the vicar had borrowed this machine on at least one occasion.

I moved across to the dressing table and pulled open the top drawer. I was expecting a pile of clothes, but to my surprise found it full of neatly stacked documents. Business papers and such like; just what I was looking for. I glanced back nervously at the door and then picked up the first folder. Inside were a series of letters on headed notepaper. Carbon copies of various correspondence, written and neatly signed by Sir Richard Villiers. The secretary would presumably have typed them out, to be signed by the man himself. I flicked through a couple of these letters, in search of the elusive "W". This was a little more difficult to find than I had first supposed. Most of the text was in lower case. But at last I found an example, in a column of figures. The misalignment Maurice had identified was subtle and not easy to make out without a close examination. So far as I could tell, however, there was nothing wrong with this particular "W". It occurred to me, however, that if the upper case was misaligned, then the lower case "w"s must also be out of place, since they were both typed using the same key. I skipped back though the correspondence. There was a fair smattering of smaller "w"s, but not a single one seemed to be out of alignment.

I looked back at the Olivetti, across the room. If these letters were typed on that machine – which they must have been – then it could not possibly be the source of all this poison. I closed my eyes for a moment. That left the secretary off the hook, then; and Sir Richard, and the Reverend Hamilton-Baynes. And, indeed, everyone else in the Reynolds Suite. Our scoundrel was an outsider, somebody looking on enviously from the wings. Unless of course there was another typewriter lying around here somewhere. Or perhaps there was one in Mrs O'Neill's stateroom. The American woman might well have one of her own. I did not seriously believe she or her companion could be behind any of this, but other people might have had access to her room and it wouldn't hurt to stick a head around the door and see. But that was a task for another day. I did not wish to push my luck. I closed up the folder and returned it to the drawer.

I was just shutting up the dressing table when I head a noise outside, in the corridor. I stepped back from the bed and was alarmed to see that the door out into the hall had swung slowly open, of its own volition. The Reverend Hamilton-Baynes, still in his dog collar but now divested of his formal gown, was progressing along the hallway outside.

'Hello!' he exclaimed, catching sight of me through the open door. 'Are you lost?'

'I…was looking for the bathroom,' I mumbled feebly. 'Sorry. The door was open. I haven't seen any of the larger staterooms. I was just being nosey.' It seemed best to make at least a partial admission of guilt.

'I don't blame you!' The vicar shot me a toothy smile. He pushed back the door, unperturbed at my distinctly dubious behaviour. 'Absolutely spiffing, aren't they? Much larger than we're used to. And so colourful too.'

'Is this your room?' I asked, recovering myself somewhat and hoping to deflect his attention in any way I could.

'No, no. This is Sir Richard's. My wife and I are at the end of the corridor. I say, would you like to have a look?'

'Er…well.' I blinked. 'If it's not too much trouble.'

'Of course not, my dear fellow.' He gestured for me to follow him. There was no let up in the animation of the man.

129

I moved out into the hallway. 'I wanted to thank you, by the way, for the service. It was very well done.'

The vicar's eyes lit up. 'That's exceedingly kind of you. I enjoyed it very much. Always a sad occasion, I know, but it helps to bring a sense of closure, I feel.'

'Very much so,' I agreed.

Hamilton-Baynes opened up the door to his own room, just to the left of the far lavatory. 'Well, this is us!' he said. 'Absolutely splendid, don't you think?'

I peered inside. The layout was similar to Sir Richard's stateroom, except there was a double bed here rather than two singles. There was more clutter too. An opened suitcase, a pair of boxing gloves on the table, a couple of shuffleboard sticks. On the dressing table stood the polished wooden box containing that flintlock pistol. A small silver crucifix rested to the left of it. There was no sign, however, of a typewriter. Not that I had been expecting one in here.

'It was exceedingly kind of Richard to pay for all this,' the reverend gushed. 'Maggie and I could never have afforded it. He can be a very generous man, when it comes to family.'

'I'm sure he can,' I said. I picked up one of the shuffleboard sticks. There was a hefty disk on the floor as well. 'Did you bring these yourself?'

'No, no. I borrowed them from the gymnasium. Frightfully helpful chap down there.'

'What, the one with the moustache?'

'That's the fellow.' The vicar beamed. 'I've promised to give Miss Wellesley a game tomorrow afternoon. Show her what's what. She's never played before, can you believe it?'

'I'm sure she'll appreciate the lesson,' I said. 'Well, I suppose I ought to get back to the throng.' Hamilton-Baynes nodded agreeably. 'Thank you once again for the sermon.' And for helping to answer all my questions, I added silently. I had now seen two out of the three bedrooms. I doubted very much that Lady Jocelyn had her own typewriter; so it appeared that the Reynolds Suite was in the clear.

'I don't suppose you stock Piccadillys?' I asked the short fellow behind the counter. It was the following morning, the fifth day of the voyage. 'Oh, yes, there they are.' My eyes had lighted on the familiar packaging before the storekeeper could reply. There was a wall of cigarette cartons behind him, some American and some British. I had just finished the last of my American cigarettes and was looking for something a bit more homely.

We were now a day and a half out from Southampton. It had been a difficult voyage, but perhaps the worst of it was now behind us. Even Maurice had looked a little less pale this morning, as he had helped me into my suit. I had taken another look at the note before breakfast, but my irritation at receiving it had cooled over the course of the night and I wondered whether it was worth continuing the investigation. It looked like nobody I knew was behind it, and exposing some random stranger was not really my responsibility, even if they had made tangible threats. Besides, he might get angry, whoever he was, and I had no desire to get involved in a fight. Nor did I wish to spend any time lurking about in the writing room, on the off chance that I might spot a misplaced "W". Better, perhaps, to let the matter go. Everyone would be heading off in their own separate directions soon enough, with no real harm done, so what was the point of poking my nose in? Was I really that upset by some tawdry letter?

'A pack of twenty, sir?' The steward turned back to look at the cartons.

'Better make it two.' The little shop was adjacent to the main stairs on D Deck, and people would often pop in here on the way to and from the restaurant. It was a useful little place, full of all sorts of knick-knacks.

'Very good, sir.' The steward reached up and produced the two packs. That would see me through the next week or so, barring any further disasters.

'Oh and a copy of the Bulletin too. See what's happening in the world today.'

The man whipped out the newspaper and folded it for me. 'Shillings or dollars, sir?'

'Er...shillings, please.' I had withdrawn some English currency from the kiosk on the opposite side of the foyer. The London and Midland Bank had its own small branch aboard ship.

'Then that's two shillings and sixpence, sir.'

I handed the loot across, grabbed the newspaper and pocketed the two packets of cigarettes. As I was turning to leave the shop, I spotted Miss Wellesley perusing the magazine rack. 'Good morning,' I called out, for once not too annoyed at having to greet a fellow passenger. I really had got out of bed on the right side this morning.

Miss Wellesley looked up, her dark brown eyes flashing happily at the sight of me. 'Good morning, Mr Buxton. You're looking cheerful this morning.'

She was not wrong. For the first time since leaving New York, I was feeling surprisingly chipper. 'Just one more night and we'll be back in the old country.'

'Yes, won't it be lovely? I'm looking forward to seeing England again. Albeit briefly.'

'You'll be heading off across Europe with Mrs O'Neill?'

'Yes, for three months. And then back to England again to resume my studies at Easter.'

'No rest for the wicked.'

'Whereabouts do you live?' she asked. 'In England?'

I rubbed my chin. 'Difficult to say just now.' I had been away for some time. 'I'm thinking of renting a property in Brighton. Or Bournemouth. Somewhere like that.' I would have to avoid my old haunts in London and the Home Counties. I hadn't given much thought yet to the practicalities of it all, but England was a much simpler proposition than the Americas. A nice seaside town somewhere, that would do me. I had spent a fair chunk of the past two years living near the sea and – the odd hurricane aside – I had come to enjoy the coastal ambience. 'How is Susan this morning?' I enquired. 'Mrs O'Neill?'

'I haven't seen her yet. We're due to meet up at eleven, in the garden cafe. What time is it now?'

I fumbled for my pocket watch. 'A little after half past

132

ten.'

She dipped her head. 'Just time to buy a few things and get back to the Reynolds Suite.'

'Oh, yes, of course. You've moved in there now.' Mrs Hamilton-Baynes had passed on my suggestion and the younger woman was now sharing a room with Lady Jocelyn Wingfield. 'How was it, sleeping with the dragon?'

To her credit, Miss Wellesley did try not to laugh. 'You mustn't call her that. She is rather severe, though.'

'I'll say.'

'But very polite. She doesn't talk much. I don't think she's used to sharing with strange women.'

'That's her own fault. Should have waited a few days before giving that girl her notice.'

Miss Wellesley's face fell. 'Jenny, yes. The poor lamb.'

'She's in with Susan now?'

'Yes. I feel so sorry for her. No references. It does seem a little harsh.'

'She's young. I'm sure she'll muddle through. What about you? What will you do, when you've completed your studies?'

Miss Wellesley smiled. She was in a good mood too, it seemed. 'I don't know. I might return to America. If I can find some work there.'

'Perhaps Susan will put in a word for you. Find you a nice office job or something. Do you type?' I couldn't help but ask the question.

The girl grinned sheepishly. 'Not properly,' she admitted. 'With two fingers, if I have to.'

'I'm not far off that myself.'

'I think it's better to write by hand, if you can' she said. 'Which reminds me, I need to buy some notepaper.' She looked down at the bottom of the magazine rack. There were several small packets of writing paper here, some plain and some with "RMS GALITIA" stamped at the head. Miss Wellesley bent down to pick up a set.

'Well, I'll leave you to get on. Any plans for this afternoon?'

133

'Yes. The Reverend Hamilton-Baynes is giving me a lesson in shuffleboard after lunch. He's lent me some equipment. Oh, I must pick that up. I left it in the other cabin.'

'Shuffleboard, eh? That should be amusing.'

'I hope so! I've told him I'm not very good at sport, but he wasn't having it. He's quite charming in his way, isn't he?'

'Yes, I suppose he is.'

'Not like a vicar at all. And then Mrs O'Neill has invited me to play whist later on, with a couple of other passengers she met last night.'

'Whist?' I raised an eyebrow. I have always been a sucker for a card game. 'I might be tempted to join her, if she has no objection.'

'There won't be any gambling,' Miss Wellesley said; then flushed at her own presumption. 'Harry...Mr Latimer...he said you were partial to the odd wager.'

'He wasn't wrong there.'

'But I don't think this will be your cup of tea, Mr Buxton. Elderly women. It's just an excuse for gossiping, I expect. Not that there's anything wrong with that.'

'No. But you're right. I think I may give it a miss.' Far better to find my own game, if I could.

Miss Wellesley moved over to the counter to pay for her notepaper and magazine.

'I shall see you at lunch,' I said. And with that I made my way out of the shop.

I would have taken the elevator all the way up to A Deck, if I hadn't spotted that retired colonel waiting outside the lift. My mood was not that much improved this morning that I wished to engage in conversation with a complete stranger. He would probably be heading for the smoking room, which was my intended destination, and I did not want to have to converse with the fellow the entire length of the ship. I headed for the stairs instead. It was six flights up to A Deck and a long walk to the Carolean at the rear. The stairs were not steep, but by the time I got to B Deck I was already starting to puff. I had eaten rather a lot at breakfast. The lift door opposite pinged open and the colonel barrelled out into the hallway, giving me a nod and heading off to his suite on the starboard side. I watched him go. I was about to head in the same direction – having decided to abandon the long walk and break out the Piccadillys in the comfort of my own room – when a sudden piercing scream ricocheted across the deck. I almost dropped my newspaper.

The sound had come from the far side of the elevators. With some trepidation, I rushed across the floor and rounded the corner into the port side corridor. A woman was standing outside the nearest of the cabins, her hand to her mouth. The door of the stateroom was open and she was staring in horror inside. At first, I took her to be one of the stewardesses, but she was not dressed in the traditional grey uniform. In fact, she was not in uniform at all, and it was this fact which prevented me from recognising her at once. She saw the movement as I appeared in the corridor and her mouth fell open again. 'Oh, sir! Come quickly. It's awful.'

'What is it?' I enquired. It was only as I moved in that I realised the young woman was Lady Jocelyn's maid. 'Jenny, what's wrong?'

'There, sir!' She pointed a trembling finger through the doorway. 'It's Mrs O'Neill, sir.'

Oh, lord, I thought, as I took in the view. Susan O'Neill was lying across the length of the stateroom. Her eyes were wide open and the carpet around her head was stained with blood. She was quite dead.

Chapter Ten

'What's going on? Is everything all right?' A couple of heads were poking out of doorways along the port side corridor. I was not the only one to have heard the maid's scream.

'I...yes. No...I...everything's fine,' I called out, trying to get a grip on myself. 'Just a...small accident.' The heads disappeared, but a steward was speeding around the near corner. I tore my gaze away from the bedroom. 'There's been an accident,' I told him, waving my newspaper at the fellow before he could catch his breath. 'You need to fetch a doctor. As quickly as you can.' The steward gazed past me into the bedroom. His eyes widened at the sight of the body, but then he swallowed hard, nodded, and raced off back in the direction he had come.

Jenny Simpkins was continuing to stare, her hand clamped to her mouth. 'She must have banged her head,' the girl breathed, trying to make sense of the bloody scene. 'Slipped and fallen.'

It was a reasonable conjecture. I folded up the newspaper and stowed it in my jacket pocket. The body was spread out across the carpet, the head lying beneath a washbasin on the right hand side. The stateroom was similar in size to my own, with its own private bathroom, but there was a separate sink as well, to the right of one of the beds. I shuddered, catching sight of a smear of blood on the side of the bowl. Jenny was right. Mrs O'Neill must have tripped and struck her head, and then crashed to the floor. And there the poor woman was, her eyes staring upwards, a dribble of blood congealing at the edge of her mouth, the carpet stained red beneath her.

The last time I had seen Mrs O'Neill, she had been positively bursting with life, gathering herself up in the aftermath of tragedy. She had gone to the Palladian last night after supper and, by all accounts, had been up on the dance floor into the early hours, waltzing away. And now this. My God, was there no end to it? I slumped against the frame of the door. Everywhere I went, it seemed, people were dropping dead, on the Galitia and elsewhere. I closed my eyes and took a moment to gather my wits. All those letters, the bomb hoax and now another fatality. One dead body onboard ship might be considered an accident, but two in a row….that was simply not plausible. I had been through this sort of affair too many times now to believe in coincidences. Mrs O'Neill could not simply have tripped and banged her head. Somebody had done this to her. And if she had been deliberately murdered, then what about Harry? Had Doctor Armstrong got it wrong? Had he been killed too? Please God no, I thought. All those suspicions I had had, in the aftermath of his death, now came flooding back to me.

First things first, I thought, trying to calm myself. Was there anything out of place inside the cabin? It was a fairly ordered space, by the looks of it. A set of garish clothes were hanging on the closet door. A pair of shoes by the bed. A couple of shuffleboard sticks. But nothing obviously amiss that I could see. It was Harry's stateroom all over again. I focused my attention on Mrs O'Neill. How long had she been lying there? An hour, perhaps? A little less? The blood had congealed somewhat on the carpet. Doctor Armstrong would determine the exact time of death, but it would be some minutes before he arrived.

The maid was caught up in her own distress. 'I've never…I've never seen nothing like this before,' she mumbled, bringing a hand up to her nose and wiping it with the back of her hand. The girl was small and blonde, dressed in a cheap but serviceable yellow dress. 'Bloody hell. What a horrible thing. Oh! 'Scuse my language, sir.'

'That's quite all right.' I pulled back from the door and took a short, hard look at the girl. Was there anything useful she could tell me?' 'You were…sharing a room with her?' I asked.

Jenny wiped her hand distractedly on the side of her dress. 'Yes, sir. I had to swap rooms with Miss Wellesley, didn't I? Her ladyship said…'

I waggled my fingers dismissively. 'Yes, I know all about that. But what time did you last see Mrs O'Neill? Alive, I mean.'

She frowned, struggling to recall. 'I dunno, sir. About eight thirty, I think. I went off to breakfast.'

Eight thirty. That sounded a little late for the servants' sitting. 'And you've only just now come back to the cabin?'

'Yes, sir.' She sniffled.

'And Mrs O'Neill...she was in good health when you left?'

'Yes, sir. Bright as a button.'

'Did she go down to breakfast?'

'I believe so, sir.' It would have been a different sitting from the maid. 'The poor bleeder. You think she was dead when she hit the floor?'

'Dead or unconscious,' I thought. It would have been quick, even if she had been attacked. Jenny was peering up at me, hoping for confirmation of her own theory. 'You're right,' I agreed. 'She must have come out of the bathroom and slipped on the mat.' I did not really believe that, but it seemed the kindest thing to say. I did not want the girl having a fit, out here in the corridor. It would only attract further attention. Besides, it was a plausible enough interpretation of the scene. The bathroom door was open and the mat in front of it did look a little ruffled. If Mrs O'Neill had been struck by someone, she must have hit the washbasin on the way down. My eye slipped sideways and caught abruptly on the dressing table. In pride of place, in front of a large oval mirror, stood a black Olivetti typewriter. I drew in a breath. I couldn't think how I hadn't noticed it before.

If I had been thinking clearly, I might have hesitated before stepping into the room. There would be hell to pay if I contaminated what might well prove to be a crime scene; and it was not as if there was any doubt that Mrs O'Neill was dead. But all thoughts of decorum deserted me at the sight of that glistening black machine. I had to get a closer look, while the opportunity was there. Gingerly, I stepped across the stockinged legs of Mrs O'Neill. A sheet of paper was spooled into position on the typewriter and something had been bashed out onto it. I leaned forward and examined the text. It was complete gibberish, a short sequence of repeated letters, all in upper case: "QWEQWEQWEQWEQWE" it said; and the letter "W" in every case was slightly misaligned.

'What on earth do you think you're doing!' an angry voice called out to me from behind. I swirled around. Mr Griffith, the security officer, was standing in the frame of the door.

The nearest available muster point was on the opposite side of the foyer, in the spacious confines of the Reynolds Suite. A steward bundled us off into the living room, while a seriously perturbed Mr Griffith remained behind to examine the scene of the crime; if indeed it was the scene of a crime. It was rather bad luck that the junior man had bumped into him first, on his way to find the doctor, but I supposed right now Griffith was the more useful of the two men. Susan O'Neill was far beyond the help of even a highly trained medic.

The Reynolds Suite was deserted as we settled ourselves in the sitting room. There was no sign of Sir Richard or Lady Jocelyn.

'Bleeding hell,' Jenny muttered, as we threaded our way around the sofa. 'I couldn't half do with a drink. Begging your pardon, sir.' She had spotted the bottles lined up on the sideboard beneath a rather stern portrait of Admiral Hood.

'You and me both,' I agreed. I pulled out my newspaper and threw it down on the coffee table. A stiff drink was definitely in order.

My mind was in something of a whirl. That typewriter. Beyond any doubt, it was the source of all these letters. But did that mean Mrs O'Neill was responsible? I ignored the stern gaze of the painted admiral and reached for one of the crystal decanters. 'I don't think, in the circumstances, Sir Richard will object,' I said, pulling out the stopper. I poured myself a hefty glass of brandy and followed it up with a half measure for the girl.

'Thank you, sir,' she said, her eyes flashing with gratitude as she took hold of the crystal tumbler. She knocked it back in one and smiled shakily. 'Gaw, I needed that.' She closed her eyes, trying to rid herself of the image of Mrs O'Neill. 'I ain't never seen a dead body before.'

'"I *haven't* ever seen",' I corrected her absently, taking a sip of my own brandy. The girl's accent was atrocious; the worst kind of East End gabble. I could see why she irritated Lady Jocelyn so much. But despite that, she did seem to have some wits about her.

'Her ladyship is always having a go at me for not speaking proper. Properly,' she corrected herself. 'Stupid cow.' She scratched the side of her face with her free hand, and then grimaced, remembering the other room. 'Gawd. Poor Mrs O'Neill.'

'It would have happened very quickly,' I assured her. 'I doubt she would have felt anything. May I get you another?'

'Not half!' She grinned, proffering the glass.

Before I could take hold of the tumbler, the far door opened and Lady Jocelyn swept imperiously into the suite. The woman's eyes widened in horror at the sight of her maid with a brandy glass in her hand. 'Jenny, what on earth do you think you're doing?' she exclaimed.

I raised a hand to forestall any confusion. 'Ah. That's my fault, Lady Jocelyn.'

'What on earth is going on?' the grand dame demanded.

'Jenny has had a bit of a shock. We both have. We… er…we needed to steady our nerves.'

'A shock?' A flicker of irritation passed across that aristocratic face. 'Who are all those people outside Susan's room? What is going on?'

'Ah.' So she had seen the kerfuffle on the far side of the foyer. Several members of staff were now buzzing about, assisting Mr Griffith. 'I'm afraid I have some bad news, your ladyship. You might like to sit down.'

Sir Richard Villiers barrelled into the room behind his sister. 'Devil if I can see what they're up to,' he said.

'Hush, Richard!' Lady Jocelyn snapped. 'Bad news, Mr Buxton? What bad news?'

I put down the tumbler on the sideboard. 'The worst, I'm afraid. It's Susan. Mrs O'Neill. There's no easy way to tell you this – your ladyship, Sir Richard – but I'm afraid she's dead.'

That, for the moment, was enough to silence the pair of them.

'I'll need to speak to all of you, in due course,' a grim-faced Mr Griffith asserted, addressing the small group now gathered in the Reynolds Suite. The Reverend Hamilton-Baynes had returned with his wife to change for lunch and they had been joined by Mr Hopkins and Miss Wellesley, the latter returning from her shopping trip down on D Deck. The mood in the room was one of understandable shock.

'Dead?' Miss Wellesley mumbled, swaying momentarily when she heard the news. 'Oh, my goodness.' The vicar had to step forward and escort her to the sofa.

Mr Griffith was in no mood to answer any questions. He was a short, stocky fellow with greying hair and a slightly ill-fitting uniform. His manner was grave but cautious, the ruddy complexion and mutton chop sideburns failing to distract from his intelligent blue eyes. He raised his hands to dampen down the speculation. 'As far as we know, Mrs O'Neill's death was an unfortunate accident. Doctor Armstrong is examining the body as we speak.'

Miss Wellesley shuddered at the use of the word "body". Her hands were gripping a glass of brandy somebody had poured for her. Mrs Hamilton-Baynes, who was now sitting by her side, put a comforting hand on the girl's knee.

'I would appreciate it if you would all remain here for a few minutes. I want to have a quick word with Mr Buxton.'

'Of course,' Lady Jocelyn agreed, before I could register any alarm.

'Thank you, your ladyship. Mr Buxton?' He gestured to an internal door.

'I...yes, of course.' I followed him into the hallway, in something of a daze. What did he want to speak to me for? Was I about to be given a dressing down? I suppose it was understandable that he would want to find out what the devil I had been up to in Mrs O'Neill's bedroom, now that the place had been properly secured. The security officer had not been at all happy to find me, *in situ,* contaminating his crime scene.

Griffith closed the sitting room door and we moved quietly to the far end of the corridor. I would have liked a moment to gather my thoughts, but it was not to be. 'In here, sir.' He indicated the far bedroom. 'I'm sure Sir Richard won't object.' He pushed back the door and we shuffled into the vicar's quarters. It was the usual clutter that I remembered. Griffith lifted a cushion off a chair and pulled it up. He gestured for me to do the same.

'Look here,' I said, anxious not to set off on the wrong foot. 'I am sorry about entering the room like that. I really didn't think. It was…it was such a shock.'

'That's all right, sir,' Griffith said calmly, pulling out his notebook and pencil. He gazed across at me with those penetrating blue eyes. 'These thing happen. However, there are one or two facts I need to establish, before I discuss anything with Sir Richard's party.'

'Facts?' I wasn't sure I liked the sound of that.

'That's right, sir.' Griffith did not feel the need to elaborate. His pencil was hovering over a blank page in his notebook. 'I understand it was the maid, Miss Simpkins, who was the first on the scene?' He had spoken to the girl briefly before sending us across to the Reynolds Suite.

'Yes, that's right. I was just coming up the main stairs when I heard her scream.'

'You weren't the only one to hear that,' Griffith said. At least it gave me an alibi of sorts. 'So you arrived at the door and the maid was inside the room?'

'No. No, she was standing at the door. She wasn't inside.'

'And what did you do then?'

'Well…erm…it was obvious that Mrs O'Neill…that there had been a dreadful accident of some kind. So I collared a passing steward and sent him off to summon a doctor. And he found you, I gather.'

'That's right, sir. And when he was gone, you took it

upon yourself to enter the stateroom?' There was no anger in the voice this time, just a calm querying of the facts. Griffith really was a seasoned policeman. He wasn't looking at me now; he was busily scribbling away.

'Er...yes. I...I did. I suppose I wanted to see if there was anything to be done.'

He looked up. 'And what was your interest in Mrs O'Neill's typewriter?'

I flinched, taken aback by the directness of the question. 'Typewriter?'

'When I found you, sir, you were standing over Mrs O'Neill's typewriter. The Olivetti, on top of the dressing table. You were examining the drum.'

'Er...yes, I was.'

'Why was that, sir?'

I gave out a sigh. There was no point concealing the truth. 'Look, Mr Griffith, you may or may not be aware of this, but there's been a...well, a spate of malicious letter writing onboard ship.'

Griffith put down his pencil. 'Go on.'

'Someone's been sending letters to various people. Nasty, distasteful letters.'

The security officer was watching me carefully. 'Poison pen letters, sir?'

'Yes, that sort of thing. You know about that?'

'Not until a few minutes ago, sir.' There was a brief flash of annoyance. 'The steward tells me there have been a few rumours flying around the last couple of days.'

'Yes, that's right.'

'But no-one has made an official complaint.'

'No, no. They wouldn't have done. But how did...?'

Griffith put down his notepad and reached into his breast pocket. 'We found this, sir, in Mrs O'Neill's stateroom.' He pulled out a piece of paper and handed it across to me.

'Good lord,' I said, unfolding the note. It was the usual typewritten monstrosity. "YOU ARE NOTHING BUT A CHARLATAN," it read. "YOUR HONEY WORDS ARE FOOLING NOBODY. YOU DO NOT CARE FOR THE

143

REPUTATION OF THE WOMEN YOU SO CASUALLY ROMANCE. YOU ARE ONLY INTERESTED IN THE SIZE OF THEIR BANK ACCOUNTS. BUT YOUR SINS WILL FIND YOU OUT AND SOONER THAN YOU THINK." I looked up. 'Good lord,' I said again. 'Where did you find this?'

'It was in Mrs O'Neill's handbag, sir. By the side of her bed.'

'Mrs...?' I stared at him in astonishment.

'And who do do you think it might be addressed to, sir?'

'It sounds like Harry,' I said, looking down at the letter in some confusion. My eye caught on the reverend's silver crucifix, which was propped up on a nearby dressing table. No, it couldn't be true. Harry had nothing to do with any of these pen letters. 'He never received this,' I said.

'No, he didn't,' Griffith agreed. 'It seems to me, sir, that Mrs O'Neill must have typed this herself at the beginning of the voyage, intending to deliver it to Mr Latimer's stateroom. But then she found him dead shortly after breakfast on the second day and she had no choice but to raise the alarm.'

That did make a kind of sense. The woman must have stuffed the letter back into her handbag before leaving the room. 'That...that might be possible. So she was...so Mrs O'Neill was behind it all? All these letters?'

'It seems likely, sir.' Griffith retrieved the note from me. '"YOUR SINS WILL FIND YOU OUT". A colourful turn of phrase. I showed this to the steward who came to fetch me. He told me there have been a few rumours doing the rounds. Canteen gossip. All quite vague, by the sounds of it. Unfortunately, nobody thought to bring it to my attention until now.'

'But if Mrs O'Neill was behind all this, do you think... do you think her death might not have been an accident?'

Griffith inclined his head. 'I am leaning towards that conclusion, sir. Best not to say anything to the others just yet. But you saw the scene, Mr Buxton. There was something not quite right about it. It was all far too neat, too carefully staged. If Mrs O'Neill was responsible for these letters and somebody realised she was the one doing it...'

'They might have reason to do her away?'

'It's a possibility, sir. This note.' He waved it at me. 'It's similar to the other ones that have been received?'

'Exactly the same,' I said. 'The same typewriter too. That was why I was looking at the Olivetti in Mrs O'Neill's room. The text has a slight misalignment. You see? The letter "W" is out of place.'

'Yes, sir, I had noticed that.' Griffith observed me with some surprise. 'You have a keen eye, Mr Buxton. More than I would have expected. The difference is quite subtle.'

'It...was my valet who noticed it,' I admitted. 'I was just following it up. And the typewriter in Mrs O'Neill's room...'

'Was used to type this letter. Yes, sir, I had already deduced that. What I haven't determined is why no-one told me about these letters in the first place. Not the stewards,' he clarified, 'but the passengers I spoke to the other day.' His eyes met mine and I could not ignore the accusation in them. 'You, for example, did not say a word to me about any of this, sir, when I interviewed you concerning Mr Latimer's death.'

'No. No, I didn't,' I admitted, with some embarrassment. This was going to be dashed awkward to explain. 'I...I didn't think it was relevant. Harry had nothing to do with any of these letters, so far as I was aware. They pre-date his acquaintance with anyone onboard ship. It was the other people here. Sir Richard's party. They've been receiving letters like this for months. I didn't think Harry had anything to do with it and they didn't want to make a fuss. But you're right. In hindsight, I...I should have told you.'

'And you, Mr Buxton? Have you received anything of this sort?'

I nodded glumly. 'Yes. But only recently. Yesterday afternoon, in fact. After...after the funeral.'

'Do you have it with you?'

'Er...yes, somewhere.'

'May I see it, sir?'

I fumbled inside my jacket. 'A very similar sort of

thing,' I said, as I handed the note across.

Griffith opened the envelope. '"YOUR SINS WILL FIND YOU OUT",' he read.

'The "LEECH" thing seems to be a common theme too. But really, you'll have to ask the family about that. They know far more about it than I do.'

The next half an hour was uncomfortable for all concerned, as we sat in the drawing room and Mr Griffith taxed the group regarding the history of the poison pen letters. 'I burnt every bally one of them, apart from the first,' Sir Richard asserted, having handed the specimen across. The security officer examined it closely. Everyone in the room had received similar letters, though the mode of attack was different in each case. Ernest Hopkins, as I had previously heard, had had his honesty impugned. The Reverend Hamilton-Baynes had been accused of impious behaviour. 'They thought I was bringing the cloth into disrepute,' he said, 'by dancing and singing, and playing sports. It was terribly vexing.' The letters Mrs Hamilton-Baynes had received had scorned her for her feebleness and her inability to restrain her husband. More significantly, however, they had suggested she was reliant on the financial support of her cousin, Lady Jocelyn. The word "LEECH" cropped up again in this context.

Griffith did his best to mask his irritation as the litany of abuse was spelled out. The fact that not a word of this had been mentioned to him during his enquiries into Harry Latimer's death understandably rankled. 'It really would have been helpful if you had told me all this before,' he said. He turned to Sir Richard's sister. The matriarch of the Reynolds Suite had been peculiarly subdued during these submissions, her face a blank mask of hostility as the focus eventually settled on her. 'Lady Jocelyn?' The man's tone was respectful but firm. 'What were the contents of the letters sent to you?'

'Is this really necessary, Mr Griffith?'

'I'm afraid so, your ladyship.'

Sir Richard cut in, anxious to save his sister from any

embarrassment. 'Look, Mr Griffith, I appreciate you have your job to do and all that. But these are delicate matters.'

'I'm sorry, Sir Richard. I'm afraid I will have to insist.' Griffith spoke with calm authority. He had to tread delicately where Lady Jocelyn was concerned – she was a friend of the captain, after all – but the question needed answering. 'If it will make it easier, your ladyship,' he suggested, 'we could discuss the matter in private.'

Lady Jocelyn's lips pursed into a thin slit. 'That would be acceptable,' she agreed.

Griffith had not quite finished with the rest of us, however. We would all need to make statements and confirm our whereabouts this morning. The security officer raised an eyebrow on hearing that Miss Wellesley had swapped rooms the previous evening. Of all the people in the Reynolds Suite, apart from the maid, she was the only one not to have received any malicious correspondence. Griffith could see how upset the woman was – Mrs Hamilton-Baynes was now comforting her on the sofa – so he did not press the point. It was not just the fact that Mrs O'Neill had died that was causing the girl distress, however. It was the clear suggestion that the American woman had been behind the pen letters all along.

'Do you really think she could be responsible?' Miss Wellesley asked, in disbelief.

Griffith nodded gravely. 'It seems very likely, miss.'

'But what about the letters she received herself? And the bomb scare at the restaurant...'

Griffith had lifted both his eyebrows when we had told him about that; but before he could reply to Miss Wellesley, there was a knock at the door.

The head steward poked his head around. 'It's Doctor Armstrong, sir. He's finished up and would like to have a word.'

Griffith acknowledged the request and glanced at his wristwatch. 'We will have to continue this later. We will need statements from all of you in due course, but that will do for now. Ladies and gentlemen, thank you for your cooperation. Lady Jocelyn, Sir Richard. You're free to head off now and have some lunch.'

'Of course,' Sir Richard breathed.

'Thank you, Mr Griffith,' Lady Jocelyn said. 'This is a dreadful business.'

'Indeed, your ladyship. If I could ask you all to keep this matter under your hat for the time being. We don't want to alarm the other passengers.'

'It's a bit late for that, old boy,' Sir Richard suggested. Half the ship would have heard the maid screaming.

'Not the fact of Mrs O'Neill's death, sir,' Griffith clarified. 'That will already be common knowledge. But this business of the poison pen letters. Better to keep that quiet for now.'

'Righty-ho,' Sir Richard agreed. He did not need telling twice.

And so for now, as far as anybody onboard was concerned, Mrs O'Neill's death was just a terrible accident.

Chapter Eleven

Miss Wellesley stared down at the plate of sandwiches, her face pale and disbelieving. 'I can't believe she's dead. I just…I can't take it in.' There were no tears, just a dumb incomprehension.

I leaned forward sympathetically. 'Did she have any relatives? People who will need to be told?'

'A sister, I think.' Miss Wellesley frowned, trying to recall. 'And a cousin in Oregon. I suppose I should write to them. Tell them….' She looked up from the plate. 'I don't know what to tell them.'

'Not the easiest thing in the world,' I agreed, 'passing on bad news.' I settled back in my chair. The garden lounge was blissfully quiet at the moment. Miss Wellesley had not felt up to the hubbub of the Louis XVI, so I had suggested coming here for lunch, while the rest of the passengers were down on D Deck. A plate of sandwiches and a pot of tea among the flowers was a more palatable proposition than the noisy restaurant; even if the flowers were looking a little depleted.

'Do you think it can really be true about…about the letters?'

'I don't know,' I said, pouring out the milk for a second cup and grabbing the strainer. I would have liked something stronger than tea, but I needed to keep a clear head for later in the afternoon. 'Mr Griffith found that note to Harry in her handbag. And it was definitely typed on her typewriter.' I put down the teapot and added a couple of spoonfuls of sugar.

'It makes no sense,' Miss Wellesley said, with some force. 'Susan wasn't vindictive. She was the sweetest, kindest woman. You should have seen her last night, in the ballroom.' She smiled at the memory. 'She was like a little girl – or a debutante even – dancing with anyone and everyone. Chatting away. And now…and now she's dead. It's such a ridiculous thing to happen. Slipping on the mat like that. And so soon after…so soon after Harry.'

'Yes,' I agreed, removing the spoon from my cup and taking a thoughtful sip. 'It's a devil of a coincidence.'

'And she really liked Harry. That's what I don't understand. Why would she write him such a horrible letter?'

'She knew he wasn't entirely sincere.' I returned the cup to its saucer. 'She wasn't quite the fool we took her for.'

'But there was no side to her, Mr Buxton. No malice. She enjoyed his attention. I'm sure of it. From him and...and from you.'

'Yes. It's a dreadful muddle,' I said.

Miss Wellesley picked up a cheese and pickle sandwich, nibbled on it for a moment and then put it down. 'You don't think...you don't think there might have been anything untoward about her death?' The question was a tentative one. 'I mean, if she really was sending such horrible letters....'

'Best not to speculate,' I advised. 'I'm sure Mr Griffith will get to the bottom of it, whatever happened. And if...if Susan was responsible for all this, well at least you can be assured she bore no ill will towards you.'

Miss Wellesley frowned, not quite understanding.

'You knew her longer than I did. And longer than Harry. And yet you didn't receive any nasty letters.'

'No. No, I didn't.' She took another bite of the sandwich.

'Did you ever see her using the typewriter?'

Miss Wellesley considered. 'Occasionally. She liked to write to her sister and one or two friends. I offered to take dictation, though I'm not really very good at it, but she wouldn't hear of it.'

'And since we boarded the ship?'

'Not that I recall. Oh, maybe once, on the first day. I'm not sure. She had the typewriter out of the case, anyway.'

'And did anyone else have access to the cabin? Any callers?'

'No. Only the stewardess, when she came in to change the sheets. Mrs Hamilton-Baynes might have put her head round the door once or twice, to say hello.'

'But nobody else?'

'I don't think so. Apart from Jenny, last night, of course. The poor thing. Finding her lying there like that, this morning.'

'It was quite a shock,' I agreed. 'Although she handled it surprisingly well, all things considered.' Mr Hopkins had been the more horrified, that his sweetheart had stumbled across a dead body. The two of them had slipped away together, after Mr Griffith had dismissed the assembly. Lady Jocelyn would not be impressed with that. 'But she would only have had access to the room in the last day or so. Logically, that would seem to rule her out.'

'And the note under the door, in the hotel,' Miss Wellesley said. 'I don't see how anyone else could have written that. I mean, on her typewriter.'

'No, it does seem fairly conclusive,' I agreed, finishing off the tea. Mrs O'Neill must have typed it herself and then dropped it on the mat after Miss Wellesley had gone to bed. It really did look like she was the guilty party. And if she was, then she had paid a heavy price for it.

My man Maurice was never far away from the facts of any case. His room was close to the scene of the crime, on the port side of the central corridor, and so I was not surprised – when I popped by his cabin in the early afternoon – to discover he knew all about it. The valet had just returned to the room after his own lunch in the canteen. There had, by all accounts, been plenty of idle speculation down there, despite Mr Griffith's stern warning. The death of this second passenger was of far more interest than the first. I had done my duty, helping Miss Wellesley to get to grips with the affair, and now it was Maurice's turn to sit and listen.

'Mr Griffith doesn't think it was an accident,' I told him, scratching my head. The valet's room was smaller than mine, without a private bathroom. There was little evidence of occupation, aside from a spare pair of shoes by the door and a biography of Florence Nightingale on the bedside table. Apart from a couple of shirts, everything else was neatly packed away. The shirts were laid out on an ironing board which Maurice had set up opposite the bed. Where he had got it from I had no idea. There was a perfectly decent laundry service

151

onboard ship, but the valet preferred the personal touch. 'It would be nice, just for once,' I said, sitting back on the bed, 'if I could travel somewhere without somebody dying like this. The gods really have it in for me.'

'Yes, Monsieur.' Maurice pressed the iron into the collar of a shirt and smoothed it down.

I had already related to him the business of the undelivered letter in Mrs O'Neill's handbag. 'Miss Wellesley is utterly baffled. She finds it hard to accept that Mrs O'Neill would do such a thing.'

'And you, Monsieur?'

'Well, the evidence is pretty damning. I didn't like the woman particularly, I admit, but she didn't strike me as venal. A little vulgar, yes, and she talked far too much. And as for her dress sense...' I grimaced, recalling the long parade of over-elaborate confections the woman had worn. 'But I never got the impression there was anything twisted there, beneath the surface. At heart, she always struck me as a decent, well meaning sort.'

Maurice stowed the iron on the edge of the board and flipped over the shirt. 'Appearances can sometimes be deceptive, Monsieur.'

'Yes, I am aware of that, Morris.'

'We all have the occasional unkind thought. The desire to strike down a friend or a family member.' He smoothed out a sleeve and pressed down on it with the iron. 'To do somebody down. Most of us would not dream of acting on such impulses. But if the desire persists and there is no outlet for it, an anonymous letter could grant a certain freedom...'

'Helping them to get it out of their system, you mean?'

'Yes, Monsieur. Giving them the ability to hurt people they know, but without any repercussions for themselves.'

'Yes, I see what you mean. And in the case of Mrs O'Neill...well, the very first letters were directed at her husband, when he was still alive. And a wife might well have reason to dislike her other half, without wanting to challenge him publicly.'

'Precisely, Monsieur.'

152

'Although, to be honest, I rather had the impression it was a happy marriage. She always talked very warmly about him; and she wouldn't be without those damned pearls he bought her. It's funny.' I expelled a breath. 'All that hot air and constant chatter, but the woman wasn't completely clueless. She had a notion that Harry was up to no good. But if she *was* behind all this, then why would she send letters to herself like that?'

'As a means of diverting suspicion, Monsieur.'

'Yes, yes, I understand that.' I waved my hands irritably. 'But the bomb hoax. The business in the restaurant, and then the note afterwards. That was a direct threat. And thinking about it, it was quite unlike the other letters. Much shorter and more to the point. More of a warning, really. And her distress, when I showed her the note; that was quite genuine. I'm sure of it.'

'But the typewriter, Monsieur...'

'Yes, that's the one thing I can't explain.'

Maurice turned over the sleeve. 'You believe that someone may have been targeting Mrs O'Neil, in retaliation for her own letters?'

'It must be a possibility. Perhaps someone got wind she was behind it all and decided to get their own back. Ah. But they would have had to have access to her typewriter.'

'And the text you saw typed on the Olivetti?'

'All those "W"s. Yes, that doesn't really fit either.' I pulled a face. 'Maybe they weren't sure it was her. Perhaps somebody merely suspected it was and wanted to examine the typewriter, like I did with the one in the Reynolds Suite. Yes, that might make sense. Perhaps they crept into her room to take a look at it, but she caught them doing it. And whoever it was crowned her and fled the scene.'

'It is an explanation that fits the facts, Monsieur.'

The pencil was poised once again above the notebook, but this time it was Mr Griffith who was providing the detail. 'Doctor Armstrong is of the opinion that the death of Mrs O'Neill was not an accident,' he confirmed. It was a couple of hours later, and I had been summoned into the great man's presence for the formal interview. The office of the head steward had been vacated, to give us a little privacy. Griffith sat behind a moulded desk, the ill-fitting cut of his uniform even more noticeable under the stark electric light. A trench coat would have suited the man better; but we were not here to discuss fashion tips. I was anxious to learn everything he had discovered.

'Somebody hit her?' I asked, leaning forward.

Griffith nodded seriously. 'We believe so, sir. A blunt instrument, to the back of the neck.'

'Lord.' So I had been right about that. 'What about the blood on the sink?'

'We believe whoever killed Mrs O'Neill tried to make it look like an accident. After he struck her, he must have lifted her up and banged her head against the bowl, to make it look like that was the cause of her injuries. He – or she – then arranged the body at the base of the sink, to make it appear as if she had fallen. But the way the body came to rest isn't consistent with a fall of that nature.'

'It did look a bit odd,' I agreed. 'But if somebody hit her and then started dragging the body around, surely someone would have heard something?'

'Unfortunately, the neighbours were away at the time. I've spoken to both of them.'

'And there's no sign of a murder weapon?'

'No, sir. Nothing that I could find. We'll keep looking, of course, but it's possible they simply threw it overboard, whatever it was'

'I see.' The perfect crime. 'What about the blood? If they were shifting the body about, they must have got some of it on their clothes.' Mrs O'Neill had not been the slimmest of women.

'Not if they were careful. But we will look into that, sir. In the meantime, the room has been sealed up, until the proper authorities can take a look at it.'

'The police you mean?' The real police, back in

England.

'That's right, sir. We've radioed ahead.' We were only a day or so out from Southampton. 'The police will want to examine the scene as soon as they get here. They're going to send a boat over ahead of time, before we dock.'

Oh lord, I thought. Another run in with the boys in blue. This was getting better and better. I sat back in my chair. 'So you have no doubt whatever that this was murder?' It was one thing to develop a theory; it was quite another to have it confirmed by the people in charge.

'I'm afraid so, sir. By person or persons unknown.' Griffith stared across at me, his penetrating blue eyes burrowing into me. Did he suspect me? I wondered. I had been close to the scene when the body was discovered.

'Did you speak to the maid?' I asked.

'Yes, sir, just before you. She's made a full statement. At face value, it seems consistent with everything else we've seen. She only spent the one night in the room, of course. We'll have to find her somewhere else to sleep this evening.'

The nocturnal arrangements of a servant were of no interest to me. There was only one question that I wanted the answer to. 'What about Harry...?'

Griffith put down his pencil. 'Well, that's the thing, sir. Two deaths on one voyage is not unusual, but with the second one being an act of violence, and the connection between Mrs O'Neill and Mr Latimer, we cannot rule out foul play.'

'You mean...with Harry's death?'

'Yes, sir. It is a possibility that we have to consider.'

'But Doctor Armstrong...'

'Doctor Armstrong is an accomplished surgeon. I'm sure he did a thorough job. But even a professional can overlook certain details. We are all capable of missing the obvious on occasions.'

'So you think Harry may have been murdered too?'

Griffith was not prepared to be drawn. 'It's too early to say, sir. The doctor insists there was nothing suspicious about his death. Nothing to indicate anything other than a natural death.'

155

'His heart was in a bad way, he said.'

'Yes, sir. Let's just say I am keeping an open mind. However, had I been aware of these malicious letters, I doubt I would have released the body for burial. It would have been helpful if I had been told about that when I was making my initial enquiries.'

'Yes, I…I'm sorry. I honestly didn't think it was relevant. And the family didn't want their dirty laundry aired in public.'

'I understand that, sir. Nevertheless, I ought to have been told. If we had kept Mr Latimer's body on ice, a police pathologist could have performed a more detailed examination. As it is, we may never know precisely how he died.'

'It's all my fault,' I said. 'I didn't think. But what if Harry *was* murdered? If someone killed him? How could it have been done? You saw the room, Mr Griffith. There was no sign of a struggle. Harry looked as peaceful as anything. And, besides, if there had been any sort of scuffle, my man would have heard it through the wall.'

'Yes, sir. I think we can assume it was not a violent death. But there are ways of killing people that are not immediately obvious.'

'I wondered at the time if…maybe some sort of poison?'

'Doctor Armstrong found no evidence of that.'

'But he's not a police pathologist.'

'No, sir.'

'Suppose…' I lifted a hand. 'Suppose somebody interfered with his drink. Or the jug of water by the bed…'

'We checked the water, sir. There was nothing wrong with it.'

'But the glass next to it. The one he drank from. Did you analyse the contents of that?'

Griffith frowned. 'The glass, sir?'

'Yes, there was a glass next to his bed. A tumbler, by the water jug.'

'I think you must be mistaken, sir.' Griffith flicked back through his notebook. 'No, there was no glass by the bed. There were two tumblers, upside down on the sink. They would have been placed there by the steward the previous day. As with all the rooms.'

'No, no,' I said. 'One of them was by the bed. I remember it clearly. Harry must have grabbed it during the night. The amount he drunk, he would have needed a glass or two of water.'

'That's not what it says here, sir,' Griffith told me. 'I examined the room quite thoroughly, and there was no glass on the bedside table.'

I regarded the fellow in bewilderment. 'But I saw it...'

'It is easy to misremember things, sir. That's why it's helpful to keep detailed notes.'

'I'm not misremembering. For heaven's sake, it was there. I'm certain of it.'

'Not when I arrived, sir,' Griffith stated firmly. 'Although I suppose it could have been moved before I got there. You didn't touch anything in the room, before I arrived?'

'No, of course not.'

Griffith consulted his notes once again. 'Well, the only people to enter the room before me were yourself, the cabin boy, the head steward and Doctor Armstrong.'

'And Mrs O'Neill,' I added. The woman we now suspected was responsible for all these letters. Had she somehow doctored Harry's drink and then fiddled with the glass afterwards? Maybe even refilled the jug? But no, that wasn't possible. She had not gone anywhere near the body when I was in the room, let alone the bedside table; and we had left together. 'She was the first one in there. I suppose she could have fiddled with the evidence before I arrived.' The jug of water if not the actual glass.

'When she was delivering the letter, you mean?'

'Exactly. But then...' I frowned. 'Doctor Armstrong said Harry had been dead for a couple of hours...' Mrs O'Neill could only have been in that room for a matter of minutes. Before that, she had been at breakfast with Miss Wellesley.

'It is very peculiar, sir,' Griffith admitted, flipping back to the current page in his notebook. 'I'll speak to the steward, and Doctor Armstrong. If there was a glass on the bedside table, perhaps it was cleared away inadvertently before I arrived. Or perhaps, as you say, Mrs O'Neill had reason to remove it. I suppose it is possible it was removed between the discovery of the body and my arrival.'

'It must have been.'

'But we're getting ahead of ourselves, sir,' Griffith said. He flipped to a fresh page. 'We should return to the matter of Mrs O'Neill's death.' He looked up at me with that steely gaze of his. 'Can you account for your movements between nine and eleven am this morning…?'

Never mind Mrs O'Neill, I thought. Try as I might, I could not get the image of that glass out of my head. My attention was now firmly back on the demise of Harry Latimer. The tumbler had been there on the bedside table. I was certain of it. And if someone had moved it over to the sink before Mr Griffith arrived then the evidence had been deliberately tampered with. Proof positive – so far as I was concerned – that Harry had been murdered.

Maurice had just returned from his regular afternoon lecture. Dressmaking, this time. The valet had worked in a draper's shop as a young man, before entering service, so it was a topic he already knew a fair amount about. I had no interest in the specifics. It was the attention to detail he had learnt in that trade that I needed now; that and his razor sharp memory.

'You were standing in the corridor outside Harry's room,' I said. 'Who went in there, after I left?'

The valet considered. 'There were three people, Monsieur. The cabin boy, Adam. He showed the doctor into the room. And then there was the head steward, Monsieur Dalton.'

'But nobody else?'

'No, Monsieur.'

'And was anyone alone in there for any time?'

'I believe the boy Adam was, for a brief moment. And, if I recall correctly, the doctor also, when the head steward came out to confer with the boy.'

'So Doctor Armstrong was in there on his own?'

'Yes, Monsieur. Although only for a moment or so.'

I grimaced. I didn't like to cast aspersions on a ship's doctor, but the question had to be asked: 'Do you think he could be involved somehow?'

'It seems unlikely, Monsieur.' A ship's doctor – like the captain – should be above suspicion.

'He was the one who performed the autopsy, though. I suppose we only have his word about the cause of death.'

'You think he may have lied, Monsieur?'

'I don't know.' I scratched my head. 'It does seem rather unlikely. So far as I'm aware, he didn't even know Harry.'

Maurice had another idea. 'Is it possible he may have been covering up for someone else?'

That was a thought. 'Those two ruffians at the funeral, perhaps? Yes, that could be it. Maybe they killed Harry and then...and then the doctor covered up for them.' A gangland hit and a doctor on the payroll? I bit my lip. It was a trifle outlandish. Armstrong had struck me as a decent, reliable sort. But then again, he had told me that Harry's heart had been in a bad way, and if Harry really had been murdered then that must logically have been an invention. 'What do you know about the fellow? Any gossip below stairs?'

The valet's eyelids flickered with distaste. 'None that I am aware of, Monsieur.'

'Ask around. See if you can find out anything. If something odd is going on, then it's difficult to see how the ship's doctor could have missed it.'

'Yes, Monsieur. Although perhaps it would be better to ask him yourself.'

I scoffed. 'What, accuse him of fiddling with the evidence? Don't be daft, Morris. I'd need a lot more to go on before I could do that.'

'Not an accusation, Monsieur. You could simply enquire about the glass in the stateroom. Was he sure he had not seen it?'

I pondered that suggestion for a moment. 'Actually,

that's not a bad idea. Perhaps he moved it without thinking? Or the steward did.' I rubbed my chin. 'No harm in asking, I suppose. One other thing that's troubling me, though.'

'Monsieur?'

'That note Harry received, over by the bar, the night before he died.'

'Did you inform Monsieur Griffith about that?'

'No. No, I didn't think to. But look, if Mrs O'Neill was our poison pen enthusiast, she must have already typed up that note in her handbag, ready to deliver. Which means that the note Harry received at the bar, logically, that must have been from somebody else.'

'Yes, Monsieur. We have discussed this already.'

'I know, but…it occurs to me now, if Harry really was murdered…then perhaps that note wasn't just a simple summons. Perhaps it was sent by the person who killed him.'

Doctor Armstrong's surgery was tucked away a few floors down on E Deck. The elevator was clear of retired colonels, so I saved myself a long walk and descended by lift to the foyer. The surgery was on the port side of the deck, opposite the gymnasium and the swimming pool. Probably quite a sensible place for it, I thought, as I approached the door. An hour of physical jerks with the gym instructor would kill just about anybody off, and having a doctor on standby might save an awful lot of time. I strolled casually into the waiting room and was pleased to see there was no-one else about. Hopefully, I could get straight in to see him.

There was a reception desk along one side of the waiting room, but no receptionist in residence. I doubted there would be enough customers to merit it. There were two internal doors. One was labelled "SURGERY", the other "DOCTOR B.S. ARMSTRONG". From this second room I could hear a low hum of conversation. It sounded like the doctor did have a patient after all. I sat myself down to wait. There were a couple of magazines on the coffee table. One was a woman's journal, the other a six week old copy of The Sporting Times.

Idly, I gazed around the room. It was clean, if a trifle cluttered. The electric lights were dim, but a last minute flicker of sunlight was sneaking in from a couple of small windows on the port side. There was a map of the world behind the reception desk, with notes on various tropical diseases and their relative distribution. A few other medical posters adorned the near wall, human anatomy and so forth, as well as various animals. A spider and a toad. Hardly reassuring fare for a doctor's surgery. A shelf containing several medical books stood beside a rather functional coat hook. On the far side of the room was a small box of children's toys.

I was just on the verge of pulling out my pocket watch, when the door to the consulting room opened and a tall, heavily suited man stepped out. He did not glance at me but instead swept through the waiting room and out into the foyer. Doctor Armstrong appeared at the door and caught sight of me on the bench. But I was looking at the man who had just left.

I couldn't be sure, but I had a horrible feeling he had been one of the uninvited guests at Harry's funeral.

Chapter Twelve

'Mr Buxton.' Doctor Armstrong greeted me with some surprise. He was looking a little flustered, his large ears seeming to flap as he moved towards me; but the professional manner quickly reasserted itself. 'What can I do for you?' He managed a quick smile.

'I just wanted to have a quiet word,' I said. 'That fellow.' I gestured to the far door, where the brute had now departed. 'Wasn't he at Harry's funeral yesterday?'

Doctor Armstrong followed my gaze. He was smartly dressed, with a mop of wavy blond hair overshadowing his small blue eyes. The hair, it struck me at that moment, was a little on the long side for an officer. 'Was he? I don't recall.'

'Him and another fellow. Turned up at the last minute.'

Doctor Armstrong considered for a moment. 'Oh yes. You're right. I do remember that, now you come to mention it. It's funny. I wouldn't have placed him, if you hadn't said.' He smiled again, but this time the expression felt a little forced. 'It's been rather a long day.'

'Was it a…medical consultation?' I asked, peering at the man thoughtfully.

'Er…yes.' Again, a small hesitation.

'He didn't look ill to me.'

'No, he was just after a bit of advice. But please, come inside.' Armstrong gestured to the door. I could not put my finger on it, but there was something not quite right in his manner. It was the first time I had seen the man even a little out of sorts and it worried me. I wanted to believe he was above reproach but his hesitant response to my questions was something short of reassuring. If I didn't know better, I would have said that the man who had just left had put the wind up him.

'So how have you been?' Doctor Armstrong enquired, settling himself behind a modest wooden desk.

I seated myself on the chair opposite. 'I'm surviving. Trying to make sense of everything that's happened.'

'Yes, it's been horrendous hasn't it?' Armstrong regarded me sympathetically, his bedside manner clicking back into gear. 'And talking these things through is always helpful.' The uncertainty of a moment ago had disappeared, as he settled into the familiar role. 'If there's anything I can do to set your mind at rest,' he said.

It was my turn to hesitate. 'I wanted to talk to you about Mrs O'Neill. Mr Griffith told me you'd completed the autopsy.'

'Yes.' Armstrong's expression darkened. 'I examined her this afternoon. The poor woman. There was no doubt as to the cause of death. A severe head trauma.'

'Somebody hit her?'

The doctor nodded gravely. 'I'm afraid so. With a blunt instrument, to the back of the head. It would have been quite quick.'

'And the blood on the sink?' I had been over this with Mr Griffith, but I wanted to get the facts absolutely clear.

'A second blow, of considerably less power. Post mortem. She would already have been dead by then.'

'Do you have any idea what sort of weapon was used?'

'No, I'm afraid not. It would have been something fairly hefty, I think.'

'And where is…Mrs O'Neill now?'

'In the cold store. We have a small refrigerated area, for food storage. On this deck, actually. There's a locker off to the side that we use for anyone who…well, who passes away, during the trip. It's not an unusual occurrence, sadly.'

'The odd death, maybe,' I said. 'But not murder.'

'No, not murder,' Armstrong agreed, with a gentle shudder. 'I've never been involved in anything like this. Frankly, it's been a bit of a shock.'

'For all of us.' I glanced around the room. Unlike the waiting area, there was very little clutter in here. The desk was mercifully free of paperwork. There was a small cabinet to one side and various items of medical equipment. The simpler tools of the trade, thankfully. No knives or scalpels here. 'Where did you perform the autopsy, if you don't mind me asking? Was it in the cold store?'

163

'No, no, it was just through there, in the surgery.' He indicated the adjacent room. There was an intervening door, which was currently locked up. 'But a police pathologist will take another look at her when we reach port. I don't think he will disagree with my diagnosis. It was pretty clear what happened.'

'Was there a struggle, do you think? Did she try to defend herself?'

Armstrong could not say for certain. 'There were no indications of a struggle. The blow was to the back of the head, so it's possible she was taken unawares. Beyond that, I couldn't really say. Mr Griffith has examined the room. He might be able to tell you a little more.' The doctor frowned. 'A murder, onboard ship. In all my years…I can scarcely believe it.'

'And he's still out there, somewhere, whoever he is. The murderer.'

Armstrong shuddered again. 'Yes, it doesn't bear thinking about. The captain's not at all happy.'

'Not good publicity for the liner, I should imagine, when this gets out.'

'No, I suppose not. But it's the safety of the passengers that's our principle concern. That's why we're trying to keep things quiet for now. To avoid a panic. But the purser has instituted a special regime, on the orders of the captain. There'll be someone patrolling the decks day and night, just to be one the safe side. And Mr Griffith is very thorough. He'll bring the fellow to book, whoever he is.'

'Let's hope so,' I said, scratching the side of my face.

'I gather from Mr Griffith that you had some concerns in respect of your friend Mr Latimer?'

I looked across in surprise. I had not expected the doctor to be the one to raise the matter. 'Er…yes, that's right. It was just…well, in the light of Mrs O'Neill's death at the hands of…whoever this scoundrel is, I couldn't help but think… couldn't help but worry that something similar might have happened to Harry.'

'That's an understandable concern,' Armstrong said. This time his manner was rock solid. I could not detect any sign

164

of dissembling. 'All I can do is reiterate what I told you the other morning. I found no evidence of foul play. His heart was in a bad way. It was a text book case, I'm afraid. I did a full toxicological analysis and there were no unexpected toxins in his blood.'

'But you're not a pathologist.'

'No, but I did study for a year at the London School of Hygiene & Tropical Medicine, as part of my training. I know the signs to look for.'

I pushed back in my chair. 'You have to admit, though, it's a hell of a coincidence. He's mixed up with Mrs O'Neill. She may or may not have been about to send him one of her letters. You know about the pen letters?'

'Yes, Mr Griffith told me.'

'Then he dies and she discovers the body.'

'And you think she may have killed him?'

'I don't know what to think.' I gazed at the fellow keenly now. I wanted to believe he was innocent, but the interview so far had been less than reassuring; and I owed it to Harry to find out the truth. 'I do know that there was an empty tumbler by the side of his bed when I entered the room.'

Doctor Armstrong nodded. 'Yes, Mr Griffith told me there was some confusion about that.' He shrugged. 'I can only repeat what I told him. I didn't see a glass on the bedside table when I arrived in the room. And as I was up close, examining the body, I'm sure I would have seen it, if it had been there.'

'And the water jug? There's no chance that someone could have slipped something into that and then refilled it afterwards?'

'I don't see how. We did examine the water.'

'Could Harry have taken a tablet or two, without knowing what they were?'

'We didn't find any medicine in the room. Any tablets or bottles. That was the one thing that did surprise me,' Armstrong admitted. 'If Mr Latimer had been aware of his condition, he would have taken something for it, if only to relieve the pain. The fact that he didn't implies that he really didn't know what kind of condition he was in. It must have come out of the blue for him, as much as it did for the rest of us. He must have ignored all the warning signs.'

'Is that possible?'

'People do have a remarkable capacity for ignoring their own bodies. It's human nature, I'm afraid. Rationalising things, putting the pain down to indigestion or heartburn, or something like that, until it is too late.'

'Maybe it's better not to know,' I thought, 'if there's nothing to be done.'

'Perhaps.' Armstrong rested his hands on the edge of the desk. 'I understand how difficult this is for you, Mr Buxton. Mr Latimer was a good friend of yours. But in all honesty, I don't believe there was anything suspicious about his death. It is an extraordinary coincidence, I grant you, but I don't think these two deaths are connected in any way whatsoever.'

I met the man's eye once again. He had such a reliable air to him, despite those pinhole eyes and the ridiculous flappy ears. He might well be speaking sincerely. But he had had years to develop his bedside manner; and the flustered response to that previous patient had given a brief glimpse of something awkward, lurking beneath the surface.

Oh yes, the manner was plausible, but I was not altogether sure that I believed it.

It might have been just me at the supper table that evening, had I not been joined at the last minute by Ernest Hopkins and Mrs Hamilton-Baynes. The Louis XVI was buzzing as the evening session progressed. The restaurant was spread out like a grand hall down on D Deck, stretching the entire width of the Galitia. It was a two storey affair, with a long winding gallery overlooking the diners; the kind of space one could easily get lost in. Waiters whirled around us like spinning tops amid the colourful painted splendour of a French court. Light chamber music wafted down from the upper levels. My regular table was on the port side just beneath the overhanging gallery, with a good view of the fountain amidships. It was common practise on ocean liners to be allocated a specific table – and a waiter –

for the duration of the voyage. On the first night out, I had shared with Mrs O'Neill, Miss Wellesley and Harry Latimer. Two of those people were now dead and the third had understandably decided to take her supper on a tray in the Reynolds Suite. I could easily have done the same, but I did not wish to sit in my cabin brooding. Neither am I the sort of person who frets about dining alone in a public space. I was not unduly surprised, however, when Mrs Hamilton-Baynes stepped across to my table, with a rather reluctant Ernest Hopkins in tow.

'Jocelyn thought you might appreciate a little company,' the vicar's wife explained with a twinkle, as the two of them came over. 'Unless you'd rather be alone?'

'No, no,' I said. I gestured to the empty chairs. 'Please do.'

The good graces of Lady Jocelyn Wingfield did not extend to joining me herself, of course. She remained with her brother and the Reverend Hamilton-Baynes over by the windows. I raised my glass in ritual gratitude and Lady Jocelyn dipped her head. Sending across the cousin and the secretary was the bare minimum that politeness dictated and it did not surprise me that her ladyship went that far but no further. Ordinarily, I have nothing but admiration for aloof, aristocratic women – in many ways, they are the backbone of England – but there was something about Lady Jocelyn that I found eminently dislikeable. I could not tell you what it was.

The presence of Mrs Hamilton-Baynes and Sir Richard's secretary did at least have the intended function of mitigating the furtive stares of the other diners. The whole ship, by now, had heard about the death of Mrs O'Neill, a woman whose hideously bright clothes and shamelessness on the dance floor would doubtless have imprinted itself on the mind of even the most inattentive passenger. People had been staring quietly at me as soon as I arrived in the restaurant. Had we been dining in second or – God forbid – tourist third class, I daresay the stares would have been even more direct. Thankfully, here in first class, despite the busy atmosphere, people had the decency to at least pretend that they were not interested.

The table's regular waiter, Jennings, a monstrous behemoth of a man with a toupee as absurd as his girth, had by now served the opening course and my new companions had settled themselves down. Mrs Hamilton-Baynes tapped the edge of the melons glace with her spoon.

'How have you both been coping?' I asked, pushing back my own plate after a token nibble. I had come for the main course: a saddle of English mutton. I had no particular interest in the starter.

'It's been a little fraught,' Mr Hopkins responded.

I was not the only one to have undergone a detailed interrogation this afternoon. 'Jocelyn's just finished talking to Mr Griffith,' Mrs Hamilton-Baynes said. The officer had conducted a full set of interviews, as he had in the aftermath of Harry Latimer's death. The results of the autopsy were being kept strictly under wraps, however. I had only been told the truth because I had seen the body and had advanced my own theories on the matter.

'How did she manage? Lady Jocelyn?' I enquired. Griffith's questions would not have been restricted to the ordinary comings and goings of the Reynolds Suite this time around. Now there was also the matter of the poison pen letters.

'Not too well, I'm afraid,' the vicar's wife admitted. As a rule, Mrs Hamilton-Baynes was a cheerful woman – the perfect foil for a lively man of the cloth – but she was looking somewhat subdued this evening. The events of the day had taken their toll on her, though her first concern was for her cousin, Lady Jocelyn. 'She came straight back to her room to change. She didn't say a word.' Mrs Hamilton-Baynes kept her voice low, for fear of being overheard, though the hum of the restaurant was sufficiently loud that her words were unlikely to carry.

'Is the maid still looking after her?' I asked.

'No, she won't have Jenny near her now. I've been helping her to change for the last day or so.' That was a bit much, I thought. A woman of Lady Jocelyn's standing would not want to be without a maid, but co-opting her cousin into the role was a little unfair. 'Well, we've been helping each other,' she clarified. 'It must have been very difficult for her, to be interviewed like that. She's not used to confiding in strangers. Even a professional man like Mr Griffith.'

'With all that's happened, I suppose it was unavoidable. Any death onboard ship has to be investigated, even if it is just someone slipping on the mat.'

'Yes, of course. It's been dreadful, though. Poor, dear Susan. That this should happen to her.' By all accounts, Mrs Hamilton-Baynes had been rather fond of the American woman. I wondered what had shocked her more: the fact of her death or the revelation that she had been behind the letters.

'It's hit the family very hard, Mr Buxton,' Hopkins told me frankly. He put down his cutlery and pushed his plate away. He was not looking too enamoured of the melons glace either. I had a sneaking suspicion that Sir Richard had given him a bit of a dressing down, for disappearing off with the maid at lunch time. Sending him over here to babysit me was probably part of the penance.

Mrs Hamilton-Baynes struggled manfully to finish off the starter and the waiter then came across to remove the plates.

'Still, it's all over with now,' I said, anxious not to let the conversation drift. I turned to the secretary. 'How was he with you?'

'He was very thorough,' Hopkins said. 'He knows his job, I think.'

'And did he...?' I peered across at Mrs Hamilton-Baynes. 'Did Lady Jocelyn give him an indication of the contents of the letters that she received?'

The vicar's wife flushed. 'Yes, I believe so.'

'They spoke to them together,' Hopkins explained. 'Lady Jocelyn and Sir Richard. A bit of moral support. I think it was easier for her ladyship with Sir Richard there.'

'It would have been very distressing for her, to have to talk about these things on her own,' Mrs Hamilton-Baynes put in.

I could not imagine a woman like Lady Jocelyn being distressed at anything. 'Sounds like the letters must have been particularly nasty.'

'They were, Mr Buxton.' She shuddered. 'How people could say such things!'

'Was it a personal attack?' I asked, out of curiosity. The vicar's wife, it seemed, was familiar with the contents of the letters. 'Somebody dredging up something from her past?'

She hesitated. 'It's really not my place to say. It was all such a long time ago. It's horrible that anyone should bring it all up like that, all these years later.'

'Was it something that happened to her before she was married?'

Mrs Hamilton-Baynes looked away in embarrassment. 'You must forgive me, Mr Buxton. It's really not something I can talk about. It's a...a private family matter.'

'Yes, of course. I'm sorry. I didn't mean to pry.' But my curiosity was peaked. What could the letters have alluded to? An indiscretion of some kind in Lady Jocelyn's youth? It was difficult to think of a woman like that ever being young. An inappropriate relationship, perhaps, before she was married? That might be enough to upset a woman of her elevated position. Or maybe – I struggled not to smile at the thought – the *result* of such a relationship? A child out of wedlock had the potential to be ruinous for someone like Lady Jocelyn, even in this day and age.

Jennings waddled across with the second course, saving Mrs Hamilton-Baynes from any further embarrassment. We waited as he carved out the beef and for the next few minutes there was a contented silence as we tucked merrily away.

Hopkins was still looking a little preoccupied, however, and it was he who eventually broke the silence. He wiped his lips with a napkin and cleared his throat. 'Tell me, Mr Buxton, do you...do you believe that Mrs O'Neill was really responsible for all of these letters?'

I put down my fork. It was an honest question and it deserved an honest answer. 'It looks like it, I'm afraid. It was definitely her typewriter. And the only other person who could have had access to it was our Miss Wellesley.' Mrs Hamilton-Baynes was about to protest but I held up my hand. 'And of course she couldn't possibly be involved. The letter writing

170

started long before she came along. But this attack on Lady Jocelyn.' I could not let the matter drop. 'The details...of course, it's a personal matter. I wouldn't dream of prying. But who...who else would have known about it? Whatever it was?'

The vicar's wife was looking a little flustered. 'That's the peculiar thing, Mr Buxton. Nobody *could* have known. It was only myself, her father and one of the servants.' Mrs Hamilton-Baynes spoke in a whisper, her eyes darting guiltily across the hall to where Lady Jocelyn was sitting; but the Reynolds Suite was well out of earshot. 'I only know the truth because Jocelyn confided in me at the time. If Susan – Mrs O'Neill, God rest her soul – if she was responsible for these letters, then how could she possibly have known about something that happened back in England such a long time ago?'

'Her late husband...what was his name? Ulysses O'Neill,' I suggested. 'He was a close friend of Sir Richard's, wasn't he?'

'Yes, he was.'

'Was it possible that he knew?'

Mrs Hamilton-Baynes shook her head emphatically. 'No. Richard would never have told him anything like that. Not about the family. And I don't think Mr O'Neill would have had any interest in discussing matters of a personal nature.'

'Did you ever meet him?'

'No, I never did. I'm just going on what Susan told me about him.'

'I met him once,' Hopkins volunteered. 'Briefly. We came over on a business trip, just after the crash.' That would have been late 1929 or early 1930. 'I'd just started with Sir Richard then.'

'What was he like? Mr O'Neill?'

Hopkins considered. 'Quite a larger than life character, I would say. Rather exuberant and full of beans. Mrs O'Neill was somewhat in his shadow, I felt.'

'Well, she certainly came out of her shell after he died,' I observed dryly. 'Perhaps Sir Richard did tell him about his sister. Or the servants gossiped. That's usually the way of these things.'

'Sir Richard doesn't usually take servants with him on foreign trips,' Hopkins pointed out. 'I only come with him because he has business to conduct. This has been a working trip for us, Mr Buxton, not a holiday.'

'Did Sir Richard know about…about whatever had happened?'

Mrs Hamilton-Baynes gave a half-hearted nod. 'But he would never talk about it. He would never discuss it with anyone. It was too shameful, for all of them.'

'For *them*?' That was an interesting choice of words. 'You mean, Sir Richard was involved in it, whatever it was?' So not a pregnancy then, or an illicit affair. 'It was something he did as well?'

'I'm sorry. I shouldn't really…it isn't…'.

'Forgive me, Mrs Hamilton-Baynes. It is none of my business.' The woman was now becoming seriously agitated. Perhaps it was time to pull back a little. 'I'm afraid I have rather an enquiring mind. Best just to ignore me.' I had no desire to cause her any distress. I lifted a hand to summon the waiter, gesturing to the empty glasses. Jennings poured out some more wine for my companions; then he took my tumbler and padded off for a refill. Mrs Hamilton-Baynes sipped nervously at her drink, clearly regretting having spoken of the matter at all.

At the other table, a little way away, Lady Jocelyn and Sir Richard were leaning in and talking to each other. Sir Richard must have said something to annoy his sister, as she pulled away sharply and threw what looked like a barbed remark straight back at him.

The waiter returned with my whisky and soda. A little too much soda, this time. That was a couple of shillings less on the tip he would be receiving at the end of the trip. I took a gulp regardless. It was time for a change of tack. 'So what is Sir Richard like as an employer?' I asked Mr Hopkins.

'Very good,' the secretary answered, loyally. 'He has his quirks, as any businessman does, but he's always very attentive.' The testimonial was well-rehearsed. 'He's been good to me. Mr Buxton.'

'When he doesn't send you off running errands for Lady Jocelyn?'

Hopkins was not smooth enough to disguise his irritation at that. That damned cat had caused him far too much trouble on this trip. A hand slipped unconsciously to his cheek. The claw marks had not yet fully healed. 'I do sometimes end up in the middle rather,' he admitted.

'They argue a lot? The brother and sister.'

Hopkins hesitated. 'It's not really my place to say, Mr Buxton.'

'I must confess, when I was first introduced to them, I thought they were married. That kind of bickering is what you'd normally see between a husband and a wife.' I gazed across at the couple. Whatever the cross words had been, they were now both sitting in cold silence. The Reverend Hamilton-Baynes was tucking into his beef in apparent ignorance, as the two of them focused frostily on their knives and forks. 'Not like a brother and sister at all,' I said.

Mrs Hamilton-Baynes choked suddenly on her wine and I thought I saw a flash of fear in her eyes as Hopkins rose up to assist her. His help wasn't necessary, however, as the woman quickly recovered. Lady Jocelyn, at the far table, looked across in concern, but I gave her a reassuring wave and mimed that everything was all right. Then I returned my attention to the vicar's wife. Brother and sister, that was all I had said. 'They *are* brother and sister?' I asked, suspiciously.

'I...yes, yes of course,' Mrs Hamilton-Baynes stuttered, putting down her glass.

I had the feeling now we were getting close to the nub of the matter. 'The letters...it was something to do with...?'

'They have always been very close,' Hopkins put in, as he resumed his seat. His frown was now a mirror of my own.

And at that moment, the penny dropped. 'They weren't...too close? Is that it?' I leaned forward, all thoughts of the beef now forgotten.

Mrs Hamilton-Baynes was staring at her wine glass. 'They were both very young,' she mumbled, her voice barely

173

audible. 'They had no idea what they were doing. It was just foolishness. The exuberance of youth.' The vicar's wife was starting to tremble, her grip tightening on the glass. She looked up at me then, in some distress. 'You mustn't…you mustn't say anything. You mustn't tell anyone. Oh my goodness. It would destroy her. It would destroy her if anyone knew.'

'She and Sir Richard?' I could scarcely bring myself to say the words. 'They were…together? I mean, *intimately together?*'

Mrs Hamilton-Baynes nodded, her face as pale as a ghost.

A brother and sister. Oh, lord.

Chapter Thirteen

'They were discovered, by the housekeeper,' Mrs Hamilton-Baynes continued, unable to stop herself now, though her voice was little more than a whisper. 'The two of them. They were... they were...' She took another gulp of wine and nearly knocked the glass over as she returned it shakily to the table. 'They were in bed together. Without clothes and...and in a state of...yes, some intimacy.'

Mr Hopkins was appalled. 'Sir Richard? And her ladyship?' It was clearly the first he had heard of it.

'How old were they?' I asked, leaning across the table.

'He was seventeen. She was thirteen.'

Not all that young then. It was not unusual for siblings to share a bed in their formative years, but this was an altogether different proposition. I do not consider myself to be a prude. I make a point of not condemning other people's sexual peccadilloes, no matter how perverted, so long as they are discreet. Lord knows, I have done some pretty disreputable things in my time, and what people get up to behind closed doors is their own affair. But some activities are simply beyond the pale. 'And the housekeeper?' I asked, trying to focus on the pertinent facts.

'She summoned their father, Sir Robert. Apparently, it had been going on for some time. Sir Robert was appalled; and he blamed Richard, of course. The boy was beaten to within an inch of his life. The two of them were separated. They weren't allowed to see each other again. Not until they were both married. And soon after that, Sir Robert died.' Mrs Hamilton-Baynes rested her hands on the edge of the table. For all her reluctance to discuss the matter in public, it was clear there was some relief to be had in speaking of it at last. 'The housekeeper is still alive – she lives in America now – but apart from that nobody ever knew.'

'But Lady Jocelyn confided in you?'

The vicar's wife nodded. 'She had to talk to someone. She was sent to stay with us, for the rest of the summer. She was just a little girl. She was so upset but she wasn't allowed to show it. But she would always confide in me. And I've kept the secret, for over thirty years.' Mrs Hamilton-Baynes wiped a tear from her eye.

'Does your husband know about it?'

'No. He has no idea. I would never tell him. How could I?'

'But somebody found out? Mrs O'Neill perhaps?'

'She must have done,' Mrs Hamilton-Baynes agreed.

Hopkins lifted a hand to his mouth, utterly aghast. The revelation had fair taken the wind from his sails. 'I knew it had to be something bad,' he muttered. 'But I never thought of anything like this.'

'You weren't aware of the contents of the letters?'

'No. And I'm beginning to understand why.' He shot a brief glance at the far table. It was difficult to reconcile the sober, bespectacled Sir Richard with the idea of such deviance, let alone the severe and aloof Lady Jocelyn Wingfield.

'You mustn't say a word,' Mrs Hamilton-Baynes pleaded, the shock of what she had told us beginning to reassert itself. 'Ernest, you must promise.'

The secretary was happy to agree. 'It's not my place,' he said, his eyes still wide. 'This business, it gets worse and worse.'

He was not far wrong. 'And Mr Griffith? She told him about all this?'

The woman gazed down at her cutlery. 'I don't think so. I overheard them talking about it beforehand. I think they may have lied to him.'

'They concocted a story?'

'You mustn't blame them, Mr Buxton. Jocelyn couldn't tell anyone about this. She just couldn't. And all the letters had been destroyed.'

'Do you know what the story was?'

'I'm afraid not. Perhaps a youthful indiscretion?' That would have been shameful enough. 'But Jocelyn couldn't have told him the truth. She couldn't bear the shame, Mr Buxton. If any of this ever came out – even a whisper of it – it would be

176

the end of her. It would be the end of both of them. That's why...that's why it has to be kept quiet.'

'Of course,' I nodded gravely. 'You can rely on us, Mrs Hamilton-Baynes.'

Hopkins and I left the restaurant shortly afterwards. The vicar's wife returned to the main table, conjuring up a weak smile when she greeted her husband.

'This is a strange business,' I reflected, after we had made our farewells. 'You really didn't know?'

The secretary was adamant. 'I had no idea.' His face was still pale from shock, as we headed out onto the foyer. 'Sir Richard...it doesn't seem possible.'

'People's private lives are always messy,' I said, keeping my voice low as we passed by the little shop. 'We all do foolish things when we're young.' We arrived at the elevator and Hopkins pulled back the gate.

'Yes, but not...*incest.*' He shuddered at the word.

'No, that's a whole other matter,' I agreed. We stepped into the lift and I pressed the button for B Deck.

'Do you have any brothers or sisters, Mr Buxton?' he asked. There was a whirr as the compartment began to ascend.

'No, no, I don't.'

'I have three brothers and a little sister. The thought of...' His face screwed up in horror.

'Best not to dwell on it,' I said. 'The past is the past, Mr Hopkins. And it won't bring Mrs O'Neill back, to rake over it all like this.'

'No, you're right,' he agreed.

The cage jolted as we arrived at the correct floor. 'Though how she found out about it all is beyond me. That typewriter of hers.' I reached forward to pull back the cage door. 'The black Olivetti in her cabin. She would have brought that with her from home, presumably.'

'Yes, yes, she did,' Hopkins confirmed, stepping out into the foyer.

'Do you remember where it was? In the house, I mean?'

I hopped out behind him onto the spotted carpet.

'I believe it was in the study. Why do you ask?'

'I was just curious.' I lingered for a moment by the gate. 'Would anyone else have had access to it?'

'Yes, I suppose so. Mrs O'Neill was often out and we had the run of the place.' He stopped, halfway between the lift and the stairwell. 'You don't think somebody else might have typed those letters?'

'No, no. I don't think that at all. Except…' I shrugged. 'No, never mind. My mind's all over the place this evening. Well…' I raised a hand. 'I suppose I should bid you goodnight.' The secretary would be heading off to the Reynolds Suite, on the port side, while I would be heading in the opposite direction. 'Try not to dwell on it all, Mr Hopkins. Whatever Sir Richard and Lady Jocelyn may have done, it was all a long, long time ago.'

'You're right, of course.' Hopkins showed no signs of moving, however. It was almost as if he were waiting for me to leave first.

'Not off to bed?' I asked, in surprise. Surely he wasn't planning on going dancing?

'No, I…' He flushed with embarrassment, indicating the starboard side. 'I thought I'd look in on Jenny. Miss Simpkins. She's moved into one of the middle rooms.'

'Ah, yes. So I've heard.'

'She can't go back to Mrs O'Neill's room tonight, now it's all locked up, and Miss Wellesley has taken her place in the Reynolds Suite.'

'You're sweet on the girl?'

His cheeks flushed again. 'Er…yes, I am. Lady Jocelyn isn't at all happy about it. But anyway, I thought I ought to…to check up on her. See how she's settled in. She's had a bit of a rough day.'

'Haven't we all?' We moved away from the stairs, heading around the corner into the starboard corridor. My room was halfway along. 'Well, don't keep her up too late,' I said, as we came to my door.

'I won't.'

'And no gossiping,' I had half a mind to call out, as he moved towards the connecting corridor. The last thing anyone needed was for Miss Jenny Simpkins to learn the truth about her former mistress. It would be all over the ship come morning. But the secretary was a sensible fellow. He would respect the confidence he had been given.

I dawdled for a moment outside my own room, my attention flicking back to the matter of Mrs O'Neill's typewriter. It had not been an idle question I had thrown at Mr Hopkins. After all I had learned at supper this evening, I was beginning to wonder if the person who had killed Mrs O'Neill might not be Lady Jocelyn herself. Incest might easily be a motive for murder, if there was a chance of the matter getting out into the public domain. Could she have crept into Mrs O'Neill's stateroom, perhaps to examine the typewriter and discover if that was the source of the letters? But why now? She would have had months to scrutinize it. Maybe it was only recently that the business of the misplaced "W"s had come to light. Not everyone had Maurice's keen eye. Yes, Lady Jocelyn might well have slipped into the cabin to look and then perhaps been disturbed. She would have grabbed the nearest solid object, whatever it might have been, and silenced the woman forever.

Of course, the same might equally well apply to Sir Richard Villiers. He had just as much to lose. As the elder sibling, he was probably more to blame than the sister; and if the scandal was made public, it could be ruinous for both of them. Who would want to do business with a man like that, knowing such a thing about him?

There was one other candidate I had to consider. Much as I was loath to admit it, the vicar's wife could just as easily be the guilty party. Mrs Hamilton-Baynes had been in a highly nervous and excitable state all evening – though "nervous and excitable" described just about everyone in the Reynolds Suite at the moment – and she had always done whatever she could to protect the reputation of her cousin. Was it possible that she had spoken out of turn – accidentally divulged the secret to Mrs O'Neill – and then realised that the woman was making use of the information? That would give her credible motive.

My head was spinning with all these possibilities. I unlocked the door to my room and stepped inside, almost missing the envelope lying on the carpet in front of me. It was only the sudden crunch underfoot as I fumbled for the light switch that alerted me to its presence. I closed the door behind me and bent down to pick it up. Somebody must have slipped the envelope under the door while I had been out at supper. I blenched, not quite believing my eyes. Was Mrs O'Neill sending letters from beyond the grave? That was surely not possible.

I moved over to the bedside table. There was no name on the envelope and the flap was not glued down. It looked just like the one Miss Wellesley had found at the Alderley hotel. I placed the envelope, unopened, on the table and poured myself a small glass of whisky. To hell with that, I thought, and made it a large one. Only when I had drained the tumbler did I retrieve the envelope and open it up. The note inside was not typed; that was the first thing I noticed. It was hand-written, in capital letters. Doubtless that was to disguise the hand. The notepaper, too, was headed, with the words "RMS GALITIA" appearing at the top. It was the same paper I had seen on sale in the shop on D Deck. Miss Wellesley had bought some this morning, though I had no reason to believe the note came from her.

The words were short and to the point: "THE SURGERY ON E DECK. 11 O'CLOCK. MAKE SURE YOU COME ALONE."

There are times in life when it pays to take a risk. As a gambler, I have on occasion been known to take this maxim far beyond the limits of common sense. When it comes to self-preservation, however, I have always held myself to a much higher standard. A late night rendezvous with a complete stranger in the aftermath of two probable murders was far beyond any risk I was willing to entertain, without taking significant precautions. Firstly, I had no intention of going alone. My man Maurice could accompany me into the depths of the ship. Secondly, I would need to be armed. I couldn't find anything approaching a cosh in my cabin, but the valet had a penknife with a six inch blade, and that would serve well enough.

'Just hang back in the foyer,' I whispered to him, as we made our way downstairs. 'If there's any trouble, I'll shout.'

'Yes, Monsieur,' he said. I was pleasantly surprised that Maurice had agreed to join me, so late in the evening. The man could occasionally dig in his heels at the most inconvenient of times and, given his experiences on the Galitia's sister ship, he would have been well within his rights to barricade himself into his cabin for the duration. But when it came to matters of life and death, Maurice would always step up to the plate. He had been on the point of retiring for the night when I had knocked on his door. I had showed him the note and explained the situation. It was his idea to take the stairs. If someone was skulking in the shadows down on E Deck, preparing to do me a mischief, it made sense not to give them advance warning of our arrival.

Our journey into the bowels of the Galitia did not go completely unnoticed. A steward on D Deck caught sight of us as we made our way down the stairs. 'Just stretching our legs,' I called out to him cheerfully. The steward smiled in return. It was the fellow who ran the little shop. Hopefully, he would not dwell too much on the improbability of a stroll down to E Deck this late in the evening. Everyone else now would be in the Palladian Ballroom, for a bit of dancing, or – if they were sensible – preparing for bed.

Neither Maurice nor I had wanted to speculate on the likely author of the note. The fact that its sender had the same capital letter fetish as Mrs O'Neill did not ease my mind in any way. The choice of meeting place – Doctor Armstrong's surgery – could not help but bring to mind those two thuggish individuals I had seen at Harry's funeral.

The valet had done a little digging with regards to the good doctor. The man was well liked among the crew, but was fond of the odd flutter, when on shore leave. In other words, he had something of a gambling habit. This was news to me. Crew members were forbidden from betting while aboard ship and Armstrong had refused to take that wager with me on the first day out. Clearly, therefore, he was not a hopeless case. But if he was in financial difficulty, that might conceivably give someone leverage over him. Had he been leant on, to fake the results of the autopsy? Perhaps that was the reason for the note. Maybe he was having cold feet, now that a second person had died. I crossed my fingers, hoping that was the case. Doctor Armstrong, at least, was a reasonable man.

We tripped down the last sets of stairs and I held up my hand for Maurice to stop before we reached the bottom. I didn't want our note writer to get cold feet at the sight of two of us. The lights had been dimmed in the foyer, but I could see that the place was deserted. The gymnasium was closed but the door to the doctor's waiting room was ajar. There were a couple of other doors, leading off into various unknown parts of the ship, but they were also shut up and were in any case out of bounds to passengers. I stepped forward onto the carpet. A line of chairs were arranged either side of the staircase, which was directly opposite the elevator. I half fancied having a nice sit down. My nerves were beginning to get the better of me. Was this really such a good idea? It might not be Doctor Armstrong lurking down here, waiting to greet me; and what if my counterpart were armed with something more deadly than a penknife?

I grabbed a nearby armrest to steady myself and heard a sudden loud screech. A small grey shape launched itself at my feet. I felt a thud against my calf and let out a yelp as I saw a small animal careering across the foyer towards the open door.

'Monsieur?' Maurice stepped towards me in concern.

'It's all right,' I breathed. 'It was that blasted cat.' Matilda must have been dozing on one of the chairs. 'She's got out again.' I scowled. What was she doing all the way down here? There would be hell to pay when Lady Jocelyn found out. 'The damn thing should be put down,' I muttered. But the cat was the least of my concerns.

I took a moment to recover myself and then held up my

fingers. 'Three minutes,' I whispered to Maurice. He nodded and I moved towards the door of the surgery. If I didn't reappear in that time, he would come in after me. I pulled the penknife out from my pocket. It was a modern blade, with a spring and a catch. My hands were trembling slightly as I flicked it open. Why did I allow myself to get into these situations? I could be tucked up now in bed, nestling in the arms of Morpheus. But it was too late for second thoughts. I grabbed the handle of the door and pushed it open.

The reception area was shrouded in darkness. Whoever I was supposed to be meeting, they had a flare for the theatrical. 'Hello?' I called out, nervously. I fumbled for a light switch and found it to the right of the door. A single bulb flickered into life. That was better. No fiends lurking in the shadows in here. The room was exactly as I had left it earlier in the day. A bench, a desk, a few illustrative posters on the walls and a box of children's toys. But no sign of life. Not even the cat. I was sure I had seen her skip off in this direction.

There were two internal doors. One was to the consulting room, where I had spoken to Doctor Armstrong earlier on. The second was through to the surgery. This door was lying open, just a crack. Matilda must have got in through there. She at least knew where she was going. Cautiously, I pushed back the door and moved into the surgery. There was a light switch just to my left which I flicked on. Abruptly, the room was bathed in artificial light. It took a moment for my eyes to adjust. Nobody here, thank goodness. The surgery was dominated by a long, functional bed in the middle of the room. There were shelves full of bottles and surgical equipment. Quite a few books too. A screen stood off to one side and, behind it, a cupboard door.

Matilda had jumped up onto the bed. 'Oh no you don't,' I hissed, smacking the creature on the hide to get her off it. She snarled and jumped down from the top, then bolted across to the screen. At this point, she stopped. Her ears perked up, and then she disappeared out of sight, in the direction of the cupboard.

I moved forward, my heart beating rapidly, and pulled

back the screen. The cupboard door, a little way beyond, was now hanging open. The light from the surgery barely penetrated the gloom, but I thought I spotted a movement inside. There was somebody in there.

I lifted my penknife defensively.

Matilda had already seen them, whoever they were. She skipped forward, purring, and began to rub up against the leg of the unknown figure.

'Who…who's there?' I called out, still unable to make out much more than a shadow. Lady Jocelyn had said her cat rarely took to anyone. And yet here she was, making merry with a stranger.

The figure stepped forward and a shaft of light cut across his face. Abruptly, I recognised him: the youthful, rounded features and the eyes twinkling in amusement.

'Evening, old man.' He smiled mischievously.

'Good God!' I exclaimed.

It was Harry Latimer.

Chapter Fourteen

The great oriental magician Chung Ling Soo once cut a lady in half at the London Hippodrome. I was in the third row, on a cold January afternoon in 1905, and I could make no sense of what I had seen. The woman's legs were sticking out of one box on one side of the stage and her head was sticking out of the other. For some hours afterwards, I struggled to make sense of it. I knew it was a trick, but I could not fathom how it had been done. My cousin Alice suggested that the great Soo had substituted two dwarves, in place of the girl, but that did not explain anything. We had both seen the woman's head sticking out of one box, smiling and nodding at the audience, and her feet wiggling out the other. I had left the theatre, emerging into the dim drizzle of Charing Cross, in something of a daze. My grip on reality had taken a severe battering. In fact, such was my disorientation that I almost stepped directly in front of a hansom cab. Only the guiding hand of my cousin had prevented a serious accident.

Imagine my confusion, then, at the scene which confronted me now. Harry Latimer was standing in the doorway of the cupboard, alive and well, a sly grin spread across his chubby face. It was impossible. It could not be true. And yet there he was.

'Harry!' I choked, unable to accept the evidence of my own eyes.

'Surprised to see me?'

I found it difficult even to stutter out a response. Harry Latimer was dead. I knew he was dead. I had seen his body. A doctor had performed a post mortem. For heaven's sake, I had even attended his funeral. And yet here he was, standing in the shadows, smirking at me as if it were all some big joke. I cannot adequately describe the shock I felt at this moment; the mixture of confusion, disbelief, anger and joy. I have never been a particularly emotional woman, but Harry was the closest thing to a friend I had in the whole world. I had spent the past three days struggling to come to terms with his death, railing against the fates, determined to unmask the fiend who had poisoned him; and now here he was, fit and well, apparently none the worse for his ordeal.

Finally, I found a voice, and managed to croak out the obvious words. 'You're...you're alive.'

'Oh, just about, old man, just about.' He smiled again, his eyes flicking down to the penknife in my hand. 'I don't think you'll be needing that.' Calmly, he stepped forward and took the blade from my hands. The brief touch of his wrist was a shock against my skin.

'But...but...you're dead,' I mumbled. 'You can't...'

Harry closed up the knife and handed it back to me. 'Just breathe, old man,' he advised me. I was starting to feel light headed. 'Just breathe.' I did as I was instructed and took a lungful of air, while Harry glanced down at his feet. 'Hey little buddy.' Matilda had followed him out of the closet. 'You're a long way from home.' He reached down and picked her up, tickling her behind the ear. The cat purred happily.

I had no interest in Matilda. 'I...I can't believe it's really you,' I said, staring at the man in bewilderment. 'I can't believe you're alive.'

Harry placed the cat gently down on the floor. 'You don't believe in ghosts, do you?'

'No, of course not.'

Matilda had come to rest a short distance from my leg and was regarding me suspiciously.

'Well, then I guess I must be alive.'

The cat hissed, remembering the earlier blow to her rump, and sprinted for the door.

'But...but...' I sucked in another heavy breath. Everything I had thought – every single thing I had come to believe over the last two or three days – was completely and utterly mistaken.

'You know me, old man.' He chuckled. 'When the grim reaper comes knocking, I make sure I'm on vacation...' He was enjoying this, that was the really galling thing. Harry was enjoying my discomfort. For the first time, my hackles began to rise.

'But how can you...?'

A loud clunk sounded from outside, before I could finish the question. Harry froze, his eyes suddenly wide and alert. 'You did come alone, didn't you?'

'Ah. Not exactly. I...'

A voice was calling to me from the outer room. 'Monsieur?' It was my man Maurice. The three minutes were up.

Harry stepped back towards the screen at some speed. It was his turn to be on the back foot.

'Don't worry,' I said. 'It's just my valet.'

'I told you not to bring anyone.'

'I was hardly going to take any notice of that.' I snorted. 'An anonymous bit of paper. I'm not a complete fool. You might have been a murderer.'

'Get rid of him,' Harry hissed, from behind the screen. The seriousness of his tone jolted me back to my senses.

'All right. Just give me a minute.' I turned to the door and stepped back out into the waiting room. Maurice was standing at the far end of the room. I raised a hand to him, to reassure him all was well; then I closed the door behind me and moved across.

The valet was watching me carefully. 'Monsieur? Are you all right?' His granite face was unreadable, as it always was, but there was a trace of concern in his voice. 'I saw the cat running from the room.'

I laughed abruptly, a sudden release of tension. 'Believe me, Morris, that animal is the least of my worries.'

'I heard voices, Monsieur. You were speaking to someone? The person who wrote the note?'

'Yes. I...look, I'll explain later.' It's all...it's all a bit confusing.' I glanced back at the door. 'I don't really understand it myself. But I'm not in any danger. I think...I think it might be best if you pop off to bed and leave me to deal with this.'

'Monsieur? Are you certain?'

'Yes, I'm sure. I've had a bit of a shock, that's all. But look, everything is fine. Well, not exactly fine but...I'll explain later.'

The valet was dubious. 'If you insist, Monsieur. You are sure there is nothing I can do to help?'

'No, nothing. Unless you fancy grabbing Matilda and returning her to the Reynolds Suite?'

That thought provoked the barest flicker of an eyebrow. 'No, Monsieur,' he responded firmly. It had not been a serious suggestion. The cat was loitering behind him, out in the foyer. But it was hardly Maurice's responsibility to retrieve her. And it would scarcely do, sitting at his mother's bedside in a few days time, to have a dirty great claw mark across his face.

'Very well. But you might at least let them know that she's down here.'

'Yes, Monsieur.'

The cat had settled once again on one of the comfy chairs on the near side of the staircase. 'Oh, maybe wait ten minutes, though.' I scratched an earhole. 'Actually, better make it twenty. I might be down here for a while yet.' Far better if my conversation with Harry Latimer was not interrupted. 'I don't think she's going anywhere.'

'Very good, Monsieur.'

'Right. Well, I'll speak to you in the morning.'

'Yes, Monsieur.' The valet peered past me one last time and then dipped his head. 'Goodnight, Monsieur.'

'Goodnight, Morris.' And with that he headed for the stairs.

I lingered for a moment in the doorway, watching him disappear. My heartbeat was beginning to slow but my head was still in a whirl. It was baffling, utterly baffling. Everything I had believed had been turned on its head. Even Chung Ling Soo would have struggled to make sense of it. How could Harry Latimer be alive? It wasn't just that I had seen him lying dead in his bed; I had seen his body being committed to the deep. If ever a man had passed beyond the veil, it was Harry Latimer; and yet there he had been, standing in front of that screen, chuckling away, as if he had been caught out in some schoolboy prank. Any joy I might have felt at his miraculous survival was being slowly subsumed by anger. Harry was playing a devilish game and I for one was not remotely amused.

I closed up the waiting room door, flicking the lock carefully behind me, and then returned to the operating theatre. I secured the intervening door and stepped over to the bed. Harry was still hovering cautiously behind the screen.

'It's all right,' I said. 'He's gone.'

The American moved back into view. 'You didn't tell him anything, did you?'

'No, of course not. What on earth could I tell him? I don't *know* anything, Harry.' The fog was gradually clearing from my mind and a little voice inside my head was pushing for answers. 'So what is this all about?' I demanded. 'Why on earth would you fake your own death? And how the devil did you do it? You were stone cold dead.'

'You saw what you wanted to see, old man.'

'I didn't imagine you lying there on the bed. You were dead, Harry. No pulse, no respiration. Nothing.'

'That's what you were supposed to think. But it was all just smoke and mirrors.'

'It was an illusion?'

'A trick of the wrist, that's all.'

'It was a little more than that, Harry. And why the devil would you go to all that trouble?'

'Believe me, I had my reasons.' Harry grabbed a chair and pulled it across to the surgical table. 'Hey, do you want a shot of brandy?' He jerked his thumb back towards the cupboard. 'I've got a bottle stashed away. You look like you could use a drink.' He disappeared inside the closet and returned with the bottle and two glasses. He set them down on the bed and poured out two fingers. I pulled up another chair and took the glass gratefully.

'So what did you do?' I asked him bluntly, knocking back the brandy in one. Harry must have been in pretty deep waters, to go to these lengths. 'It must have been something really bad.'

Harry drained his glass. 'You could say that.'

'You were in trouble with someone?'

'Yeah. Let's just say I trod on a few toes, back in New

189

York.'

That did not surprise me. 'Who was it? The mafia?' An obvious guess.

Harry confirmed that with a nod. 'They don't like people muscling in on their territory.'

'Lord.' I returned my glass to the table top and Harry poured out a second shot. 'And those gorillas who turned up at your funeral?'

'They were the hired muscle.'

'They followed you here? Onboard the Galitia?'

Harry nodded sourly. 'They wanted to fit me up with a concrete overcoat. I thought I'd save them the trouble.'

'But what did you do to upset them? It can't have been bootlegging, surely?' Almost everyone in New York was involved in the liquor trade.

'It was a little more serious than that. Hey, I don't suppose you've got a cigarette?'

'Er...yes.' I reached into my jacket and pulled out my case. 'So what was it then?' Harry took a Piccadilly and I offered him my lighter. 'Not gunrunning? Again?' That had been the caper Harry had been involved in the last time we had met. I pulled out a cigarette for myself and pocketed the case. 'Selling guns to communists. I'd have thought you'd have learnt your lesson last time.' I lit the cigarette and took a lungful of tobacco.

'Not guns,' Harry said quietly. 'Something a little more...explosive.'

I frowned, exhaling a cloud of smoke. Harry could be maddeningly oblique at times. I took another puff of the cigarette. 'Explosives?' My jaw fell open, as I suddenly caught the inference. 'Oh God, Harry. You didn't?' The dynamite, for the bombing campaign in New York. 'Those anti-Mussolini fanatics. Don't tell me you supplied *them* with explosives?'

Harry shrugged; a small boy caught scrumping apples. 'I may have given them a little help. Don't look at me like that, old man.' He took a drag of his cigarette and then spread out his hands. 'You know me, I'm not political. I'm just a salesman. An ordinary guy looking to make an honest buck. Or a not so

190

honest buck. If someone needs a piece of merchandise and I can supply it, why wouldn't I help them? Anything they want. Moonshine, medicine. Fluffy toys for the kids.'

'But *dynamite*?' I regarded the man in horror. 'Good God, Harry. You sold sticks of dynamite to the anti-fascist brigade?'

Harry rose up from his seat and moved across to one of the shelves, to find an ashtray. 'I guess so.' He returned to his chair with a small metal dish and placed it on the bed between us. He could see the disapproval on my face. 'Look, I happen to know one or two guys in the construction industry. It's no big deal. Easy enough for a few sticks to go missing. It happens all the time.'

'But this is the dynamite that was used in the parcel bombs? The ones that have been terrorising New York since Christmas?' I made no attempt to disguise my disgust. Harry had been involved in some pretty dubious activities over the years, but this took the proverbial biscuit.

'Don't get upset, old man.' Harry's face was the picture of wounded innocence, as he tapped out the end of his cigarette. 'I was just providing a service. I had no idea what they wanted it for. They might have been planning to rob a bank, for all I knew.'

I scoffed at that. 'Why would the anti-Mussolini league want to rob a bank?'

'Every organisation needs capital.'

That was too much. 'But people *died* Harry. Innocent people. Those poor postal workers. People who have nothing to do with Mussolini.'

'Yeah, that was too bad,' he admitted, scratching his left cheek. 'But it was hardly my fault. Like I say, I'm just the guy in the middle. If I sell you a gun and you kill someone, does that make me a murderer?'

'It makes you an accessory, if you had some idea of what I might be planning. Good God, Harry. You've done some pretty despicable things in your time, but this…'

Harry put down his cigarette. 'Okay, look, in hindsight, it probably wasn't the greatest idea I've ever had. Sure, it was lucrative, but there were too many complications.'

'You mean the whole thing blew up in your face?' It was my turn to smile. By the sounds of it, it served him right. 'Harry, how could you be so stupid?'

'Oh, I took precautions, old man. It was all done at arm's length. No names, no come back. None of these people had any idea who I was, even what I looked like.'

'All done under cover of darkness, down by the docks?' I had seen enough American films to understand the *modus operandi*.

Harry smiled quietly, and took another drag of his cigarette. 'Something like that.'

'And thanks to you, innocent people have died.'

'But hey, the good news is, the people responsible are under lock and key. They'll pay for their crimes, old man. Justice and the American way will prevail.' His eyes twinkled mischievously. 'I don't know what you're complaining about.'

'You're not worried they might tell the police where they got their dynamite? Skipping the country won't save you if your name is read out in court.'

'That's not going to happen. Those schmucks don't know the first thing about me.' Harry was dismissive. 'Oh, sure, the cops will put the thumbscrews on them, but they can't tell them what they don't know. And I was real careful not to let them see anything.'

'So the police are clueless, but the mob realised that you were behind it?'

'Yeah. They have better lines of communication than the NYPD.'

'You mean, they recognised your handiwork when they saw it.'

'Uh-huh.' Harry stubbed out the end of his cigarette. 'They're all over the construction sites. I should have taken that into account. They'd already given me a friendly warning, about the bootlegging. And when I say friendly, I mean *unfriendly*, But this was something a little more serious. So far as they were concerned, this was a direct attack on them. You know, some people can be so sensitive.'

'You can hardly blame them, Harry. Italian Americans. Lord, what were you thinking?'

'I was hoping I could get out of town before any of them were any the wiser. I figured I had a week or two before they followed the chain back to me.'

'And so you booked a ticket on the Galitia?'

'It was the quickest ride out of here. It always pays to quit while you're ahead. I've made a fair bit of dough, these past few months. But I thought I had a little time in hand.'

'They caught up with you sooner than you expected?'

'Yeah, that was a real blow. I heard a few whispers, the last day or two in New York. And when the bomb hit the restaurant that evening – or didn't hit it – I was sure it had to be meant for me.'

'Except it wasn't,' I pointed out. 'It was all a hoax.'

'Yeah, I should have realised that straight out. It's not the way these guys operate.'

'Blowing up a restaurant full of people, to kill one man? No, I suppose not.' An Italian restaurant, to boot. Harry had some nerve.

'But even so, I was pretty spooked, I can tell you.'

I took a last puff of my cigarette and stubbed out the end. 'And yet while all this was going on, you still found the time to serenade Mrs O'Neill?' That was the part I couldn't quite understand. Harry had spent most of his last day in New York courting a rich widow, engineering a meeting with her in the morning and conspiring to steal her pearl necklace. 'Why would you bother doing that, if you were about to skip the country?'

Harry shrugged, sitting back in his chair. 'I had a day in hand, before the Galitia set sail. It was just a little side project. I needed something to take my mind off things. You know me, old man. I'm not the kind of guy to sit in a hotel room, waiting for something bad to happen. And I figured once I was onboard the Galitia, everything would be plain sailing. Plenty of time for a little fun. I took a quick look at the passenger list a day or two before and I recognised the name. Susan O'Neill, widow of the late, great Ulysses O'Neill, one of the richest men in the county. You'll think me sentimental, but I always like to keep a fatherly eye out for vulnerable widows travelling on their own. There are so many sharks about. Beside, I needed something to occupy myself with on the long trip across the Atlantic.' He chuckled again. 'And when I heard about those pearls….'

'You thought that might be a nice little bonus on the way out?'

'That's about the size of it, old man. Doesn't do to let the grass grow. But to be honest, my heart wasn't really in it. Oh sure, I set the whole thing up, engineered the meeting, took her out for dinner – the usual routine – but when it came to it…'

'You couldn't concentrate. You were too concerned about your own damned neck.'

'Well, I have always been rather attached to it. And a con like that, you need to be properly focused. This time, there were too many distractions…'

'What, like Miss Wellesley?' I laughed.

'Not that kind of distraction. The morning we were due to leave, I got word that they were coming for me. Pierre, the guy who did the pearls, he warned me ahead of time. Happily, I'd already taken a few precautions. For one thing, I'd doctored my passport, and booked the passage under a different name, so it didn't flag up with any of the usual suspects.'

'G Harrington Latimer. Yes, I remember. Not exactly a world class alias.'

'It was never intended to be. If they looked hard enough they were always going to find me.'

'And put someone onboard to finish you off?'

'That's it. Of course, if it had just been the one guy, I could probably have dealt with him, but if it was more than one…well, let's just say, I needed a contingency plan.'

'A contingency. You mean, faking your own death, just to put them off the scent?' I boggled. 'Isn't that a bit over the top, even for you?

'You don't know these guys, Hilary. Jeez, do they bear a grudge. And I had one or two friends onboard who were happy to help out.'

'Like Doctor Armstrong?' That was an obvious assumption, given that we were sitting in his surgery. 'He agreed to help you?'

'Him and one other guy, Al. He was the one who smuggled the pearls onboard. He owes me a couple of favours. And the doc is a good friend. I met him on a trip over to Europe a few years back. We would go for a drink from time to time, whenever he was in town.'

'But why would he help you on something like this? It's one thing to socialise, it's quite another to help a man fake his own death.'

'Oh, he had his reasons. The guy has this one big weakness. He likes to gamble.'

'Yes, so I've heard.'

'And he's even worse at cards than you are.'

My eyes narrowed. 'So what did you do? Set up a game and bleed him dry? Or were you blackmailing him?'

Harry pretended to be offended. 'It was nothing like that, old man. What do you take me for? He's a friend. I wouldn't do anything to hurt him. But the last time we met up, he was in a bad way. I was back in town after a run down from Canada. A few crates of whiskey in tow. Anyway, he'd lost a lot of money at the card table, between trips, and taken out a loan to cover some of the debts. And not from a bank, if you follow my meaning. The people he owed the money to, well, they wanted paying back real soon. Or else. So I helped him out.'

'Helped him? I regarded Harry dubiously. 'You mean, you paid off his debts?'

'Of course, old man. You know me. I'm a sucker for a sob story.'

'Right.'

'I was pretty flush after that last run, so I lent him the money, but on better terms. Sure, he'd have to pay it back, but in his own time. And meanwhile, if there was any little job I needed him for, he'd be on hand to help me out.' Harry grinned. 'A doctor on the payroll is always useful. Getting hold of medicines. Procuring a few chemicals without arousing suspicion.'

195

I shook my head. 'Oh, Harry…'

'It's handy to have a guy like that in your pocket.'

'And you knew in advance that he'd be aboard the Galitia on this trip?'

'Sure I did. Why do you think I booked it? He stopped by to say hi, when the ship arrived from Southampton just after Christmas. We had a couple of drinks, but it was only in the last few days that I began to think it might be a good idea for me to disappear. As I said, it was a contingency plan.'

'But then you realised someone had been planted onboard?'

'At first, I thought I'd got away with it. It wasn't until that evening that I heard the truth. Two of their goons were onboard and looking for trouble.'

'That was the note you received in the ballroom, during the dance?'

'You noticed that, huh? Yeah, that was the doc. I'd asked him to check the passenger lists, to see if there were any last minute additions. If it had just been the one guy, I could have dealt with him. Arranged a little accident.'

'You'd happily have killed the fellow?'

'It would have been him or me, old man. What else was I going to do?' In a straight fight between a mafia hit man and Harry Latimer, my money would be on Harry. 'Someone falling overboard, it happens all the time. No-one would be suspicious. But two of them.' He sucked in his cheeks. 'That's never good odds. You saw what they were like. Gorilla doesn't cover it. There was a pretty good chance they'd be able to get the drop on me. And I couldn't allow that. You'll think me sentimental, old man, but I'm not in any hurry to meet my maker.'

'So you decided discretion was the better part of valour?'

'I decided to remove myself from the board. It wasn't a last minute decision. Like I said, I'd been mulling over the idea for a few days. If I could convince these schmucks that I was dead, then all my problems would be over. And then, what do you know, I bumped into you, and found out you'd done exactly the same thing, back in England, in 1929.' He laughed.

196

'I don't believe in fate, but that was a hell of a coincidence. You know, I always figured there was something funny about that death of yours. It was all too neat. All too stage managed. I had a suspicion it might be a put up job. But it was still a shock, to see you like that, out of the blue, the night before we departed.'

'You didn't look surprised.'

'Poker face, old man. Poker face. Never let on what you're thinking.' He chuckled. 'To tell you the truth, I'd been having second thoughts about the whole thing. It wasn't without an element of risk. But seeing you there, in perfect health, it made me think, what the hell, maybe it's not such a crazy idea.'

'But how exactly did you do it?' He had still not explained the mechanics of the affair. 'This scheme of yours, the death. How did you pull it off? When I saw you lying there...'

'It was all down to the doc. He's not just a pretty face, you know.'

'Hardly that. What was it, though? Some kind of drug?'

'More of a toxin than a drug. A little concoction of his that put me to sleep.'

I scoffed. 'What sort of toxin could put you into that state? It wasn't even a coma. You were stone cold dead, Harry. There was no temperature, no pulse, no respiration.'

'That's not strictly true. There was a pulse, old man, but you'd have had a hard job finding it. The doc explained it all to me. You know he studied toxicology at some college in London?'

'Yes, I remember him saying.'

'He knows all about that stuff. Different types of poison. The dosages. What they do to the body. There's this one particular one he told me about. It's scraped off the back of a toad.'

'A *toad*?'

'Yeah, a little fellow. It's used in religious ceremonies in the Caribbean.' There was a picture of a toad, I recalled suddenly, on a poster out in the waiting room. 'It slows down your heartbeat and gives the impression that you're dead. It's fatal in large doses and it's a bit of an hallucinogenic. But if you get the dosage right, the heartbeat slows and you hardly need to breathe at all. At least for a while.'

'And that's what Doctor Armstrong provided. A toxin?' I blinked. 'From a toad?'

'That's it. Oh, don't get me wrong, it wouldn't fool a doctor. But your average passer by wouldn't be able to tell the difference.'

'Like me, you mean?'

'Don't beat yourself up, old man. It would have fooled most people. They use the drug in some places to bring people back from the dead. It's a trick, of course, but a good one. I thought I could adapt it for myself, as a last resort.'

I sat back in my chair. This affair was becoming ever more bizarre. 'Well, rather you than me. It sounds lethal.' I wasn't sure I would be willing to risk taking a drug like that, even if half the hounds of hell were after me.

'It was a calculated risk, old man. And the doc said it was safe enough. Well, reasonably safe. Like I say, he knows his stuff. He'd tried it himself, back at medical school. A student prank. He was researching poisons at the time and figured he might as well have a go at it.'

'Lord.' I shook my head. The things that students get up to.

'Anyway, he reckoned it would be safe enough. The natives use it all the time. And it was either that or going over the side. This way, when the goons came calling, they'd find mother nature had beaten them to it.'

I leaned forward and grabbed the brandy from the table. 'I think I need another,' I said. Harry waved away the offer of a refill. 'And Doctor Armstrong just happened to have a supply of this drug onboard ship?'

Harry gestured to the many bottles on the shelves. 'He's got a drop of just about everything in here.'

'But how did you administer it?'

'He provided me with a small phial. I just mixed it in with a glass of water.'

'From that jug on the bedside table?' I sipped my

brandy.

'That's right. But the doc didn't want to be around when I did it. We'd had a bit of a talk, that evening, after supper.' When Harry had left the dance floor. Miss Wellesley had said he had been gone for a good twenty minutes. 'We agreed to go ahead with the thing, and he said he'd prepare the phial for me and stash it in one of the cisterns in the men's bathroom, just opposite. That way, no one would see him going anywhere near my cabin. Anyway, I went to bed and then sneaked out in the early hours to pick it up.' That would have been at about six am, according to the steward. 'Then I waited until I heard them knocking on the doors later on, to change the bedsheets. That must have been about nine. I drank the potion and that was that.'

'Did it hurt?' I asked, finishing off the brandy.

'No. I was out like a light. I don't remember anything about it. The plan was for the steward to find me, lying there. He'd knock on the door and open it up, and then see the body.'

'He was in on it, was he?'

'No, no, it would just be the regular cabin steward. He'd raise the alarm, and the doc would be along to pronounce me dead.'

'But as it transpired, it was Mrs O'Neill who found you, not the steward.'

'Yeah, that was unexpected. But it didn't matter. Armstrong was on the scene straight away, just as we'd planned. He was able to clean everything up.' Including, presumably, washing the glass tumbler and returning it to the sink. He had lied outright to me about that. 'He examined me, with the head steward watching, and then got me moved downstairs for the autopsy as quick as he could.'

'You mean, before the drug wore off.'

'Yeah.'

'But he couldn't have carried you all the way down here on his own. Didn't anyone notice anything amiss, when they moved the body?'

'No. He had a little help from this other guy, Albert Staines.'

'The man who helped you with the pearls?'

'That's right. He's one of the crew. I've known him for a while. He owed me a favour and he was happy to help out, no questions asked.' That was how Harry operated, of course. Favours given and returned, with the odd bit of cash to oil the wheels. 'A bit of dough on top, and a drop of Canadian whiskey.' It seemed to work well for him, most of the time.

'So he and Armstrong brought you down here and then the doctor pretended to perform a post mortem?'

'Sure. And it all went like clockwork. I woke up in the early afternoon, with one hell of a headache. And Al had prepared a room for me in the closet back there.' He jerked his thumb at the cupboard behind the screen. 'He makes sure I'm comfortable. There's a wash room just over there, when no-one's about. And there's plenty of food. I've slept in worse places.'

'That I can believe. But what about the body? They must have still needed a corpse, to put on display. Surely you couldn't just disappear completely?'

'No, not entirely. But nobody keeps tabs on the deceased. They have a special place set aside for passengers who've croaked – a cold store – and the doc is in charge of the key. And that, you'll be happy to know, was where the late G Harrington Latimer came to rest. At least, temporarily.'

'But what about the funeral. How on earth...?'

'Well now...' Harry smirked. 'The doc is a man of many talents. You know, every trip out, he gives a lecture to some of the passengers, out of the kindness of his heart.'

I frowned, not quite following. 'On human anatomy. Yes, I know. My man was there the other day. But I don't see...'

'He has a special demonstration model, a mannequin he uses to illustrate the talks. Usually, it hangs on the hook out there in the waiting room. It's one of those anatomical models, you know the sort, cut open so that you can see the insides.' Maurice had mentioned to me that they used models to illustrate their talks. 'He drags it out for each lecture, so that he can explain exactly what he's talking about.' Harry chuckled. 'I guess he's going to have to get himself a new one.'

'You wrapped up a mannequin and got them to bury that instead of you?'

'Neat, huh? We had to add a bit of ballast, to get the right weight distribution, But yeah, essentially, that was it. We wrapped up the dummy, Al and I, and we were ready to go.'

'And nobody noticed anything odd about that either? Nobody asked any awkward questions?'

'Why would they? Nobody touched the body except Al and the doc. The other guys just helped to carry the litter. And if anyone asked about the mannequin, he could just tell them it was on its last legs and had to be put into storage.'

'So the whole funeral, the body, the sea burial, it was a complete sham?'

'An important sham. It convinced those goons that I really was swimming with the fishes. And it meant there would be no awkward questions when we got to Southampton.'

'It was Doctor Armstrong who convinced the captain to allow a sea burial,' I recalled.

Harry laughed. 'Now you understand.'

'But dear God, Harry don't you realise what you put us through? What you put *me* through?'

'Hilary! I didn't know you cared.'

'I don't,' I snapped. 'I just didn't want to have to deal with all the paperwork.'

'Hey, don't be short with me, old man. I only did to you what you did to me.'

He had a point there, I supposed. 'Yes, but at least I turned up to your bloody funeral. You only sent a bunch of flowers.' He looked away. 'You did *send* a wreathe to my funeral?'

'Of course I did, old man. Well, I intended to, but things ran away with themselves. And besides, you weren't even dead.'

'No. No, I wasn't. And neither were you.' I shook my head angrily. I had never met such an insensitive soul. 'So what's to stop me going outside now and announcing to the whole world that Harry Latimer is alive and well?'

The smile vanished. 'I don't think that would be a good idea.'

'People are dead because of you, Harry.'

'Hey, I had nothing to do with what happened to Mrs O'Neill.'

'I'm not talking about Mrs O'Neill. I'm talking about those postal workers.'

'Yeah, that was too bad. But sneaking on me won't bring anyone back now, will it?'

I let out a sigh. 'I'm not going to "sneak" on you Harry. You're the biggest scoundrel I've ever met, but I...' I closed my eyes. 'I wouldn't want to see you disappearing over the side of the ship. Not while I'm onboard, anyway.'

He grinned. 'I knew I could rely on you, Hilary.'

A sudden, awkward thought occurred to me. 'But what the devil am I supposed to tell London? They asked me to keep an eye on you. They'll have heard about the funeral. The police in New York will have passed on the information, and they're going to want to talk to me, when I get to Southampton, to find out exactly what happened. What on earth am I going to tell them?'

'Tell them I'm dead. What harm can it do?'

'That's all very well, Harry. But what happens when you turn up in a year or two, alive and well? I know you. You're not the type to keep a low profile for long.'

Harry was unperturbed. 'Hey, just do what I do, old man. Deny everything. You thought I was dead. That's true enough, isn't it? You saw the body being laid to rest. What else were you supposed to think?'

'You don't leave me a lot of choice, do you?'

'Hey, look, I just need a bit of breathing space, away from America. These things always blow over.'

'And you're sure these mafia fellows are convinced you're dead?'

'I'm sure. The doc was a bit spooked this afternoon when one of them called on him, but I figure the guy was just sizing him up, making sure he was on the level. When you turned up five minutes later, he was properly spooked. He thought you must have guessed the truth.'

'I was becoming suspicious, after what happened to Mrs O'Neill. But I would never had imagined he could be involved in anything like this. Poisonous toads, for goodness sake. No, I thought he must have been in league with those two men. I thought they might have leaned on him to help cover things up, after they'd bumped you off.'

'Not a bad theory.'

'But nowhere near the truth' I stared down at the brandy bottle. 'I don't seem to be getting any better at this sort of thing.'

'You found me.'

'You sent me a note. Or one of your accomplices did.'

'That was the doc. I got him to act as postman.'

'And I certainly wouldn't have been creeping about on E Deck at this time in the evening if you hadn't done.' I pulled out my pocket watch. It was just gone eleven thirty.

A clunk echoed from somewhere out on deck. It sounded like the elevator, across the way. Harry rose up from his seat in alarm.

'It's all right,' I reassured him. 'It'll just be someone from the Reynolds Suite coming down to fetch the cat. I told my man to let them know she was here. Don't worry, I've locked both the doors. They won't look in here.'

Harry resumed his seat.

'So why did you bring me down here anyway? Why confess the whole sordid truth, after all this time? It's not like you to own up to anything, Harry. It can't just be because Doctor Armstrong was spooked.'

'Oh, it was partly that. You telling Griffith about that glass on the bedside table didn't help either. The doc was worried if you kept fishing, you might draw the wrong kind of attention. If anyone finds out he's faked a death certificate, he won't just be struck off the medical register, he'll end up in jail. And I still need him to get me off the ship when we get to Southampton. But you're right, I had another reason for wanting to talk to you.'

'You wanted to confess your sins and apologise to me

for all the grief you've caused.'

'Well, of course, old man. That goes without saying. But no, it's this business with Mrs O'Neill.'

'You saw her, did you, when…when they brought her down here?'

'They laid her out on the table here.' He patted the top gently. 'She's in the cold store now. But yeah, I had a quick look. Afterwards, when the place was empty. It wasn't pleasant. She was still wearing those pearls of hers, when they wheeled the body in.'

'I'm surprised you didn't whip them.'

Harry pretended to be hurt. 'I do have some scruples, old man. Respect for the dead and all that. Besides, they'd have been missed.'

'And you didn't have the reproductions to hand, to swap them with.'

'No, they were back in my cabin.'

'Actually, Mr Griffith confiscated them. I think he guessed what you'd been up to.'

'Smart guy. But sadly, it was too late for that. And the last thing I wanted was to draw any attention to this place.'

'And Mrs O'Neill? How much do you know about all that?'

'As much as you do, old man. A little less, probably. I didn't know about the pen letters until the doc mentioned them to me. I wish you'd told me about that.'

'I barely knew myself, the first day out. Only the note your Miss Wellesley showed me.' I grimaced, remembering how upset the young woman had been to learn of Harry's death. 'What would she think if she could see you here now?'

'Kinder not to tell her. One thing I don't understand, though. Why would she confide in you, rather than me?'

'She obviously thought I had a more sympathetic ear. Your charms are not universal, Harry.' I gazed down at the empty glasses on the bed. 'No, in point of fact, it was because I already knew something about it. About the hoax, I mean. Miss Wellesley gave me an account of their conversation with the police, the night of the bomb. She knew I would understand.'

'I figured it was something like that. But these letters, all these crazy notes that have been going around, it got me thinking...'

'How you'd misjudged Mrs O'Neill? How she wasn't the light touch you thought she was?'

'That's just it,' Harry said. 'I reckon I'm a pretty shrewd judge of character. In my line of work, you have to be. Usually, I can size someone up in a couple of minutes. And this just doesn't sit right with me. Mrs O'Neill wasn't the brooding type. She wasn't one to sit on her feelings. It was all on the surface. Or most of it.'

'Don't be so sure. She had you sussed out, Harry. She knew you were a bounder. She just didn't care.'

'Everyone loves a scoundrel.' Harry grinned. 'She thought I was after her money. She teased me about it, thought I was looking to marry into it. She had no idea I was after the necklace.'

'So she wasn't that bright after all.'

'Well, that's what I mean. I don't think she was capable of writing these sorts of letters.'

'The evidence is pretty damning. It was her typewriter that was used.'

'I know, I know. But from what I hear, everybody had access to that.'

'Yes, back at her house. But...'

'And that's what got me thinking. It was something I saw, the morning we boarded the ship. I didn't think anything of it at the time. I didn't know about the letters then. That's why I thought I ought to talk to you, old man. You see, I'm pretty sure Mrs O'Neill wasn't responsible for any of it.'

'If not her, then who?'

'You'll think I'm crazy, but I think it may have been the Reverend Hamilton-Baynes.'

'The vicar?' I laughed. 'But he wouldn't....'

'Oh, I can't prove it. But the thing is, I saw him. That morning, after the hoax. We were all staying at the Waldorf Astoria. I couldn't sleep that night, so I came down early to the bar for a coffee. It must have been half past five, six o'clock in

205

the morning. And I saw him out in the foyer, leaving the hotel.'

'Leaving? At half past five in the morning? That is odd,' I admitted. 'Did he see you?'

'I don't think so. I was over at the bar. He was dressed kind of funny, though. Not wearing the dog collar, or even a coat. I mean, Jesus, at this time of year. '

'Perhaps he was going out for a morning run,' I suggested.

'In New York? Are you serious?'

'Some people do, I understand. He is the athletic sort. I wouldn't put it past him.'

Harry shrugged. 'I suppose it's possible. But anyway, forty, forty-five minutes later, I was still at the bar, and he comes back in, looking pretty beat up. Face all red, what you could see of it with that great beard of his. And it occurred to me: the Alderley Hotel – where you and Mrs O'Neill were staying – it's only a few blocks north of the Waldorf. What if he slipped out of the hotel, delivered that note Cynthia found and then came straight back?'

I considered the idea. 'It's not impossible. But it would have have been a hell of a risk. Anyone might have seen him, if he was creeping about the Alderley at that hour.'

'He might not have gone up to the room himself. He could have just slipped the bellboy a dollar or two.'

'And risk being identified?' That seemed unlikely to me.

'But he had the opportunity, that's what I'm saying. And if he did write that note, then he must have been behind the bomb too. The two things were connected, weren't they?'

'Yes. "NEXT TIME IT WILL NOT BE A HOAX". That's what the note said.'

'Well, exactly. And if the padre was targeting Mrs O'Neill before we even set sail, then I figure he might just as easily have bumped her off a day or two later.'

The vicar's raised posterior was not a sight I expected to see at any time of day, less still at a quarter to midnight. The

206

Reverend Hamilton-Baynes was on all fours, shuffling across the carpeted floor at the base of the central staircase. I hesitated at the sight of the strange, bearded man as he moved, an arm extended, towards the beechwood chair on the nearside of the stairs. 'Here puss, puss!' he cooed, oblivious to his own absurdity. 'Here puss, puss!' I regarded him for a moment in the half light, his beard visible from the side, as he waggled his fingers unselfconsciously in front of him, unaware that he was being observed from the door of the doctor's waiting room.

I slid a hand down into my trouser pocket to make sure Maurice's penknife was still accessible. I was not wholly convinced by Harry's theory – the business of the typewriter was an obvious sticking point – but there was no point taking any chances.

I coughed politely to alert the vicar to my presence. 'You've found her then?' I called out across the foyer. It was just my luck that the older man had been sent down to retrieve the cat.

Hamilton-Baynes looked round, unperturbed at the sudden noise. His face lit up at the sight of me, his large white teeth a veritable lighthouse beaming out of that heavy beard. 'Never trust a man who smiles that much,' Harry had said, which was rich, coming from him; but at the moment, I could see his point. The American, of course, was now safely tucked away in his cupboard, while I was out here a couple of yards away from a potential source of danger.

'Yes, at last. You've led us a merry dance haven't you?' The reverend chuckled. Matilda was hiding under the chair. Hamilton-Baynes reached a hand underneath the seat, but the cat hissed and spat at him, before retreating to the next chair along. 'Dear me. I think this may be a little tricky.' His teeth flashed again. 'Cats. Not really my field. Beautiful animal, though. A gorgeous coat, don't you think?' He pulled back his hand. 'I don't suppose you're any good with them?'

'No, I'm afraid not. That little monster would gouge my eyes out if she had half a chance.'

The vicar rose to his feet, and dusted down his kneecaps. 'She is rather a handful,' he agreed, cheerfully. He was quite a tall fellow, Hamilton-Baynes, lean and well-balanced. All that exercise had put him in good stead. He was not someone I would want to face in a boxing ring. 'Jocelyn didn't want the stewards handling her, so of course I volunteered to help out. Spot of cat and mouse before bedtime. Super fun. Although I suspect Mr Hopkins doesn't agree. He was running all over B Deck looking for her, until your man came and told us she was down here.'

'You came down together, did you?'

'Yes. Ernest is in the gymnasium.' The vicar gestured to the opposite side of the stairs. 'He thought she might have slipped in there. We didn't see her under the chair here. Naughty puss! I suppose I ought to go and tell him.' He glanced down at the carpet and then across at me. 'And what brings you here at this time in the evening?' He smiled. 'I'd have thought you'd be in bed at this hour.' There was no edge to the question, but in light of what Harry had told me I could not help but interpret it in a sinister manner.

'Er…just having a word with Doctor Armstrong,' I lied. 'He's retired for the night now, though.'

'As will we all soon enough, God willing. We do need our beauty sleep.'

'No dancing this evening?'

'Sadly not.' It was the last night of the voyage and, despite the death of Mrs O'Neill, a dance had been organised at the Palladian on A Deck. 'We popped up for a coffee after supper, but it wouldn't have been right to join in. Not on a day like this.'

'No, of course not,' I agreed. Try as I might, I could detect nothing sinister in the man's demeanour. He was as lively and cheerful as ever. I did not doubt that Harry had seen him leaving the hotel that morning, but it was difficult to accept that this beaming vicar could possibly be a cold-blooded murderer. Perhaps he had just been out for a morning run after all. Nevertheless, I did not wish to tarry here any longer than I needed to. 'Shall I fetch Mr Hopkins? He might have more luck, getting Matilda under control.'

'That's a splendid idea,' the vicar agreed. 'I'll keep an

eye on her in the meantime.'

'He's in the gymnasium, you say?'

'Yes, just across…' Hamilton-Baynes stopped.

There were footsteps clomping down the stairs from the deck above; rather loud footsteps. A group of three figures came into view. One of them was Mr Griffith. He was looking particularly dishevelled. He was flanked by two solid and rather burly crewmen. 'Stay where you are!' he ordered, in a surprisingly aggressive tone.

'Mr Griffith?' The reverend stepped backwards in surprise. It was clear the security officer was addressing him rather than me.

Griffith reached the bottom of the stairs. His two companions spread out.

'Reverend Joshua Hamilton-Baynes. I'm arresting you on suspicion of murder.'

The vicar regarded the fellow in astonishment. 'Murder? I…I don't understand…'

One of the crewmen grabbed him from behind, and pinned his arms behind his back.

The security officer was grim faced. 'I'm arresting you for the murder of Margaret Hamilton-Baynes.'

Chapter Fifteen

For a moment, I thought I must have misheard him. 'You mean Susan O'Neill?'

Mr Griffith shook his head emphatically. 'I'm afraid not, sir.' The security officer spoke with dark authority. 'Mrs Hamilton-Baynes was discovered dead in her bedroom some twenty minutes ago. She was battered to death.'

'*Dead*?' I breathed, in disbelief. 'Mrs Hamilton-Baynes?'

The vicar was equally incredulous. 'Maggie? No, that can't be...'

'I'm afraid it's true,' Griffith confirmed. 'She was struck from behind by a blunt instrument, sometime within the last hour.'

The vicar let out a cry of horror.

'My God,' I said. Another murder.

'With a metal disk from a shuffle board set,' Griffith added. 'We believe the same instrument was used to murder Mrs O'Neill this morning.'

'Good grief.' It was difficult to take in. Margaret Hamilton-Baynes dead. I had only been dining with the woman a couple of hours ago. While I had been getting to grips with Harry Latimer's unexpected resurrection, events appeared to have moved on elsewhere. It was something of a rarity for me to learn of an event like this second hand. I was so used to being close to the scene of a crime. 'And you think the reverend here...?'

Hamilton-Baynes was refusing to accept the truth. 'It's not possible,' he cried. 'Maggie. She can't...she can't be dead...' His face was deflating like a soufflé beneath that heavy beard. 'I only just...no. Oh, God, no. Not Maggie.' The vicar staggered suddenly and the crewmen had to keep a firm grip on him to make sure he did not collapse. At a nod from Griffith, they manoeuvred him over to a chair. 'Not Maggie. My darling Maggie. She...she's really dead?' Hamilton-Baynes stared up at the security officer, his whole body trembling.

'I'm afraid so, sir,' Griffith confirmed. 'But I have reason to believe you were already aware of that fact.'

'But...but...no. I...I would never hurt her.' The vicar's eyes were now wet with tears. 'I would never hurt my darling Maggie. I would never hurt anyone. It can't be true. It simply can't.' In less than thirty seconds, the Reverend Hamilton-Baynes had become a gibbering wreck. Could he really have killed his wife, not half an hour ago?

Mr Griffith, at least, was in no doubt that he had got his man. 'We have a *prima facie* case against you, sir. It'll be up to the courts to determine the truth. But in the meantime...' He gestured to his men. 'We're going to take you down to the hold.'

Hamilton-Baynes was barely listening. His eyes were flicking randomly left and right. 'Maggie....my sweet Maggie. I must go to her. I must see her.'

'I'm afraid that's not possible at the moment, sir. The crime scene cannot be disturbed.'

'But I must...I must...She can't be...'

Griffith gestured again to the crewmen. 'Lift him up.'

The vicar was helped shakily to his feet, his arms once more held behind his back. The security officer produced a pair of handcuffs from his pocket and handed them to one of his underlings. 'It's been a while since I've had any use for these,' he confessed, catching my eye. Hamilton-Baynes was weeping loudly now, great wracking sobs, as tears flopped down onto his grey-black beard. 'Get him down to the brig,' Griffith said. He glanced at his wristwatch. 'I'll be along shortly. The formal interview might have to wait until morning.'

The vicar was led slowly away, through one of the out-of-bounds doors, and down into the bowels of the ship. I watched him go with some consternation. Minutes earlier, the man had been as right as rain. Could he really have held himself together like that, shortly after bludgeoning his wife to death?

'This is a queer business,' Griffith asserted. 'I've never known anything like it.'

'You really think the Reverend Hamilton-Baynes killed

211

his wife? A man of the cloth like that?'

'He's human, like anyone else.'

'But what possible motive could he have? He adored his wife.'

'That's as maybe,' the officer said. 'We think she may have discovered what he did to Mrs O'Neill.'

I boggled. 'You mean, he murdered her too?'

'We believe so. He must have realised she was behind the poison pen letters. He was verifying the truth when she found him in her stateroom. He probably didn't intend to kill her.'

'But he struck her? With this…shuffleboard disk?'

'It seems likely, sir. Mrs O'Neill's stateroom contained a few items of sporting equipment borrowed from the gymnasium.'

'Yes.' I remembered seeing them there. 'The reverend was planning to give Miss Wellesley a lesson or two.'

'We believe he grabbed the disk from the shelf, struck Mrs O'Neill with it, then fixed up the body to make it look like an accident. He then hid the disk in his bedroom.'

'Why didn't he just throw it overboard?'

'He probably didn't have time to get out on deck, sir. People don't often think logically in these situations.'

'But you searched the rooms, didn't you? This afternoon?'

'Yes, but not as extensively as we should have. It was the clothes we were looking at, for signs of any blood, not the gym equipment.'

'And Mrs Hamilton-Baynes?'

'We believe she must have found the disk. It's got a slight dent, perhaps from the first blow. Easy to miss at a glance but not up close. She may well have suspected her husband before that, but the disk confirmed it. She knew what he had done and she confronted him.'

'When she came back to the room after supper?'

'That's right, sir. She must have threatened to tell the police. In a panic, he battered her to death.'

I puffed out my cheeks. It was a hell of a story. I was

not altogether sure I believed it.

'Sir Richard stuck his head around the door, to say goodnight. He discovered her, lying there in a pool of blood. He raised the alarm and I was on the scene a couple of minutes later. It wasn't at all pretty, sir. Lady Jocelyn confirmed that the reverend was the last person to speak to his wife. Her cat had got out onto the deck again and she asked him to help Mr Hopkins find her. Apparently, the reverend made a display of talking to his wife as he closed up the bedroom door, saying he wouldn't be long and not to wait up. All an act to disguise what he had done. Doubtless he was hoping that no-one would look in on the scene until he got back. Your valet confirms that the two of them left together.'

'Yes, I sent him there to tell them about Matilda.'

'And what were you doing down here, Mr Buxton? Not searching for the cat.'

'No, I…wanted another word with Doctor Armstrong. Then I saw Matilda and thought I'd better wait here until someone came to retrieve her.' I was quite pleased at how plausible that sounded. I was getting better these days at thinking on my feet. 'But look here, Mr Griffith, are you absolutely sure you've got the right man?' Despite what I had learnt from Harry, the reactions of the Reverend Hamilton-Baynes did not strike me as those of a guilty man.

'I'm as sure as I can be, sir. I'll need to take a statement from you and the others, but that can wait until morning. I'll see the vicar settled in, make sure he's properly locked up. We may have to leave the body *in situ* for now. Wait for the arrival of the police tomorrow. I'll have to talk to the captain about that.' He grimaced, glancing at his wristwatch. 'He's not going to be at all happy.'

'Lord, no. Three deaths on one trip.'

'The press will have a field day. It won't be pretty. You should get back to your cabin, sir. Best not have anybody wandering around. Get some sleep, if you can.'

'What about the cat?'

Griffith almost smiled. 'She's the least of our concerns.' He made to leave, but stopped himself briefly. 'Did you say Mr

213

Hopkins was down here somewhere?'

'Er…yes, in the gymnasium. At least, according to the reverend. Lord, he won't know anything about any of this. Do you want me to fetch him?'

'If you would, sir. I'd feel more comfortable if everyone was back in their rooms.'

The sky was dark as pitch through the windows on the starboard side and a handful of shipboard lights did little to alleviate the gloom. The gymnasium was an eerie place after dark, the wall bars and mounted horses casting strange shadows across the room. 'Mr Hopkins?' I called out, but there was no response. Where the devil was he? It couldn't have taken the fellow this long to have a look around; but there was no sign of him. Perhaps he had gone through to the swimming pool.

The adjoining door was shut up but not locked. I grabbed the handle and entered. The swimming pool seemed larger than before, without a crowd of spectators lining the edge. The changing cubicles were curtained off, but the under pool lighting was switched on and the crystal water glistened in the half light. A couple of dim lamps were also in evidence, and it was these which served to illuminate the figure of Ernest Hopkins. He was sitting halfway along, not on a chair but perched on the edge of the swimming pool, his legs dangling over the side. I stopped for a moment, surprised to see him there. 'Mr Hopkins?' I called out again. By the look of it, he had not even rolled up his trousers, plunging his socks and shoes straight into the water. 'Are you all right?' I asked, stepping forward in concern. 'What are you doing in the dark?'

Hopkins did not look round. He was staring at the gently lapping water, the lower half of his trousers completely submerged. It was most peculiar. His tone, when he spoke, was entirely matter-of-fact. 'I was trying to decide whether to throw myself in,' he said. 'Or to give myself up.'

I did not understand. 'Give yourself up?' Good grief. What was the fellow blathering about?

'I've been such a fool, Mr Buxton.' He turned his head

214

then, to look at me. His eyes were alive with bitterness and regret. 'I should never have listened to that...to that man.'

'Look, Mr Hopkins...' I had no time for theatrics. I had important news to impart. 'There's been a development. You need to come away now.'

'A development?' The man frowned, not understanding.

'Another murder,' I said.

That got his attention. 'A murder?' He stared up at me, a sudden spasm of alarm flickering across his freckled face. I could perhaps have broken the news a little more delicately. His peculiar manner had disconcerted me somewhat.

'I'm afraid so. Mrs Hamilton-Baynes.'

His eyes widened in shock. 'Margaret?'

'Not half an hour ago. I'm so sorry.'

'But...how did...?'

'Bludgeoned to death, just like Mrs O'Neill.'

'My God.' Again, I could perhaps have chosen the words a little more carefully. 'He did it then?' Hopkins muttered, in disbelief. 'He really did it.' The young man let out a sudden low howl and clutched his face in despair. 'It's all my fault. I should never have listened to him. I should never have...Oh, please God, no. Not Margaret, of all people.' His hands dropped to his lap and his eyes scanned the water in front of him. 'It's my fault. I told him, you see. I told him I knew what he had done. I didn't think...I didn't think for a minute...' He stopped abruptly. 'I didn't know, Mr Buxton.' This time, the bitter note had returned to his voice. 'I didn't realise before today. I didn't realise it was him. And now...oh God in heaven, he's killed Margaret.'

I was struggling to keep up. 'You have nothing to reproach yourself for,' I assured him. The fellow was babbling somewhat. 'You can't be held responsible for anything the Reverend Hamilton-Baynes has done.'

The secretary threw me a puzzled look. 'The reverend? What do you mean?'

'Well, he...' I coughed. 'I'm afraid he was responsible for the death of Mrs Hamilton-Baynes. At least, according to Mr Griffith. He's been arrested for her murder.'

215

'But that's...' Hopkins shook his head vehemently. 'Joshua didn't kill her. He adored his wife. He wouldn't lay a finger on her.'

'That's what I thought.'

Anger flashed across the young man's face. 'Oh, he's clever. Mr Buxton. You've no idea how clever. But you've got it all wrong. Don't you see? The Reverend Hamilton-Baynes wouldn't have killed his wife. He has nothing to do with any of this.'

'But...if not him then who?'

'I only found out the truth today. Oh, if only I'd known. Mr Buxton, it's not the reverend who killed her. It was Sir Richard.'

I regarded the secretary in astonishment. 'Sir Richard? Sir Richard Villiers? You think *he* killed Mrs Hamilton-Baynes?'

'I'm certain of it. It's all my fault. I told him, you see.'

'You *told* him?' A dim light was beginning to flicker in my mind. 'You mean, about...?'

'I told him what Margaret...what Mrs Hamilton-Baynes told us at supper. About...about him and her ladyship.'

'Good grief.'

'I was so angry, don't you see? I'd trusted him. I'd believed in him. And the things I'd done.' He shuddered. 'But now I saw the truth of it. The sort of man he really is.' Hopkins lips curled up in disgust, the same look I had seen on his face when we had left the restaurant together that evening. 'And I knew I had to get myself away from him.'

'You confronted him? About...?'

'I told him exactly what I thought of him. What I knew about him. He was behind it all, Mr Buxton. Don't you see? Those stupid letters. He tried to blame it on Mrs O'Neill, but she had nothing to do with it. It was all him. The pen letters. Everything.'

'Wait a minute, you're saying *he* was the letter writer?'

Hopkins nodded vigorously. 'He admitted it to me, when I challenged him. He even crowed about it.'

'Good lord.'

216

'He's deranged, Mr Buxton. He must be. The man has no shame at all.'

'And you think he murdered Mrs Hamilton-Baynes?'

'I'm sure of it. Oh God...' Hopkins let out another sob. 'It really is my fault. I should never have spoken to him like that...'

'And Susan? Mrs O'Neill?' Had Sir Richard been responsible for her death too?

Hopkins looked down. 'No. He didn't lay a finger on her. But he might just as well have done.' The bitter tone had returned.

'If not him then who?' I asked, still utterly confused. 'Who killed Mrs O'Neill?'

Hopkins buried his head in his hands. 'God forgive me,' he said, his body convulsing in despair. 'It was me.'

Chapter Sixteen

As a general rule, I try to avoid cosy pool-side chats with self confessed murderers. Far safer to remove oneself from the potential source of danger. Better yet, one should summon the forces of law and order, and have them restrained. It was clear to me, however, that Ernest Hopkins was no threat to anyone. He was a wretched figure, with tears now staining his cheeks.

I slipped off my socks and shoes and sat myself down on the tiled floor next to him, rolling up my trousers and swinging my legs into the cool blue water. The freckled secretary was staring numbly over the edge. Whatever had driven him to such an act – to murder, no less – it had not been an easy journey. I regarded the fellow with some confusion. In the short time I had known him, Hopkins had always displayed a calm and business like demeanour. He had kept his emotions in check; not just with me but in front of everyone. Only the occasional run in with Matilda the cat had dented his professional veneer, and then only slightly. Those scars were healing now, but it appeared there were other scars, buried far beneath the surface, which were finally bursting out in a wave of anger and despair. Ernest Hopkins was a broken man; and, so far as I could tell, it was Sir Richard Villiers who had broken him.

I cleared my throat, not quite sure how to proceed. It is never an easy thing, to discuss a murder, especially with the murderer himself. 'How did it happen?' I asked, tentatively. 'Mrs O'Neill? How did you come to…?'

Hopkins wiped his eye and let out a weary sigh. 'The pen letters. We thought it was her, you see. Sir Richard, he had a way of…' His voice trailed off. 'I didn't know, until this evening. I didn't have any idea.' He closed his eyes and shuddered.

'Perhaps you'd better start at the beginning,' I suggested, settling myself on the edge of the pool. 'The pen letters. How did all that start?'

Hopkins took a moment to collect his thoughts. 'It was

last October, when we arrived in New York.' His eyes were fixed on his boots, submerged in the water. 'The trip out was uneventful. It was only when we…when we got to Mrs O'Neill's house in Boston that things began to sour.'

'The letters started to arrive?'

'Yes. Anonymously, through the post. Typewritten letters, in capital letters. Well, you've seen them.'

'One or two. But these weren't the first letters, were they?'

'No. Mrs O'Neill's husband had received something similar, a few years before. I never saw any of those, but Sir Richard had heard all about them. I think…I think now that must have been the start of it.'

'You think that's where he got the idea from?'

'I suppose it must have been.' A seed had been implanted in his mind, all that time ago. 'If only I had realised…' Hopkins swallowed again.

'You don't think Sir Richard had anything to do with those original letters?'

'No. At least, I don't see how.' It was clear that the fellow was still trying to work the matter through himself. I suppose he had not had that long to reflect upon it. 'As I understand it, those letters stopped some time before Mr O'Neill died and only started up again when we arrived in America late last year.'

'You met Mr O'Neill, didn't you, before he passed away?'

'Yes, briefly. But there was no talk of the letters then. I think by that point, whoever it was must have stopped sending them. Mrs O'Neill said she thought it was a disgruntled employee, from one of the businesses her husband had acquired.' That was the line she had taken with me. 'Some poor chap who lost his livelihood or something of that order. The letters Sir Richard sent…the first ones, I think they were intended to mimic the originals.'

I coughed slightly. I was having some difficulty accepting that the businessman was behind any of this, but I was willing to be persuaded. 'Why would Sir Richard start sending people nasty letters, though? What would be the point?'

'I don't know,' Hopkins admitted, his booted feet tracing a circle in the water. 'Sir Richard has always been bad tempered. I don't think I fully appreciated until recently just how much bile there was beneath the surface. Not until this trip, anyway. I suppose, to start with, writing the letters must have been...I don't know, a...a way of letting off steam.'

'A release valve of some kind?' That sounded plausible. My man Maurice had suggested something similar to me when we had discussed the matter. 'You mean, he saw the opportunity to settle a few scores, while he was away from home, when no-one would be able to connect it to him?'

'I think so. In some twisted way, I suppose he might even have found it amusing, to begin with. A bit of mischief making, like at school. He always did have a dark sense of humour.'

'And once he saw the consternation it caused, it became an addiction?'

'I think it must have done,' Hopkins agreed. Evidently, Sir Richard had gained a great deal of pleasure from watching other people squirm; and once he had started he was unable to stop. 'I should have seen it. I should have realised...'

'You didn't suspect him, when the letters started to arrive?'

'Not for a second.' Hopkins was clear on that point. 'He seemed as outraged as the rest of us. And the first letter was addressed to him.'

Sir Richard had shown me that particular missive. 'That was clever,' I thought. Getting in his alibi ahead of time.

'That was the thing. It was all so calculated. And when he showed that first letter to us, he seemed genuinely rattled by it.'

'But really, it was all play acting?'

'It must have been.' Hopkins scratched his head. 'In business, Mr Buxton, you always have to put on a bit of a performance. It's the way everyone operates. It's what gives you the edge over your rivals. I think...I think he must have seen it in those terms. And it worked. We were completely taken in. I didn't...I didn't even consider the possibility that he might have written it himself. To be honest, if you'd suggested it to me then, I would have thought you were mad.' Hopkins did not try to hide the bitterness in his voice. He was a man, evidently, who had been comprehensively deceived. 'He showed the letter to Mrs O'Neill and she said it was exactly like the old ones. He'd mimicked the style exactly.'

'Do you think he might have seen any of those earlier letters?'

'I don't know. Mrs O'Neill didn't keep any, but I suppose it's possible her husband showed them to him, way back when.'

'And presumably if the original letters came from somewhere outside the house, they wouldn't have been typed on Mrs O'Neill's typewriter?'

'No. I think Sir Richard just copied the style.' And since those first letters had all been destroyed, there would be no opportunity for anybody to make a forensic comparison. 'At first, when the letters began to arrive, we assumed they must have been sent by the same person. But then, gradually, they became more personal. Lady Jocelyn received a letter, in the middle of November. I remember Margaret – Mrs Hamilton-Baynes – telling me how upset she was about it. The reverend got a couple too, attacking him for his irreverence and his lack of piety. He wanted to inform the police, but Lady Jocelyn wouldn't hear of it and Sir Richard was of the same mind. It was far too personal, she said. It's only now that I understand why.'

'You had no idea? About the contents of Lady Jocelyn's letter?'

'No, none at all. She didn't show it to anyone, except Sir Richard. I knew it had to be something pretty bad, but not... not that bad.' His face twisted in horror.

'Do you think she might have suspected him? Of sending it?'

'No, I don't think so. I don't think it would have even crossed her mind. He had just as much to lose as she did. And

Sir Richard would never say a word against her ladyship, that much I do know.'

'You don't think he might have still been holding a torch for her, after all these years?'

The secretary shuddered. 'I don't even want to think about it. She always kept him at arm's length. If he was…if he did still think of her in that way, I don't think it could have been reciprocated. But she wouldn't have thought him capable of anything like this. If anything, she was far more likely to have suspected her cousin Margaret. Mrs Hamilton-Baynes.'

Hopkins took a moment to consider that possibility. 'Yes, now I come to think of it, there was a bit of a cooling between the two of them at that time. But it soon passed. Sir Richard…he has this way of deflecting attention, you see. He'd have found another explanation. Something that didn't involve a member of the family.'

I scratched my chin. 'The only other person who knew about that business was the old housekeeper, wasn't it? And she would have moved on decades ago.'

'Yes. Although I believe she settled in the United States when she retired. He might have used that, somehow.'

'You mean, thrown some suspicion her way?'

Hopkins shrugged. 'It's possible.'

'But none of you wanted to contact the police?'

'No. Mrs O'Neill agreed with Sir Richard that they should be kept out of it. Her husband had always impressed on her the importance of avoiding bad publicity.'

'She was certainly upset when the police came calling on her at our hotel,' I recalled, 'after that business in the restaurant.' She had reported the attempted bag snatch earlier in the day, but that had been a trivial matter in comparison.

'Mrs O'Neill was so embarrassed, that we had been targeted while we were guests under her roof. Nobody wanted to involve the police, but Sir Richard said he would make a few discreet enquiries, through other channels. He is a man of great influence in certain circles.'

That much was definitely true. 'And did he? Make enquiries?'

'After a fashion. But not quite in the manner he promised. By this time, of course, I had also received my first letter.' Hopkins brought a hand up to his face and wiped a spot of dribble from his nose. 'It accused me of things that...it knew things about me that I didn't think anyone could possibly know...'

Now we were getting to the heart of it. When I had first raised the business of these letters with Sir Richard, in the Carolean Smoking Room, he had let slip that Mr Hopkins had been accused of theft. Both men had laughed the matter off, but could there perhaps have been some truth in the accusation? 'You'd been stealing from Sir Richard? Is that it?'

Hopkins nodded, his cheeks red with shame. 'I'm not proud of it, Mr Buxton. I should have had more sense. We had two sets of books, you see. The official accounts and the real ones. That was Sir Richard's doing. It's the way he always does business.'

'That doesn't sound strictly legal.'

'It isn't. The transactions themselves are all above board. All the contracts. The bookkeeping, though...that's just for tax purposes. One set for the tax man, the other set to keep a proper account of things. It's common practice. Everybody does it.'

'That's hardly an excuse.'

'No. No, I realise that. But what could I do? That was the business. I was an employee. I had to toe the line. You must believe me, Mr Buxton: before I started with Sir Richard, I was an honest man. I'd never stolen from anyone. I'd never deceived anyone.'

'But you got into the habit?'

'That was what he taught me. And if one set of money can disappear, it's just as easy to make it happen to another. But I wasn't just...I wasn't doing it for myself. I was trying to set up a new life. I'd become...well, I'd become rather fond of Miss Simpkins. Of Jenny.'

I nodded sagely. 'You started courting her?'

'As best I could. We couldn't be open about it. If Lady Jocelyn had known, that would have been the end of it, she would have been out on her ear, long before now.'

'But you were rather taken with the girl?'

'I've never met anyone quite like her. She's so honest and down to earth.'

'Not quite in the same class as you, though.' Hopkins was a decently educated, middle class bookkeeper and Miss Simpkins was little more than a skivvy. Those sort of relationships were rarely successful.

'I didn't mind about that. I loved her. I do love her. We were going to get married, when we got back to England.' He let out a sudden sob. 'And I've ruined it all. We'll never be together now. It's all my fault.'

'But the bookkeeping,' I said, anxious not to be side-tracked by unnecessary emotions. 'You needed the funds.'

'If we were to marry, we would have to have some money put by. We both agreed about that. But Jenny earns a pittance and I don't earn enough to support a family.'

'You could have asked for a raise.'

'I did, but Sir Richard wouldn't give it to me. He said I hadn't been with him long enough, and, in any case, I was too young to merit it. Even though I was handling all of his day to day accounts by then.'

'Do you think he might have suspected the reason you wanted a raise?'

'I…don't know. I think he may have done.'

'But you started to take money from him anyway?'

'Yes. I'm not proud of it, Mr Buxton. I've always been very good with figures. Money in and money out. It wasn't difficult to make the odd shilling disappear. Sir Richard trusted me implicitly. At least, I thought he did. And it was only ever small amounts. But then, these horrible letters started to arrive, and they accused me of thieving. They seemed to know everything. Not just the money, but about Jenny and me. I didn't understand how anyone could possibly know.'

'Did you tell Sir Richard?'

'I didn't dare. At first, I didn't even admit that I'd received a letter. But then the second one came, and the third. They were delivered through the mail, so everyone saw them when they arrived and who they were addressed to. We came to recognise the envelopes. And the threats became ever more specific. They were going to tell Sir Richard what I had done, and I would be thrown out on the street. "YOUR SINS WILL FIND YOU OUT", that was what they said.'

'And Miss Simpkins? Did she receive any threats?'

'No, none of the servants did. Sir Richard never paid much attention to people below stairs. Mrs O'Neill had a housekeeper and a couple of maids, but they were never mentioned. None of that mattered to me, though. I was so scared, don't you see? Somebody knew exactly what I was up to and they were going to reveal the truth. I didn't know what to do.' His hands gripped the top of his knees. 'My whole life was crashing down around me.'

'Did you confide in Miss Simpkins?'

'No. I couldn't bear to tell her. I didn't want to upset her. Jenny...she didn't know that I was stealing money. She wouldn't have approved. She knew I'd received a couple of letters, but I put a brave face on that. They were just insults, I said, pathetic ravings. But the truth was, they could have ruined me. They could have ruined us both.'

'So what did you do?'

'The only thing I could do. I threw myself on Sir Richard's mercy.'

'Lord.'

'I asked for an audience, and I confessed everything.'

'That was a brave thing to do.'

'I didn't have a choice. I was so ashamed, so appalled by what I had done. I had been sucked into it all, without thinking.'

'And what was his reaction? Sir Richard?'

Hopkins frowned, recollecting the moment with some embarrassment. 'He didn't...he didn't lose his temper. He didn't shout at me. It was very strange, Mr Buxton. He just...he looked disappointed.'

I sympathised. 'That's always the worst reaction.'

'I thought he would give me my cards, sack me on the spot. But he didn't. He was more concerned to take a look at the letters, all the horrible things they said. He showed me the latest one he'd received and it was every bit as vile as the others. It mentioned the bookkeeping, seemed to know all about his business practices. I was shocked when I saw that. He destroyed the note shortly afterwards. But it seemed like we were both in the same boat, don't you see? We had to stick together, he said, and I agreed with him. I really did. I would have to pay back the money I had stolen, of course, but the most important thing, he said, was to find out who was behind all this. He wanted to get to the bottom of it. He seemed completely sincere. He must have been laughing at me all the while, at my stupidity, but I believed him. I really did.'

'He's a man who is well practised in deception,' I said. 'Which is doubtless why he is so successful in business. But, even so, he must have put forward some kind of theory as to who might be behind the letters?'

'Yes, he did. It shames me to think of it now, the lies he spun. But yes. He suggested that somebody in Mrs O'Neill's household must be responsible.'

'And what did you think of that?'

'It seemed unlikely to me. I couldn't see how anyone could know such personal things, but Sir Richard said it was an easy enough insinuation to make, to accuse an employee of stealing, or a businessman of falsifying his accounts. Even if it weren't true, it would put the wind up anybody.'

'So he tried to lay the suspicion on Mrs O'Neill's people?'

'Not just the household. He began to suspect Mrs O'Neill herself. At least, that's what he told me. After all, she knew far more about us than anyone else, certainly more than any servant. And the first letters were sent to her husband. Perhaps she had written those too. She had always been in his shadow rather, though she spoke fondly of him after he died. Anyway, we started looking about the house, searching for evidence. Very discreetly. It seems such a farce, now. We checked the envelopes that the letters were delivered in. There was a stack of them, the same type, in a drawer in the study. That only reinforced our suspicions.'

'And the typewriter?'

'I checked that too. Mrs O'Neill's Olivetti. At that time, we hadn't noticed the inconsistency in the lettering. Or I hadn't anyway.'

'It's not that easy to spot,' I said. 'But you saw enough to convince you of Mrs O'Neill's guilt?'

'Not entirely.' Hopkins grimaced. 'She'd received a couple of letters too, you see, and from what I understood, they were almost carbon copies of the earlier ones sent to her husband. If she was behind it all, why would she send letters to herself like that? Sir Richard said it had to be a bluff. He was becoming ever more confident that she was the guilty party. He was never overly fond of Mrs O'Neill. He was much closer to her husband. But they were tied together by business – which is why we came over here – so he had to be nice to her in public.'

'There were tensions, though? With regards to the business?'

'A few,' Hopkins admitted. 'We were meant to be disentangling it all. Mrs O'Neill wanted to sell everything off, to divest herself of all her husband's stocks and the various assets. She didn't have the aptitude to keep it up. She wanted to cash everything in.'

'That's understandable.'

'Sir Richard saw it as a golden opportunity. He thought she would leave it all to him to sort out and he would make a mint, but it turned out she wasn't the soft touch he supposed. She brought in a lawyer to handle the contracts, someone who knew what they were doing.'

'Lord. Sir Richard can't have been happy about that.'

'He wasn't. The last thing he wanted was a level playing field. He had hoped to make a tidy profit. He was very angry about that. With a lawyer involved, he wouldn't receive a penny more than he was entitled to.'

'And you think that may be why he chose Mrs O'Neill as a scapegoat?'

'I think it must have been, at least partly. She was the obvious person to blame. The letters to her husband; the references to his business practices; the personal attacks. It all fitted. And so, gradually, I came to accept what he said, that she must be behind it all. By the time Christmas came, Sir Richard was sick of the sight of her. When she announced that she would be coming with us to Europe, he was apoplectic. That was the last thing he wanted. I heard him discussing it, with her ladyship, and Lady Jocelyn felt exactly the same way. She was no fonder of Mrs O'Neill than he was.'

'Ironically,' I said, 'I think the poor woman only wanted to go to Europe to get away from all these malicious letters.'

'Yes, I suppose that must be true. But it didn't seem that way at the time. The atmosphere over Christmas was stifling.' Hopkins shivered at the memory. 'We *all* wanted to get away from that damned house. Excuse my language. And when we came to New York, Sir Richard made sure we stayed in a separate hotel. But somehow, the letters continued to arrive.'

'Through the post?'

'Yes. And that was proof positive as far as Sir Richard was concerned. Mrs O'Neill had come with us and the letters had come too.'

'They were sent from New York?'

'Yes, for the two or three days we were in town.'

'And all the time, Sir Richard was typing them up himself?' My mind boggled at the audacity of the fellow.

'He must have prepared them ahead of time, before we left Boston. He would have had plenty of opportunity. People were often out of the house during the day. '

'Did no-one ever see him using Mrs O'Neill's typewriter?'

'I imagine so, but we all used it. That was the thing. Sir Richard had his own typewriter, but I was on that most of the day, typing up his correspondence. The Reverend Hamilton-Baynes did a fair amount of typing too, as did his wife. We wouldn't have thought twice about see anybody on it. At that point, we hadn't connected any of the letters to that particular typewriter. But then, when we got to New York, things changed. I mean, with Sir Richard. Enough was enough, he said. He wasn't going to put up with this nonsense any longer. It was time to teach Mrs O'Neill a lesson.'

'I see.' That sounded ominous. 'And what did he suggest?'

'He wanted to give her a dose of her own medicine. Imagine her face, he said, if she started receiving letters that she hadn't written herself. Think how that would unnerve her. He almost laughed when he suggested it. But even that wasn't enough. I didn't realise at the time how deeply Sir Richard must have hated that woman.'

'It sounds like, by this stage, the whole thing had become far more than mischief making.'

'It had,' Hopkins agreed. 'He was getting more and more audacious. More vindictive.'

The release valve was becoming an open sewer. 'He must have been bottling up his anger for years,' I said. 'Not just at the people here, but at the world in general. At his sister, and perhaps his own guilt, over what he had done all those years ago.' I suppose it did make a kind of sense. 'But to send letters to Mrs O'Neill, in retaliation for the letters he had written to himself…that's insane.'

'And the worst of it is, Mr Buxton, it was all just a preamble. He was drawing me in, I see that now. It was part of the game, slowly entangling me in his schemes, getting me more and more involved with it. Against my better judgement, I agreed to help with the letters, to give Mrs O'Neill a taste of her own medicine, as he put it. But that wasn't enough. Sir Richard had something much more unpleasant in mind. We really needed to put the wind up her, he said, make her fear for her life.'

'Lord. You mean, threaten to kill her?' I had known the conversation would be heading in this direction, but it was still a shock to hear the words spoken out loud.

'I'm afraid so. He wanted to make her sweat, to make her think the whole world was conspiring against her, to pay her back for everything she had done to him. He had read the papers over Christmas, about the bombings on Boxing Day and afterwards…'

'The *bombings*?'

'Yes.' Hopkins drew in a breath. 'He'd read about the

anti-Mussolini campaign and he thought…oh, Mr Buxton, it was mad, but he thought…why not make use of that?'

'Good God.' I blinked in horror. 'You mean the bomb? The hoax bomb at Leopardi's? That was Sir Richard?'

Hopkins nodded shamefacedly. 'It was his idea.'

'Good grief.'

'It wasn't intended to cause any actual harm. The idea was to frighten her off. That and the note sent to her hotel room. It would put an end to this nonsense altogether, he said. Put a stop to her odious campaign.'

'But in reality he was just feeding his addiction?'

'The letters weren't enough any more. He wanted to frighten her half to death.'

'But to go to such lengths…' I shook my head.

'It was madness,' Hopkins agreed. 'And I told him so. I said I wanted nothing to do with it. Sir Richard didn't like that at all. He said I was nothing but a coward. I had no backbone. What was I worried about? No-one was going to get hurt. It was just a practical joke. But you know what the atmosphere was like in New York, these last couple of weeks. The paranoia, when the bombs started going off. We could have ended up in jail, or worse. It was mad. Utterly insane. But Sir Richard wouldn't take no for an answer.'

'He threatened you?'

'He told me he had no use for someone who wouldn't obey orders. I'd be out on my ear. Me and Miss Simpkins. He'd make sure neither of us ever worked again. He even threatened to call the police and accuse me of theft. Have me hauled away to prison.'

'That was a lame threat,' I suggested. 'You had as much on him as he did on you. Massaging the books.'

'But who would believe me? That's the thing, Mr Buxton. Sir Richard is a peer of the realm – he has friends in parliament – and I'm just a secretary. They'd side with him. I'd end up in prison and he'd walk away without a stain on his character. I didn't know what to do.'

'You could have said no.'

'I tried to, please believe me. I did try. But you don't

understand how persuasive he can be. How frightening.'

'I know a bully when I see one.'

'One moment, he'd be raging and the next he was utterly reasonable. It was just a prank, he assured me, time and time again. Nobody was going to get hurt. It was just a bit of fun. And it would teach Mrs O'Neill a thorough lesson. She would never write another letter to anyone ever again. He kept telling me that, over and over.'

'And so you finally agreed to help?'

'He wore me down. And I agreed to it, yes. God forgive me. I wish I could say it was the worst thing I'd done. Oh, Mr Buxton, that man. The way he twists everything.'

'But you did it? You prepared the package?'

'Yes, to my shame. It wasn't that difficult. We'd read all the details in the papers. I made it the same size and shape as the original bombs. Even gave it the same return address.'

'But with Mrs O'Neill's name plastered across the front?'

'Yes. That was the most vicious part of it. Sir Richard wanted there to be no doubt it was aimed at her. And then, that last evening, I...I put on a heavy coat and a pair of gloves, and I left the parcel at the side door of the restaurant, where someone was bound to notice it. I was so scared that I would be seen. But I was lucky. Nobody saw me do it.'

I pursed my lips in distaste. 'That was a damned foolish thing to do. You heard what happened when the package was discovered?' All hell had broken loose. 'Somebody might have been seriously injured.'

'I know. I know...' He sniffled. 'It was so stupid. I should never...I should never have agreed to do it. If it wasn't for Jenny...'

'Miss Simpkins, she knew nothing about this?'

'No, nothing at all. At least, not until today. She would have been appalled. She could see how distracted I was, but the same was true of everyone. We were all out of sorts because of these letters.'

'And after the bomb, you sent the note to Mrs O'Neill at her hotel?'

231

'Yes. That was what we agreed. By this time, we'd noticed the misalignment of the key on Mrs O'Neill's typewriter. The misplaced "W". Sir Richard had spotted it. I suppose he must have known about it for some time. We didn't have access to her typewriter any more, so we typed up the note on Sir Richard's Olivetti, adjusting the barrel slightly when we typed the "W", to mimic the style of the original.'

'And you delivered the letter?'

'Yes. I passed by the Alderley later that evening and handed it to a bellboy, with instructions to deliver it after everyone had gone to bed.'

'That was risky. Letting him see you.'

'I did my best to disguise myself. I told him it was a *billet-doux*. A love letter. I gave him a few coins. I even put on an American accent when I spoke to him. Not a very good one,' he confessed.

'He might still have recognised you, if Mrs O'Neill reported the matter to the police.'

'We didn't think she would. The police would have interviewed her already, about the bomb. That was part of the punishment. Or the mischief. But she wouldn't be able to tell them anything about the letters, without incriminating herself. That was what I thought, anyway. As for Sir Richard, it must have amused him no end, frightening the life out of her like that, but knowing full well she wouldn't say a word to anyone.'

'And as it was a hoax, the police wouldn't waste too much time investigating,' I said. 'Even so, Sir Richard was sailing pretty close to the wind.'

'He was. He was becoming more and more reckless.'

'And having terrified Mrs O'Neill half to death with the bomb, you then sent the note to add salt to the wound?'

'It was intended to underline the message: stop now or suffer the consequences. I hoped...I hoped that would be the end of the matter.'

'But it wasn't?'

'No. Far from it. Things seemed to get worse, when we boarded the Galitia. Sir Richard became ever more erratic.'

'You began to suspect him?'

'I began to worry about him. Other letters started to arrive, ones that apparently came from Mrs O'Neill. And then Sir Richard took exception to your friend Harry Latimer. He didn't like the cut of his jib. Or yours, Mr Buxton, if I'm honest. He didn't like the way Mr Latimer flirted with Mrs O'Neill. Wouldn't it be funny, he said, if he were to receive a nasty letter too, warning him off. I couldn't understand that. Why would Sir Richard want to send a letter like that to a person he hardly knew? It made no sense at all.'

'Not if he was the innocent party,' I agreed.

'But he kept telling me how necessary it was. Think how perplexed Mrs O'Neill would be, he said, if other people started receiving letters she hadn't written. It would help to put an end to this nonsense. And despite myself, even then, I believed him.'

'And so you became his post boy?'

'Yes.' Hopkins grimaced. 'It seems absurd now. He had me skulking about the ship, pushing envelopes under doors. I said to him, it will look suspicious, me creeping about like that, so he suggested I let Matilda out of the Reynolds Suite and pretend I was trying to find her. He's never liked that cat. And she was always getting out anyway.'

'So that was what you were doing, when I bumped into you after breakfast on the first morning? You were delivering one of these letters?'

'To Mr Latimer, yes. I was mortified, later on, when I heard he had died. But Sir Richard wasn't at all ruffled about that. He didn't seem to care that Mr Latimer had passed away. Forget it, he said. We had nothing to do with his death. But he was becoming ever more unstable. When Mr Griffith came to talk to us, I didn't know what to say to him. I managed to keep my nerve. Thank goodness, he didn't ask me about the letter. He didn't seem to know anything about that, or any of the correspondence.'

'No. There was a wall of silence. Sir Richard even asked me to keep quiet about it,' I recalled, with some embarrassment.

'And somehow the note ended up in Mrs O'Neill's

handbag.'

'Yes. That must have been when she discovered the body,' I said. 'Perhaps she tripped over it when she entered the room, before she even realised Harry was dead. She read it, thinking he was still asleep, and decided it was better for him not to see it. When she realised Harry was dead, she probably forgot all about it. And later on, she couldn't say anything, because she had knowingly tampered with the evidence.'

'Mr Latimer...his death...do you think that was really an accident?' Hopkins asked. 'You don't think...?'

'I'm sure it was,' I said, the lie coming easily to my lips. 'Doctor Armstrong did a thorough examination. It's a devil of a coincidence but I don't believe his death had anything to do with your affair. It certainly had nothing to do with Sir Richard.'

'I hope not,' Hopkins said, staring down at the water. 'We've done enough damage, him and I, these last few days.'

'But you say he was becoming more erratic?'

'Yes. I was beginning to think that perhaps everything was not as he had told me. I'd spent some time with Mrs O'Neill, and she had never seemed in the least bit venal. Unfortunately, I had become so caught up in Sir Richard's web of lies that I didn't trust my own instincts. And now I had had enough. When Jenny got given her notice, he refused to lift a finger to help her. And it was partly our fault, letting the cat out like that. But he didn't care. He didn't care about anyone. And I was beginning to think he had been lying to me all along.'

'So what did you do?'

'I confronted him. This can't go on, I said. It has to stop.'

'How did he react to that?'

'He said I was a fool. Everything he had told me was true, but if I wanted proof, it was Mrs O'Neill I should be talking to, not him. Get the truth from her, he said. I didn't know what to think about that. But his story never wavered. And I was angry too, to be put in this position, to have become so entangled, to have done such stupid things. If Sir Richard was right, and Mrs O'Neill really was behind it all, then it was all her fault.'

'So what did you do?'

'I had to determine the truth, one way or another. Sir Richard knew I wasn't likely to confront Mrs O'Neill directly, but there were other things I could do. The typewriter, for example. I hadn't seen it since we left Boston. Back then, I didn't know about the misalignment of the keys. But now I could take a close look at it, and see if it really was the one that was used. And maybe I could find some other evidence in her cabin which might prove her guilt.'

'You broke in there, this morning?'

'Yes. I waited until everyone was down in the restaurant, first thing. The door was locked but I slipped a piece of card down the side.' His face flushed with embarrassment. 'I've seen it done in the pictures. I didn't think it would work, but it did. I was worried that someone might see me, but there was no-one around in the corridor and I closed the door behind me. The room was empty. Just lots of clothes and some sporting equipment. I couldn't think why she would have that. I scoured the room and found the note Sir Richard had written in her handbag. Then I checked the typewriter. I tapped out the letter "W" and a few others to see if it was out of step. And it was. And then...and then...Mrs O'Neill returned to the room.' Hopkins was staring at his lap now, his body shuddering, his lower legs causing small ripples in the water below.

'And what did you do?'

'I...I hit her. Oh God, I hit her. I grabbed a shuffleboard disk from the shelf. It was all her fault, you see. She'd placed me in this impossible position. She'd forced me to confess to Sir Richard. And now she was going to find me rifling through her things. She would know that it was me who sent the bomb to the restaurant. She would know it was me who delivered the second note. I wasn't...I didn't really think about it. I just grabbed the disk with both my hands and...and bashed her with it, like a rock, to the back of the head. She fell straight away. A single blow. I didn't intend to kill her. I really didn't. I just wanted to knock her out. But...but it didn't work out that way. I knew as soon as she hit the floor that she was dead.'

A brief silence fell. I didn't know what to say. The poor idiotic fool. 'So what did you do then?' I asked quietly.

'I pulled myself together, as best I could. I tried to make it look like an accident. I pulled her up against the sink and… and banged her head against it…'

'To make it look like she had fallen.'

'Yes. And then I left her there and…and hurried back to the Reynolds Suite. No-one saw me.'

'What did you do with the shuffleboard disk?'

'I tried to clean it. Then I slipped it into the reverend's bedroom. I remembered he had his own set. It wouldn't look out of place among them.'

'Why didn't you just throw it overboard?'

'I was too scared of being seen, out on deck. There was a slight dent in the disk, so I turned it around to the wall, to make it less obvious. I knew someone would see it eventually, though.'

'And what did you do then?'

'I left the suite and went and sat in the reading room, trying to calm myself down. I even did a bit of work, just to keep myself busy. I returned to B Deck an hour later, when the body was found. Mr Griffith didn't show much interest in me then, thank goodness. And the interview, later on, was very brief. Somehow, I managed to hold myself together.'

'And Sir Richard? What did he make of Mrs O'Neill's death?'

'He understood exactly what I had done, right from the off. It was obvious, even though we didn't get to talk about it until later. But he didn't seem to care. It was Mr Latimer all over again. Mrs O'Neill had got what she deserved, as far as he was concerned. He told me not to worry, he would look after me, so long as I kept my nerve. I couldn't understand it. I didn't understand. Not until…not until this evening…'

'When you confronted Sir Richard?'

'When Margaret…Mrs Hamilton-Baynes told us about…about everything. It was only then…only then that the scales really fell from my eyes. I finally understood just what sort of a man I had been working for. It made me sick just to

236

think of it. I could scarcely believe I had been so deceived.' The young man had certainly been agitated, when we had left the restaurant together. 'But now, it all made sense. The way he had manipulated me. I talked it over with Jenny, after I said goodnight to you. I'd spent the whole day trying to keep myself calm, trying not to show any trace of emotion, but now everything was unravelling. And when I realised...when I finally understood how Sir Richard had misled me, how he had exploited me, I was so angry, so upset.'

'And you discussed all this with Miss Simpkins?'

'I...told her about the letters, about the money I had stolen, how Sir Richard had manipulated me.'

'And Mrs O'Neill?'

'No.' His face fell. 'I couldn't tell her about that. I couldn't bear to.'

'What about Sir Richard and Lady Jocelyn?'

'Not that either. It was shocking enough, just talking about Sir Richard. All the upset he had caused, all the letters he had sent. The way I had been deceived. Jenny was as horrified as I was, to discover how he had manipulated us all. She didn't blame me. It was all his fault, she said. I needed to get away from him. Tell him you want nothing more to do with him, she said.' He frowned at the memory of that. 'And she was right. Somehow, I had to disentangle myself from all the mess. So I went to see him, fool that I was. He had come back to the stateroom alone after supper. I think he'd had a disagreement with Lady Jocelyn. They are always having minor tiffs. She had gone to the Palladian with the others, as it was our last night onboard, so there was no-one else around in the Reynolds Suite. Well, Miss Wellesley was there, but she was asleep in her ladyship's room. We could hear her snoring. We went out onto the verandah, just to be on the safe side. And then I told him, as firmly as I could, that I wanted nothing more to do with him; that I knew he was behind the poison pen letters, that he had been lying to me from the very beginning. This time, he didn't deny it. He just laughed in my face. He didn't care.'

'He admitted it to you?'

'He did. His eyes...I could see the cruelty in them; how

237

much he had enjoyed deceiving us all. I confess, Mr Buxton, I wanted to strike him down. But instead, I told him what Mrs Hamilton-Baynes had told us, about the affair he had had with his own sister all those years ago, and at that point everything changed. Sir Richard was outraged, appalled that Margaret would betray his confidence, after all these years. I had never seen him so angry. He wasn't shouting or snarling. He knew he couldn't afford to be overheard. But she had betrayed him, he said. Stabbed him in the back. Him and Lady Jocelyn. And she would suffer for it.'

'He threatened to hurt her?'

'Yes, he did. At the time, I thought it was all hot air. He wouldn't lash out at her physically. I was sure he would find some other way to get back at her. And then, before either of us could say anything else, people started arriving back at the suite. Lady Jocelyn and the reverend. And then Matilda escaped again. I think that may have been Sir Richard's doing – trying to divert attention – and I was despatched to look for her. And then, a while later, your man came along and said she was down here, on E Deck. And I was in such a whirl, not knowing whether I was coming or going. Nothing had been resolved. Sir Richard was furious but trying to hide it. And her ladyship insisted we go and look for the cat, the reverend and I. All I could think about was…what I had done. Everything that had happened. Mrs O'Neill. My God. I had killed her. And for what? I came down here and I just…I just sat.' He gazed disconsolately at the pool. 'I didn't know what else to do. I needed time to think. To decide…to decide what to do next.'

'Killing yourself won't help anyone,' I pointed out quietly. 'And I don't think it's as easy as it looks.'

'No…no, you're right. I have to take responsibility for what I've done. I have to give myself up. Not just…not just because of what I did. But because of him. Sir Richard. He can't be allowed to get away this. Mrs Hamilton-Baynes, of all people. The most harmless, defenceless woman. And he just…' Hopkins pulled himself up. 'I won't let him get away with it. The world needs to know what sort of a man he is. Even if I have to go to prison. Even if…'

'That's the trouble with young people these days,' a voice boomed suddenly from behind us. 'No backbone.' Sir Richard Villiers was standing calmly a few yards away from us. Hopkins jerked backwards in surprise and I almost lost my grip on the edge of the pool, as I scrabbled to take him in. 'In my day,' Sir Richard continued, his voice dripping with scorn, 'people knew how to hold their tongue, how to keep things under their hat.'

Hopkins recovered himself quickly, pulling his feet out of the water and swivelling up onto his knees. 'You killed her, didn't you?' he cried, lifting himself up. 'You killed Margaret!'

Sir Richard curled his lip. 'I put her out of her misery, if that's what you mean. That bloody woman.' He scowled. 'She was nothing but a leech. Living off my hard work, my enterprise. Just like all the others.' Sir Richard was carrying a small leather bag with him. He stepped forward, his attention focused on the younger man, and quietly placed the bag down on the tiles. 'We've supported her for all these years, Jocelyn and I, after marrying that damn fool of a vicar. She'd have been penniless, if it wasn't for us. And this is how she pays us back. Telling everyone our secrets. Telling everyone things she has no business talking about.'

'It wasn't her fault,' I protested, rising up beside Mr Hopkins. 'It just slipped out over dinner. It was quite by chance. And no-one else will ever know.'

'I shouldn't have said anything,' Hopkins realised, with a trembling voice. 'I shouldn't have told you.' Water was now dripping from his trousers onto the marble floor. 'I should have gone straight to Mr Griffith and thrown myself on his mercy.'

'Don't be a fool, boy!' Sir Richard barked. 'Do you want to hang?'

I was more concerned with Sir Richard's behaviour after the secretary had spoken to him. 'But why kill her? Why kill Mrs Hamilton-Baynes? She wasn't any threat to you.'

'She's always been a threat,' Sir Richard spat, his face red with contempt. 'She's had that hold over us for years. It's a question of honour, old boy. Family honour. You wouldn't understand.' He shook his head and growled. 'I wasn't intending to kill the damned woman. I was going to give her a piece of my mind. But I opened the bedroom door and what did I see? She was kneeling there, in front of the bed, praying for forgiveness. It made my blood boil to see her like that. The hypocrisy of the woman. Always so virtuous, always so kind and mild mannered. Keeping our secret for so many years, like a good little nun. But inside she was lording it over us. Enjoying our discomfort. Well,' he chuckled. 'I put an end to that.'

The man was mad, quite mad. He had lost whatever grip he had once had on sanity. Even so, it had taken some nerve, to grab that shuffleboard disk and batter the woman from behind; and then, a short time later, to move back to the doorway and call the alarm. The fellow might be unhinged, but he was a quick thinker too.

'And the best of it is,' he crowed, 'I can blame it all on the Reverend Hamilton-Baynes. They've already arrested the damn fool.' He smiled sourly. 'I've never liked that man. Too lively by half. In my days, vicars were quiet, humble people. He deserves everything that's coming to him.'

'You won't get away with this,' I said, my own anger beginning to flare. 'Mr Hopkins here has told me everything. Every little detail. You won't keep a lid on this.'

'Won't I now?' He regarded the pair of us with some amusement, his eyes wide behind those chunky spectacles. 'I've managed perfectly well so far. And what kind of threat are you? Look at you, the pair of you. Pathetic. Ernest here will do exactly what I tell him.'

'I won't. I won't.' The younger man was staring at his employer, his hands clenching and unclenching, as if trying to decide whether to launch himself at the fellow. I would not have blamed him if he had.

'Of course you will. Use your brain, Ernest, for goodness sake. You don't want to hang do you? He's good with figures,' Sir Richard explained to me, in a disconcertingly casual tone, 'but everything else in there is hot air. You'll keep quiet, lad, for all those fine feelings of yours, because you want to *live*. You can marry that girlie of yours, live happily ever after. And as for you, Mr Buxton.' He regarded me shrewdly. 'I know your sort well enough. You're out for what you can get. I've bought dozens of people like you. How much do you want? A hundred pounds? Let's say two hundred. I can write you a cheque here and now.'

'You're offering me *money?*' I spluttered. 'To keep quiet?'

'Why not? I had you sized up right from the start. A "gold digger", that's the term they use these days. Attaching yourself to rich widows, bleeding them dry. Oh, I know your type well enough. In my day, you'd have been given a good thrashing and thrown over the side.'

'I don't want your money,' I snapped.

'Bartering, are we?' Sir Richard looked at me in surprise. 'Very well. Three hundred pounds. That's my last offer.' He reached down to the bag resting by his leg.

'I'm not interested,' I told him firmly. 'Look, Sir Richard, what you got up to with your sister all those years ago, that's your business. We can put that down to an error of youth.' I had turned a blind eye to worse things in my time. 'Even the letters you sent I could overlook, those vile, cowardly letters.'

'Cowardly?' Sir Richard riled at that.

'You talk about plain speaking, Sir Richard. The good old days. But when you really want to spew your venom, what do you do? You hide behind the printed word. You take refuge behind it, like a little boy hiding behind a tree. And that's cowardice in my book.' The words were designed as a provocation and they seemed to be working. Steam appeared to be coming out of Sir Richard's ears. It was a risky strategy – he was a hefty fellow, after all – but there were two of us and only one of him; and the more he raised his voice in anger, the more likely it was someone would hear him and come to investigate.

'It's not cowardice,' he spat, his thin face red with anger. 'But you're right, Mr Buxton.' His voice calmed abruptly. The inconsistency in his tone was alarming. 'It is better to speak frankly when you can. In my day, we called a spade a spade. But some things are too personal, too damaging. They can't be spoken of out loud, but they need to be said all the same.'

'I'll take your word for that,' I said. 'Like I say, I could forgive the letters, but Mrs Hamilton-Baynes…Mr Hopkins is right. She was the gentlest, kindest of women; and you murdered her, Sir Richard. You crossed that line. And that is unforgivable. I'm going to make sure you are held to account for it.'

'Not if I have anything to do with it,' the man snapped, rising up from his bag. In his hand he was holding a flintlock pistol, the one belonging to the Reverend Hamilton-Baynes. He cocked the weapon. 'You have a choice, the pair of you. Do as I say, or this ends now.'

I swallowed hard at the sight of the gun. If I had known he had been armed, I would not have spoken so harshly. 'You're bluffing,' I asserted, more in hope than conviction. 'That's not loaded. You don't have any ammunition.'

'Mr Buxton,' Hopkins whispered urgently, 'there was a pouch of ammunition in the box. Gunpowder too.'

Sir Richard smirked. 'And don't doubt I know how to use it,'

I closed my eyes and suppressed a shudder. It appeared the day was determined to end on a low note. 'If you fire that, Sir Richard,' I said, clutching my hands together, 'people will come running.'

The man shrugged. 'Self defence. Young Hopkins here was in league with the reverend. Or you were. He wrote the letters, you were his accomplice.'

'That'll never wash. Sir Richard, you're deluded. Give it up, while you still can.'

He was not listening. 'What do you say, boy?' He addressed the secretary. 'We can still walk away. Blame it all on the vicar and this damned fool.'

Hopkins shook his head. He had been through too much already. 'No, Sir Richard. I won't do it. I won't do anything for you ever again.'

'You can only shoot one of us,' I pointed out, my voice trembling now despite my best efforts to keep it level. 'Put the gun down, Sir Richard. It's over. You can't win now.'

'Maybe not,' he conceded, reluctantly. 'But I have no intention of dangling from a rope. If it has to end now, then so be it.' And with that, he pulled the trigger.

Chapter Seventeen

I am pretty sure he was aiming for Mr Hopkins, but flintlocks are tricky things to fire.

Before I had even heard the bang, I felt something hard thud into my right shoulder. A spasm of pain shot up the back of my neck and my body spun under the impact. Hopkins was standing just to my right and I careered into him, losing my footing on the wet tiles. The impact knocked Hopkins off balance. I crashed to the floor, blood spurting from my shoulder, as Hopkins fell sideways, plunging into the swimming pool, a cry of surprise cut short by the heavy splosh.

Sir Richard, meantime, had discarded his musket. Even if he had extra ammunition to hand, it would take him too long to reload. Instead, as I struggled back to my feet, he strode across the floor towards me, his eyes blazing with anger. The intention was clear: he was going to finish me off. I had barely managed to recover my balance when he reached me. His hands grabbed hold of my throat. My shoulder was already throbbing with pain; there was a tear at the top of my jacket and blood on my waistcoat. I pushed back at Sir Richard as best I could, but his grip was like a vice. I did not have the strength to get him off me. I gasped for air, my vision beginning to blur as he squeezed at my windpipe. His face – what I could see of it – was twisted into a cruel smile, those hideous bulging eyes magnified to infinity by his enormous glasses.

I stopped pushing, an idea bubbling up in my mind. I dropped a hand from his chest down to my trouser pocket and fumbled inside. I confess, I nearly dropped the penknife as I pulled it out. Sir Richard must have seen the movement but he was too slow to react. I flicked the blade open and, with all the strength I could muster, I plunged the knife into his right thigh. It cut through the fabric of his trousers with surprising ease and slid directly into his flesh.

The reaction was instantaneous. Sir Richard let out a growl of pain. His hands dropped from my neck and I staggered backwards, letting go of the penknife, which plopped down into the water. Sir Richard clutched his leg, blood already spooling across his knee. 'You'll pay for that!' he snarled. But he was off balance and I saw my opportunity. I stepped forward, ignoring the pain in my right shoulder, and launched a fist directly at his head. It was impossible to miss, but somehow I managed it. In the brief moment it had taken me to make the move, a dripping figure had risen up from the swimming pool and grabbed Sir Richard. The knight cried out in surprise as Mr Hopkins yanked his leg hard from below. Sir Richard lost his footing and came crashing down, just as my fist hit the air where his head had been a moment earlier.

Sir Richard thudded heavily into the water, on top of the poor secretary, who disappeared beneath the waves.

I might have avoided the same fate, had I not at that moment collided with a pair of empty shoes – my shoes, to be exact, with socks stuffed into the holes – which were lying by the side of the pool. I tripped across them, staggered backwards and then hit the water hard, the back of my left leg thudding against the glazed brickwork. All at once, I disappeared into the depths. It happened so quickly, I had no time to think. I did not even have the presence of mind to keep my mouth shut. Before I knew what was happening, my lungs were filling up with water. I started to panic, pushing myself desperately up to the surface. I have never been the strongest of swimmers, but my head broke the water a couple of seconds later and I coughed and spluttered, grasping for the side of the pool to support myself as I attempted to regain my breath.

Hopkins was slower to recover. Sir Richard, who had fallen on top of him, had surfaced first. His bloody leg was out of sight and his chunky glasses had been swept away, but the older man was not done yet. This time, it was the secretary who was the focus of his anger. As Hopkins resurfaced and gasped for air, Sir Richard grabbed hold of him and smashed him hard in the face. The young man reeled under the impact and, as he did so, Sir Richard grasped his head and forced it under the water.

Hopkins was fighting a losing battle, but I was gradually recovering myself. The pistol Sir Richard had abandoned had come to rest by the edge of the pool. My eyes lit up at the sight of it. I was only a few feet away from the struggling pair and the pistol would make a perfectly serviceable club. I grabbed hold of it with my free hand and edged along. Sir Richard had his back to me. I gritted my teeth, my poor arm grasping the side to keep myself afloat while I steadied myself and then raised the pistol above my head. The older man was too intent on drowning his secretary to notice me creeping up on him. With the length of the barrel, I whipped Sir Richard hard across the back of his head. This time, the blow struck true. The man yowled and spluttered, instantly releasing his grip on the secretary. But the effort had winded me too. The pistol dropped from my hand and sank uselessly into the depths.

The game was not over. Sir Richard took a couple of seconds to steady himself and then, with superhuman strength, spun himself around and, with his spare hand, launched a fist directly at my face. I barely saw the blur of it, but I felt the impact as the knuckles cracked solidly against my jaw. My head jerked backwards and there was a loud crunch, as the back of my head collided with the brickwork. The pain was indescribable. I must have blacked out for a moment, as my body slipped beneath the surface of the water.

I woke to find myself several feet under, with blood starting to spill out around me. I had cracked my head pretty severely. Once again, I found the strength to kick my way to the surface, but I had lost my orientation. I was now in the middle of the pool, well away from the support of any ledge. I worked desperately to keep myself afloat, but my energy was beginning to flag.

Sir Richard had his own problems. A howl of anger echoed across the hall, as Hopkins resurfaced and went on the offensive. The wound in Sir Richard's leg was beginning to take its toll and, as the two men locked together, he was struggling to hold his own. Hopkins had his hands firmly around Sir Richard's throat.

For my part, I was battling just to keep my head above the water, coughing up half the liquid I had already swallowed.

My battered cranium was shrieking with pain and my legs were kicking feebly beneath me. Try as I might, I could no longer keep my face clear of the water. Abruptly, I found myself falling and, this time, there was nothing I could do to prevent it.

The last clear image I had was of Mr Hopkins, doing to Sir Richard what Sir Richard had done to him, holding the man's head savagely beneath the surface.

My foot bumped the bottom of the pool. All around me the water was swirling red. I could barely focus my eyes. My chest was tightening under the pressure and the last of the air was bubbling up from my lungs. I flapped my good arm about as best I could, but my energy was spent and I realised, in despair, that I no longer had the strength to propel myself back to the surface. A strange calm came upon me then, as my knees scraped the base of the pool. I was going to die. If my mind had not been so fogged over, I might have railed at the indignity of it. I had survived a hurricane and a tidal wave and now I was going to pop my clogs at the bottom of a swimming pool. But in truth, I felt a strange kind of peace wash over me. What was the point of struggling against it? Everything was beginning to darken. I stared numbly up at the glistening surface, so far above me. If my time had come, then so be it.

I fancied I saw a figure rushing along the side of the pool, but it was almost certainly a trick of the light. If I then heard a heavy splosh behind me, I was sure I must have imagined it.

The next thing I was aware of were the arms that seemed to be grabbing hold of me. Strong, silent arms. An angel had come to collect me, I thought, an emissary from the hereafter, though whether from above or below I could not begin to imagine. Regardless, I surrendered myself into his embrace. I could feel myself being tugged upwards through the water. Someone or something was pressing against me, a firm, heavy trunk of a body. Not an angel, then. Together we broke the surface and the whole horrible world and its choking pain came back into focus. I found myself coughing and spluttering, the agony returning to my head, while an arm around my neck kept my mouth gently above the water line.

'Careful, Monsieur,' a voice whispered in my ear. 'I have you. Try to keep calm.'

I was dreaming. It was my man come to save me. It had to be a mirage, a phantom to comfort my deluded brain. 'Morris…' I spluttered vaguely. And then, once again, everything went dark.

I was sitting on a cork board floor, my back against the side of a changing cubicle, my head throbbing like the devil himself as I shivered into consciousness. A gentle hand held me in place as my eyes cranked open. I coughed loudly, momentarily gasping for air and starting to panic. I was in pain everywhere, my arms, my shoulder, my neck, my head. But then I saw the vague outline of my man Maurice crouching next to me, and gradually my heartbeat began to slow.

'How do you feel, Monsieur?' Maurice asked.

I coughed again. 'I…I…' My throat felt raw and constricted. I was having difficulty finding a voice. A chill came over me, adding to the sense of disorientation. My clothes were dripping wet. My jacket had been removed, but the waistcoat, trousers and shirt sleeves were absolutely sodden; and stained red with blood.

Maurice held up his hand, a gentle blur in front of my face. 'How many fingers, Monsieur?'

I tried to focus but a wave of nausea swept across me. 'I…I think I'm going to be sick.' Bile rose up from my gut, my body convulsing under the strain, but nothing came out. After a moment, the trembling subsided and, with a supreme effort of will, I forced the hand into view. 'Three…three minutes,' I said. 'Then come and…no.' I frowned. That wasn't right.

'Monsieur?'

'I…three, three fingers.' That was it. There were three fingers.

He removed one of them. 'And now, Monsieur?'

'Two.' The gesture sparked something in my mind, and I almost laughed, before a coughing fit engulfed me again. 'That…that's considered very rude in England,' I said, after I finally managed to settle myself.

'If you say so, Monsieur.'

I slumped back against the wall of the cubicle, the world gradually coming into focus. I was alive. My God, I was alive. 'I thought...I really thought I was a goner there,' I said, gazing up at the valet in wonderment. 'You...you saved me.'

'Yes, Monsieur.' Maurice had a cloth in his left hand. Carefully, he began to wipe the side of my head. I flinched at the sudden sting as the fabric made contact.

'Is it...is it bad?' I asked, not really wanting to know the answer.

'I do not think so, Monsieur.'

I gazed down at my shoulder. The waistcoat and part of my shirt had been pulled back. Evidently, Maurice had already taken a look at that. 'He shot me,' I recalled in dismay, remembering the moment but still not quite believing it. 'Sir Richard, he shot me.'

'Yes, Monsieur.'

I had faced quite a few lunatics over the years, but none of them had ever managed to put a bullet in me before. It was not a pleasant experience. My right shoulder was still throbbing and any movement of the arm caused a fresh spasm of pain. 'Is the bullet still in there?'

'Not a bullet, Monsieur,' the valet corrected me. 'A musket ball. Do not concern yourself. It merely grazed the top of your shoulder.'

I grimaced, not quite believing him. 'Are you sure? It nearly knocked me for six.'

'I am certain, Monsieur. The wound is superficial. The ball is embedded in the wall of the cubicle behind you.'

I tried to glance round but the movement provoked another wave of pain. 'I'll...I'll have take your word for that.'

'Better to stay still, Monsieur. I believe the wound to your head may be a little more severe.'

'Yes, I...I cracked it on the side of the pool, when Sir Richard hit me.'

'You have lost a little blood.' Maurice finished wiping my head and then produced a roll of bandage from his jacket, which was lying on a bench at the back of the cubicle. The man always carried a set of bandages with him – and some cotton wool – but this time it was not my bosom that needed restraining.

As the valet set to work, I took a moment to gaze beyond the open curtain of the cubicle, across the hall. The slippery tiles leading back to the gymnasium were awash with crewmen. Doctor Armstrong was in the water, at the shallow end of the pool. I struggled to bring the man into focus. He was in his shirt sleeves, the water up to his waist, engaged in the grim task of manoeuvring a body towards the edge of the pool. Two crewmen were assisting him. The body was that of Sir Richard Villiers. Mr Hopkins had got the upper hand in that last, desperate struggle.

The secretary was now standing by the side of the pool, dripping wet, a towel around his shoulders. Mr Griffith, the security officer, was standing next to him, overseeing the recovery of the corpse with his usual dour efficiency. Hopkins did not seem to be under restraint – Griffith had probably run out of handcuffs – but two further stewards were standing by at the far door, making sure nobody tried to leave.

Maurice had finished wrapping the bandage around my head and was tying off the end. I coughed loudly and wiped a spot of phlegm from my mouth; then I returned my attention to the valet. 'You saved my life,' I breathed, still not quite believing it. The fact that I was alive, even, was nothing short of a miracle. The last I had seen of Maurice, he had been heading off to bed. 'What on earth brought you back down here?'

'I did not wish to retire, Monsieur, without first making sure you had returned to your room.' That was typical of Maurice, never following instructions. 'When midnight came, and there was no sign of you, I decided to come looking. Then I saw Monsieur Villiers stepping into the elevator on B Deck, with a curious expression on his face, and I alerted the stewards.'

'Well, I'm glad that you did,' I puffed, observing the man with some gratitude. His clothes were as wet as my own, apart from his jacket, which he must have taken off before he jumped in. 'You dived into the pool,' I realised belatedly, finally connecting him with that blurry figure I had seen earlier on. 'You dived in and....' I stopped myself and frowned. 'I thought you hated water.'

'Yes, Monsieur.' Maurice's expression was neutral – that is to say, grim, which was his version of neutral – but I understood only too well the anxiety any large body of water provoked in the man. And yet somehow, on the spur of the moment, he had set aside his fears and dived straight in.

'I didn't even know you could swim,' I said.

'I am a good swimmer, Monsieur,' he assured me, matter-of-factly. 'My father taught me when I was a boy. If I had not been able to swim, I would myself have drowned many years ago.'

'You mean, when the Lusitania went down?'

'Yes, Monsieur.' He buttoned up the front of my shirt, covering over the wound in my shoulder. Even now, there was so much that I did not know about this peculiar, grim-faced Frenchman.

'You were in the water, then?'

'Yes, Monsieur. For three and a half minutes. A minute longer and the cold would have killed me.'

'And yet...' I regarded him with something close to admiration. 'And yet you still jumped in and saved me today?'

'Yes, Monsieur.' He closed up the flap of my shirt. 'I did not wish to have to find another employer.'

I laughed abruptly and the sudden movement provoked a fresh round of coughing. 'Morris, you never cease to amaze me.' I rested my head against the back of the cubicle. 'That's one hell of a way to ask for a pay rise.'

Maurice dismissed the idea. 'That will not be not necessary, Monsieur.'

'I'm not taking no for an answer.' I coughed again. My God, if any action was beyond the call of duty, it was this. 'How long has it been since you last had a raise?'

Maurice considered. 'I believe it was last April, Monsieur.'

251

'Ah, yes.' I remembered. 'Oh, you mean…?'

'Yes, Monsieur.' I swear there was a ghost of a smile on his face as he added, 'the last time I saved your life.' But if it was there, it was gone in an instant.

The pain in my shoulder had lessened slightly by now but my head was still throbbing. Had I suffered any serious damage, I wondered. 'How is it looking, the head?'

'I believe you will live, Monsieur,' the valet responded, peering carefully at the bandage. 'But I am not a medical man. You should perhaps allow Doctor Armstrong to examine you.'

I grimaced at that suggestion. I have always done my best to keep doctors at arms length, for obvious reasons. But Sir Richard's body had now been retrieved from the pool and Armstrong was heading in our direction. 'Not the shoulder,' I insisted. Even a cursory inspection of that area might prove troublesome. 'I suppose it can't hurt to let him have a look at the head, though.'

'Yes, Monsieur.' Maurice finished buttoning up my waistcoat.

By now, the doctor had come to a halt outside the cubicle, his large ears flapping despite the absence of a breeze. 'How are you, Mr Buxton?' he asked, observing the bandage Maurice had wrapped around my head.

'I'm all right, I think. It probably looks worse than it is.'

'I ought to be the judge of that.' Armstrong crouched down in front of me. 'You have been in the wars. That looks quite nasty.' He reached forward and placed a gentle hand on the top of my head. 'What happened? Did you hit your head against the side of the pool?' I nodded, trying not to flinch as his fingers moved across, probing the scalp for any abnormalities. 'I apologise for not getting to you sooner. I was helping with Sir Richard. We had to see if there was anything to be done.'

'That's quite all right. Is he…?'

'Dead? Yes, I'm afraid so. Drowned, poor devil. That's three bodies I've had to examine in the past twenty-four hours. Can you credit it?' Armstrong's pin hole eyes were shrivelled up even further than usual. 'Keep your head still, please.' He peeled back a section of bandage and scanned the interior; then he returned the bandage to its proper place, and rocked back onto his haunches. 'Well, it doesn't look too bad, all things considered. What on earth happened down here? Mr Hopkins hasn't been very coherent, so far.'

'It's a long story. We've all had a difficult evening.'

'Evidently. You've done a good job with the bandage, Monsieur Sauveterre,' he said. His eyes flicked down to my bloodied shirt. 'I ought to take a look at that shoulder, too.'

'It is a flesh wound, Monsieur,' Maurice cut in calmly. 'Nothing more. The musket ball merely grazed the top of the skin.'

'Yes, we heard a gunshot.' He shuddered. 'Even so, I ought to take a look at it.'

'There's really no need,' I assured him, waving the doctor away with my good arm. 'Maurice has cleaned it up. He knows what he's doing.'

'You have some medical experience?' Armstrong gazed across at the valet.

'He was a...hospital orderly during the war,' I improvised. 'Don't worry. He can take care of me.' Maurice was not a qualified doctor, but he had recently attended a lecture on human anatomy; and he was currently reading a biography of Florence Nightingale. 'I'm more concerned about my head,' I said.

Doctor Armstrong raised a hand to his ear and gave it a good scratch. 'Well, there's no sign of a fracture. We'll have to keep a careful eye on you, though. Always better to err on the side of caution with these things.'

'Absolutely,' I agreed. 'I could do with a little something for the pain, if you've got it. It's still throbbing.'

'Yes, of course. I'll see what I can find. If you start to feel at all nauseous, though, anything out of the ordinary...'

'You'll be the first to know.'

'Good man.' He lifted himself up. 'We'll get you back to your cabin. I'll send one of the stewards over to help. There's quite a lot of cleaning up to do here.' He wiped his hands on his shirt sleeves, which were almost as wet as my own. 'Try and get some rest, Mr Buxton. Sleep if you can. And please make sure the wound is kept clean, Monsieur Sauveterre. I have some surgical spirits, if you need them. And some tablets for the pain.' Doctor Armstrong gave a quick smile and then departed, heading back to the far end of the pool, where Ernest Hopkins was being led away by a couple of crewmen.

Two minutes later, with a bit of help from Maurice and a rather tired looking steward, I was also on my feet and shambling barefoot towards the exit. Mr Griffith was loitering at the edge of the swimming pool, examining the discarded pistol, which had now been recovered from the water.

'You've had a lucky escape, Mr Buxton,' he observed.

'I don't feel all that lucky,' I said, wincing slightly.

'I don't suppose you happen to know anything about a knife, do you, sir?' he asked. Griffith was looking rather perplexed. 'There was a gash in Sir Richard's leg,' he explained. It appeared they had not yet found the penknife.

I was about to answer, but Doctor Armstrong cut across me. 'The questions will have to wait, Mr Griffith. Mr Buxton has had had quite an ordeal. He needs rest.'

The security officer inclined his head. 'Very well. But I will need a full statement in the morning.' He glanced down at my sodden clothes and the red stained shirt. 'When you've properly recovered, that is. One little thing, though, sir,' he added, as we were about to move past him. 'That lad, Hopkins. He seems to think Sir Richard was behind it all. The pen letters. The death of Mrs Hamilton-Baynes. Is that really true, sir?' In other words, had Griffith arrested the wrong man?

'I'm afraid so,' I confirmed. 'I heard it from his own lips. Sir Richard's, I mean.'

'And the Reverend Hamilton-Baynes? He had nothing to do with any of it?'

'Nothing at all,' I said, shaking my head sadly. 'Just another victim of Sir Richard's madness.'

The police launch was hovering along the port side. A small gangplank connected the vehicle with the mother ship. The launch had been hauled to and securely attached, but it looked a little precarious to me. Unlike Maurice, I had no particular fear of the sea – despite one or two disastrous incidents in my recent past – but I could recognise a degree of risk when I saw it. Nonetheless, I steeled myself and made my way quickly across the plank. A hefty young constable on the far side gave me a hand over the lip of the boat and onto a wobbly approximation of terra firma. I looked back at the Galitia and glowered up at the stream of passengers lining the port side. They were not here to see me off; they wanted to catch a glimpse of the fearful murderer Ernest Hopkins, as he was escorted across the gangplank in chains. They had already enjoyed the splendid entertainment of the corpses being loaded aboard. The ghoulishness of some people never fails to astonish me.

I had been spared the feverish gossip that had rippled across the ship the morning after my unfortunate dice with death. I had spent most of that day in my cabin, recuperating as best I could. Adam brought me my meals and Maurice saw that my wounds were properly cleaned and dressed.

The police launch arrived from Southampton at midday, several gruff looking officers from Scotland Yard clambering aboard. I have never had a high opinion of that particular organisation, but these men set about their duty with surprising diligence. Our arrival in Southampton was to be delayed by twenty-four hours, to allow them time for a proper examination of the ship.

By mid-afternoon, I had recovered sufficiently for Doctor Armstrong to allow one of the detectives to speak to me. As the principal eyewitness to events on E Deck, my testimony was considered particularly important. Thankfully, the man in question was content to come to me, rather than dragging me from my bed to some soulless office. At the same time, a couple of sergeants were handling the other interviews, and the crime scene and the bodies were being examined by various experts. I chuckled at the thought of Harry cowering in his locked cupboard, as the police pathologists swarmed over the doctor's surgery, conducting their post mortems. The poor fellow would not be able to get to the bathroom all day.

I did not have to tell too many lies to the detective. In truth, I had very little to conceal, beyond the real reason for my journey down to the doctor's surgery at that time in the evening (and I had already provided Mr Griffith with a perfectly acceptable excuse for that). I could state in all honesty that I had not known Sir Richard was behind the letter writing campaign or that Mr Hopkins had colluded with him in its later stages. I had only seen two or three of the letters first hand, after all. In the matter of Harry Latimer, everyone seemed content to accept Doctor Armstrong's assessment that the man had died of natural causes. Somehow, the doctor managed to keep his nerve, his professional demeanour maintained more easily in the face of officialdom than when confronted by two burly Mafioso. He assisted the police pathologist with a preliminary examination of Mrs Hamilton-Baynes, but still found time to visit me, to make sure that my wounds had been properly attended to. He was a decent sort, Armstrong, for all his obvious flaws. Not once, as he was checking my bandages, did he mention Harry Latimer; and, for my part, I did not feel inclined to drag it all out into the open and embarrass him.

As the day progressed, I had several more visitors, Miss Wellesley among them. She was horrified to see my head swathed in cotton. I assured her that it looked a lot worse than it was. The Reverend Hamilton-Baynes had been released from the brig, she told me, and his place taken by Mr Hopkins. 'Jenny – Miss Simpkins – she's absolutely distraught,' Miss Wellesley lamented. It cannot have been easy for the girl, to discover her sweetheart had been arrested for murder, even if there were mitigating circumstances.

The one caller I did not expect came by shortly after breakfast the following morning. Maurice had packed up my things and left me to my own devices. I was alone, therefore, sitting with a book by the bedside, when Lady Jocelyn Wingfield arrived.

There was not a trace of emotion on the woman's cold, narrow face as I invited her into the room and she accepted a chair opposite me. The great woman regarded my little cabin with practised disdain – an air of superiority that I could not help but admire – but her words at least were polite. 'I was so sorry to hear what happened to you,' she said. 'This is a dreadful business. I hope you have not been too badly injured.' Her voice had all the regret one might have felt at having stubbed a toe on a door frame. To a casual observer, it would have been impossible to guess that anything of significance had occurred in the past forty-eight hours, less still that this woman had just lost a dear cousin and a brother. To add salt to the wound, her beloved cat Matilda had now been confined to the hold and would be spending the next six months in quarantine. That, I suspected, would be the cruellest blow of all. Without Sir Richard to pull a few strings, there was no chance of getting the animal past the customs men in Southampton. But any signs of distress the lady might have felt were buried so deeply beneath the surface that they might as well not have been there at all. Lady Jocelyn was an aristocrat of the old school. I did not like the woman, but I admired her stoicism.

'It was nothing,' I lied, my hand reflexively touching the bandage. 'I'll be up and about in no time.' I gestured to the teapot on the bedside table but Lady Jocelyn declined the offer politely. 'I'm sorry about Mrs Hamilton-Baynes. And…and your brother. It was…the way things happened. I'm afraid there was nothing to be done.'

Lady Jocelyn nodded. 'Richard was a difficult man. I fear I did not understand him as well as I ought to have done.' It was a rare admission of failure, and it pained her to have to say it. Like everyone else, she had been entirely ignorant of her brother's many vile schemes.

'Families are always a bit tricky,' I observed, lamely. 'Mr Hopkins…don't think too harshly of him. There was a…a degree of provocation.'

'I am aware of the circumstances,' Lady Jocelyn replied. 'And poor dear Margaret.'

'It's been a difficult few days for all of us. How is the reverend?'

'As well as can be expected.' Hamilton-Baynes had been released from prison but he was still coming to terms with the death of his wife. 'It is not an easy thing to lose a wife or a husband,' Lady Jocelyn said. 'He is with Margaret now, down in the surgery. He wanted to say his goodbyes, before she was carried away.'

'I understand.'

'The next few months will be difficult for him, I daresay, but time is a great healer. I will make sure he is properly looked after. In the circumstances, it is the least I can do.' Whatever her personal feelings towards the man, Lady Jocelyn was not a woman to shirk her familial obligations.

'Of course.' I sat back in my chair and a brief pause fell upon us.

Now that the social niceties were taken care of, Lady Jocelyn decided to address the real reason for her visit. 'Mr Buxton, it may be that things were said, the other night. That you became aware of certain matters…' All at once, the great lady was floundering.

'I don't know anything about that,' I assured her. I had no desire to cause the woman any further embarrassment. 'Family matters, family history. They're not my concern.'

'The pen letters I received…the letters that it appears my brother sent to me.' Lady Jocelyn pressed her lips together. 'They related to an incident in my youth. A regrettable incident.'

'Lady Jocelyn, you don't have to…'

'I had an affair,' she cut across me, 'before I was married. Richard knew about it, of course. But it was distasteful to be reminded. And Margaret, my dear Margaret, she knew all of the details.'

'An affair?' I said.

'An affair,' Lady Jocelyn repeated firmly. That, it was clear, was going to be the official story.

'Of course.' That was what Mr Griffith had been told, when Mrs O'Neill had died. With Sir Richard now dead and Mrs Hamilton-Baynes too, the only people who knew the truth – apart from an elderly housekeeper – were Ernest Hopkins and myself. 'I'm sure Mr Hopkins will be discreet,' I said. The young secretary had no reason to want to harm Lady Jocelyn and the precise details of her past were not that relevant to the case against him. Her life would be a matter of public scandal whatever happened, but there was no need to grind the poor woman into the dirt. Would Lady Jocelyn attempt to talk to Mr Hopkins before the trial? Would she even be allowed in to see him? It probably did not matter. 'And for my part,' I assured her, 'I knew nothing of the contents of any of your letters.' That was the line I had taken with the police, and it was a line I intended to stick to. 'The past is not my concern, your ladyship.'

'I appreciate that, Mr Buxton. You are very kind.'

'I do have one favour to ask, though.'

Her forehead crinkled momentarily. 'A favour?'

'Not for myself, you understand.' I had been reflecting a little on what Miss Wellesley had told me the day before. 'The young maid, Miss Simpkins.'

At the sound of the name, Lady Jocelyn narrowed her eyes. 'What about her?'

'I gather she is rather upset by everything that has happened.'

'I don't see what she has to be upset about...' The tone was dismissive.

'She and Mr Hopkins had developed something of a romantic attachment, I understand.'

'Yes, I am aware of that,' Lady Jocelyn said. 'It was not at all appropriate.'

'But now it looks like he's going to hang. You must see how distressing that will be for her. And to have lost her position too. It might seem like her whole world has fallen apart.'

Lady Jocelyn had little sympathy. 'The feelings of a servant are not my concern. She has been dismissed and that is the end of the matter.'

'That's your prerogative, of course. I can see that she was less than satisfactory as a maid.'

'So what is it that you are asking, Mr Buxton?' Her tone was now as cold as ice.

'A reference, nothing more. An acceptable character, so that she can find herself another position. That's not too much to ask, is it?'

Lady Jocelyn gazed across at the curtains. 'I suppose that would not be unreasonable,' she agreed, reluctantly. In the circumstances, she could hardly refuse.

'Thank you, your ladyship. That's most kind.'

'I will see to it when we arrive in Southampton.' The great lady rose up from her seat. 'Thank you, Mr Buxton, for your consideration. I will not take up any more of your time.' She moved towards the door and turned back. 'I doubt we will meet again. Except perhaps in court.' That last word was spoken with particular distaste.

'Ah, yes.' I gave out a sigh. In truth, that was a matter of some trepidation for me too.

The police had made it clear that I would be expected to testify against Mr Hopkins, when the time came. I was the principal witness, after all, in the killing of Sir Richard Villiers, and I would not be allowed to avoid the limelight. That was going to be rather awkward, to say the least. There was, however, one useful consequence to this unfortunate state of affairs: it afforded me pride of place on the police launch.

Mr Griffith had suggested the possibility to me, the previous evening. 'I can arrange for you to go with them,' he had said, 'if you would like to avoid all the attention tomorrow.' The gentlemen of the press would be lying in wait for us at the docks when the Galitia finally pulled into port and I had no desire to be put on public display. Needless to say, I accepted the offer at once.

And so I found myself aboard a much smaller ship that afternoon, on the seventh day out from New York, bouncing up and down as we sped across the water, away from the great iron bulk of the Galitia, towards the industrial docklands of Southampton. For a brief moment, as I stared out of the window, the past few days were forgotten; the murders, the brushes with death, the sheer inconvenience of shipboard life. All my thoughts now were of home.

Chapter Eighteen

The edge of the paper narrowly missed the top of the teapot as I folded back the Times and scanned the day's headlines. The item I was looking for was on page twelve: "DEATH SENTENCE COMMUTED." I had been alerted to the news already, but it was nice to see it confirmed in public. The Home Secretary, Mr Herbert Samuel, had commuted the sentence to twenty-five years. That seemed about right to me. Ernest Hopkins had been found not guilty of the murder of Sir Richard Villiers but guilty of the murder of Mrs Susan O'Neill. An inquest into the death of Margaret Hamilton-Baynes had concluded that Sir Richard had been responsible for her demise.

I settled back in my chair, in a reflective mood. Hopkins was in his mid twenties. He would be older than I was now when he got out of prison; but he would still have a life of some sort ahead of him, once he had paid his debt to society.

I reached for the toast and took another crunch. The marmalade was a bit off this morning. I would have to have a word with Mrs Middleton. She was my housekeeper, a stout grey haired woman in her late sixties. I had rented a small property on the seafront in Brighton and she had come with the house.

I was about to move on to another article in the Times when I heard a knock at the front door. For a moment, I dismissed it. Mrs Middleton was upstairs, changing the bedsheets, but she could waddle down to answer it easily enough. That is what servants are for, after all. Then I remembered the poor dear was as deaf as a post and, reluctantly, I hauled myself up.

I suppressed a smile as I moved across the hallway and caught sight of the figure behind the frosted glass. The man was instantly recognisable, even in silhouette. I opened the door and adopted the sourest expression I could manage. 'Morning, Harry,' I said.

Harry Latimer beamed at me across the doorstep. 'Morning, old man.' He was dressed in a smart tailored suit, a rakishly angled fedora atop his head. His eyes twinkled and his mouth split into a wide grin.

'You managed to find the place then?' I stepped back and gestured him inside.

'A little off the beaten track.' He removed his hat and moved into the hallway. 'I didn't expect you to answer the door yourself. Has somebody died?' He flicked his hat across to the hook by the door.

'Yes, as a matter of fact. My valet's away in France. Please come through. His mother passed away last week and he's gone for the funeral.'

'I'm sorry to hear that.' Harry followed me through into the sitting room.

'She's been ill for a while. He was there at the end, which is the main thing. Well, this is me.' I gestured to the room. 'I was just having breakfast.' The sitting room and the dining room were all in one. 'I wasn't expecting you until eleven.' The carriage clock on the mantelpiece indicated that it was barely half past nine.

'I caught the early train.'

'You don't mind if I finish my breakfast?'

'No, no. Be my guest.' We settled at the table. 'Did he fly out, your valet? To France?'

'I offered to book him a flight. Least I could do after everything that had happened. But he decided to go by boat instead. Finding his sea legs at last. Or confronting his fears. Something like that, anyway. It's a dashed nuisance, having him away.'

'You're on your own here? Harry looked around the room. I could tell what he was thinking. It was hardly the Ritz. The flowered wallpaper was particularly uninspiring.

'Not quite. I have a woman in twice a day, to cook and clean. She's upstairs at the moment. Oh, don't worry.' A mild flash of concern had crossed his face. 'She's half blind and deaf as a doornail. And she won't know you from Adam. Would you care for some tea? The pot's still warm.'

'That's okay.' Harry smiled as he slid into his seat. 'I brought my own refreshment.' He pulled a small flask from his jacket pocket.

'Bit early,' I said, taking the canteen when he offered it and adding a touch of brandy to my own tea cup. 'We're not in America now, you know. You could have brought a bottle.'

'I'm not staying that long.'

'I'm surprised to see you at all.' I had not expected to hear from Harry again for at least a year or two. He was supposed to be lying low. 'I suppose Doctor Armstrong gave you my address, did he?' I had written to the good doctor with my current details, so that Harry would be able to get in touch when he needed to, but I had not expected to hear from him quite this soon.

'Yeah, he said you'd settled down here, in Brighton. Nice town. Bit quiet, though.'

'It livens up in the afternoons. How is Doctor Armstrong? I haven't seen him since the trial.'

'Oh, he's fine. Better than ever.'

'I'm glad.' I crunched on my toast. 'I think it was all a bit of a strain for him. Lying on oath like that.'

'The guy has too many scruples for his own good. I keep telling him, truth is just a matter of perspective.'

'I think it was more a question of whether somebody would find out. I don't think he was the happiest of accomplices.'

'I guess not. Still, he can't exactly lose his job. Leastways, not any more.'

'How do you mean?' I picked up my cup and took a quick slurp.

'Haven't you heard? The doc resigned his commission a couple of weeks back.'

'Really? He's left the Galitia?' This was the first I'd heard of it.

'He's taking up a new position, in East Africa.'

'Good grief.' I put the cup down.

'He's heading off there in a few days time. Out in the middle of nowhere, catering to the natives. And you'll never guess who's going with him.'

I had no idea.

'The delectable Miss Cynthia Wellesley.'

'Good lord.' I laughed. 'You can't be serious?'

'I wouldn't lie to you, old man. They got to know each other, apparently, during the trial.'

I grimaced, trying to remember. 'Yes, I did see them talking together once or twice.'

'You know what they say…' Harry smirked. 'Romance can bloom in the strangest of places.'

'Evidently. And now she's run off with him?' I smiled. The sensible botany student. I wondered if she would ever manage to complete her studies. 'You're losing your touch Harry. You had quite a thing for her yourself, didn't you?'

Harry shrugged. Women were a "dime a dozen" as far as he was concerned. 'It was nothing serious, old man. Besides. it's difficult to compete when your body's at the bottom of the Atlantic. I figure she'll be good for him. Keeping the guy away from temptation.'

'The gambling, you mean?' I rolled my eyes and took another sip of brandy and tea. 'He just has to learn, everything in moderation.'

Harry would not be shedding too many tears for Miss Wellesley. He had already found a replacement, by all accounts. That was what had brought him down to Brighton in the first place.

At the moment, however, he was eyeing my newspaper, which I had left folded on the table. 'You see they commuted the sentence, for Hopkins?'

'Yes, he was very lucky. I think it was the reverend who made the difference. Hamilton-Baynes. Speaking up for him like that. It was a brave thing to do, after losing his wife.'

'Yeah, he's a decent guy.'

'If only he would shave off that ridiculous beard. The maid, Miss Simpkins, she was there as well, to see it all happen. Kept herself together. Rather surprised me, actually. She says she's going to stick by him. Mr Hopkins, I mean. She's going to wait for him.'

'Do you think she will?'

'I think she believes it. But twenty-five years is a long

time.'

Harry took another swig of brandy, 'So how was the trial, anyway? Armstrong didn't say much. I only read the reports in the paper.'

'It was pretty grim,' I said.

'I can't believe you actually testified.'

'I didn't have a choice. I was the principal witness. Believe me, it was the last thing I wanted, appearing in public like that. At the Old Bailey for goodness sake. I was terrified someone would recognise me, being dead and all. Well, you'd know all about that.'

'Sure. So what did you do?'

'Everything I could. Put on a pair of glasses and a false moustache, and hoped the court room artist would do a really bad job. I am happy to say he obliged.' I chuckled at the memory. I could laugh about it now, but at the time I had been a bundle of nerves. 'And so far as the press were concerned, I was the mysterious "Mr X".'

'Yeah, I saw that.' Harry grinned. 'You must have pulled a few strings to make that happen.'

'Oh, I did. Had to go to Kensington on my knees. An audience with the Colonel, no less.' My former boss at MI5. 'He was pleased to see me, anyway. I still have a bit of currency in London, believe it or not.' The Zeppelin business the year before had put me in good stead with the powers that be. 'They asked about you.'

Harry put down his flask. 'I figured they might. What did you tell them?'

'The truth.' I raised my hand as Harry made to protest. 'They already knew, Harry.' I would hardly have betrayed his confidence otherwise. 'Don't ask me how, but they knew you were alive. You might pull the wool over the eyes of a few mobsters, but this is the British secret service. They're not so easily fooled. You should know that by now. You've worked for them.'

'Yeah, a long time ago.'

'And you weren't going to keep this a secret forever, now, were you?'

265

'I guess not.' Harry shrugged. 'It would have been nice to lie low for a year or two. Things are a lot easier when nobody's looking over your shoulder. But I guess it's no big deal. I'm in the clear with the mob.'

'They fell for it?'

'Those two goons of theirs. They got off the ship at Southampton, had a little walk around and then got straight back on again. Didn't see me slip away. Just headed right home to New York. I don't think I'll be seeing them again.'

I drained my tea cup. 'You've had a lucky escape, Harry. I hope you've learnt your lesson.'

'Oh, sure, sure. Next time, I'll be more careful.' He grinned and raised his canteen.

'So what's all this about a girl you've met?' I was wary of asking, but it seemed only polite. Harry had mentioned the young woman when he had first got in touch.

'Her name's Constance. A real looker. Nineteen years old and loaded too.'

I laughed. 'You dirty devil.'

'Oh, it's all above board, old man. Her family lives down here in Brighton. They've invited me over for the weekend.'

'You have your foot in the door, then?'

'Well and truly. I'm an eccentric millionaire. A property tycoon from New Jersey.'

'Of course you are. Lord, Harry. You don't change, do you?' I had the sneaking suspicion some rather expensive jewellery was going to go missing in the next few days.

'A guy's got to earn a living. And what about you? You're not going to settle down here for the rest of your life, are you?' He gestured vaguely to the room, but he meant the town, of course.

'I'm not altogether sure. It's been nice to have a bit of peace and quiet. The Colonel says he might have a little work for me, in due course, but I'm not sure if I can be bothered with all that. I've had my fill of secret service work.' I sighed. 'The money would come in handy, though. I can't afford all this luxury indefinitely.'

Harry chuckled. 'Hey, I might just be able to help you with that.'

I waved my hands at him. 'Oh no, I'm not getting involved in any of your schemes.' Whatever he was up to with this young woman, I wanted nothing to do with it. 'I've had enough of that for one lifetime.'

'Don't worry, old man. I'm not trying to rope you into anything. You deserve a bit of a rest, after all you've been through. I just figured I owed you a favour, that's all. That's why I stopped by.'

I laughed again. 'You mean you came all this way, out of the goodness of your heart, just to pay off a debt?'

'Well, of course. I always pay my debts.'

'Eventually,' I conceded. 'But usually at the point of a gun.'

'Not this time, old man. This couldn't wait. Like I say, I was coming down here anyway, and I thought I might as well kill two birds with one stone; pass on a bit of useful intelligence.'

'Intelligence?' My eyes narrowed. I wasn't sure I liked the sound of that.

'Give me that paper, will you?' He gestured to the Times. Dubiously, I handed the newspaper across. He unfolded it and found the page he was looking for; then pulled a pencil from his jacket pocket and circled a small area of text. He handed the paper back to me and I looked down at it, a slow smile spreading across my face. 'The three o'clock at Newmarket,' he said. 'Put everything you've got on "Coster Boy".'

Acknowledgements

The RMS Galitia is a fictional ship but I have based it closely on a real life Cunard liner, the RMS Aquitania, which was in service between 1914 and 1950. I am indebted to Mark Chirnside for his book "RMS Aquitania - The Ship Beautiful" (The History Press 2008) and to the British Library for copies of the ship's early promotional material. Special thanks to jclarkdawe, bolero and several others on AbsoluteWrite for providing many extra details. Thanks also to my beta readers, Steve and Gemma, and to my family for their continued support. Finally, thanks to the Times Archive for the racing results. Coster Boy came in at 30-1.

Jack Treby

For news of future releases visit the website:

www.jacktreby.com

Available Now On This Imprint

The Pineapple Republic
by
Jack Treby

Democracy is coming to the Central American Republic of San Doloroso. But it won't be staying long...

The year is 1990. Ace reporter Daniel Parr has been injured in a freak surfing accident, just as the provisional government of San Doloroso has announced the country's first democratic elections.

The Daily Herald needs a man on the spot and in desperation they turn to Patrick Malone, a feckless junior reporter who just happens to speak a few words of Spanish.

Despatched to Central America to get the inside story, our Man in Toronja finds himself at the mercy of a corrupt and brutal administration that is determined to win the election at any cost...

271

Available Now On This Imprint

The Scandal At Bletchley
by
Jack Treby

*"I've been a scoundrel, a thief, a blackmailer and a whore,
but never a murderer. Until now..."*

The year is 1929. As the world teeters on the brink of a global
recession, Bletchley Park plays host to a rather special event.
MI5 is celebrating its twentieth anniversary and a select band of
former and current employees are gathering at the private estate
for a weekend of music, dance and heavy drinking. Among
them is Sir Hilary Manningham-Butler, a middle aged woman
whose entire adult life has been spent masquerading as a man.
She doesn't know why she has been invited – it is many years
since she left the secret service – but it is clear she is not the
only one with things to hide. And when one of the other guests
threatens to expose her secret, the consequences could prove
disastrous for everyone.

Available Now On This Imprint

The Red Zeppelin
by
Jack Treby

*"You'll never get me up in one of those things. They're
absolutely lethal."*

Seville, 1931. Six months after the loss of the British airship
the R101, a German Zeppelin is coming in to land in Southern
Spain. Hilary Manningham-Butler is an MI5 operative eking
out a pitiful existence on the Rock of Gibraltar. The offer of a
job in the Americas provides a potential life line but there are
strings attached. First she must prove her mettle to her masters
in London and that means stepping on board the Richthofen
before the airship leaves Seville. A cache of secret documents
has been stolen from Scotland Yard and the files must be
recovered if British security is not to be severely compromised.
Hilary must put her life on the line to discover the identity of
the thief. But as the airship makes its way across the Atlantic
towards Brazil it becomes clear that nobody on board is quite
what they seem. And there is no guarantee that any of them will
reach Rio de Janeiro alive...

Also Available On This Imprint

Murder At Flaxton Isle
by
Greg Wilson

A remote Scottish island plays host to a deadly reunion...

It should be a lot of fun, meeting up for a long weekend in a rented lighthouse on a chunk of rock miles from anywhere. There will be drinks and games and all sorts of other amusements. It is ten years since the last get-together and twenty years since Nadia and her friends graduated from university. But not everything goes according to plan. One of the group has a more sinister agenda and, as events begin to spiral out of control, it becomes clear that not everyone will get off the island alive...

Also Available On This Imprint

The Gunpowder Treason
by
Michael Dax

"If I had thought there was the least sin in the plot, I would not have been in it for all the world..."

Robert Catesby is a man in despair. His father is dead and his wife is burning in the fires of Hell – his punishment from God for marrying a Protestant. A new king presents a new hope but the persecution of Catholics in England continues unabated and Catesby can tolerate it no longer. King James bears responsibility but the whole government must be eradicated if anything is to really change. And Catesby has a plan...

The Gunpowder Treason is a fast-paced historical thriller. Every character is based on a real person and almost every scene is derived from eye-witness accounts. This is the story of the Gunpowder Plot, as told by the people who were there...

Printed in Great Britain
by Amazon

35061075R00168